REMNANTS OF MAGIC
VOLUME I

Alicia R. Leslie

Michelle,
Enjoy!
Alicia Leslie

For my parents
James and Diane Chapin

Prologue

The powerful animal's hooves hit the soft sand on the beach in a perfect cadence of a full-fledged gallop. The hooves churned the earth sending streams of damp sand flying. Each glimmering hoof sank into the white sands with tremendous force, leaving welts to be washed away by the crashing waves of the sea. With each step the animal's snorted breaths misted in the cool morning air. His eyes were wide and alert and sparkled with hope. His long tail floated on the breeze, a ray of silky, iridescent threads. His coat was without equal. It was the purest white, dazzling to the eye and as sleek as blue ice on the cool bays of the Nortarwin Sea far to the north. Nothing thrilled the great beast more than running with the salty winds of early morning.

The round, yellow sun rose above the watery horizon in the east. His hooves shone coppery and his prismatic horn sent all the colors of the spectrum dancing across the beach as the sun's rays shone through. He flipped his mane from the pleasure of the sun warming his cool back. He galloped on, his movements smooth and quick. He was Apollos, an advisor of the country of Shelkite. He had promising news to report to Prince Alkin and his mother Lady Adama, waiting for him at the castle in the city of Fordorn.

Chapter 1

A dark lock of hair fell across his damp forehead. He impatiently swiped it away and rubbed his brow with anxious fingertips. The young warrior bit his bottom lip as he felt for the hilt of his sword. His hand found it right where it should be, at his side in its sheath. He breathed out, letting his broad body relax.

His ears heard the light laughter of a woman behind the closed door of which he stood in front. His uncommonly bright azure eyes shifted around the long corridor for anything abnormal. There was nothing. He started to pace, his black riding boots tapping quietly across the floor. *When is he going to be done?* Bryan rolled his eyes upward.

Being Prince Alkin's personal guard did have its advantages, but waiting around for him to make social calls was ridiculous. Bryan wanted action, battles, even blood, anything but tag along with the Prince to visit pretty lady friends of Fordorn— the city where his castle was built upon the outskirts of in the country of Shelkite.

Blah! Bryan let out an annoyed breath and paced the hall quicker. *Women! All they ever do is get their skirts in the way.* Sure, he had had his fair share of girls, but that was all done and over with. No more for him, thanks! Sure, he liked Prince Alkin. He was one of his closest friends. However, it was getting annoying that he met with Lady Evelyn every week. She was a beauty known around the city as the Chaos Goddess. And, in Bryan's opinion, she was kind of silly.

The latch clicked on the oak door. Bryan spun around to face it. The handle turned ever *too* slowly. *"Come on,"* he whispered through clenched teeth. He stood at attention as he heard the Prince say his farewells from behind the door. The door opened and a blonde, handsome prince stepped out. Alkin smiled at his waiting guard. Bryan nodded his respects to the Prince as a shapely woman stepped in the threshold.

Alkin turned to face the brunette. "Thank you again for your time, Lady Evelyn." He bowed.

"I'll see you next week then?" the Chaos Goddess replied.

The sugarcoated words sickened Bryan. As he stood

silently waiting, she briefly flicked her brown eyes over him. Bryan was growing more impatient every second. He clenched his jaw in annoyance.

"Yes, my lady." Prince Alkin took her pale hand and landed a kiss there. He smiled, and then turned briskly to start down the staircase to the lobby below.

"Goodbye, Sword Bryan," Evelyn said sweetly.

Bryan was just turning to follow the Prince. He spun back and bowed politely, "My lady." He smiled the best he could at the moment. He caught a glitter of amusement in her cow eyes before she closed the chamber door. Letting his gaze linger on the door for a second, Bryan rolled his eyes. He then started down the creaky stairway after his master, the tip of his sheathed sword clinking on the tops of the steps as he jogged down. He pushed his way through the crowded lobby to the front porch of the inn. Standing under a weathered sign that read 'Snowed Inn', Bryan looked up and down the main street of Fordorn City.

This part of the city was lower class, bustling with hard working people. Teams of mules and oxen pulled hefty carts loaded with goods through the muddy streets. Women shouted at children causing havoc. Men hollered orders to their employees. The residents of the city were merrily going about their everyday business. *What a great place the city is.* Bryan breathed in the dingy air, happy to be away from inside the tavern and females.

"Well, are you coming?" Prince Alkin asked from atop his bay warhorse. The burly horse flipped his black mane causing the metals of his bridle to clink. Alkin was leaning casually on the pommel of his saddle. "For acting so impatient, you're not moving very fast," he joked.

Bryan smiled at the smirking prince before untying his black mount from the Snowed Inn's hitching post. He couldn't hide anything from him. Bryan liked to fancy himself an impassive man, though when he was impatient it was well-known. Patience was not one of his strengths. "I'm coming, my prince." He mounted quickly and gracefully despite the bulkiness of his weapons and saddle. He turned his burly stallion around to follow the Prince down the road out of town.

Bryan and Dragon, his mount, slowly made their way around the bustling citizens. Dragon weaved from side to side of the sloppy road intently trying to catch up to his stable-mate. Bryan bumped Dragon lightly with his heels when he saw the Prince disappear around a bend. The game horse responded instantly, his huge hooves kicking out clods of dirt.

"Hey! Watch it, dim-wit!" An angry shout came from behind them. Bryan shifted around in his saddle to see an irate, mud-splattered woman. When she caught sight of him, she bowed immediately remorseful. "S-sorry, Master Sword, I didn't know it was you!" she apologized, holding her gaze down to her feet, which were rapidly disappearing in the muck. Bryan apologized graciously for his lack of thought, and then clucked to Dragon to move on.

As they reached the bounds of the city, Dragon quickly drew abreast with the Prince's mount. The stallion gave a loud snort to make known his arrival. Prince Alkin's green cloak flowed over the rump of his horse. It made him appear regal even though he was trying to blend in more today by not wearing his usual hue of blue.

The Prince softly hummed a familiar, light-hearted tune native to Shelkitens. He glanced over to his friend as he rode up beside him. "You know your horse has about as much patience as a *real* dragon. And, I fear his master isn't far behind," the Prince said nonchalantly, looking up to the next bend in the road, which led them past the last of the city homes.

Bryan snorted. "Humph! We've more important things to do than have tea with the ladies."

Prince Alkin looked at him surprised. "Really?" he said sternly. "Do you ever recall me stopping by just to make social calls with the ladies in the past?"

"No," the rebuffed Bryan answered slowly.

"Then maybe you should assume there is more to my visiting Lady Evelyn than just a social call." Prince Alkin heeled his horse into a faster gait.

They rode on, entering into the firmer, grassier country roads. The winding road was about six miles to the castle. The landscape was beautiful, wide-open rolling fields with crop and livestock farms settled along the way.

Up until the last couple of years, Alkin and Bryan had always been good friends. The Master Swords—a select number of the Prince's elite warriors and advisors—had appointed Bryan two years ago to become a Master Sword and Sword-Guard to Prince Alkin. The necessity of this position was because of an assassination threat to the Prince. But ever since Bryan's promotion he and Alkin squabbled more than they ever had as childhood pals. It didn't help that Bryan would be happier if he was back training the other warriors rather than being a Master Sword and a part of the Prince's council. What good was his ability if he could never use it alongside the other warriors? At any rate, Bryan worked hard to keep fit and hold his place of high stature. Moreover, because of his skills and hard work Bryan had quickly moved up in rank within the Master Swords. He was now the Head-Master Sword. He often thought he should be honored, but he didn't feel that way. He felt bored, bored with life. He needed action or something new at least.

Bryan patted Dragon's strained neck as they passed a mare hitched outside the noisy Blue Mermaid Tavern. It was the only decent place a traveler could get a drink for miles until the city. Many men assembled there to tell their stories of lost girls and distant lands. It gathered quite an interesting crowd. Bryan himself had been there many times.

The stallion nickered, but did nothing more than crane his neck to get a better look. "It's just better off to stay away from those," Bryan said to his horse as they passed by. "They end up being nothing but trouble." Dragon shook his head and pulled at his bit.

The sun was beginning to set below the hilly horizon. They wouldn't reach the castle until after dark. Bryan nudged his horse to catch up to the singing Prince. Alkin's shoulder length blonde hair was down and tousled. It lifted gently from the wind as he turned to his companion to sing part of the chorus to him. Bryan smiled and listened to the words that spoke of Shelkite's beloved rolling hills and farmlands.

"Sing with me, oh Great Master Sword Bryan!" the Prince called over joyfully, but his voice was tainted with mockery at his austere friend. Bryan stared at him as if he were mad. "It will pass the time better." Alkin smiled at his always-resistant guard.

Bryan finally cracked a grin. He didn't mind that occasionally the Prince slipped into a child-like demeanor. Alkin was just a few years younger than himself. Bryan was in his early twenties. What was important was that Prince Alkin had a good heart and was a clever and fair ruler. No country could ask for more. So, he proudly joined in.

For the remainder of the trek the two young men's voices, Prince Alkin's practiced tenor and Bryan's slightly off key baritone, resounded clear over the foothills of the Haiparian Mountains—a chain of mountains to the north just below the snowy country of Vtalmay.

As they neared the grounds of Shelkite's castle, the two men's singing voices died down. Formidable stonewalls appeared through the dusk. Prince Alkin gazed at his castle as he halted Sapharan, his blood bay, before the gate. Alkin moved his hazel eyes over the high walls thinking of his departed father. His ancestors had built the castle strong. Alkin had been thirteen when his father had passed away leaving him the ruler of Shelkite. Alkin's father had been a demanding, but just and popular ruler. After his death, the guidance and wisdom of Alkin's mother, Adama, prepared the young prince for the rest of his ruling era.

Bryan sat motionless on Dragon as he watched his prince scan the walls of the castle while they awaited the appearance of the gateman, Lycil. As Prince Alkin identified them, Bryan felt the damp of the night fade away. He thought of escaping to the warmth of the castle. The two horses stomped their hooves as the gate opened. Dragon snorted; a puff of mist sprang into the cool air. He arched his neck, prancing in anticipation of his awaiting dinner. The two riders guided their mounts through the gate and onto the flagged-stoned courtyard.

"My prince, I have some news!" Lycil called down. He was holding a torch. The flame was high above his head looking like his hair had caught fire. With Lycil's usual luck he probably *would* catch his hair on fire. Bryan chuckled at the thought. He was prone to accidents.

"What is it?" Prince Alkin answered him merrily.

"Apollos is back!" Lycil answered as they dismounted and handed their reins to the Stable Master's daughter.

Bryan watched the Prince stare dumbfounded at Lycil. Apollos hadn't been seen or heard of for two years. He was the Prince's most trusted advisor. He'd been an ally to the crown of Shelkite for many years. Though, the most extraordinary thing about Apollos was that he wasn't human. He was a unicorn. Unicorns in Eetharum were a rare sight. In fact, other than Apollos no unicorn had been seen for centuries.

Prince Alkin whispered something inaudible. Looking troubled, he turned and quickly ran to the castle's door. Since Bryan didn't have to guard the Prince as closely in the castle, he'd been looking forward to a pleasant night in his room away from all disturbances. Perhaps taking a hot bath and reading an old war book. Now, however, Prince Alkin had him worried. He was curious as to why the unicorn's sudden appearance had brought fear into his friend's eyes.

Hardly before Bryan settled in his room, even before his pleasant young servant could bring him dinner, he was summoned to come to the Council Hall. He heaved a sigh and grabbed his knife, sliding it back into his boot buckle and donned his sword. The servant girl gave him an understanding look as she helped him back into his uniform. His Master Sword garments comprised of tan trousers, riding boots, a lightweight, white shirt, and a silver trimmed blue overcoat. Once dressed, he started reluctantly down to the meeting hall.

He was late. The other eleven Master Swords were already gathered around the rectangle oak table. It sat in the center of a grand circular room. The hall was magnificently made. The thick walls rose high into a domed ceiling. Through a large window on the northeast was a spacious balcony overlooking Shelkite's precious grazing land.

Gracing the walls were murals telling the tales of ancient battles. The paintings consisted of thousands of mystical creatures that had been long forgotten or become extinct. The magical world of Eetharum and its creatures were now of the past. Only a few remnants of it still lingered. The unearthly power that had ruled Eetharum had waned at a great velocity after the Lost War. Magic and its counterparts had subsided against the multitude of humans. And humans went on, no longer bothering to remember their mystical brethren. Or the power that once dominated the world.

The room, however, was not the magnificent aspect that caught Sword Bryan's bright azure eyes. In the far right corner of the room, near the balcony, Prince Alkin stood conversing with none other than a unicorn. The creature was like nothing Bryan had ever seen. Its coat was of heavenly white and looked of satin. Each single iridescent, pearly thread of its mane and tail glimmered one of the colors of the rainbow when the flickering lights of the hall hit them. Its hooves were a bright copper-gold. And the slender, crystal horn dazzled the Sword's eyes.

The creature bobbed its flawless head and flipped his shimmering mane as he spoke. The Prince, listening intently, nodded and answered in low tones. Bryan stood gaping stupidly. Apollos had left on his mission after Prince Alkin had been threatened and before Bryan had become a Master Sword. Before he had moved to the castle and had had nothing to be concerned with other then his everyday warrior life in the camp. He had never seen a mystical creature in person before.

The other Swords spoke quietly, sitting around the table eyeing the unusual guest with suspicion. Bryan listened to the older men's murmured gossip of the possible reason for the Prince's sudden apprehension.

"Please sit down, Sword Bryan." Prince Alkin strode over eloquently. Apollos followed close behind. No sound echoed from the beautiful creature's hooves.

Bryan brushed a lock of dark hair from his eyes and took a seat at the end of the table, bracing himself for the bad news he knew he was about to hear.

Prince Alkin stood at the other end of the table looking out over his Master Swords. His earlier child-like behavior had vanished into maturity. He was now clad in robes of blue. His blonde locks were pulled away from his tense features. He looked kingly wearing his silver circlet. He placed his hands lightly on the table. The unicorn watched impassively from behind. Alkin eyed the group pragmatically. "I've kept a secret from you all." The Swords looked up to him perplexed. "I didn't want to announce something before I had facts. So, please forgive me. It wasn't something I should have spared." The Swords glanced at one another thoroughly anxious. "I have evidence of a threat to Shelkite—as well as Eetharum. King Ret of Zelka appears to have decided that he should set himself up as an emperor over Eetharum." Alkin paused. The Master Swords just stared at him. Eetharum was the united allies of their continent. The Prince continued, "I'm not sure if you all know, but King Ret is a wizard…" Alkin stopped and allowed a few murmurs to slither around the table. "I'm just going to say this plainly. I have to stop him. He's a threat to Shelkite and the peace of Eetharum. It could mean an all-out war, but there's still a chance we can stop him before it gets to that. I've learned of his clandestine plan from reliable spies in contact with the Chaos Goddess. She informed me that Ret usurped the throne unlawfully." Alkin sighed sounding like an old, worn out warrior, but pressed on. "He wants to dissolve the countries, and supplant the rulers with his own lackeys. And that's not half of it…" He hung on the sentence, re-snagging drifting attentions, "He…sacrifices to the Demon." He plunged on before anyone could interrupt, "So, that means he'll be using soiled magic against us. We won't be able to fight him with just swords and arrows." The Master Swords looked on him in heavy consternation. The hardy weapons they wielded were all they knew. "The Chaos Goddess says he has managed to dupe some Zelkans into his plan. But he has also recruited some mystical beings. I believe only Galeon is aware of this threat. Our task right now is to inform the rest of the allied countries and ready our military."

"Ready a military ignorant of magic? We'll be slaughtered," Sword Keavin blurted, hissing a bit in his anxiety.

Alkin held up a calming hand, "Apollos has just returned from trying to find our own magic to fight back with. I'm not naïve enough to think that we would succeed without manipulating magic ourselves. But, as you know, magic and its beings are not something we can readily get our hands on anymore. However, Apollos has discovered that there are magical keys we can seek out to aid us in his defeat. The good news is they're in Eetharum, though under watchful eyes."

"What are these keys—or counter magic?" Sword Xercan asked.

"We don't know..." Tense silence thrummed in their ears. "Apollos got this information from the Guidance Naiad."

"The creature from the Faded Sea in Carthorn?"

"Yes. She's a mystical being, that if found, will give a few trustworthy words of guidance."

"What if her magic is soiled? How do we know if we can trust her?" Sword Keavin was dubious.

"Apollos says she's trustworthy," was the Prince's curt response. He took a breath and continued, "Already many Zelkans have died in rebelling against Ret. He's covered up their deaths. He's very clever…and from my own experience I know he has a likable, though deceiving demeanor. This is urgent. He might be able to convince other countries to join him. It's our duty to protect Shelkite and our honor to protect our fellow countries. We can't let him cross Zelka's border. And if we can root him out and save Zelka, all the better. I beg for your pledge to stop him before he destroys the peace of Eetharum and our beloved Shelkite. Can I count on my Master Swords?" The Prince ended with an emphatic plea in his eyes.

The Swords looked upon him stunned, voiceless, and breathless. Bryan gulped down a lump of air. *How ironic, here's my adventure.* It definitely was a slice of an unexpected circumstance to stir his adventure lust. But he would have never wished *this* kind of adventure on anyone. Perhaps he was a little too bored with life; now it was paying him back. It was as if the buried powers of the world had come back to haunt them for forgetting they existed. For Bryan's cautious mind it was almost unbelievable to think that magic still resided in the present. If it wasn't for a unicorn standing before his eyes, he would have scoffed at the Prince's insanity. But there, at Alkin's side, a live magical creature stood. Bryan rose from his chair staunchly. "My service belongs to Shelkite and all it believes worthy," he said resolutely. Prince Alkin gave his friend a sad, appreciative smile. Bryan glanced nervously at the regal unicorn. Apollos gave the slightest nod of approval.

Another Sword stood. "I second that." Two more followed. Then the rest stood. Prince Alkin smiled a cheerless thank you.

"But, here is the main thing." He looked down at his fingers lying lightly on the table.

Bryan and the others took in a breath. He hadn't told them everything before he made them vow. *How deceiving.* Bryan narrowed his eyes. But he quickly pushed the angry feeling away. He would do his duty anyhow.

"Apollos has learned from the naiad that there's only one person that can control the counter magic against Ret." They stared bewildered, a few mouths opened. All wondered who it could be. And though no one mentioned it, they wondered if this person was even trustworthy. "We were told where we could find this magic user. She's from Eastern Kaltraz. I'm sorry to say that it seems we must enter this battle depending almost exclusively on a single soul…"

The word 'she' echoed in all their minds, an endless word resounding on and on. At least to Bryan it did. The Swords continued to stare, impassive to the world around them. Bryan was the first to come back. "A woman?" he nearly shouted in disgust.

Prince Alkin looked scared. "I'm afraid it's worse. We must not put our trust and lives in the hands of a woman, but a girl of only seventeen, a shepherd's daughter."

Chapter 2

A small figure sat confidently on a slender white horse in a small assembly making its way across the grassy foothills. It was nearing dusk. The white looked petite and fragile compared to the large warhorses striding nearby. But the poised rider of the white knew of the animal's abilities beyond those of the warhorses. The rider flipped her waist length black braid over her shoulder, looking warily around to the Shelkiten warriors with whom she had traveled with for so long. During their time together the warriors had made sure they took good care of her. However, they had spoken seldom to her. They had mostly conversed with one another in their own tongue, which, for the most part, was an obsolete language now, even for them.

Their journey, which had started more than a month ago, was now nearing its end as the large Shelkiten castle loomed ahead. The young rider knew little of what the Prince of Shelkite wanted with her. She was of the common people. What possibly could royal blood want with a dirty shepherdess? Even her own country's princesses had not known she had existed until two months ago. That was when she had received a notice she was to leave her home and come quickly to the castle of Kaltraz in the city of Sansdela in Western Kaltraz. From there, she was hurried through an explanation of her aiding Eetharum and how she must go see Prince Alkin of Shelkite. She hadn't even been able to give a suitable goodbye to her family. Her departure had been unexpected and heavily rushed. The warriors would have whisked her away with or without her permission. Nevertheless, though Alexandra was from a family of shepherds and inn keepers, she was spontaneous at heart. She was ready for anything that came her way. As long as she had her faithful mount, Zhan, and her handy bow and arrow.

The group halted in front of the towering, stone-mortared walls of the castle. Alexa surmised that rocks were a readily available source of construction material for this area considering all the stone fencing she had seen on her trip. It gave the country an alluring atmosphere. It was vastly different from the sandstone of Kaltraz.

To the west the sun slowly slid behind the rolling hills as if the grass were a sheet for the hot sphere to rest in for the cool night. Alexa watched it set. Her blue eyes glittered in the adventure and wonder of the moment. She had never been outside her country before.

The castle gates opened for the small procession to enter into the courtyard. Alexa looked around, curious to see how the foreigners lived, or rather how their prince lived. Then, she suddenly realized that *they* were not the foreigners. *She* was. She raised her chin haughtily, taking up her guard as a handsome man with dark unruly curls falling over his brow strode up from the stables. He wore a uniform of lightweight clothes to enable him to move freely. Alexa guessed he was high in the rankings of the prince's warriors. He was obviously skillful with the sword that hung at his side. Two austere warriors followed in his path. He came to halt in front of Zhan and her. With bright blue eyes he eyed her and her strange horse suspiciously. To Alexa he looked cocky. She was determined to not allow anyone get the better of her right away, especially after having to endure her escorts' impoliteness. She was on her own here. No one would do her any favors.

Sword Bryan strode up to meet the assembly and the girl they had escorted from Kaltraz. For some reason he felt like starting a grapple. He was still annoyed over the fact that a girl was appointed to do the perilous job. When he had defiantly walked over to the waiting lot, he half expected to see a petite, helpless child clad in a white dress riding sidesaddle. However, when he came to pause in front of the girl he was quite surprised. He saw a young woman, yes she was petite, but strangely enough she looked as if she could pull the horns off a dragon. Unlike the women from Shelkite, who always wore dresses and adornments, she wore dark, figure fitting pants, tall, black riding boots and a light worn out shirt and cloak. Slung over her shoulder was a bow and quiver. At her side hung a sheathed dagger fastened to her belt. She was obviously a ruffian. He looked her up and down, noting a single raven-black braid fell to the center of her back. Her features were angular and plain, but not completely unpleasing to the eye. Her

16

skin was lightly colored by the sun, causing a soft sprinkle of freckles to lie across her nose.

Bryan noticed with alarm her horse. A beast like that was not known around this country. He was too slightly built. His head small, but finely shaped. *He won't last a day of hard riding.* Bryan thought of his burly Dragon with pride.

The girl eyed him carefully back with vivid, sapphire eyes. Her eyes felt as if they saw straight through him. As if *he* were the one being evaluated not her. Bryan returned the challenging stare levelly.

"Am I sufficient, Sir Knight?" Alexa asked exasperated. She was tiring of his judgmental glances.

Her tone fell on Bryan's ears like bitter chocolate. "Master Sword," he corrected firmly. "A Master Sword is not quite the same thing as a knight. We're more superior in many aspects."

Alexa nodded tersely. "Pardon me, Master Sword. I didn't mean to offend you," she replied. Though, her inflection revealed she was not completely sincere.

"You're to meet our prince soon. Why aren't you clothed appropriately? And what kind of animal is that?" Bryan blurted, ignoring her apology. His brash statement even caught him by surprise. The words were over his tongue and out before he even realized that perhaps his comment was blatantly rude. It, in fact, did not matter how she dressed. The difference, actually, was something like a fresh breath of air to him. However, the horse had to go.

"I'm sorry if you don't approve of the way I dress. This is how most women in my country dress who are under Princess Athena's rule. If you want a girl in a silk gown, I suggest you find one of Princess Livia's followers. And this is a noble animal, quick witted and fast. He's bred for the deserts of my country," she answered curtly. Shouldn't she be the one asking the questions here? She was the one taken abruptly from her homeland. "In Kaltraz women are allowed to dress and do as they please. And the horses are high caliber. Isn't that so here?"

"Not exactly. Although, nothing is stopping the women, they just don't find it proper. It's untraditional. And, as for the horses, they have excellent bloodlines." Bryan smiled smugly. Sure, she was a cute thing, but a thorn. He felt his lip twitch. He was strangely being drawn to her oddities. He resisted it.

"I see, Master Sword." Alexa inclined her head, struggling to hold back a biting remark. This man needed to be put in his rightful place regardless whether or not he was a Master Sword and older than her. "I may be in your country, but I don't plan on changing myself just to please you."

"And we wish it to be that way." A pleasant voice came up from behind the Sword and his silent followers. Alexa looked up to see a handsome young man stroll up to stand next to the Sword. He was slightly shorter than and not as broad as the Master Sword, but looked fit just the same. His hair was golden blonde and pulled slightly back from his fair features. He smiled warmly. He wore no crown. His conduct and attire were the only indications that perhaps he was royalty. "Welcome, Alexandra. I'm Prince Alkin. I hope my Head-Master Sword hasn't frightened you?" His hazel eyes shone with kindness as he bowed to her. He wasn't much older than she was.

"Thank you, dear prince. And I'm not at all frightened by your mighty Sword," Alexa replied a bit haughty. She dismounted Zhan lithely, who was eyeing the nearby stables and its occupants with interest.

"We're very glad to have you. I'm sure you're tired. You can rest, have dinner, and a tour of my castle before we get into details as to why you're here." Prince Alkin took her sun-bronzed hand into his and landed a soft kiss there. Alexa smiled gratefully at the Prince. His grasp was warm and friendly. She had at first worried that the whole country was going to be unpleasant to her, but he had proven otherwise. He was their leader; and in her situation that was the most important. They started for the castle's doors. "I hear you're the daughter of a shepherd. Is this true?" Prince Alkin asked eagerly. Alexa followed him closely down the flagged-stone path, glancing back to see Zhan being led to the stables. The warriors had departed and returned to their business, but the cocky Master Sword followed close behind. Alexa could sense bitterness flowing from the man, masking any other feelings she might derive from him. Though, from the Prince she felt nothing but sincerity in his heart, giving her confidence.

"Yes, my father's a shepherd. He's also a wizard. But he prefers the quiet life of a shepherd and inn keeper." Alexa offered the information unabashedly.

"Oh, really?" The Prince seemed surprised. "That's intriguing. I can tell by the way you speak that you prize your father highly."

"Yes. He's a good man," she replied.

"Well, no more inquiring now. Let's get you settled, and then we can speak some more. I'm sure you're feeling a little lost and confused. I want to make sure you're as comfortable as possible." Prince Alkin's smile widened as they stopped in the castle's grandeur foyer. He called a servant to show Alexa her room. "I'll have Sword Bryan come for you in a couple of hours. In the meantime, you may make yourself at home in your chamber." He bowed and kissed her hand. He turned to leave her in the servant's care. Sword Bryan also smiled, though it looked forced, and bowed. He then followed the Prince down the corridor.

She glanced over her shoulder to the departing Prince Alkin and Master Sword. They intrigued her. She smiled and shook her head to free her thoughts. The people here were certainly different from hers, less personable, if she had to describe it. She quickened her pace to match the servant's quick short steps, all the while wondering why *she* was needed by a foreign prince.

Alexa found her chamber to be decorated warmly in the latest styles of western Eetharum. It was elegant. Being very fond of the sun, Alexa gleefully noticed that the adjoining washroom had large windows encircling two sides facing the vast hills of Shelkite. Although at the moment, it wasn't the sun shining through the windows but the moon casting its silvery shadows about the room. Alexa took it upon herself to soak in the awaiting, perfumed, hot water of the large tub. Her muscles, tight from the long days of riding, slowly relaxed. She closed her eyes, relishing the comforts of the castle.

When she had dressed in a clean set of her boyish garments, she braided her hair, letting the long raven plait fall down her back.

While she was gazing out across the fields of Fordorn there was a firm knock on her door. Poking her head out, she spotted Sword Bryan, who was trying his best to look his austere part. He didn't fool her. She smiled in spite of his set face. "I'm instructed to give the guest of honor a tour of the castle." Bryan bowed, clutching the sword at his side. "Would you like one, Miss Alexandra?"

"You can call me Alexa, or even Lex as my brothers do. And I'd very much like to see the castle." She looked back to her bow and quiver sitting on the bed, pondering whether she should bring them. She touched the dagger at her side encased in its sheath. If she got into any trouble it would be enough.

Bryan led the young woman through the castle, making only brief stops to explain murals or various statues. The higher levels of the castle consisted of Prince Alkin's personal wing, his family's chambers and the Master Sword chambers. The guest chambers were found just below. The servants had their own rooms in the southern lower wing. On the ground level were the ballrooms, dining halls, meeting rooms, throne room, library and of course the kitchens and laundry rooms.

Bryan began to lead Alexa down the staircase to meet with the Prince in the dining hall when she caught his arm. "What's down that wing? You didn't take me down that way." Alexa pointed beyond the staircase to the right.

"That's the Swords' conditioning rooms. I didn't think you'd want to see them," Bryan said. Although, he knew the girl would have probably liked them best. They were exquisite rooms and modernized for the age.

The girl's eyes lit up. "Can I see them?" she asked earnestly, unconsciously clutching his arm.

Bryan smiled reticently down at her, "Of course." He led her down the long corridor to one of the many rooms. He took her into the combat room to have a look around. One large window was the whole wall on the east side. The west wall in the rectangular room was lined with mirrors. All different kinds of swords, knives, daggers and other menacing looking weapons adorned the end walls: lances, maces, and battleaxes. Some blades of the swords were slim and straight, while others were thick and jagged.

Bryan watched as the young woman looked around purely amazed. She was unlike girls from Fordorn, he noted. Their pleasures were of clothes and jewelry, but Alexa seemed to be enjoying herself quite enough here. Bryan walked down to the end wall and pulled a sword down. Alexa followed him. The two eyed the sharp, glinting metal and delicately designed hilt.

"It's a Galeon sword," Bryan stated admirably. "In fact, all these swords are Galeon made. They're very highly regarded."

"Yes, Galeon borders my country to the northwest. I've heard of their impressive sword-makers. Many say that Galeonics are the best smithies and masons in the world. Though, I've never owned one of their swords myself." Alexa hesitantly touched the hilt of the weapon, a sense of awe in her voice.

"Yes, but it stills baffles me why any woman would enjoy a warrior's practice room and his weapons," Bryan stated, a little maliciously. He looked down at the girl touching the blade.

Alexa's head shot up, a glint of blue fire sprung into her eyes, turning her awed face into a dire stare. "Why shouldn't I? I'm not from here anyway. I could win any fight," she said icily.

"All right then, Alexandra of Kaltraz." He pulled down a sword and tossed it to her. "Fight me. I'm the Prince's best. By your fighting you will represent every woman that believes she's a warrior." The Master Sword honestly meant this sarcastically. He just wanted to irk her. He had heard and read of many great female warriors fighting in the Lost War, and thought highly of them. However, he wasn't about to let this arrogant girl know his true mind-set.

"It's Alexa!" she shot back, catching the sword by the hilt. "I'm my best at bow and arrow."

"So you lied then." Bryan smirked. He advanced toward her holding out his sword. The girl began to nervously back away from him. "All show, eh?"

"You have bitterness in your heart." Alexa frowned, taking up the sword. She didn't fear him, but she didn't want to fight him either. "Did something happen, *Sword Bryan*? Did some lady snare you on a hook only to throw you back?" She snickered. Bryan advanced on her and thrust. She blocked the hard blow. His features had turned sour. He grimly struck again, his footwork precise. Alexa parried it with a sly smile; her words had worked.

The two circled each other in the center of the room. Their eyes fixed for any slight movement. The full moon shone through the dark windows. The sconces lining the walls cast flickering shadows across them.

Bryan seethed inside. She was a little beast of a girl. He was beginning to wish it *had* been a lady to come save Eetharum. At least they were not deranged on what gender they were, as this girl seemed to be. Bryan attacked her with a series of hard thrusts. She blocked them effortlessly. He knew he should not use his full potential on her. It wouldn't be a good idea considering she was the Prince's guest. *Plus, it's an unfair fight anyhow.* His inner conscience nagged him.

Alexa bit her lip. She was forced to concentrate more on protecting herself then advancing on him. She couldn't let her mind go at ease, lest he strike. He *was* good. The best she had ever gone up against. She tried to thrust a blow, but failed. Alexa sneered at the Sword. "I hit the spot didn't I? Was she pretty? Did she dump you on your backside? Or did she just out smart you?" she said through gritted teeth.

Sword Bryan snarled at her and launched a swing. The swords sang when they connected. Bryan held his sword strongly on hers. Alexa strained under his strength, unable to make a move. With their faces inches apart, the Master Sword shoved. Alexa fell hard. Her sword skidded across the room, and he quickly put his blade to her throat. She glared up at him. Bryan smirked. "How do you think you know so much?" he said through a tense jaw. *I cannot stand this arrogant witch!*

"I don't *think* I know. I know!" she spat at him, feeling chagrined. His clear blue eyes narrowed. "You can't fool me, *Bryrunan*! My father is a full-blooded wizard. I have inherent senses," she snarled, rushing to get up. The tip of Bryan's sword glanced across her cheek. Alexa clenched her jaw and gave him an ill-fated look. *What a pig!* She seethed.

Bryan stared surprised down at the girl's face now reddened by a crimson scratch. How had she known his birth-name? He took a step back from her, perplexed. Her blood was only half-human? What had they gotten themselves into? Wizards lived to be very old, but most all had died out. Could this girl possibly be related to or conspiring with the wizard in the north?

A figure came to stand in the room's threshold, prying the twos' piercing glares away from one another. "Am I interrupting anything? Or do I remember correctly that Alexa is my guest and we were to meet for dinner now," Prince Alkin said. The Prince was doing all he could to contain his laughter. He had had a notion that the two would have to battle out their state of minds, but he had no idea that it would be so soon. He knew that ever since his friend had had a horrific experience with a former love he held little patience for the female gender, let alone a strong-minded one.

"Yes, my prince." Bryan took his weapon from Alexa's face. Stepping back, he sheathed it. Alexa straightened and went to stand next to the Prince, while Bryan replaced the sword she had used. Prince Alkin started down the corridor. The Master Sword slipped up behind Alexa. "How'd you know my true name?" he hissed in her ear. Very few knew his birth-name.

Alexa grinned, and whispered out of the corner of her mouth, "I told you. I have abnormal blood in my veins. Be careful what you think. I might be able to hear you." She smiled sweetly and bounded up to walk next to the Prince, leaving the Sword to wonder. She could of course sense feelings because she *was* part witch, but she had only known his name because it was a common name in the east. And she had actually only guessed his bitterness was because of some woman, perhaps it wasn't. She didn't think Sword Bryan posed any threat to her in a bad way, just an annoyance mostly. She would show him up later with her exceptional archery skills. Right now, though, she was anxious to speak with the Prince. She would deal with the arrogant Sword later.

Chapter 3

"Well, I must tell you that I'm a little relieved that you're a follower of Princess Athena and not Princess Livia." Prince Alkin leaned over the table grinning at Alexa. "It saves a lot of time and energy. I didn't want to have to train a duchess to fight." He chuckled. The princesses were twin sisters; Livia was known to be the more refined.

They were seated at one end of a long oak table in the oil-lamp lit dining room of the castle. The Prince was at the head. Alexa sat at his left, and Sword Bryan ate quietly at his right. The other Swords had eaten earlier while he had been giving her the tour.

Alexa smiled at the Prince and stuffed an ungodly amount of ham in her mouth. The dinner was like a feast to her. Having traveled for so long the food seemed exceptional. The servant had set in front of them platters of bread, cheese, ham and sweet potatoes. Alexa's mouth watered just at the sight of it. "I am a bit confused about why I'm here," she said after she had swallowed. "Why would you have to train me to fight?"

Bryan watched her disgustedly and a little flabbergasted. Why was she jamming so much food in her mouth, and more notably where did she put it all? She was so slender she could be used as a lance. Did she come from a family of heathens? He had to tell Alkin as soon as possible that she had witch blood in her. Bryan was not biased, but it made him feel uneasy considering the circumstances.

Prince Alkin smiled at Alexa understandably. He set down his mug and sighed. "That's reasonable." The Prince searched the girl's face. She had a veiled beauty that he figured many men had foolishly overlooked. He could have punched Bryan for being so rude and spoiling his guest's face.

Alexa watched the fair prince's features turn from cheery to unsettled, his brow creased in thought. She listened intently as he explained the situation and why and how she was a part of it. The Master Sword seemed to be ignoring them. He was busying himself munching on a buttered slice of bread, watching a candle's flame.

Alexa leaned toward the Prince eager, her curiosity running deep because of her connection with the wizard. Ret was her uncle. Her father's estranged twin. But she didn't find it wise to mention that just now. She set down her mug, which was filled with a sweet drink she had never tasted before. "So you got my name from…a nymph," she said.

"Yes, the Guidance Naiad from the Faded Sea in Carthorn. It's the only territory where magic still can be found. Apollos, my friend, brought this news." Prince Alkin motioned to the entrance of the dining room.

Alexa turned in her seat to see nothing other than a unicorn standing in the threshold. Her eyes widened and she almost choked on her ham. She had only ever heard meek descriptions of the beauty of unicorns in children's stories. This creature surpassed all imagination. She had never seen a unicorn; they didn't live in her country. She supposed that the desert climate was not their preferred habitat.

The heavenly creature nodded to her and stepped silently into the room. His pearly mane and tail shimmered in the flickering light. Alexa's mouth dropped open. The unicorn came and stood next to the Prince. Bryan stopped chewing to watch the girl's reaction. In spite of his dislike of her he had to smile. Apollos was truly a remarkable sight.

Once Alexa overcame her surprise and noticed that Prince Alkin was grinning at her, she snapped her jaw shut. "I'll try my best to live up to your expectations. Although, I don't know what to do this second; I think it'll come to me…eventually," Alexa stated tentatively.

Bryan snorted from across the table. Alexa, Alkin and the unicorn turned their attention to the Sword. "This is absurd, certainly *not* the way to win a war. We're being led by a girl that doesn't know anymore what's going on than the army itself. And, she'll be fighting against her own likeness. Sounds like we'll crush the enemy for sure," he said sarcastically, a flicker of flame in his eyes.

The Prince looked down, licking his lips thoughtfully. Bryan was accurate. It seemed all odds were against them. But he had nothing else to work with. They needed magic to fight the wizard, and this girl had magic bloodlines.

Apollos snorted chidingly, breaking their despondent thoughts. "Have a little faith. Don't begin hopeless." Apollos shook his head disapprovingly; his mane flipped to the other side of his satiny neck. "We're taking the correct steps. We're taking the only steps we know of. It does seem we're entering this a bit handicapped, but we *do* have a lead. Right now we have to be patient. Use your brains and sense! Plan where to begin finding the keys, decide where to place the first contingent of troops, and discover with whom we can ally ourselves with. We have to *do* what we know we *can* do."

"Yes," Alexa piped up. "I'll look for the keys the naiad spoke of. I wonder what kind of magic they are?" she pondered aloud.

"But how do we know where to begin? The naiad never said," Bryan asked. His azure eyes bored intensely into the others.

"We wait until I know; and then we ride. My magical senses give me an extraordinary intuition," Alexa stated. She felt more confident every minute. If only her brothers could see her now. They would be so jealous of her. She smiled at the thought.

"Intuition? We place our lives on your intuition? Foolish! And with that scrawny beast you're riding you won't get very far," Bryan stated flatly.

Prince Alkin sighed and rubbed his forehead. Why did Bryan have to be so difficult? If he were not such a good friend and Master Sword Alkin would have demoted him real fast. He knew Bryan's blatant suspicions were all for the best and just a precaution, but they were still exasperating at times.

Alexa felt heat rise in her face. She clenched her teeth. "Magical intuition is different, Master Sword. It can't be defined the same way as a normal person's intuition," she shot back, "And Zhan's a more worthy animal than any beast that's bred here," she added frostily. "He's built for speed and distance. He's smart and knows me well."

"His color also stands out more than our horses. It'll draw attention. He'll stand out like a dragon in the city." Bryan sat back, feeling pleased with himself, although he had no idea why.

Prince Alkin rubbed his brow in frustration. "I'm sure her Zhan will serve her just fine." He glared at the Master Sword, feeling that this was a detrimental argument to their forward progress.

Alexa looked admiringly on the Prince for using her mount's name.

"His coat is of no matter," Apollos said to Bryan. "I can easily make his coat appear as dark as a raven's feathers. Besides," the unicorn's eyes twinkled, "I can't imagine he'd stand out more than me."

The Head-Master Sword didn't answer.

"Then it's settled." Prince Alkin smiled. "I still have to decide how to order my troops and find our allies, but as soon as Alexa gives word we will send a team out in search of the keys." Prince Alkin slapped the table and leaned back in his chair content for the moment. He never stayed in a suppressed mood for long. Things were going as smooth as they could. He would send out emissaries to the surrounding countries to notify them and advise them to prepare for battle and defense. He would also discuss battle plans with his advisors in the coming days. He felt a tad less tense having a more solid plan now.

Alexa looked at the Prince, her senses discerning him. He was such an optimistic young man. Quite the opposite of his Sword-Guard, but she also knew that Sword Bryan was not pessimistic. He was just cautious, realistic…and perhaps a bit bitter.

Bryan sighed and leaned back, relaxing. Alexa turned her attention to watch him, trying to discern his disposition. He was not at all what he appeared. He only played that he didn't like her. She could tell that he certainly cared deeply for his younger companion and master, the Prince. Suddenly Bryan's glittering azure eyes caught her gaze; they quickly turned dull. Alexa swiftly pulled her eyes away.

The unicorn nodded his finely shaped equine head in approval of the plan at hand. His eyes had a spark of assurance in them. Alkin stood, pushing back the heavy chair. The others followed suit. "Oh, one more thing," Alkin grinned inwardly, "Since, Sword Bryan, you're the best of the best you will be Miss Alexandra's personal Sword-Guard for the time being. It isn't as urgent for me to be protected as it is for her now." Alkin knew this would not go over well with the Master Sword, but it was the logical thing to do.

Bryan's jaw nearly dropped, but he kept his composure well underhand. He'd imagined that he would be leading the warriors into battle, not following the girl around, babysitting.

"However, I also hope you will accompany Alexa on the mission, but that's to be decided later. I'm putting Sword Xercan in charge of the warriors." Prince Alkin smiled knowing Bryan's thoughts. He hated doing the opposite of what he knew his friend wanted, but he had a feeling this was the best place for Bryan.

Alkin looked to Alexa and smiled. She nodded. "Get some rest and make yourself at home. Don't fret too much over knowing what to do. It'll come to you. You were meant for this. And, also, tend to your wound. We don't want you ill." Alkin inclined his head in goodbye and gestured for Apollos to follow him. At the threshold he added, "You have a guardian now. I'll not have to worry about you." Then with a glance at the austere Bryan, he said, "Give him lots of trouble. He likes it." With that, he laughed and left the two.

Alexa chuckled and bowed as the prince departed. Dead, awkward silence engulfed the dining room. The two antagonists stood silently, feeling an invisible barrier grow between them.

"Come on. I'll move my things in the chamber next to yours," Bryan declared and headed out. He must press on and do his duty as much as he despised it.

When they reached Alexa's chamber, Bryan stopped at her door as she was entering. "If you need anything, I'll be in here." He gestured to the room across the hall. He stared dryly as the girl's bright sapphire eyes gazed straight into his. They caused his nerves to unravel. They had a peculiar deep, penetrating feeling to them. They were clever bewitchment tools he was certain.

Then, surprising even himself, he grabbed her chin roughly and turned her cheek. "I'll send up a servant to care for your cut."

He examined the irritated pink skin around the slash. It was harmless; she would be fine.

Annoyed with his sudden rough contact, Alexa jerked her chin from his grasp. "I can take care of myself, thank you," she said coldly.

"As you wish, but I'll still send a servant. Good night." He bowed, agitated with his own coarse behavior. He couldn't help himself. He couldn't say why he disliked her. The arrogant witch just did all the right things to elicit an attitude from him.

Alexa watched the tall man stride down the corridor to retrieve the servant. She sighed, a sly, half smile curving her lips. She closed the door softly and went to undress for bed. Her body felt so weak and worn from the news and travel. She missed home desperately. Before she fell asleep that night, she came to the obvious conclusion that it was going to be a long, baffling journey. One that she wasn't quite certain she was prepared for.

Chapter 4

During the next couple of days, Alexa took it upon herself to investigate the castle grounds. She wanted to visit the workers that served under Prince Alkin in order to see if she could gather any information about this country and its prince.

The castle was certainly a grand one, bigger than Kaltraz's, but not as exquisite. Kaltraz's palace was made of red brick, a clay-like substance. It was open to the sun in many places, but cool when inside. Its décor was beautiful. Sparkling, colorful mosaics of the country's history lined the walls. Cool fountains bubbled among lush gardens around every bend. Alexa had only been there when she'd been summoned to Shelkite. She'd been awed.

Alexa's country was divided in to two separate states, Western and Eastern Kaltraz. Eastern Kaltraz was ruled by the Princess Athena. Western Kaltraz was ruled by Athena's twin sister, Princess Livia. The country had been divided thus upon the death of their mother the queen. The princesses knew many countries had been torn apart by quarrelling twins fighting for the throne, so they concluded they would have mutual power. Instead of declaring themselves queens, the twins crowned themselves princesses, dividing Kaltraz into two united states. Each princess ruled the best way she saw fit, but any chief decisions were made by the combined councils of the princesses.

There was a great river that sliced through the country dividing it into western and eastern halves; so the division had been rather simple. The people were welcoming to the idea. The citizens from each state lived in friendly co-existence with each other. They came and went freely between the two states. The currency was the same, but the industrial exports of the two states were different. Western Kaltraz consisted of many grand cities. Its population was full of aristocrats and wealthy merchants. It was well known for its fine cloths and beautiful clothing. Eastern Kaltraz was more rural. It was best known for breeding fine horses and raising sheep for wool.

Alexa's family was under Princess Athena's influence. Princess Athena loved the desert sun. She could often be spied relaxing at many of the luxuriant oases. She disguised herself in a red hooded cloak and traveled with her guards—some of which were rumored to be her lovers. Though the cities were sparse and the countryside consisted mostly of desert, she could often be found traveling through her land upholding her own laws and mingling with the people. However, the more refined and fashionable Princess Livia kept mainly to her palace and left the law upkeep to her trained men.

Athena's people were allegedly said to be more of a crude crowd than those of Livia's. Thus, they were dubbed warmly by Livia's followers as the Ruffians. Eastern Kaltrazians referred to Livia's followers, a group of more etiquette peoples, the Dukes. Alexa was proud to have Athena as her princess; and by all standards Alexa fit the stereo type of Athena's people perfectly.

Prince Alkin's castle was different. Tall, formidable walls encircled Prince's abode, giving it an aloof feel. Sentinels marched impudently across the walls holding their crossbows forebodingly. However, there was a large, pleasant courtyard to the right of the main entrance of the castle. Alexa deduced this gate was the only entrance in or out except for the probable secret passageways. Aside from the castle itself, within the walls there were cabins to house guards and a decent sized stable with lush paddocks.

Coming out of the slightly gloomy castle into the sunny courtyard, Alexa paused to view her surroundings. The pleasing sound of the fountain in the center of the courtyard filled the atmosphere. The water plopped and sprayed onto the flag-stone walk. Alexa discovered the fountain wasn't just for embellishment; it sat on a fresh water spring, and the castle's residents collected their drinking water here.

Various bushes lined the walkways and small blossoming trees scented the air sweetly. Alexa walked to the fountain and bent to dip her hand in the silky waters. The sun glared off the rippling water and sent her mind into dreamy thoughts. A familiar whinny broke her daydream. She looked up to the stables across the garden, promptly forgetting her silly fantasy. Cupping her hands with the sparkling icy water, she took a refreshing sip. Wiping her mouth with her sleeve, she strode over to the stables.

There she met Rhik the Stable-Master and his daughter.

They exclaimed, to a very pleased Alexa, how exquisite Zhan was. After a few minutes of exchanging good horseflesh talk with Rhik, Alexa tacked Zhan up with his lightweight saddle and bridle. She led him out and mounted by the fountain.

At the sound of heavy hooves clopping across the stones and the jingle of metal, Alexa shifted in her saddle to see Sword Bryan ride up beside her. She eyed him a little sourly. "I'm just taking a look around. Do I really need a guide?" she stated. Zhan curiously touched noses with Dragon.

Bryan smiled. She would never consent to his power over her. "Someday you'll be glad of my presence when you so boldly get yourself in a fix." Bryan's azure eyes sparkled in the sun. "My orders were to take care of you, so that I will. Come on, I'll show you around." Bryan had determined he would be nice to the arrogant girl, if only for the Prince's sake. He heeled Dragon forward before the dominate stallion could squeal and strike at Zhan.

Annoyed, Alexa gave her mount a sharper jab than she intended. Zhan, not accustomed to such rashness from his rider, leapt forward startled. Alexa rode ahead, muttering under her breath through gritted teeth, "I don't need a babysitter."

Bryan shook his head and smiled. Her narcissism would soon get the better of her. "Hey, Lycil! Open the gates!" he heartily called up to the Gate-Master. The day was sunny and beautiful despite the cool breeze. He wasn't in the mood to let anything bring him down. The castle gates creaked open and the horses clopped through.

They had a fairly pleasant ride as they cantered around the circumference of the castle. The emerald hills rolled away from them in all directions. Nothing was located for miles except for the nearby extensive warrior's quarters and training grounds.

Alexa carefully scrutinized the towers, walls and sentinels. Bryan rode along her side, watching her carefully. Every now and then he would state the history of the castle and Fordorn. When they came around again to the main gate, Bryan stopped his lesson and they halted the horses.

"Everything safe, warden? Where would you like to go

now?" he asked sarcastically.

Alexa nodded her head and looked up to Lycil at the sound of a clatter. He'd been resting quietly and humming to himself right before he'd accidentally knocked his mug over with his elbow. "I'd like to see the city. Is that okay?" she asked, looking back to the Sword.

For the first time the girl sounded unsure of herself. Bryan pondered this. Maybe she was finally realizing she wasn't as important as she thought she was. "It's over six miles." Bryan shrugged. He didn't care what they did; the horses were warmed up for the trek now.

"I'd like to see it," she said cordially. Sword Bryan wasn't so bad. He may be bitter inside, but he'd offered information kindly on any questions she'd had as they circled the castle.

"All right then, let's get started." Bryan glanced briefly down at her. Dragon was much bigger than Zhan. The two horses looked odd alongside each other, like dam and foal.

The Master Sword led the way down the grassy road to the east and Fordorn. "It'll be early afternoon when we reach the city." He turned in his saddle to speak to her. "We can find something to eat at one of the taverns and then head back. Prince Alkin's mother wants to speak with you later tonight." Alexa nodded and flipped her braid over her shoulder. She scanned the hilly terrain and farmlands.

Bryan picked up the conversation again as Alexa drew abreast with him. He spoke of legends and strange things seen in Shelkite. He also spoke fondly of Prince Alkin and Shelkite's history and a little of the Lost War. He was very knowledgeable in history, obviously because of a fondness of it. Though, Alexa noted he carefully veered away from anything personal, his past or anything he did before he had become the Head-Master Sword. She studied him closely. He merely stared to the road ahead as he spoke.

Bryan could feel the girl's peculiar eyes on him. He distinctly tried not to look at her. He spoke of the country's supply of crops, including the profitable tobacco plant, and livestock, beef and dairy cattle. He explained how all the surrounding countries depended heavily on Shelkite's agriculture. "We're proud of our farmland and that we can contribute a lot to Eetharum. It gives Shelkitens a sense of pride." Bryan squinted as he looked adoringly over the rows of young, growing crops. The sun shone on them as the wind rippled over the fields, giving an illusion of a verdant ocean.

"What about you, Sword Bryan? Your name isn't of these parts. It sounds more eastern." Alexa paused, eyeing his reaction carefully. "The shortened version actually sounds of the origin of Kaltraz's old language. Why do you shorten your true name? Did your family migrate from somewhere? Undoubtedly you would never admit it…"

The Master Sword scowled and didn't look at her when he answered, "For as long as I can remember I've lived in Shelkite. My parents were farmers. They died when I was very young," he said. He shut his eyes briefly, attempting to clear a vivid memory. Then he added more proudly raising his chin, "I don't know why I have an eastern name." He turned in his saddle to look at her. "If I had it my way I wouldn't," he retorted. Of what he knew of the easterners they were rude and absurdly proud. In his opinion, the west was the pride of Eetharum. He knew this was judgmental, but it'd been his experience. He had traveled a lot.

Alexa bore him with a shallow gaze at his attempt to slash down her people.

Bryan swallowed tensely and didn't say more. Sometimes his tongue galloped away with him. *So much for trying to get along with her.* He rolled his eyes up in exasperation with himself. It bothered him that he didn't have a more Shelkiten name, being the Head-Master Sword and all. The other Swords seemed to bristle at this aspect, too, for some reason. It was a sore spot. *She would point that out wouldn't she?* He made a sour face.

They traveled in silence the last miles to Fordorn. With every mile Bryan seemed to get hotter inside, until he felt like he was boiling with irritation. She had no business prying into his life. He was her Sword-Guard. That was all. Not her long-time friend, or even for that matter his acquaintance. As far as he was concerned she was on a need to know basis; and she was asking too many questions. There was something underhanded about this eastern girl, and he wasn't about to let it go.

A bit later they entered the bustling city. Alexa looked around amazed as their horses carefully made their way through the crowded, cobbled streets. The Master Sword had taken her to a higher class section of town. Fordorn was so different from the small villages she knew in Eastern Kaltraz. It was large, with a mixture of new grandeur buildings and some older quaint buildings lining the main street. Well-kept cobbled roads branched off the main street to lead into fancy neighborhoods and other businesses. They passed by a well-manicured square where some of the citizens were strolling and enjoying the refreshing afternoon.

They turned down a side street where people, mostly commoners, bustled about in their daily routines. Merchants' carts were set up alongside the road and they called out to them as they passed.

They rode by a rotund man guarding a booth with pearls and other fine jewels. "Hello, beautiful!" the suave-looking man grinned beseechingly at Alexa. He held out a pearl necklace. "How would you like some Yoldor pearls to grace that radiant neck of yours? They're imported straight from the Elendace Sea. They say *mermaids* grow them." Alexa smiled and declined politely. But the gentleman regarded Bryan with a sly smile, "Master Sword, why don't you treat your pretty girl to a special gift?"

The Sword shook his head, and rolled his eyes upward.

They continued on and Bryan carefully maneuvered Dragon around a group of gossiping women. Alexa heeled Zhan to his side. "So, this is Fordorn," Bryan commented. They halted the horses to let a crowd of people cross. They were now in more of a working class part of town.

Alexa looked up and around. Tall apartment buildings towered above her. Women left their laundry out to dry stories above. Young girls hung out the windows to call to their friends below. Rebellious boys raced each other, knocking into booths, causing angry merchants to curse them away.

"Marki's Tavern is up the road a bit." Bryan nudged Dragon forward. "I think it'll suit you." He looked over his shoulder at her. "They have delicious food. I don't usually find too many bugs…" he added casually, then rode away.

Alexa nodded absently, not losing her zest for the city's sights. He was just trying to agitate her.

They passed more taverns, shops and inns. A young woman approached Dragon and Sword Bryan as they stopped for another throng to pass. Her pale hand stroked Dragon's dark neck. The stallion craned his head around to investigate the new touch.

"Master Sword," the girl whispered.

Bryan looked skeptically down at her. His dark locks drooped over his bright eyes. He towered over her atop Dragon. Alexa halted keeping her distance. The young woman had long blonde, wavy tresses and a small piercing in her nostril. She was not at all homely, and she wore a revealing gown. Alexa watched the encounter suspiciously with a furrowed brow. *Peculiar.*

The girl spoke for only the Master Sword to hear, "Care to come and savor the last hours of day with me?" She caressed Dragon's reins and laid a gentle hand on Bryan's polished boot.

Bryan's handsome features were troubled. He looked into the girl's brown eyes and said, "Don't care to, but, here." He dug into one of his blue overcoat's many pockets and pulled out two silver coins. He dropped them into the girl's hand.

Alexa stared, shocked. The girl looked purely overjoyed with unbelief.

"Oh! Thank you, Master Sword! Thank you!" She turned and dashed away.

Wordlessly, Bryan moved on.

"A friend of yours?" Alexa said, raising an accusing eyebrow.

Bryan clenched his teeth, looking intently ahead for the worn, painted sign of Marki's, trying desperately to choke his impatience. "Nope," he replied tersely, and then mumbled, "Sorry, poor wretch."

"Oh," Alexa said with a frown.

"Think I'm the kind to keep company with brothel girls?" Bryan glared at Alexa.

Alexa shrugged, feinting wide, innocent eyes. "Wouldn't

think it was below you," she said casually while patting Zhan. *How was I to know?* She sulked inwardly.

The Master Sword turned in his saddle to face her, a scathing look in his eyes. "You had better be careful what you say, Miss Alexandra. You've a lot to learn. Remember *you* are the foreign one here." The words dripped, seething from his mouth. If she'd been a man he would have punched her right off that gangly beast of hers and into the mud. "It's my country's duty to help others. Whether they be a brothel girl or not," he said hotly. "Even though she is a slave, she still had more manners than you'll ever have. Maybe if you subjected yourself to her life style you wouldn't be so vain and we'd all be better off."

His words bit deeply. Alexa's head snapped around to face him. He glowered at her, his eyes bright and sizzling. She stared contemptuously back, her jaw clenched. Thought he was smart, did he? What a scoundrel! She should curse him. She knew a few. Though, her father always warned her never to use them in anger. But certainly something good to send Dragon bucking his master off into the mud wouldn't hurt.

Bryan felt spiteful. *Maybe now the self-righteous so-called Savior of Eetharum will keep her obnoxious trap shut.* What she needed was a good kick in the rear. He knew Alkin would be furious with him if he knew how he was treating her. *But, the vain little witch threw her own insult first.* He defended himself.

When they finally reached the tavern, the Master Sword heaved a sigh. He dismounted Dragon and tied him to the hitching post underneath the battered wooden sign.

Alexa hopped down from Zhan, her boots sinking deep into the sloppy mud. She screwed up her face and followed the Sword into the noisy tavern.

The two ate mostly in silence. Bryan felt a little irritated as he sipped his drink carefully and watched Alexa stuff food in her mouth. "Does it have your approval?" he asked, with a wry raised eyebrow.

Alexa nodded her head vigorously. She wiped her mouth with her sleeve. "What do Shelkitens do for entertainment?"

Bryan sat down his mug. "Pretty much the same as

anywhere else, I suppose. They hold dances and have circuses, play games, drink…enjoy the pleasures of the flesh," he added with a roguish smile. She ignored it and he continued, "Prince Alkin doesn't really care as long as they behave themselves. There's also a fine theatre in the south side of town." He stood, putting down a few copper coins.

Alexa got to her feet, picking up her much-needed cloak. The air in Shelkite was much cooler and damper than in Kaltraz, probably due to the ocean on the western border.

Bryan waved and thanked Marki as they parted the tavern.

As they stepped out on the front porch, a curvy woman holding up her sweeping skirts came trudging through the mud breathless to greet them. "Oh, Head-Master Sword! I'm so glad you're here!" she called in relief. She went to step on the porch, but left a delicate boot behind in the mud. She turned exasperated and tugged at the shoe a few times before finally releasing it from the muck. Placing it back on her foot she said, "I must speak with the Prince at once. Is there a way you could escort me to the castle?"

Bryan nodded and quickly mounted Dragon. "Do you have a mount?" He reined Dragon around to face Lady Evelyn.

Evelyn shook her brunette curls. "I tried the local stables to rent a pony, but they're all rented out," she replied. "My horse," she continued, straightening her stance and looking vexed, "is unfortunately missing in action. I'm going to have to have a talk with the inn keeper," she said a little frostily.

"Well, then…." Bryan offered his arm. Evelyn smiled gratefully and swung herself up behind him. If he must do it for Alkin's sake, he would. It was his duty whether he liked it or not. *How much worse can it get?* He was in the company of two women who couldn't have been more different from each other and both of which he despised.

"We aren't seeing more of Fordorn?" Alexa protested from atop Zhan. She felt annoyed with the new company.

"Nope, Miss Alexandra," Bryan answered. "We have to get back. Remember Lady Adama wants to meet with you? And Lady Evelyn has to speak with the Prince," he said authoritatively.

Alexa clenched her teeth as Evelyn landed her big, curious brown eyes on her. Was that a flare of competition in her eye? Alexa wondered. Well, she certainly had nothing to worry about. Alexa stared moodily after the departing back of the Master Sword and his warhorse's big rear. She muttered under her breath, "It's *Alexa*!" She steered the prancing Zhan to follow him up the street and out of Fordorn.

As they rode outside the city, Lady Evelyn chatted cheerily. Her words were being mostly wasted, as Sword Bryan didn't answer her often and Alexa was too busy trying to use her witch senses to discern the woman. She seemed to be a flirt, but of some importance, Alexa figured. She wasn't going to see the Prince for personal matters. She was going for a sincere, important reason. The woman seemed to be honest, yet Alexa sensed dishonesty in her also. She seemed like she posed no ill will. She obviously had a liking for idle chatter, fine clothes, and from the looks of things Master Sword Bryan.

As they passed the Blue Mermaid, Evelyn stopped her chattering momentarily. With her magical senses running rampant, Alexa sensed Sword Bryan desiring to make a stop there. He would no doubt return later if he could. There was something bothering him and she sensed him wishing to drink it away.

As they passed the tavern's sign swinging and creaking in the breeze, Alexa felt a strange stir within her being. The buzz started in her chest and spread out to her fingertips. Her breath seized inside of her. She squelched a startled gasp and cringed at the awkward sensation as it flooded into her brain. She stared at the faded, cracked paint of the sign as if it were at fault.

The sign was of a bare-breasted, golden-haired mermaid with blue fins, holding up a mug of ale to good cheer. Alexa did a double, baffled look at the sign. For just a split second the combination of her light-headedness and swinging sign made it look as if the mermaid was beckoning to her. Alexa stared wide-eyed as she rode closer and closer to the apparently very happy, intoxicated mermaid. When she came within reaching distance of the sign, another more powerful shudder shot through her viscera, causing Alexa's body to tense almost uncomfortably.

Alexa rode in mute surprise. Craning her neck around, she blinked befuddled at the sign as it swung squeakily in the wind. After she recovered from her initial shock, she sat pondering for several long minutes. She finally concluded she had had an episode of magical intuition. The buzz swimming through her body was the rush of magic.

The others seemed completely oblivious to Alexa's experience. Evelyn had started to chat again and Sword Bryan would occasionally throw a disgruntled look over his shoulder to see if his responsibility was still riding safely behind.

Then the clue suddenly became clear to Alexa. She grinned to herself. She would find the magical key for the counter magic in the underwater world of the merpeople, if such a place still existed. The hint was now so obvious to Alexa that she didn't doubt it. She knew her witch intuition had kicked in, for it was undeniably magic ebbing hotly through her veins.

It seemed to Alexa that her father had mentioned merpeople before, that they could be found in the Elendace Sea. *"But the most inhospitable creatures you'd ever come across,"* he used to mutter. Alexa hummed to herself, happy to have found a clue. She would tell the Prince immediately.

Bryan glanced at Alexa from the corner of his eye. *What is she so happy about?* he grumbled inwardly. If only he could be back in the camp with the other warriors, sword fighting and training instead of here. Alkin would surely give him the rest of the night off, hopefully. He sighed, ruefully missing the warrior camp.

The Sword decided to make a visit back to the Blue Mermaid. He just had to get these females off his hands first. Alexa would be completely safe in the castle with another Master Sword to guard her for the time being. It would be just time enough for him to have a quick drink. Only, though, if she didn't decide to go off and do something stupidly brave, as was her wont he suspected.

Chapter 5

To Bryan's delight Prince Alkin released him from his duty for the evening, charging Sword Boraz to guard Alexa until his return.

Alkin was overjoyed to see Lady Evelyn. He waved Bryan off and led Evelyn into the library to talk. Alexa, however, huffed out a noisy grunt and strutted away man-like to her room to retire until the Prince's mother called for her. Bryan shrugged unconcerned as he watched the silly girl walk away. He then sent for Sword Boraz. Being released, Bryan started out immediately for the tavern.

Alexa had been raised with eleven older brothers. They lived with her wizard father and human mother in the outer, rocky lands of Kaltraz. Eastern Kaltraz was known for its horse breeding. However, Alexa's family was shepherds, albeit they had several broodmares. They also owned a well-to-do inn. Most of their customers were travelers, the majority merchants, going to and from the Kalcala Desert. The weary travelers always welcomed good shelter and a hearty meal after a trek through the vast, unforgiving desert. The Kalcala began in Eastern Kaltraz and reached to the far east.

Alexa was favored as the only girl and the youngest. Although all her siblings shared the wizard blood, Alexa was the only child their father had begun to teach how to utilize her magical powers. Alexa's father, Erec, had left his magic behind when he had decided to settle down at the age of one-hundred sixty. The reason was because he had fallen in love with a beautiful human woman. He and the young woman named Dara had married right away. They immediately started a family. That was forty years ago.

Even though Erec no longer had magical powers, he had over time decided to teach his only daughter some tricks of his blood. Alexa was glad he had. But, she was still a novice at best. Her powers hadn't completely manifested either. By wizard years she was still young and maturing. At this time she could utilize her senses well, but the innate senses were also something her brothers possessed even without being trained.

Of her brothers Alexa was the sharpest arrow shot of the family, one of the best at dagger throwing and the second to best rider. But none of these talents had anything to do with her semi-trained witch blood. She had grown up with a throng of tough, harassing brothers, and she had learned how to take care of herself. Her family was competitive among each other. So she had always strived to be better than the boys.

As Alexa lay on her bed, she thought of her best accomplishment; winning the highly prized Arrow Trophy just last season at the annual archery match in the city of Sansdella. She was proud. Her whole family had been proud.

She rose to splash cool water on her face and glare at her reflection in the mirror, wondering just how good she really was. Perhaps she was taking this competition thing with Sword Bryan a little too far. Though, he did think that he was the best thing since Galefen, the greatest warrior ever in all of Eetharum. He was a legendary general in the Lost War. The war had ended five hundred years ago. The people, blinded by fear, hate, and blood lust had driven the war on for a whole century. A hemorrhaging Eetharum was left in its wake. It had taken many long years of reconstruction to heal the countries, though some wounds in old enough hearts had yet to be mended.

Alexa rolled her eyes at the thought of comparing Sword Bryan to Galefen. She should be thinking of more important things than trying to outdo that egocentric pig! Why did it seem so important anyway?

There was a knock on her door. Expecting to hear the deep voice of Sword Boraz coming to retrieve her to speak with Lady Adama, Alexa snatched up her dagger to strap around her waist. But instead of Sword Boraz, a feminine voice floated through the door.

"Miss Alexandra?" Another light tap sounded.

"Come in." Alexa finished strapping her dagger and looked up to see a woman open the door. She was perhaps a few years older. Her bronze-gold hair was concealed tightly in a plait wrapped around her head. She held a tray of steaming food. "I take it Lady Adama isn't ready for me yet," Alexa stated, eyeing the food.

The girl shook her head and walked over to set the tray on the table. "I'm Melea. I'll be your servant while you're here." Melea's brown eyes swept briefly over Alexa.

Alexa plopped down in her chair and pulled the tray toward her and said, "Which hopefully won't be long." She took a swig of her drink, discovering the sweet liquid to be famous Zelkan wine. Wiping her lips with the back of her hand, she looked up at Melea who was standing quietly, hands folded in front of her. "Do you happen to have anything stronger?" Alexa asked through a mouthful of food. Melea nodded her pretty head and turned to retrieve it. "Wait. Never mind. It's all right." Alexa waved her back, taking a bite from her seasoned chicken leg.

"Anything else I can do for you, Miss Alexandra?"

"Yes." Alexa motioned for Melea to take a seat. "Please tell me about Sword Bryan…and Prince Alkin." Melea's pale cheeks flushed. Alexa looked at her curiously, raising an eyebrow.

Melea cautiously lowered herself across from Alexa. "What would you like to know, Miss Alexandra?"

"Alexa," she corrected her, "if you please. Would you like something to eat?" she offered, feeling rude for eating in front of the servant.

"Oh, no thank you. I just ate." Melea smiled gratefully.

"Just tell me what you know about Sword Bryan." Alexa said, setting down her massacred chicken bone. Melea turned a deeper shade of crimson. Alexa stuffed a mouthful of mashed potatoes in her mouth to keep from snickering at the older girl.

"He's the best of the Prince's men," Melea started a little hesitantly. Alexa nodded encouragingly for her to continue. "He's also the youngest of the Prince's Master Swords. He's an excellent warrior, swordsman, and was top student in his academics." She paused, raising an arching, suspicious eyebrow.

Alexa took a drink of her wine knowing the girl thought she was up to something dubious. How was she to help anyone if they acted like they couldn't trust her and kept things from her? She had to find out somehow. Alexa prodded, "Was he born in Shelkite?"

Through the chamber window the girls could see the sun slowly slip into its hilly blanket for the night. Pregnant storm clouds began to accumulate, promising rain.

Melea straightened in her chair. "Oh! He had to be to even been accepted as one of the Master Swords," she said a little defensively. "All the warriors accepted in the school take an oath claiming their blood was born for Shelkite and will die for Shelkite. It's a strict oath, but it's stricter yet if they become Master Swords. They have to be pureblood Shelkitens, born on Shelkite soil; and if they marry it has to be a woman native to the land—to bear true Shelkiten sons." She stopped briefly, and then continued slowly, "Bryan's—I mean *Sword* Bryan's family died when he was just a child." Melea's brown eyes lowered. "It was very tragic. Prince Alkin's father, the late Prince Izsum, found little Sword Bryan and brought him back to live in the warriors' camp. During that time he was taught in the arts of swordsmanship, war strategy, and horsemanship. He was tutored and excelled in many other academic studies. He was given more than any commoner child could hope for. He graduated at the top of his class. Prince Alkin, only the heir at the time, visited the warrior camp often and they became friends. Sword Bryan and he played together and trained together." Melea was wistful as if she was retelling a story told to her many times. She went on, "When Prince Izsum died, Prince Alkin became ruler, and Sword Bryan began traveling and sword fighting competitively. The two kind of drifted apart after that." Melea stopped and searched Alexa's face, wondering.

Alexa wiped her hands on a linen napkin. She was curious how Shelkite's government worked. "So you have no kings, no queens, just princes and heirs to the title of prince?" she asked a little befuddled.

Melea nodded. She now seemed at ease, realizing Alexa was only curious about her country and its people. "Yes, the high ruler of our land is entitled prince. After the Lost War Shelkitens decided 'prince' was less domineering sounding than 'king'. 'The Peoples' Prince' was the idea. They set up the court of counselors and advisors for the ruler on the peoples' behalf. Other countries are starting to follow our lead. For instance, the rulers of Vtalmay and Yoldor call themselves chancellor and chief and have advisors. Anyway, if Lady Dorsa would have been born first she would have been the ruler and princess."

"Prince Alkin has a sister?" Alexa stopped Melea's explanation.

Melea smiled, displaying small, perfect teeth. "Yes. The power and title goes to *only* the first-born. The current wife or husband of the ruler is the only other allowed to be referred to as either princess or prince," she said, thoroughly enjoying speaking of her country. "In all of Shelkite's recorded history only one blood princess has ruled, Princess Alhanna. She was a great woman. She ruled just after the Lost War era. She helped with the reconstruction of Shelkite," Melea said fondly. "In the main hall there are canvases of all who have ruled. I'll show you if you want to see them," she added bright eyed.

Alexa smiled, "Maybe sometime. But, tell me, is Prince Alkin a good ruler?"

Melea smiled sincerely. "He has a truly great heart. He does his best to rule justly. He has hearings once a month, and keeps track of the regions via the Master Swords, who visit the dukes constantly. He treats his people kindly and cares for the poor. Shelkite's relations with other countries are healthy. He's currently working on abolishing owning the pierced slaves. We servants are very fond of him."

"And all the Master Swords like him, too? You don't know of any who are displeased with him?" Alexa asked. There was a rumble of thunder outside the window and falling rain began its sweet chorus against the panes.

"As far as I know everyone loves the Prince. The Swords are his most trusted companions. Some of the older Swords served under Prince Izsum; but they're all good-hearted men. Sword Bryan is the Head-Master Sword and the youngest of them. He suffers a lot from the other Swords' unintentional envy," Melea said. She sighed and looked out the window and added wistfully, "All he wants is to be back in the camp and train the new warriors. He prefers that over being a Master Sword."

Alexa stared thoughtfully at the woman, deciphering her without using her senses. "You love him," she announced, slouching back in her chair.

Melea looked aghast. "I'm only his servant," she shot back defensively.

Alexa smiled. She hadn't called her his whore. Alexa chuckled inwardly; and thought better of saying anything. Using her special senses, she searched the girl's mind and heart. Melea was more than she let on. She was complex, appearing dainty and naïve, but in reality she was strong. She had courage and a powerful mind. She was a good person to have on her side.

"Of course." Alexa smiled slyly. "But you can't hide it from me."

Melea sighed. "I suppose so." She narrowed her eyes and leaned forward. "I heard that you were a half witch and a ruffian. I didn't believe it until now. I didn't know there were any wizards still alive. But," she added desolately, "I mean nothing to him. I'm just his pleasant servant who he confides in…sometimes."

Alexa feigned a sympathetic noise that bordered on mocking. "I am sorry," she said half-heartedly. She leaned forward and changed her tone, "Melea, I feel I can trust you. You're a good person. Can we be friends?" She was essentially asking if she could trust her.

"Well, of course."

"I know you felt I was untrustworthy when you first saw me. But I'm just as concerned as everyone else. I'm only trying to put pieces together. I sense evil here. I didn't want to admit it before. But it *is* here, lurking." Melea had a sudden look in her eyes as if she had seen a dragon. "I need a favor."

"Yes," Melea replied hesitantly.

"I want to know more about Lady Evelyn. Could you do some spying for me? Nonchalantly. It'll be easier since you're a servant. What do you know about her?"

"Oh, Lady Evelyn…" Melea faltered. "Not much. She's just a northeastern girl of some status I think. She's comes and goes from Shelkite on business. Everyone calls her the Chaos Goddess. Prince Alkin visits her often. I don't know anymore. She seems like a dim-witted flirt. I hate those kinds of women," Melea ended sulkily. No doubt Melea had noticed Evelyn's fondness for Sword Bryan.

Alexa bit her lip thoughtfully. Lady Evelyn had to be a spy of some sort, the dim-wittedness an act. She was an intelligent woman. Alexa had sensed the qualities of one in her at once, or at least what she figured were the qualities of a spy. Why was Prince Alkin keeping so much from her? She didn't like being kept in the dark.

A heavy knock interrupted them. "Miss Alexandra, Lady Adama will see you now," Sword Boraz's bass-toned voice said.

Alexa turned to Melea, and they both stood. "We're friends?" Melea nodded cheerfully. Alexa smiled. "Thank you! I'm glad to have found a trusting heart in this country aside from the Prince." Alexa turned to follow the awaiting, austere Boraz.

Master Sword Boraz led her up a few levels of stone stairs and down a sconce lined corridor. The candles flickered, casting shadows along the cold walls. Alexa looked around suspiciously; evil's presence vaguely pricking her heart.

Outside thunder cracked louder and lightning, through various windows, lit up the corridor in intense flashes.

Alexa strode confidently a stride behind Boraz, her dagger gently tapping her thigh. Boraz glanced back at her and smiled. He was a handsome middle-aged man. Alexa sensed extreme loyalty and evenhandedness in him.

"Almost there. Lady Adama resides in the west wing of the castle. Ah, here we are." He stopped in front of an elegantly designed oak door. "I'll be right out here if you need me." Boraz took his post beside the doorway.

Alexa knocked firmly on the thick door. A gentle voice beckoned her in. She stepped into the receiving room of the chamber. Its décor was red velvet and black oak. One large window on the far wall revealed a spacious balcony outside. The room contained a number of chaise lounges and chairs. A roaring fire was ablaze in an elaborate stone hearth. A regal looking woman sat in a cushioned chair. She wore a gown with shades of purple, and held herself proudly. Expensive jewelry adorned her neck and slender fingers. She was middle-aged, and soft frosted auburn locks were piled upon her head elegantly. She sat quietly, smiling at Alexa.

"Come and sit, my dear." She motioned to a soft chair across from her.

Once Alexa's foot crossed the threshold, she felt something cool spill through her body. It was as if her blood had turn suddenly to slush. Her senses slowed. Startled, she shivered, feeling a pang of fear. Then as suddenly as the cold feeling had stung her she felt warmth wash over her. She was extremely comfortable and relaxed, almost drowsy.

Recovering, Alexa smiled respectfully at the lady. She took a seat in the chair; sitting a little slumped compared to the poised woman across from her. Alexa glanced at a canvas above the fireplace. It was of a man much of the likeness of Prince Alkin, but more matured. Blonde locks of braids fell onto his broad shoulders. His fair face smiled curiously as if he could actually see under her clothes. She eyed the canvas suspiciously.

"Ah." Lady Adama smiled, regarding the painting. "My husband, Izsum. A wonderful man." Adama turned her gaze back to Alexa.

"I'm sure he was." Alexa replied. She was struggling with the odd feelings she was receiving trying to decipher the lady. She found for the first time she couldn't see into the regal woman's heart. *She must be very complex*. She contemplated. But there was something else that seemed to muddle her senses. *Is she ill?* Alexa wondered. Sometimes when an individual was ill, in either mind or body, it was hard to see into their hearts through the murkiness the illness created physically and mentally.

"Traveled far, I hear," Lady Adama stated, her voice was calm and gentle, but there was an unmistakable tone of authority in it. Alexa nodded, feeling uncomfortable in the straight-backed chair. "Kaltraz is quite warm, you must be chilled here," Adama continued.

Alexa eyed the lady and forced a smiled. "At home the desert nights can sometimes get bitter."

Adama raised her chin with a slight nod. She peered at her

skeptically for a moment. "You appear to be decent for a commoner, educated somewhat. A bit of a handsome face…but a tad ruthless and crude in conduct," she said superiorly.

Alexa raised an indignant eyebrow at the woman and retorted frostily, "You say this because of my dark blood? My evil heritage? And, surprisingly educated for a mere shepherdess?"

Despite the cold remark, Lady Adama leaned forward, flashing her most beautiful smile yet, and said with a chuckle, "I can tell you are truly a half-blood. I knew a wizard once. They're such defensive, temperamental beings." Lady Adama cocked her head and looked at Alexa cryptically, as if she were waiting for another reaction from her.

Alexa leaned defiantly forward, her eyes glinting sapphire flames. "A tad ruthless I may be, but wholly trustworthy. You don't need to provoke me for any test."

Lady Adama beamed. "One must not be too careful around strangers right now." Adama gestured to Alexa's dagger, referring to Alexa's own cautiousness. "I was indeed just testing you," Adama said sincerely. She motioned for her to kneel next to her chair. Alexa smiled, understanding the woman's precautions. She knelt by the chair. Adama reassuringly patted Alexa's hand. "I'm glad my son has someone like you to put his trust in." Adama's hazel eyes sparkled with gratitude. "Sad days are pending for the future. Eetharum needs strong hands to place its hope into. I see that no hands are as good as yours, Alexandra." Adama's eyes searched Alexa's features adoringly. Feeling strangely awed by Lady Adama's praising and mothering persona, Alexa was bewitched. No wonder Alkin was such an admired prince. "Alexandra, Eetharum's deliverer!" the lady said happily.

"Hardly," Alexa smiled modestly, a little embarrassed. "I'm intelligent enough to know not to put too much trust in creatures or humans, but only in the High Power." This woman was hoping for too much from her.

"But you'll be the one to achieve victory." Lady Adama reached for a little box sitting on the table next to her and opened it. She pulled out a golden chain. A pendant swung lightly from it. "Here."

Alexa narrowed her eyes to see the small adornment better. It was a tiny, golden key. "It's a lovely charm," she commented.

Adama unlatched the chain and held it out in the palm of her hand. "Given to me by the only full-blood wizard I've ever known. It's a good luck charm, to keep the wearer safe. I want to give it to you." Alexa stared astonished at the charm. Adama carefully latched the chain around Alexa's neck. "A key to unlock the intangible. Hope it's useful, my dear," Adama stated gravely.

Alexa bowed her head solemnly. "Thank you, Lady Adama."

Adama smiled. "You go now and get some rest. That was all I wished of you. Take care."

Alexa nodded, stood and left, closing the chamber door quietly behind her. Sword Boraz greeted her with a smile. Alexa looked sternly to her right down the hall, sensing another's presence. A young woman had come out of a room farther down the hall. Sunshine-blonde locks curled sweetly around her pretty heart-shaped face. The locks cascaded down her back, where the curls bounced gaily in cadence with her step. Her jade-colored eyes glowed, reflecting brightly from her emerald gown.

Down the corridor she whisked, smiling slightly at Alexa as she passed, and flashing a friendly grin at Boraz. No doubt she was Alkin's sister, Lady Dorsa. Alexa raised an amused eyebrow at the girl's back. She then strode quickly after the departing Sword, determined from there on to be all business.

Chapter 6

Bryan casually lifted his over flowing mug to his lips. The feathery foam slid soothingly down his throat. The Blue Mermaid was crowded with country folk and townspeople mingled with the more uncivilized: wanderers, swindlers, mercenaries and entertainers. The storm had driven unruly bands in from over the countryside.

A loud crash and clatter came from the far side of the tavern as two men stumbled to sit back down from a minor brawl. Laughter erupted and jests were made as more and more drinks were consumed.

Bryan sat silently at the bar on a three-legged stool, which felt at any moment it might give way. He was letting his mind wander. Wander much like many of the men drinking at his side did for a living. They were wayfarers, taking up jobs along the never-ending road. Sometimes he thought that would be the perfect life, something new always around the next bend, always leaving the past behind.

Bryan let his mind weave in and about many thoughts as he sipped. He watched the cold rain beat against the windows and the lightning streak the starless night sky. Men on either side of him became merrier as their insides became warmer. Paying no heed to the Master Sword next to them they often bumped him in their outbursts. Bryan disregarded them and took another swig, draining his mug.

"Master Sword?" a voice hoarse from years of bartending said. It halted Bryan's thoughts. "Ya all right?" Binz asked.

Bryan smiled and slid his mug over for the old bartender to fill, "Never better."

Binz filled it, "Jest never seen ya so quiet and thoughtful like. Come to think somethin' was the matter. Ya're usually out there jesting with all the boys, sharin' stories and all that nonsense."

"No worry, Binz." Bryan casually took another sip. He sat with poise and self-assurance; one would only have to look at him to be intimidated.

The man to Bryan's left let out a booming laugh and

slapped him on the shoulder. His meaty hand gripped his overcoat and gave the Sword a jolting shake. Bryan gazed at him bemused. "No worry?" the man chuckled. His laugh was low and melodious, "Looks to me like this young man has lady problems. I've seen it written on many youngin's faces."

Bryan shook his head and gave the older man a crooked smile. He was an obvious foreigner. His burly body was covered in weathered clothing. His auburn beard was flecked with foam. Bryan looked into his mug; the bubbles swam haphazardly. Considering the weight of his commitment to his country perhaps he did have something like lady problems.

He pondered; these men knew nothing of the growing threat to their countries and lives. Everything was as it would be on a holiday, merry, without any cares of tomorrow. Bryan began to wonder if all the said troubles were true. Life seemed normal. All else felt like an intangible dream, the Kaltrazian, half-blood witch, the cryptic naiad, the sly wizard…and the sacrifices. It felt unreal, something that belonged in the past, not the present. Why should he trust a naiad or a unicorn? Weren't they magic just like the wizard? Or why should he recognize an assassination threat to Alkin as a declaration of war on Eetharum? And what was this nonsense of counter magic? It all seemed like a bunch of childish tales. How could a bunch of hidden magic and one young half-witch save Eetharum? It wasn't logical! If it was true, maybe it was time he once again believed in the High Power, the deity he had long ago lost faith in. Where there was evil there must be good, right?

Bryan shook his head and cleared his thoughts. He was Prince Alkin's Head-Master Sword and friend. If Alkin summoned him to do this job, then no matter how foolish and unrealistic it seemed he would do it. He would do it not only for his friendship to Alkin and loyalty to Shelkite, but also for gratitude to Prince Izsum. Bryan knew he wouldn't be in his high position if it weren't for Izsum.

Bryan couldn't remember much of his blood family. He was very young when his parents had moved to the little farm on the rolling prairies of Fordorn. He had called it home for only a short time.

Bryan closed his eyes, took a drink, and struggled to bring back distorted images in his mind of his blood family. He had had two older sisters. Bryan fell into the old memory as he remembered vaguely running through rows of crops with the girls, their gleaming dark hair flying carelessly around their young faces.

Their mother called to them from the small, cozy cottage for supper. The oldest girl ran first, calling to her younger siblings. "Come on, Magdalena, Bryrunan, mama wants us for dinner!" The eldest girl's blue eyes sparkled not unlike the little boy's she held hands with.

The toddler Bryan tittered alongside his sisters. Bending to his level the eldest smiled blissfully. "Mama says the land is good here and we're going to stay. No more moving. We'll have a real home!"

Little Magdalena clasped her hands together joyfully, "Forever?" she squealed.

"Yes. Forever and ever!" the eldest answered, picking her sister up in a tight hug and swinging her around. They laughed merrily.

"Time to eat!" their mother called again from the doorstep. "Kids, get your father in the barn. I don't think he heard me," the auburn haired woman ordered. At that moment, a tall, muscular, dark haired man appeared from around the house. Worry creased his sun-bronzed brow.

"Riders from the northeast," he said tensely. His wife looked at him quizzically. "Thirty or more coming fast. Get the children inside. I think it's the Galeon warriors that raided Tilicon earlier this month looking for renegades. Hurry," he ordered. She obeyed at once. The dark haired man stayed outside.

Bryan's memory of the tragedy was forever seared on his brain. He remembered a group of men riding onto the property, and hearing raised voices, his father's included. He recalled strange noises, screaming horses, the breaking of glass and the heat of an intense fire. Above all, he remembered the terrified screams of his mother and his sisters and the horrid smell of burnt flesh. He could still hear the clank of metal and rumbling of hooves as

Prince Izsum's warriors rode into the fray. Lastly, he remembered being whisked up and carried away never to see his family again. Sadly, the only things he couldn't remember were his eldest sister and parents' names. It bothered him at times.

The Shelkite warriors had saved him. They had been too late for his father, mother and sisters. Most of the images of his family were lost and hard to bring up to actual thought, but he could feel them. He knew that they were in his past, forever lingering and haunting him.

Life Bryan had known after that had been as the child of a warrior in the camp of Prince Izsum. There he had grown to be the best fighter and most educated young warrior in all of Shelkite. Despite its rough beginning, he had had a good childhood. He didn't feel sorry for himself. In the camp he had been loved and admired by all, especially by the daughter of the Head-Gate Master….

"Master Sword Bryan." Binz shook the robust Sword. "Ya blanked out. Ya feelin' all right?" Binz didn't wait for an answer. "Back to the castle wit ya. The storm is worsenin'."

Bryan rubbed his eyes, cleaning his thoughts. "I'm fine!" he said gruffly, a tad annoyed. "But, I should get back…to baby-sit," he mumbled resentfully to himself.

"Shall I send a rider wit ya?" Binz asked.

"I *don't* need an escort." He stood defiantly from his stool.

"Of course." Binz left to clean up a mess farther down the bar.

Bryan shoved his wobbly stool in and gave one last grumpy look around the tavern before setting a generous amount of copper coins down and leaving.

Dragon was tethered in a lean-to outside the tavern. He nickered to his master when Bryan neared. "Hello, pal." Bryan mounted and pulled his cloak tighter around himself, pulling the hood down over his head. He nudged Dragon out into the pounding rain.

The sun had long disappeared. The night had settled like a heavy, black coat on the earth. The dark sky was periodically interrupted with intense glitches of platinum-colored lightning.

Dragon's strides were steady and sure as he carried his master homeward. Slopping along the road, Bryan felt for the hilt of his sword. It was there. He only felt secure with it by his side. He had been born to carry a sword. He believed he belonged nowhere but clasping a hilt and facing an opponent.

Wind bitterly swept over the open fields. The rain beat down hard on the Master Sword and his mount. As lightning sliced through the bleak night sky and the atmosphere trembled, Bryan rode past lit up cottages; the occupant's safe and warm from the rampant storm.

The burly horse shook his large boned head and snorted as the rain stung him in the eyes. Bryan patted the thick, soaked neck reassuringly. He let his thoughts wander lazily, from warrior camp to women.

Feeling the cold spring rain bite through his cloak, Bryan nudged Dragon to move into a faster gait. Instead of shifting to a faster pace, Dragon suddenly planted his hooves and snorted uneasily.

"Come on," Bryan urged. No amount of asking made Dragon take a step farther. Bryan bumped the horse harder, but Dragon snorted and sidestepped nervously. Confused at his horse's odd behavior, Bryan growled, "Don't be such a mule! It's cold out here!" He gave him another decisive bump. Dragon popped forward, snorting, his gait jarring. His wide eyes rolled, showing the whites. He broke into a fast canter. "That's better," Bryan said satisfied.

All too soon Bryan found out the explanation for his stallion's hesitance. A beast jumped out of the dark roadside and charged at them. Dragon reared, letting out a threatening squeal. He came down hard, attempting to drive the creature's skull into the earth. The beast evaded the horse. Dragon swung around to send a hard blow at the animal with his hind legs, giving off a loud battle neigh.

Caught off guard by his mount's sudden shift into battle moves—and feeling his whisky a bit—Bryan lost his balance. Groping for the slick reins, he caught sight of the creature. *A howler!* Fear jumped into his chest. He bumped Dragon with his heels to escape the dreadful creature. Dragon didn't hesitate to go this time.

Bryan knew howlers were not ordinary animals, but queer intelligent creatures that only appeared after dark. They had ghastly sounding calls, and were deadly. Where there was one, there were more. They hunted their prey in packs.

As Bryan galloped Dragon, three more howlers came charging out of the hills. Their screeches were terrifying and piercing. Bryan glanced over his shoulder to see their snapping fangs and hideous, fervent eyes. They looked dreadfully similar to large furless dogs, though their front paws were akin to human hands, with long claws. Their bite was deadly, as was their blood if it touched the skin. Two short horns protruded from their skulls. They whined, screamed and snarled after the rider and horse.

Bryan yelled angrily at the revolting creatures, feeling fear for his mount as well as for himself. They paid no heed. Their hairless bodies felt no cold as the rain pounded down on them. They chased vigorously, eager for a fresh meat.

Dragon raced along the sloppy road as fast as his hooves could carry his burly body and Bryan. He huffed out heavy breaths and his sleek coat became frothy with sweat, but he didn't let up.

Soon Bryan and Dragon were surrounded by a dozen screeching and snarling howlers. Suddenly, with a vicious neigh, Dragon skidded to a halt and reared. He came down kicking out and flinging his body around in attempt to ward off the creatures as he was trained to do in battle. Bryan lost control and fell head long to the muddy earth; thinking ironically to himself that he shouldn't have drank so much as he crashed down. Dragon bolted, still trying to ward off the howlers as a trail of them followed.

As soon as Bryan had hit the earth, a pack of howlers began surrounding him. They circled, eyeing their prey carefully. Saliva dripped from their fangs and their screeches caused Bryan to unconsciously clasp his hands over his ears.

When they attacked, Bryan was ready. His drawn sword swiped at them as each force charged him. Blood poured down on him like rain; the sting of it causing him to yell out in pain. He was angry. He was furious, far past being logical. He hewed and hacked at the beasts for what felt like hours. He felt his strength begin to ebb, but pushed harder. They hissed and pulled at him with their horrid human-like hands, and swiped at him with their thick tails.

Feeling as if days had passed, the sound of pounding hooves siphoned into his dark world like a moonbeam. He had no time to divert his attention to see the source. It came from behind him. A sharp whiz spilt the air near his ear. A howler shrieked and fell, an arrow piercing its side. A white blur came hurtling out of the darkness, and two more whizzes zipped past Bryan. Two more howlers fell.

It was the Kaltrazian witch! Bryan, unable to let down his guard at his surprise, downed two howlers attempting to shred his skin; their claws caught in his cloak.

As Alexa let her arrows fly, Bryan hacked away at the creatures, beheading as many as he could. Soon they found they had killed many of them. They watched as the rest fled back into the shadowy fields.

Struggling to breathe, Bryan heaved in gulps of the moist air. The air was cold, and a damp mist sprouted from his lips and nose. He stumbled over to a place clear of howler bodies on the roadside. He knelt in the stinking muck that was quickly becoming saturated with howler blood.

Alexa hopped lightly from Zhan's bare back, her quiver still strapped across her back. She stepped over to the kneeling Sword's side and looked down on him. Bryan swiped his sword in the wet grass to clean the blade. His dark hair was disarray. His cloak was painted with gleaming, scarlet blood.

"You all right?" she asked breathless. She squinted from the smacking rain.

His attention focused on cleansing his sword, the Master Sword nodded solemnly. He stood and sheathed his weapon. He found himself starring straight into the girl's fiery, sapphire eyes. He quickly shifted his gaze, noting curiously that she must have left in a hurry. She appeared a little rumpled, but poised. She stood tall and strangely elegant for just surviving a battle with howlers.

Bryan suddenly felt sick. The rain was freezing, and he

began to shiver. The spots where blood had touched his skin began to seethe. He looked down to the young woman staring up at him. His brow furrowed questionably. "How'd you—" he faltered. He stepped onto the muddy road.

Alexa, ignoring his question, turned and whistled to Zhan. The horse trotted over. He wore no bridle or saddle. She turned back to Bryan and answered, "I sensed evil."

Bryan looked at her skeptically. "Dragon?" he inquired.

"Headed for the castle. I shot the howlers after him. He's safe." Alexa placed a soothing hand on the white horse's slender neck.

Bryan nodded approvingly. The two began to trudge through the thick mud, their boots sinking. Alexa reached down to pull an arrow from a howler's body. Bryan quickly grabbed her wrist stopping her. She yelled out in pain as the blood seeped from his hand to hers. She pulled her hand protectively toward her body.

"Sorry," he muttered apologetically. "But don't take the arrows. They're poisoned."

Alexa stared at him, her jaw clenched in pain. "I know that now!" she snapped.

Bryan glared at the girl with narrowed eyes. "Wipe your hand on the inside of my cloak if it makes you feel better." He held out his cloak. She brusquely wiped her hand off. As she began to turn on her heel, Bryan felt his head begin to swim. He stumbled into her.

She caught his arm, refusing to yell out as the blood touched her skin again. "You will ride Zhan," she said.

Bryan's head felt hazy. "I will not ride that...*runt*."

"I've saved you, and you insult me?" Alexa snarled at him, letting go of his arm.

Bryan shut his eyes in pain. He had to get back to the castle quickly so he could receive aid for the blistering wounds. He started to walk, ignoring her comment.

"You left in a hurry." He gestured to the unsaddled horse. They walked side by side up the road. Zhan followed alongside Alexa.

She turned and looked him straight in the eyes, challenging

him. "Yes," she stated.

"I don't understand how you knew?"

"I told you *Sword* Bryan," she answered slyly. "My father is a wizard." She stopped dramatically and held his level gaze with a futile attempt to unnerve him. "My blood isn't all human." She gave him a smug, half smile.

The Master Sword stared at her sharply. He wanted to fall to the ground laughing despite his increasing weakness. She was such a little wisp of a girl. His stature towered over her, but she stood unflinchingly, challenging him in a silent match of dominance.

Bryan's hand rested lightly on his sword, "I see." The corners of his mouth curved into a suppressed grin. Turning, he flipped his hood down over his soaked head and began walking. "But my *dear*, little girl, you left without a guard and without permission." He stopped and turned to face a fuming Alexa. "*Don't* do it again." His voice held all the finality of an ending conversation that only the Head-Master Sword could deliver. He then strode away feeling her loathing him. *It's for your own well-being, girl. And you* will *learn who's in charge.*

Chapter 7

Stumbling along the muddy road, the walls of the castle soon came into view. They luckily had traveled with no other mishaps. Alexa, at Bryan's bidding, rode silently beside him as he walked. The stubborn Master Sword stumbled over his own feet. His mind had become cloudier; and he was having trouble remembering things. The howlers' blood had begun its evil work. He struggled against falling into unconsciousness.

Once in the courtyard, Alexa slipped from Zhan's back to assist him to the entrance. Bryan's strength began to ebb quickly and he leaned on Alexa, his eyes rolling dangerously. Streams of sweat crept down his forehead and dripped off his chin.

Alexa hurried him along the best she could. It started to rain again; the pounding droplets impaired their vision. Making her way clumsily through the heavy doors Alexa cried out for assistance as Bryan slipped from consciousness and fell to the floor in a heap.

From a room on the left, Sword Boraz's large frame appeared along with Prince Alkin's slighter form. There was a woman's gasp—Lady Evelyn.

"What happened?" Alkin inquired.

"Ugly…creatures…" Alexa was short of breath. She felt dizzy. "Attacked," she gasped. Her eyes felt weird.

"Howlers! Sword Boraz, get the Head-Nurse quickly," Alkin ordered. Boraz left immediately. "Alexa, are you hurt?" Alkin asked.

"Not terrible. S-sword Bryan is sick," she stammered. Her hand burned. Her veins and blood seemed to writhe and boil within her.

"Don't worry we have a salve that may stop the poison before its work is finished."

Alexa nodded, her forehead covered with sweat and eyes twitching. Then her eyes rolled back and she fell into a slump next to Bryan. Evelyn let out another gasp and ran to assist, but Alkin held her back. "Evie, don't touch them! The poison will affect you, too. Wait for the Head-Nurse."

A while later, after giving the initial treatment, the Head-

Nurse wiped her hands on a rag and said, "Keep bathing his burns in warm, clean water with the salve. It will draw out the poison. Hopefully the fever will break soon with the draught I've given him. Keep an eye on him and notify me if anything changes." The stocky woman straightened from leaning over Bryan. He was unconscious in his bed. The nurse looked over to the worried prince and smiled. "He needs rest and care. Don't worry. I believe we caught it before it was too late." She turned her stern gaze on Melea, who had been standing quietly by. "Stay with him. Howler poison is not to be fooled with. He'll need constant care for at least a night and day. Make sure he keeps drinking this to flush out his system." She held up a bottle of liquid. She nodded her head curtly and abruptly left the chamber.

Alkin regarded Melea and smiled kindly. Then before exiting the room he gave Boraz a scolding glance. No doubt the Sword would hear of his mistake of letting Alexa slip away. Smiling weakly at Melea, Boraz followed Alkin.

Melea quickly went to the bedside and knelt, looking into Bryan's pale face. His skin was moist and pasty. The blood from the howlers had burned through the arms of his cloak and onto his skin. His bare hands had borne most of the damage. Melea took the rag by the bedside and soaked it in the warm salve and water solution. She gently dabbed the raw burns. The poison had already seeped through his skin and begun its deadly journey through the veins.

Bryan's forehead was covered with sweat. He groaned. "I don't trust her," he mumbled and attempted to roll over. Melea stopped him from moving, looking at him perplexedly. She wiped his forehead, frowning. "Witch…no…good," he foundered.

She stopped her caretaking to listen. Bryan grimaced and his eyes flew open. He glanced around the room before spotting Melea at his side. There was a moment of silence; and his eyes dumbly searched her. "Please, leave," he stated flatly.

Melea was shocked. "No. I can't. You need care."

"I don't. Go away."

"Bryan don't be stubborn."

"*Sword* Bryan," he corrected hoarsely even in his delirium.

61

"Him? Be stubborn?" Someone said from behind.

Melea spun around at the sound of Alexa's voice. The raven-haired girl stood tall and proudly in the doorway. Her frame was slender and almost queenly. Bryan convulsed and then coughed. Melea turned quickly back to him.

"Prince Alkin sent me." Alexa walked to the bedside. Melea looked puzzled. "I can help. I have some healing knowledge."

Melea nodded, but she was hesitant after hearing Bryan's mistrust of the girl. She glanced at Alexa's hands. Linen had been wrapped around one; it was stained crimson. She didn't seem to be affected by the poison. "Are you better?" she asked.

"It's not bad," Alexa answered.

"It doesn't affect you?"

"I've got something that really helps."

"I *don't* want your help. Leave me alone, both of you." Bryan came to and glared at the two women. He now seemed fully aware of his surroundings.

"What is it?" Melea asked dubiously.

"Don't worry. It won't hurt him," Alexa replied, moving closer to assist.

Bryan thrust his arm forward, warding her off. "I'll have your hide if you touch me, girl."

"All right then, Master Sword." Alexa glowered at him, and then briskly turned, leaving the chamber.

Melea regarded Bryan. "She was going to help heal you. Why'd you do that?"

"I don't trust her. There's something underhanded about her." His bright eyes beckoned Melea; and she leaned forward to listen closely. "Keep an eye on her when I'm not around."

"I don't think she's evil. She asked me to keep a watch on Lady Evelyn," Melea whispered back, feeling oddly elated he was confiding in her.

Bryan started and his face turned sour. "Lady Evelyn is loyal to Prince Alkin. But I'm not sure of Miss Alexandra's loyalties yet."

Melea bit her lip undecidedly. She usually trusted his

judgment; but she didn't think Alexa wicked. "Look, you have to rest. Forget about your duties for a while." She pushed aside the conversation.

Yielding, Bryan shut his eyes and endured the pain the best he could. He soon fell into a fitful sleep.

Leaving Bryan's chamber, Alexa wandered the halls searching for Prince Alkin. The long corridors were lit by fancy sconces and lanterns. They cast eerie, dancing shadows around her. Alexa stopped in the spacious foyer of the castle and paced restively, biting a short fingernail.

"Can I help you with anything, Miss Alexandra?" Sword Boraz appeared next her.

She turned on her heel. "Yes. Could you please take me to see the Prince? I have to speak with him."

Boraz nodded, his gaze curious, and said, "He's in the library. In here," he gestured to a double doorway.

Alexa stepped through and immediately found herself in an intriguing atmosphere. The room was lavishly decorated. She was surrounded by walls of books, comfortable reading chairs and lounges. She looked up. There was a second floor of more books, and the high, domed ceiling was paneled with glass, showing the gloomy night sky. On the opposite wall from the doors, there was a cheerful fire blazing in a large stone hearth.

Prince Alkin and Lady Evelyn stood speaking in low tones by an oak desk in the corner of the library. Alkin looked up. "Alexa!" his fair face broke into a smile, "I'm pleased to see that you're well."

"Yes. Thank you." Alexa nodded. She glanced hesitantly at Evelyn, and said, "I need to speak with you."

Alkin nodded solemnly. There was silence, and then he said, "Anything that you have to say about our big predicament can be said safely in this company." He smiled assuredly.

Alexa nodded still unsatisfied, but willing to go on. "Today," she began. She was uncertain how they would react to her story of the mermaid. They would think her crazy. "On the way back from Fordorn I got an answer to at least one of our problems. I suspect it was from my witch intuition. Without a doubt I know

my inclination is trustworthy. I have to go see the merpeople."
Alkin and Evelyn looked thoughtfully at one another for a
moment. Alexa stirred, shuffling her feet.

"Is there such a people?" Evelyn asked quietly. "I heard
that their kind lived a long time ago in the Elendace Sea. Or maybe
it was the Nortarwin Sea. But did the kingdom really exist? And if
so, would they still be there? What could they do for us on land
anyhow?"

Alkin was silent, his face troubled.

"I know it sounds strange, but believe me, dear prince,"
Alexa pleaded. She knew she had to go. The magic pulsing
through her veins told her so.

Alkin finally spoke. "I believe there was once an
underwater city. Though, the merpeople were rumored to be highly
reclusive. It's possible they could be a fabled race. But Apollos is
akin to them, and the howlers also. And, too, here stands a young
woman that has magical blood." He smiled sadly and looked at
Evelyn. "I think there's a chance they did exist and are still there.
What chances do we have to throw away? If these people can help
us, why not make the trip? It's all we have right now."

Evelyn nodded. Wisps of her brown hair fell into her big
eyes. "Yes, I suppose you're right." She regarded Alexa, studying
her.

Alexa noted the woman's face was not as it was earlier in
the day, flirty and giddy. She had somehow matured by just a
change in her demeanor. Alexa figured that Evelyn was at least ten
years her senior. She sensed deep intelligence, accompanied with
sadness within the woman. Using her senses on her, Alexa realized
she wasn't prone to wickedness as she had thought.

Resolved, Evelyn nodded her approval and said to Alkin,
"Okay, but gather the council for a discussion." She turned to
Alexa, "The reason I rushed here today was because my sources
tell me we are running out of time. Some of the border villages in
Galeon have been ravaged. People have gone missing. They're
beginning to panic." She looked down at her folded hands, her
brown eyes becoming watery. "And, I worry about my people still
in Zelka left with no one to protect them from Ret and his *vile*

sacrifices," she said bitterly. Alexa stayed respectfully mute.

Alkin nodded firmly in agreement, and said, "When Sword Bryan is on his feet again, we'll hold a council." He patted Evelyn's hand. "We'll do all we can to help your people and the rest of Eetharum, hopefully before Ret has gained too much influence." He turned to Alexa, his face changing from sympathetic to quizzical. "Tell me," his voice boomed to the top of the dome with attempted enthusiasm. "How is the Head-Master Sword?"

"I don't know. He looked really ill when I went to help him. He would have none of it, though."

Alkin heaved an exasperated sigh. Evelyn turned her head to hide a smile. "Well, so be it. If he wishes to suffer longer than he must, let him," Alkin concluded.

"I don't believe he trusts me," Alexa acknowledged.

Alkin smiled and gently took her hand. "Well, I do, and he's under my orders. I want you to feel free to ask questions and explore as much of my grounds as you want while you're here."

Alexa smiled widely. "Thank you."

Chapter 8

A day later Sword Bryan sat uncomfortably in the council hall, slouched down in his usual chair at the end of the table. Alkin's seat at the head was empty. Bryan felt a trickle of sweat slide down his face. He was still not entirely well. His blood coursed through his veins with an abnormal heat. However, he was well enough to withstand the council.

Today the council table didn't seat just its usual company of Master Swords. Among the twelve men there were two women. Alexa sat to the right of Prince Alkin's chair and Lady Evelyn sat to the left.

Bryan eyed Alexa with dislike. She sat slumped, yet proudly. Her long raven hair was braided as normal, resting over her shoulder. She looked preoccupied. Her brow was furrowed as she drummed her fingers on the table, staring into space. *Probably amused by a floating speck of dust.* Bryan snickered inwardly.

He shifted his gaze to Lady Evelyn. She sat up right and dignified. Her demeanor was quiet and assured. Her brown hair was down in soft, wavy locks. Her big cow eyes flicked over and met his; he looked away.

Echoing footsteps came from behind; Bryan peered over his shoulder. Prince Alkin strode in with Apollos at his heels. No sound came from his hooves. All in the room stood and bowed as the Prince took his seat. Apollos stood silently nearby.

Alkin folded his hands together and rested them on the table. All were quiet and expectant. He looked around to each face: the two women, the elder Swords whom had served under his father, the Swords he had appointed, and to Bryan, his Head-Master Sword and old friend. He thought deeply before he uttered a word, his hazel eyes troubled.

"Soon we'll all have to set out on missions," he began seriously, "Tonight we'll decide what actions to take to carry this out." He paused. "I want everyone to freely speak their mind. Please don't hold anything back." Pushing back his chair he stood. The dark blue overcoat he wore and his small, silver circlet studded with three simple jewels, a sapphire with two emeralds on either side, made him appear more regal and old beyond his years.

66

"I'll go first. On my left is a lady who has been a longtime friend of mine. She came to me two years ago seeking Shelkite's aid. She's a loyal citizen of Zelka. Lady Evelyn is of noble blood and was a close counselor of the former king."

The Swords and Alexa looked suspiciously around to one another. A few leaned together to hide a whisper.

Alkin cleared his throat. "When she heard of her king's unfortunate and unanticipated death, Lady Evelyn wasn't deceived. She had long been wary of her fellow counselor, Ret. She was one of the few who fled when he overtook the throne. He's not the lawful heir. He tricked the sickly king into handing over the crown on his death bed. He also obtained the approval of many Zelkans with his eloquent speeches; which have been all lies wrapped up in the simple truth. Before Evelyn escaped, she stationed behind people loyal to her and the country. Secretly they've been able to send regular updates to her. She's learned through them of the covert, hostile happenings. Ret practices soiled magic. It's been verified that he's been sacrificing humans and animals to appease the Demon. As I've said, he intends to enslave the people of Eetharum and make himself supreme emperor. Some of his doings are more gruesome than I care to delve into. But we've evidence of torturing methods he uses in his underground dealings. Until now he has managed to deceive the majority of Zelka's population, hiding his odious doings with his sly speeches and seemingly generous demeanor. But his nature is beginning to show. And Zelkans are frightened and suffering. Lady Evelyn came secretly to me for help because our families are old friends. She's the niece of the deceased king and the *rightful* heir to the throne of Zelka. But a foe caught wind of her meetings with me and I received a murderous threat." Alkin looked at Evelyn with a small smile. She smiled sadly back, looking fondly at him, sharing a memory. "Ret knows we're mobilizing a plan against him, so his evil doings have increased."

Alkin regarded Apollos standing a step behind his chair. "Apollos is probably the last unicorn. He has served loyally to Shelkite for many years, as most all of you know. After I received the assassination threat, he swiftly left for the territory of Carthorn, in hope to obtain answers from the Guidance Naiad." Apollos bowed his head in acknowledgment. "This brings us to the lady on my right." Alkin gestured to Alexa.

Alexa looked up to the Prince gazing down at her. She sat calmly, allowing no thought of fear or worry form in her mind. Bryan looked up from his thoughts still feeling suspicious toward her. He focused his gaze and undivided attention on her, listening intently.

"The naiad advised us by the High Power to seek her help. Okay, now," he petitioned, "it's your turn to speak." He sat down.

Silence reigned in the hall for a long moment. Bryan fidgeted; he had plenty to say. But he didn't think now was the time.

Alexa's eyes flicked over to Bryan and were met by his level gaze. She felt something brewing inside him. It would come out soon. She cleared her throat and spoke calmly and confidently. "My first task is to travel south to the merpeople. Where I hope they'll lead me to the counter magic. But, I would like to ask," she regarded the Prince, "if I could take a small company with me."

Alkin nodded. "Definitely, I wouldn't send you alone, Alexa."

Sword Xercan, a broad and war-like man, stood. He was of the old council of Swords under Izsum. His face held weathered lines and his dark hair was streaked with gray. "Though we don't have the means to summon mystical creatures like Ret, we can't wait for him to harm more people even while Alexandra is away on her mission. We have to assemble Shelkite's army and go to Galeon. We must confirm the allegiance of Eetharum's countries with us so that we're not unprepared for the impending attack. My prince, while serving under your father I was in charge of the warriors for many years, so I ask that I may lead the Warriors of Shelkite."

"Yes, Sword Xercan I had in mind that you would. Prepare the men to mobilize. Every warrior *must* be ready whether he stays to protect Shelkite's borders or goes to Zelka," he instructed. "Lady Evelyn and I have discussed ideas of battle strategy; she's knowledgeable in this area and knows Zelka's terrain. She'll go with you, Sword Xercan, and assist. Her people still loyal will welcome you and most definitely join us. They camp just across the southern border of Zelka in Galeon."

Xercan bowed to the Prince and nodded a salute to Evelyn before he sat.

Bryan wanted to growl. He clenched his jaw in irritation. Lady Evelyn was to go to? He wanted to be the general of the mobilized army! How did she suddenly become so high in command of Shelkite's warriors?

"Sword Gyqua," Alkin addressed another Sword. A slender, fair haired man straightened and acknowledged the Prince. He was the head of Shelkite's Messenger Company, "Send men as you can spare to Eetharum's countries to warn and gather allies, but first send out scouts. I want to see what countries, if any, are allied with the Ret. Send emissaries next to explain the trouble. After you've done this, go to our battlements in Galeon. Your warriors will be used to dispatch messages and keep the battalions in full contact."

Gyqua nodded his understanding, his green eyes sparkling with anticipation.

Alkin continued, "I'm leaving a Sword stationed here to watch over the castle. Sword JaVin will reside here to oversee castle duties, though I give my mother top authority." The Prince turned to regard another older Sword, "Sword Devlon, you will be in charge of the homeland warriors left to protect our beloved Shelkite and its citizens. The rest of my Master Swords shall fall into the army ranks as colonels."

"Where are you going, my prince?" Sword Boraz inquired the question that was on all their minds.

The Prince looked at Alexa. "I'm going with Miss Alexandra. After the mission is finished, I'll be in Galeon at the battlements."

There was sudden chaos. Everyone spoke at once, fervently voicing questions and warnings. All the Master Swords advised strongly against his rash idea.

Alexa stared astonished at the Prince.

Bryan sat furious in his seat, grinding his teeth. Finally, he stood with defiance, "How are we to be assured *she* is not in league with this wizard?" his authoritative voice boomed across the room causing everyone to quiet. "Ret is the same race isn't he? She's been wandering freely about the castle and grounds, I might add, asking a lot of questions. She's had plenty of time to contrive and send information to Ret! My prince, think of what you're doing." Bryan gazed wildly at Alexa. She stared levelly back at him with a defiant, raised eyebrow.

Alkin opened his mouth as if he were going to rebuke Bryan, but Apollos stepped forward and spoke. Abrupt silence fell. "I came from Carthorn with only the name of this girl for help. My kind knows well of her kind. Our ancestors were fierce enemies and brutality spilt the blood of each other. If you don't trust me or this young woman then we're back to the start. Her father may be a full-blood wizard, but he's chosen exile from the evil tendencies of his kind. He's bound by an enchanted, unbreakable promise to the Power. He's taught his daughter the wisdom of integrity. Alexandra is good because she chooses so, you have *my* word. Don't fight each other. We'll most certainly fail if we're divided." Apollos gave them a penetrating stare.

Silence reigned. They had listened as if their own lives depended on his words. Even Bryan had been humbled. He sat down, feeling weak with his illness again. He wondered where his place would be. He looked at Alexa. She was holding him with a strange gaze. He felt his eyes lock to her features and for all his wishing he couldn't remove them. Finally, she let his gaze go, and suddenly, inexplicably, he knew she wasn't evil. It was as if she had told him so by showing him all that was within her, every thought, every motive, every feeling, every hate and love. Though, he couldn't put a finger on them. She somehow had poured her soul right out through her eyes into him. *No.* He finally decided. *She's not evil, but she feels no love for me because of my mistrust. It doesn't matter. I don't care much for her either...the little haughty witch.*

Tenseness clouded the air. Alkin spoke first, breaking it. "Three of my good warriors shall go with you, Alexa, at your choosing." Alexa nodded her approval. "And, as I've said, I'll

70

accompany you. I also implore you to take my advice and pick a Master Sword to come," Alkin advised.

Bryan's heart gave a sudden jolt. Where was he in this tale? Surely not with her. He wished to go to battle. That didn't mean he wished to follow this girl aimlessly over the countryside. Yet, the witch had the choosing. She surely wouldn't choose him, for all her loathing of him. Would she?

Alexa looked around the table to the many unfamiliar faces. Who would be the best? Who had what she needed? A fierce loyalty, skill and everything possessed within that was needed for this journey. She knew who even before she had to search with her senses. She could feel and see all their hearts. However, she didn't speak of him first. "I would like to ask something else," she began.

All eyes were on her, curious. The Chaos Goddess looked at her with a strong sense of respect. The Master Swords waited on the edge of their seats for her to speak. Alkin watched her closely. Apollos stood calmly as if he knew her thoughts.

"That I can be assured that I'll have the right in making every final decision. Even in your presence, dear prince," Alexa said this without a hint of hesitance. After all he was not *her* prince

The Swords were stunned. Evelyn looked at her with grave interest. Alkin stared blankly. Apollos said nothing and moved nothing but his gleaming tail with a slight flick.

"What for, may I ask? Safety purposes?" Alkin asked perplexed and a little dazed, but surprisingly not offended.

Bryan unknowingly leaned forward to hear better. He was greatly intrigued.

"Please don't take me wrong. I don't want to control the company. I just feel that with my senses I'll be a more adequate decision maker. Everything of course will be discussed amongst us first before any decision. It's for your own safety. I believe that since my name was given to help *all* of Eetharum, and that I was pulled from my home I should have at least this," she said. Plus, she felt it necessary to establish her status. She would *not* be overpowered and used. Alexa liked Prince Alkin, but she was still a bit wary of them all. She had to watch her back.

How bold and brash of her, Bryan thought. She should

never speak to the Prince that way. He glanced at the stricken Alkin. Bryan sat back with a thump, snorting his disapproval. An older Sword gave him a look of disgust at his child-like behavior. Bryan diverted his gaze.

"As you wish," Alkin stated, "But *everything* must be discussed. And I'm still acting as the Prince of Shelkite none-the-less," he added sternly.

"Trust me. I don't want any trouble," Alexa said.

"I do trust you," Alkin said, a true smile creased his face for the first time that night.

Apollos spoke. All ears were sharp to listen to his fluid voice. "I'll come, too."

Everyone in the room seemed to take in a breath. Bryan let his boot drop to the floor from where it had been resting on his knee. He received another disgusted look from a fellow Sword. Bryan ignored it and looked at the unicorn gravely.

"You're clever, Miss Alexandra," said the unicorn. "But you've yet to pick your choice of the Master Swords. Who will it be? Tomorrow you'll go and choose your warriors, but tonight a Master Sword must be chosen. One that's skilled, intelligent and creditable."

Bryan held his breath. He had a strange feeling…

Alexa looked up, for her head had been bowed in thought. Her blue, flaming eyes searched each man. They landed on the Head-Master Sword. "I choose Sword Bryan."

"An astute choice," approved the unicorn.

Bryan huffed out the pent up breath, eliciting another scolding glare from the older Sword. It was just as he worried. He smiled weakly at the others. He nodded his acceptance.

"Good," said the Prince, "I was hoping you'd pick him. I didn't want to pressure you. Sword Bryan will continue to be your Sword-Guard until the mission is completed."

Three hours later, when many details had been discussed and debated, Prince Alkin stood and dismissed them. Bryan was the first to leave, but he hid himself outside the chamber doors in the shadows. Listening intently, he overheard the whisperings of his departing fellow Swords as they filed out.

"…he probably bribed the girl just so he wouldn't have to stay behind. Now it's my duty, he knew full well Xercan would be general. Mark my words there's a scam…thinks he's all high and mighty…brash young cock…just because he's the *Head*-Master Sword. He's always strutting around here like he has the biggest— well, you know…"

Bryan glared at their departing backs. Suddenly, Alexa's willowy figure appeared in the threshold; it paused. Bryan stayed silent, attempting to hold his breath. *How childish of me.* He felt odd.

"I know you're there, my Sword-Guard. Planning to attack me?" Alexa spoke wryly.

Bryan stepped out from behind the door and shadows. Heels together and back tall, he bowed. "No. I've waited to escort you to your room, as it is my duty as your Sword-Guard." Alexa nodded curtly and started at a brisk pace down the corridor. Bryan followed.

After clambering up the flights of shadowy stairways and striding in awkward silence down the dimly lit corridors, they finally reached her chamber. Turning to shut the oak door, Alexa nodded a terse dismissal. "Good night," she said firmly. But the Master Sword stepped over the threshold and into her room. Alexa glared at him turning her back to him. He obviously had some business he needed to discuss. She sighed inwardly.

Calmly, but with an edge in his voice Bryan began, "You did that deliberately just to spite me." His words dripped with apparent disdain.

"Of course, I *deliberately* chose you," she spat back. She began to unbuckle her dagger, her eyes zapping dangerously.

"You're a witch. You had to *know* I wanted to go to the battlements." He stood stiffly, but he looked menacing and resolute. His wrath and his want to fight were pent up, boiling, held at bay by some inward dam. It showed only through the quivering tenseness of his body.

With sudden abrasiveness, Alexa threw her belt and dagger down on her bed. She strode toward him; her long, fixed strides brought her quickly to him. She stood before him staunchly. The top of her head barely passed his nose. A menacing blue fire blazed in her eyes. She was small, but foreboding. "I'll ask you *once* to never call me that again in such a way," she said through clenched teeth.

Bryan's voice lowered. "As you wish, but I do *not* wish to be your comrade on this little jaunt," he persisted more calmly, but sternly.

"Aren't you loyal to Prince Alkin and Shelkite? Then go for them and not me, if that pleases you." She turned and paced agitatedly.

Bryan watched her closely, trying to decipher the peculiar girl.

"I didn't pick you to torment you. I had other reasons. You're selfish Sword Bryan, but very fitting to this. You must know that." Her strides quickened. "If blood and battle is what you want then you won't be deprived of it following me. The end will be a bitter taste for you…and me." She paused reflectively, her brow puzzled. Then she looked up to him, adding, "You have no ties. You're free to choose what you want. Your voice must be heard. *You are* the Head-Master Sword after all. But I've made my decision."

Her gaze upon him was bewitching. Bryan stared blankly back; his azure eyes seeing a new light and understanding. He pondered for a moment. "You're more sensible than you act at times. Forgive me. I'll do my duty now, with no more complaints. I'll protect you as your Sword-Guard until this is over…that's a promise." The words had been hard to choke out; but in her eyes he had seen a fear. He could see the dread of the blackness of death and loss in the depths of her sharp sapphire orbs. He turned to exit. "I'll leave now." He bowed and closed the door behind him firmly.

Pausing in the dim corridor, Bryan attempted to sort through his feelings. Perhaps this wasn't all a ploy. Maybe she was sincere and the counter magic, too. It was difficult to believe in things he had only known from his childhood as fireside tales. And more so difficult to believe that she was the one to do this perilous job. Though, he wasn't sure why.

Stubbornly raising his chin he took two strides and came to

his chamber door and flung it open. Why did she cause him so much inner-strife? She acted so childish at times and then other times when she opened her mouth it was as if she were old and wise. She was an enigma.

Troubled with his thoughts, Bryan had expected to walk into an empty room, but found Melea standing by the bedside with a steaming teapot. "What're you doing here?" he asked a little harshly. "You're to attend Miss Alexandra now." He unbuckled his sword and set it on his bed.

"You're still unwell," Melea said. She set the pot down on the bedside table.

He turned to face her. "I'm fine now. You can attend to your other duties."

Melea came to him, placing a soft hand on his brow. "You're still warm. You need to drink this."

Bryan moved from her touch. Heaving a sigh, he sat down and began removing his riding boots, taking the knife from the inner flap. Melea knelt to help.

"I don't need your help," he said sternly. Melea raised her face to look him in the eyes. He was surprised to see a troubled set of brown eyes searching him.

"Oh, Bryan!" she suddenly cried, resting her hand on his knee. Bryan stared wide-eyed and astonished at the woman's outburst. "I know something is wrong. No one has told me anything yet. All I have to do is look at everybody's faces. Please tell me you're not leaving!" Her eyes welled with tears. Bryan said nothing. He continued to take his boots off, an eyebrow arched. "If you leave, I'll just die!" she confessed.

Bewildered, Bryan jerked his head up to look her in the face. What was she talking about? "Don't say that," he demanded. Despite his warning it seemed for the first time he saw her as a woman instead of his steady servant. She had light brown eyes that were intense. Her long, dark-blonde tresses curled softly around her pretty features. Her face was flushed pink, and a fat tear rolled down her cheek.

"Please tell me what is going on."

"Attend to the person you're supposed to be. She'll tell

you," he answered softly, turning away.

A tear slid down Melea's cheek and dripped off her chin, plopping onto Bryan's knee. "Could you tell me?" she said. He stared dumbfounded at the girl's unforeseen affection.

Bryan could see the girl trembling as she spoke. She clutched his knee. Bryan sprang to his feet and began pacing. He didn't feel like discussing the situation, or the more surprising situation that was surfacing. "Leave me alone…please."

"What, my Master Sword?" She slowly rose.

"Melea, I said go. Tend to your other duties."

"But, Bryan…" she blubbered. "I—"

"Master Sword," he corrected stubbornly. He kept his features stern. He then turned his back on her. He had had no idea she had feelings for him. He didn't want her; she would have to learn the hard way.

She came to him, placing her hands on his turned back. "Sword Bryan, I understand why you're doing this…but please don't."

"Just leave, Melea," he commanded hoarsely.

She turned him around by the shoulders to face her. "Please, open your heart once again…to me this time. Forget about the past," she pleaded softly. Bryan stared passively over her head to the wall, saying nothing. Searching his face, Melea nodded solemnly. "All right then," she said reluctantly. Turning quickly, she left without a word or a glance back.

Bryan stared at the closed door in shock. "What in Shelkite just happened?" he mumbled. Then, as if being woken, he shook himself and went to his washbasin to splash water on his face. He wiped his clean-shaven face dry and grumbled, "Crazy girl."

Chapter 9

Gladness flooded Bryan's heart as he entered through the main gate to stand in the courtyard of the warrior camp. He was home. The camp was surrounded by large barricades much like the ones surrounding the castle. It was located about two miles from the castle and was a lot like a small city. The warriors and their families lived there day after day, coming and going as they pleased.

Shelkite's line of princes had always put an emphasis on a good military. So it was important everything ran smoothly in this town full of warriors. The streets were lined with small diners and shops, mostly ran by the warrior wives. Almost everything a person would require could be found. When supplies were needed, a company was set out to Fordorn, or elsewhere, to retrieve them. It was a simple life. And Bryan loved it.

Feeling happy, Bryan waved at warriors as they passed. They called back merrily, and some came over to slap him on the back like an old friend and not their superior. Alexa hung back, silently waiting for the Sword's next order. She watched him curiously. At seeing him genuinely smile for the first time, she fell silent and thoughtful. He was a different person here where he liked it.

Bryan's attention eventually turned back to his duties. Still grinning, he turned to Alexa, "Ready, girl?"

She smiled back, "Yes."

"There's about an hour before the warriors gather on the great field. I'll show you around beforehand." He strode off down the main street. Pointing to his left at a large, domed building, he said, "That's the hall. The top warriors gather there." A light seemed to shine in his eyes as if a fond memory was embedded there.

Stride for stride, they walked down the way passing immaculate homes and shops. On their right were roomy stables and paddocks. A number of large horses, much like Dragon, hung their heads over the stall doors. Bryan patted a brown, curious nose as he went by. "Look," he said, a spring was in his step as they neared a large, older looking building. "There's the school.

Everything I know I learned there. That's where the warriors are made."

"Fordorn's School for Young Warriors," Alexa read from the sign in the front of the building. Bryan nodded, a smile spreading across his handsome face. They walked by a practice ring, where two young warriors, supervised by an instructor, clashed in full combat mode.

As they marched on, they came to a more rural part of the camp. Paddocks lined the roadway on either side with all sorts of animals roaming about. Spotting two small ponies in a field, Alexa pointed, "Brave warrior horses no doubt," she said good-naturedly.

The Master Sword grinned and gestured farther up the road where two children were riding similar, fat ponies. "Great learning mounts," he stated. The children were fencing each other from atop their mounts with wooden swords. The ponies, however, had a different idea. They were insistently pulling their young riders to greener patches of grass.

Alexa laughed openly. As they passed the playing children and persistent ponies, she noted that one child was, in fact, a little girl. "Ah, the future heroine of Shelkite," she said, making it a point to the Sword.

"Perhaps," was all he said, his voice holding no coldness.

"And where is the great Head-Master Sword taking a lowly foreigner like me?" Alexa asked with only slight sarcasm. She gave a girly skip up the road, happily taking in the sights. The day was bright and the sun shone its favor on the green earth. The sweet-scented wind blew gently, pushing plump clouds across the cerulean sky.

Stopping in front of a medium sized cottage, Bryan said, "Right here." He stepped up to the door and knocked firmly. A moment later the door creaked open and a middle-aged woman stood there.

"Bryan!" she gasped, her face alight.

Bryan's features were broken by a wide grin. "Hello, Mother."

The woman gave him a tight hug around the neck and called over her shoulder, "Dear, Bryan's home!"

"He is? Well, tell him to get in here," a male voice called excitedly back, "I have so much to show him since the last time he was here!"

Bryan's mother rolled her eyes. "He's taken up on inventing things in his spare time again. The whole camp is wondering when he'll be burning down the house," she said exasperated. "Well, come on in." She quickly ushered them through the door. Stopping in the hall, she inquired, "So, who is this young lady, Bryan?" A significant grin spread across her face.

"This is Miss Alexandra of Eastern Kaltraz. Here on business with the Prince. I'm her Sword-Guard." Bryan introduced her with respect and formality. "Alexa, this is my mother, Catha. And my father is around here somewhere, I suspect. Theroe is his name."

"Nice to meet you, Alexandra." Catha smiled and shook Alexa's hand.

"Same to you, Catha." Alexa inclined her head. "And, you can call me Alexa."

"That's fine, Alexa." Catha smiled.

Catha was a small stature woman. Her golden hair was tied back into a tight bun. She wore kitchen clothes adorned with puffs of flour on them. She didn't look old enough to be Bryan's real mother. Alexa surmised the couple must have been very young when they took him in.

Sniffing the air appreciatively, Bryan asked, "Mmm, what are you making?"

"Ooo, you're just in time for lunch. Come in. You can eat before you run off again. I'll go get your father." She hurried away, disappearing down the hall.

Unbuckling his sword, the Master Sword hung it on a hook on the wall. Reluctantly, Alexa did the same with her dagger. Following him, Alexa entered into a modest kitchen with a round wooden table. Bryan took a seat and motioned for Alexa to do the same.

"What're you doing now?" Catha's stern voice rent the air. Alexa started at the sudden outburst. "You'll blow the whole camp up with all that nonsense. Get rid of it, Theroe, now!"

"But, Catha, think of the possibilities!" Bryan's father's voice echoed excitedly back.

Looking quite flustered, Catha bustled back into the kitchen. Taking up a platter of sandwiches and fresh cookies, she placed it on the table. "Thinks he's doing Prince Alkin a favor." She shook her head. "He's trying to start a science program for the warrior school. Pish, I say. Him trying to invent things? We'll all be blown to next year!"

"Oh, you're too critical. Last time I was home I thought his ideas were great. The school could really use a science program. Besides, the medical program we all thought would fail is up and running successfully. There are already a few students that have specialized in it and have graduated." Bryan served himself some food.

"Yes, well, I thought his ideas were good, too." Catha plopped down in her chair breathless, "Until some of whatever he was doing decided to blow up in the dead of night, got the whole camp in an up roar. Thought we all were being attacked!" Then, abruptly, she turned her attention to Alexa and added, "Eat up, girl. You're far too skinny I think for Bryan's taste."

Alexa almost choked on her sandwich. She shook her head vigorously at Catha with wide eyes. Bryan merely snorted and ignored his mother's comment.

An hour later, the great field was packed with all the top warriors in the camp. The multitude stood at attention, looking crisp and business-like. It was magnificent to behold. The Shelkiten warriors were all outfitted in rich green and silver, two of their country's colors.

The Master Swords, whom were lined up facing the mass, wore their blue overcoats trimmed in silver. This displayed their higher rank. Sword Bryan stood at the head. Sword Xercan, now Sword-General, stood to his right, and Alexa stood to Xercan's right, feeling quite small. However, she stood proudly, a reflection of Sword-General Xercan and the Head-Master Sword's stance: feet braced apart, upright and hands folded in front and chin high.

Sword Bryan's explanation was brief and to the point. He left out many details. He informed the warriors of the necessity of a select few to join Miss Alexandra on an important mission. The nature of the mission would remain undisclosed until only the men chosen would be briefed. He also succinctly explained they would be preparing for battle. Sword-General Xercan would give them a thorough briefing and orders later.

There was tension in the air. Alexa felt it and breathed it. It was suffocating. Sword Xercan leaned over and whispered to her, "How would you like to go about choosing, Miss Alexandra?"

Giving him a sidelong glance, she stated, "Let them mingle. I'll just observe. No need to make it like a slave auction." Sword Xercan met Sword Bryan's eyes quizzically. Bryan nodded his confirmation. Sword Xercan ordered the company to relax and have a friendly chat with each other.

Bryan and Alexa mingled among and around the various groups of men. Alexa barely looked them over. She was feeling them out through her senses. "Him," Bryan gestured toward a muscular, middle-aged man. "He would be good."

Alexa glanced at him and shook her head. "No. He's not good."

Bryan stared at her obstinately. "What do you mean?" he said through gritted teeth.

"I mean, I like him." Alexa pointed to a young, lanky, dark haired warrior chatting with others his age.

Sword Bryan looked. "This is *not* a gathering for you to find a beau. He's too young and inexperienced," he scoffed.

Alexa glared at him, clenching her jaw. "I choose him. The others you pick are no good."

Snarling, Bryan hissed in her ear, "I do not need a little wisp of a girl like you telling me who is a good warrior or not."

Turning with a clever glint in her eye, she stated, "I chose *you*. Remember? Wasn't that the best pick? You of all people should know how it is to be persecuted for being young." She stalked away.

Growling, Bryan followed. "So be it. Warrior Eelyne will be informed."

A bit later, he pointed another out. "What about him?" The man in question was tall and strong, with a mop of red, curly hair.

"It is Warrior Hazerk."

Alexa took a look, a smile spreading across her face. "Very good, Sword Bryan!" she said mockingly, as if she was praising a child who had just learned a new task. "I *will* take him on my little outing," she said merrily, but it dripped heavy with sarcasm. Bryan nodded his approval. On they looked. "One more man," Alexa asserted thoughtfully, "and, he should do it." She pointed to another warrior. He was laughing forcefully, and had light blonde hair. He was tall, broad and looked intimidating.

Bryan glanced his way and nodded his approval once again. "So be it. Our business is done. Warrior Warkan will be the last."

Chapter 10

Darkness obscured their vision. It filled their eyes with the unknown as the newly formed company passed from the lit courtyard to beyond the gate. South was their path, across the farmland of Shelkite, through Charad Forest, to tropical Yoldor and the Elendace Sea, where they hoped to find in the depths of the waves, no matter how unwelcoming, the merpeople. Where the road after would lead was a mystery. Respect of the numinous was ever present in their minds.

From atop the stone walls of the barricade, torches threw an orange glow into the chill morning air. Guards peered down to watch the silent company depart, their eyes glistening with wonder in the light.

The company of six humans, cloaked in black, took with them six mounts and a pack mule. A strange light emitted from the seventh in the company; the horn of Apollos led them off the road across grassy terrain. His sleek body shone with a ghostly light. The soft hue of his hooves glistened through the long, shadowy grass.

Fog swirled around the hooves of the beasts, the morning dew wetting their legs. The only sounds were the soft breaths of the horses and the quiet shifting of the humans.

Alexa sat astride Zhan with her cloak wrapped closely around her and her hood drawn up. She glanced over her shoulder to the watchtowers for one last look. Her eyes wandered to the Prince riding alongside her on Sapharan. His gaze met hers. Sadness and worry manifested within him. He had been strongly advised not to join the company, but he had refused to listen. Turning her eyes ahead, she saw ominous clouds let loose the drizzle of rain they had promised. Alexa felt the heavy hearts of her companions sink a little lower.

It would take them a number of days to reach the southern border of Shelkite. They then would enter the land of Yoldor, ruled by Chief Bahjahn. They hoped to pass through the country as disregarded travelers in order to reach the seashore on the outer eastern boundaries. Back at the castle, after an adequate amount of time that ensured the company passing through Yoldor, Sword

Gyqua would dispatch Shelkite messengers to inform Chief Bahjahn of Ret's intentions. The protection of the company was most important. If the chief turned out to be an ally to Ret, the company would then be safely out of his territory.

Riding in the lead, Sword Bryan kept mostly to himself. He was followed closely by the Prince and Apollos, who were now side by side speaking softly to each other.

Warrior Warkan trailed them, riding a mount nearly as intimidating and austere as he. Warkan and his granite-colored warhorse towered over all the company, both wearing constant set scowls. Quick tempered and one to never take back talk from anyone, Warkan was a natural leader. But under the Head-Master Sword he followed orders well.

The light hearted and witty Warrior Hazerk rode next in line. Like Warkan, he was broad and strong. Though, he hummed a soft tune into the bleak morning. His coppery-colored warhorse arched his neck and had a spring in his step not unlike his master.

At the tail of the company, young Warrior Eelyne traveled on his sorrel just behind Alexa, leading the sweet-tempered pack mule. As boastful as he must have felt to be a part of such an important mission, he didn't speak of it, knowing he was less experienced than most there. He had an innocent air about him, and seemed to have much to prove, but Alexa knew outside appearances were sometimes deceiving. She could see deeper. He was needed here.

The soft, pattering drizzle bounced off the riders' eyelashes and slid down their noses, slowly dampening their cloaks. The low rumble of thunder in the distance promised more severe weather. The riders were quiet. The awkwardness of being thrust into traveling with new acquaintances—practically strangers—had yet to be dispelled.

The silence of the group was much to Bryan's delight. As he led the company, he felt briefly as if he was leading a legion off to war. His heart lightened at the thought. However, when he turned to survey his grand army, his fantasy melted away. It was merely a small crew following him, which unfortunately consisted of Alexandra. He rolled his eyes at his own eccentric imagination and discontinued to think about his dream of commanding warriors.

Looking to the east, Bryan saw the faint glow of Fordorn in the early morning. The city never completely slept, but the light told that it was awakening from its slumber. As much as he esteemed Fordorn, his heart leapt gleefully at the thought of leaving everything familiar behind.

Keeping a steady pace, they stopped only once for a short lunch in a grove providing them protection from the rain. They ate swiftly and mostly in silence, with only small attempts at friendly conversation.

Later, pushing his hood aside, Bryan stole a glance over his shoulder to spy on Alexa, just to see if the girl was percolating any havoc. His carefully planned glance was met by a steady gaze from her. Startled at seeing her already looking at him, his curious features turned to a cold glower. In return, she narrowed her eyes and stared rigidly at him. From beneath her hood her wicked sapphire eyes seemed to brighten intensely, piercing him with uneasiness. He turned, giving Dragon a reassuring pat. "Her blood is black," he muttered. "She'll be the death of us."

Prince Alkin perked up. "Did you say something, Sword Bryan?" He rode Sapharan up next to Dragon.

"Nope."

"Just grumbling, I suppose," Alkin concluded. "You know you should lighten up a bit. Life would be a whole lot easier."

Bryan grunted. "Tell that to Miss Alexandra."

The Prince didn't answer, but gazed at the Master Sword perplexed.

As the day waned, the thunderstorm came and passed. The atmosphere was filled with a warm breeze gently brushing their faces. Before night fell, the sky cleared into a brilliant, clear midnight blue. The company set up camp at the base of a cluster of boulders. Hazerk took kindling collected from a nearby grove and hummed an upbeat tune as he built a fire large enough to scare anything that may have been lurking and scheming.

For the evening meal the three warriors sat close to the fire with Prince Alkin. The four laughed and jested merrily, finally breaking the skulking uneasiness.

Apollos stood a distance off, silently gazing at the stars. Alexa watched the unicorn as she sat on a rock next to the tethered horses. The unicorn's coat gave off a chilling, ethereal glow. His crystal horn glittered immensely in the firelight, casting shards of light. He held his head high and moved as if he was counting the stars…or perhaps reading them. He paced through the damp grasses alone, muttering to himself.

Looking over, Alexa spotted the Master Sword sitting on a log by himself, shoveling food into his mouth absently. *I wonder why he separates himself from the warriors if he wants that life so much,* she thought. The Sword paused his eating when he spotted her watching. She looked away.

That night it was cool. Bryan unfurled himself from his blankets and relieved Hazerk from watch. It was quiet. The Master Sword didn't suspect any trouble this early into the trip, but yet one could never be sure. He paced.

A few days travel and they would come to a forest road. There was a small town just outside the forest. They would make a brief stop there. He wanted to replenish certain supplies before they started the long trek through the forest.

He looked around to his companions. The warriors were out cold. Alkin was curled up sleeping soundly and peacefully. The glow of the fire lit his features almost majestically. Apollos was nowhere in sight, but Bryan felt assured he had good reason to be off by himself. The unicorn could take care of himself. The Sword looked over to the tethered horses and Alexa. He stopped pacing.

The girl looked distressed even in her sleep. Her features were contorted and she muttered incoherently. Zhan stood over her protectively. He gave his mistress a gentle nudge with his muzzle as if he desired to wake her from her restless sleep.

Taking interest and feeling a little odd, Bryan crept over to where she lay twisted in her blanket. When he approached, Zhan tossed up his head, flattened his ears and snapped his teeth. "It's okay, skinny man. I'm just checking on her," Bryan whispered, holding out a hand for the horse to sniff. Bryan's reassurance seemed to calm Zhan; the horse allowed him to approach.

Bryan wondered if he could decipher the puzzling witch by her mutterings. But he could make nothing of her moans, and decided to wake her. He put a heavy hand on her shoulder, giving her a shake. She groaned and tossed violently. "Wake up, girl!" he hissed in her ear. He gave her another unsympathetic shake. Alexa jerked up, her eyes wide with fear, and sweat trickling down her brow. Locks of her black hair were torn from her usually tight braid.

Kneeling on the ground, Bryan leaned back as she turned briskly toward him. Her fear turned to a smirk. He narrowed his eyes knowing exactly what she was going to say before it past her lips.

"*So*, you've a repulsive habit of watching people sleep. Young girls, preferably?" she said while untangling herself from her blanket.

"No." Bryan stood.

Alexa stumbled to a stand. She straightened herself, finding her composure. Even in her defiant stance she looked tiny compared to the Master Sword.

"With all that groaning you were doing, I didn't want the others thinking we could be…up to something. If you get my drift." He smiled a genuine boyish smile, knowing it would anger her. It had been too good of an opportunity to pass up maddening her.

Alexa snorted and hastily brushed a stray hair from her face. "Not even in your dreams, Master Sword." She stalked off to fetch her water pouch.

"Yep, but in *your* dreams," he chuckled, and received another murderous glare from her. Bryan let out a loud laugh. Realizing his noise, he quickly stifled it. "What would make you think that *I* would want *you*, a scrawny, little, haughty girl like yourself? That's the funniest thing I've ever heard." Snickering, he turned to warm himself over the fire. He could feel her icy stare on his back. It shot right through to his fingertips causing them to ache. The fire felt like it wasn't providing any kind of heat at all. He shivered; magic…

A minute later, Alexa stood by him, holding her hands over

the glowing coals. "I'm sorry that you don't like me. You aren't exactly my choice of company either," she said as they gazed into the pit.

Bryan rubbed his hands together, the stinging cold dissipating as Alexa calmed. He sighed resignedly. "I think we need to call a truce," he stated. Alexa looked up at him, surprise across her narrow features. He continued to talk to the coals. "Whether either of us likes it or not we have to work with each other. And it looks as if it's going to be a long time…and probably not an easy one at that." He stopped and raised his eyes to look her straight in the face. She stared at him passively with an arched eyebrow. "We just have to get along," he pressed on. "I don't like you doing this job any more than you want to do it."

"I want to do it," she protested.

"I guess the real problem is you being so smug about everything."

"There you go. You *were* talking about a truce…and I'm not smug," she snarled.

"All right, all right, we work together. I won't harass you…more than my job requires. And you won't be so self-righteous. Sound good?" he stated.

"Fine."

They shook hands, briefly.

"Now," Bryan started. "Speaking of dreams, what was all that about?"

"Nothing I prefer to discuss."

"Fine." He let it hang for a moment, and then persisted, "Magical intuition?" She shrugged. There was a moment of silence. "Do you dream like that often?" Bryan ventured.

"No, definitely not like that. But, like I said, I don't want to talk about it."

"Do you have an idea what you're looking for?" he asked. "No."

Then with an accusing edge, he asked, "Do you even know what we're up against? Can you wield this so-called counter magic?"

"No." She sighed exasperated. "I don't know

anything…yet," she snapped.

"Well, how in all of Eetharum did that naiad pull your name out?" he stated. It was meant as a question of puzzlement, but it had come out offensively. Alexa turned a pair of cool, sapphire eyes on him. They glittered dangerously in the firelight. "I mean…just how is someone who knows less than others about this ordeal supposed to help?" His tongue tripped over the words in his attempt to reconcile his already forgotten truce.

"I don't know," she said. There was a vague falter in her voice. "But I was thinking maybe it has something to do with my blood more so than my abilities." She didn't look up at him. She was embarrassed she was letting him see she wasn't as strong as she hoped others to perceive her. She despised weakness. She had always prided herself on her skills, especially because her fighting techniques were rarely practiced by females in Eetharum. Female warriors were an eastern thing. But some inclination told her it wasn't her being a female warrior that brought her here to do this job. It went deeper than that. Perhaps it had to do more with her magic blood. She wasn't sure. The dream had led her to believe that much. But, then again, it was just a dream. Nightmares often reveal a dreamer's worst fears or desires.

Bryan didn't answer. Though, he felt relieved discovering that she knew she wasn't some kind of immortal savior. The naiad may have given her name, but she wasn't the only key in fixing this problem. She *needed* help from others as well. She would be less apt to fail knowing this about herself. Being too confident in her abilities would have most definitely brought her closer and quicker to trouble. This was the path he had thought she was on, but Bryan was suddenly contemplating whether he should change his mind about her. Not yet. *So, she's covered up her fear with fake confidence. True, she is annoyingly arrogant. But some of it has to be a mask. She's young…she has to have some insecurities. And neither witches nor humans are perfect.* He gave her the benefit of the doubt.

Alexa took the Sword's drawn silence as a hint he didn't want the conversation to continue. *Fine.* She clenched her teeth resentfully. She didn't feel like talking to him anyway. Opening up to him would be like throwing herself over a cliff anyway. She stood and said tersely, "Well, I'm going back to bed or I should say back to my bedroll."

Bryan straightened his stance next to her. He nodded, still letting his silence reign. The girl was hesitant to leave. "Yep," he finally said, pretending to survey the site in order to pass the suddenly awkward moment. *Why isn't she leaving?* He was a tad annoyed. She stood next to him almost fidgeting on the spot. He turned his steady gaze on her. "Okay," he said pressingly. He was in a rush to pass the weird moment.

"Well…night." She backed away and sauntered over to her staked out spot. Settling herself with her back toward him, she pulled the blanket up to her neck, sighing. It was soothingly quiet, except for the night creatures' soft sounds.

Her dream had been disturbing. She couldn't bring herself to feel sleepy or even close her eyes. She stole a furtive glance over her shoulder. Why? She didn't know. The Master Sword was moving slowly around the site. He was currently on the opposite end. She watched him as he moved almost gracefully. Not a sound came from his footfalls. He was so tall, broad and strong. The metal on the tip of his sheath and the hilt of his sword glistened in the low light. He held himself upright and proudly. He was the epitome of what a Master Sword should be.

As Alexa watched, an unbidden thought crept into her mind, one that she furiously regretted immediately. She quickly turned over to look the other way. Feeling vulnerable to her thoughts, she became angry as if she had somehow betrayed herself. She absolutely disliked the cocky Sword. Dislike wasn't even a strong enough word. But—she couldn't even bear to think it now—she had just looked at him with desire. She had admired how soft his unruly, dark curls were in the light and how his square jaw was chiseled so perfectly and how his bright azure eyes seemed to radiate. He seemed so *deadly* and *appealing* altogether. Alexa shuddered, glaring into the dark, staring unblinkingly at the hooves of the horses tethered near her. It had just been a childish, silly, lusting girl surfacing in her for one split second. A trait she disliked in other girls her age. One that she never or would ever let take over. She refused to be that way, a silly, dumb, flirtatious woman—weak. She was a warrior. She reached a hand up to pet the lowered muzzle of Zhan to distract her wandering mind. Soon, she drifted off to a restless sleep where she dreamt of wielding the mysterious counter magic.

Chapter 11

Several uneventful, though successful, days after leaving Fordorn the company reached a small town bordering Shelkite's vast southern forest. The forest was uninhabited except for a few secluded woodsmen and a single lumber company located across the border of the small, eastern, neighboring country of Burgah.

Sword Bryan halted the company just outside the town's boundaries. "There's no need for all of us to go parading down the main street, especially with the Prince of Shelkite. It might cause suspicion or worse yet, panic. I'll pick up the supplies we need quickly so we can be on our way. Warrior Hazerk you'll join me." Bryan's voice held an unquestionable command. Hazerk nodded and guided his big chestnut mount next to Dragon. "The rest of you stay together and try not to do anything attention grabbing." He stopped and looked at Alkin a little uneasy. "Of course, I don't mean to be bossing you around, my prince. You do whatever you wish." Alkin shrugged his shoulders, a careless smile across his features. Bryan nodded. "Good. Warrior Warkan, Warrior Eelyne, I'm putting you both in charge of Alexa's protection while I'm away. All right, Warrior Hazerk, let's go." He nudged Dragon, reining him around.

"Wait," Alexa called.

Bryan sighed and rolled his eyes upward. How did he even think he could get away without her having something inane to say? He turned Dragon around, bumping Hazerk's mount in the process. "Yes, Alexa?" He tried not to sound exasperated, but failed.

She heeled Zhan to stand in front of the others. Her face suddenly held uncertainty at seeing everyone waiting curiously on her. "I would like to pick up some things of my own," she said with resolve.

"We'll be picking up everything you'll need," Bryan replied. Dragon tossed his head, snorting and stomping a large front hoof as if to show his master's impatience for him. Bryan groaned inwardly. She was probably just irritated for not being his choice partner to go with him. Alexa stared at him, giving him a challenging gaze. Everyone waited. "What?" he huffed out. "What is it you need?"

Alexa swiftly reached behind her back for her weapon. Surprised at her sudden movement and taking it for an act of violence, Bryan's sword was drawn even before Alexa had a chance to pull out one of her arrows.

"Relax, Master Sword, I'm not going to attack you," she scoffed, holding out a slender arrow in her hand. Bryan snorted and sheathed his sword.

The others stared in shock at them, unable to register exactly what had just happened. Prince Alkin was blinking rapidly and staring at Bryan dumbfounded. He had thought the two of them were coming to blows. It hadn't escaped his notice that they always spoke to each other as if they thought the other was some kind of vermin. He tried to restrain an amused smile that the confused Eelyne noticed.

The company watched wordlessly as Bryan reluctantly maneuvered Dragon up next to Zhan. Alexa handed him the arrow. "I need more of these. I don't want just any arrow. It has to be like this," she said. "I lost a lot of them fighting the howlers."

Bryan examined the arrow. The shaft of it was long and slender and of a peculiar hard, black wood. The blue feathers were attached at a precise angle and the tip was obsidian, sharpened to a lethal point. "Very nice." He handed it back. "I'll do my best."

"No, you don't get it. I want to pick them out. If they don't have this specific type, I want to choose a kind just as worthy," she argued.

Bryan snatched the arrow back. "Like I said, I'll do my best." He turned Dragon away from her zapping eyes that were narrowed intensely as if they were the only thing holding back her fury.

He looked back at her. "You stay," he ordered.

Alexa watched with an angered set jaw as the handsome Master Sword and Warrior Hazerk, with his bright, bouncing red curls matching the color of his horse, cantered away until they disappeared into the streets of town. She let out a low frustrated growl.

*****

93

"You know it's smarter this way. Better to not start a panic." Prince Alkin was trying to console an irritated Alexa a little while later. He squatted down next to her, where she sat on a rock hunched over, flipping her dagger continuously at a mutilated patch of grass between her feet. She stared at the overturned dirt, silently ignoring the Prince, her frustration evident. "That will come soon enough when warriors reach here looking for recruits...." he trailed off. Then looking wistfully into the hazy late afternoon horizon, he added, "But hopefully, we'll be able to resolve this mess before it turns into a full-fledged war and there will be no need for civilians to fight."

After a moment he sighed heavily at his failure of eliciting a pleasant response. He stood and walked back to Warkan and Eelyne who were watering the horses in a nearby creek. Eelyne seemed to keep his distance from the older warrior on the count that it appeared he was frightened by him. But even Alkin was a little intimidated by Warkan's size and constant scowl.

The warriors gave a reverent nod as Alkin approached. "Has anyone seen Apollos?" he inquired. He always made it a point to speak to his subjects as equals. It wasn't in his demeanor or ideals to use his royal blood to make others feel insignificant. The warriors had taken to him quickly because of this attribute.

Eelyne spoke, "He said he couldn't resist a tasty looking patch of clover not far from here."

"Did he say when he'd return?"

Warkan scratched his square chin quizzically and turned his austere eyes onto Eelyne.

"He'll meet us at the entry into Charad," the young warrior said, giving his sorrel mount a firm pat. The warhorse turned and fondly nuzzled his young master.

Alkin nodded, sighed and began to pace. He was mostly concerned with Alexa's sulky attitude and not the whereabouts of the clever unicorn, but he didn't want to voice his unease with the others. Alexa acted immature sometimes, throwing little tantrums. And other times she was rational and thoughtful, seeming almost otherworldly in her mannerisms. He wondered if he should have given the girl any power concerning the company. However, what would stop them from protesting her if they decided she was leading them faultily? The Prince hoped it wouldn't come to that, to overriding her. Who knew what she might do? What magic she knew….He needed her as an ally. He couldn't afford another magical adversary. He knew the history of wizards and witches. He knew they weren't particularly a peaceful or likeable lot. Alkin was beginning to feel apprehensive of her after seeing her childish pouting party. He prayed her blood wouldn't turn bad. She was still so young; she had yet to mature into herself.

He paused his pacing and stared off into the hilly horizon to the north, back toward his home, feeling sad at the prospect of a war. *Well, she'll grow, learn, and no doubt become powerful. Hopefully it will be for the good.* He sighed at his resolution.

He would just have to continue to trust her until that time came. After all she was only *half* witch. And if a pure creature such as a unicorn could trust a descendent of an ancient enemy, then certainly Alkin could trust her. He *had* to trust her and her witch intuition as she called it. He had no choice. Or at least he knew he had to trust he had made the right decision in listening to the Guidance Naiad. He glanced at her. She continued to repeatedly pitch her dagger into the dirt and pull it back out with a set scowl on her face. Alkin heaved a sigh that brimmed thick with many unspoken worries.

At twilight, the mounted silhouettes of Bryan and Hazerk appeared moving leisurely from the southeast. As they approached, the group rose from their places around the campfire to greet them.

Alexa had calmed and she looked on the forthcoming men with anticipation for her new arrows. Now relaxed, she felt a slight qualm for her behavior earlier, but only because the Prince had always been so kind to her. She had made a fool of herself. She hadn't apologized. She wouldn't. Instead, she settled to kick herself mentally and endeavor to rein in her problematic witch temper better in the future.

Bryan and Hazerk each had a satchel with goods and other supplies strapped to their saddles. Bryan also carried a curious long, slender object carefully wrapped in a cloth across his lap.

Hazerk steered his chestnut mount to stop next to Alexa.

He dismounted and pointed to the satchel. "Your weapons, my lady." He bowed slightly and grinned devilishly at her.

Feeling mocked, Alexa self-consciously fumbled to open the satchel. She drew out a bundle of elegant arrows, much like her own, but not exact. She carefully examined them, running her fingers over the black smooth shafts and gently fingering the sharp-tipped arrowheads. She eyed the feathers closely, checking all the angles for any flaw. She didn't notice the others' observation of her actions.

"Will they work?" Bryan asked as he watched Alexa. Her brow was furrowed in deep concentration and her head was cocked close to the arrows. The girl looked up, startled out of her thoughts. Her face changed quickly from a serious focus to her normal set features, but Bryan thought he caught something in between the transform. His own brows furrowed as he tried to decipher it. Her dark blue eyes once squinted in scrutiny had widened, but in one brisk moment he caught a glint of remorse. Or so he thought, perhaps it was the breaking of a spirit. Whatever it was, it was gone now and her wicked sapphire eyes had returned. They stared him down with the same acid power they always held.

"They will be fine," she said resentfully, then added anxiously, "Thank you."

"Yep." Bryan dismounted, carefully reallocating the slender package he held.

The others, who had been watching in apprehensive stillness, let out a relieved breath. Alkin, Eelyne and Warkan sauntered back to the fire as Alexa continued to inspect the arrows. Bryan and Hazerk began to repack the satchels, discussing traveling plans and the like.

As the company sat down around the simmering coals and ate their evening meal, the sun set beyond the hills, whispering its good-bye with a lavender hued horizon. They sat in a companionable silence, letting each have his thoughts. For they all knew in the morning, the real journey would begin.

Chapter 12

They rose early. The Master Sword was the first up since he had been on watch. They packed and made ready to enter the forest. The Prince and the warriors started single file toward the entrance to Charad Forest, their horses snorting in anticipation of the coming blustery day.

The wind had picked up through the night and now whipped with increasing speed over the grassy plains, rippling the green like a soft blanket. When it reached the outer trees of the forest it tossed their tops as if they were mere flowers in the breeze.

Bryan waited impatiently, holding a prancing Dragon's reins, as he watched a kneeling Alexa fumble around in her small sack she always carried. She was unmindful of the others' missing presence. Zhan stood with her, his head over his mistress' shoulder, curious of her doings. Though, he soon lost interest and tried to spin around in attempt to follow the others. It was to no avail; he merely received a sharp reprimand to stand still.

"Misplace your crystal ball?" Bryan asked smugly. Alexa's head shot up, startling an already jittery Zhan. She glared at the Master Sword contemptuously. Bryan snickered and held up his hands submissively, "Just joking, relax." Dragon bobbed his head enthusiastically, his black eyes glinting playfully. He tugged at the reins and flung his head over to whinny to his departing fellows. "Come on. They're already almost a half a mile up the road." Bryan turned to mount Dragon. The burly horse pranced in place, swinging his hindquarters around. Bryan settled in the saddle with ease.

Alexa glanced up from her pack, "Oh, they are not. Don't be so impatient," she retorted. She fumbled for another second and then finally tied up the bag. Straightening and flipping her long raven braid over her shoulder, she attached the bag quickly to Zhan's saddle.

Bryan sighed and rolled his eyes lightheartedly. The fine blustery day had put him into a somewhat genial mood. He lightly guided Dragon to face south. The horse pulled at the reins, but Bryan held him, turning in his saddle to regard Alexa. *Women!*

They can always be counted on to hold up things. He exhaled a little exasperated. "Come on, Sand Queen! We're burning day light!" he hollered above another gust of wind.

Alexa situated her things and prepared to mount. Zhan pawed at the earth and impatiently chewed his bit, tossing his silver white mane as the wind whirled about him. Alexa placed her foot in the stirrup and gracefully swung into the saddle. No more than a second before her backside hit the leather seat Zhan sprinted off, neighing loud and clear to alert the others of his coming.

They zipped by the standing Dragon and Sword Bryan in a whirl of light and dark and continued to race down the path. Alexa glanced over her shoulder and cracked a devilish grin at the Master Sword before turning back.

Bryan lingered only a moment to watch the girl's long raven braid bounce in the breeze and her willowy body move smoothly with the graceful horse. But before Dragon would allow his master watch a second longer, he snorted noisily, stomped a large hoof and shot off after them with his own thudding four beat gait.

On reaching the chatting warriors and prince, Alexa reined Zhan into a walk to the front of the company. A moment later, Bryan pulled Dragon down to an exhilarated walk. The horses were puffing with excitement. Alexa looked over to the Sword, who was already looking at her. "If you must know, I was rearranging my herbs," she said.

"Herbs?" Bryan simpered.

"Yes, ones that you so naïvely disregarded when the howlers got the better of you."

The Sword raised an eyebrow. "Oh. So, now the Sand Queen is an expert herbalist…hmm," he teased.

Alexa smiled, taking the banter with ease. "I may be from the desert, but it doesn't mean we don't have markets. My father believes the best healing comes from nature itself. So, he made sure his children knew the basic kinds. I just took it a step further than my brothers and actually applied the knowledge. Anyway, with all the jostling from riding, I didn't want them to mix or even touch each other. It taints them." She shrugged.

"I see." Bryan looked ahead and gazed at the massive outer trees of Charad Forest. Prince Alkin trotted Sapharan over.

"Sword Bryan, we're entering the forest by the Lumberman's Path. Apollos is supposed to be meeting up with us," he stated.

"Yes, my prince."

When they reached the outer edge, they stopped and waited. The wind had not let up; it raced through the trees and tossed them with such exuberance it was almost frightening. The clouds overhead, however, were white and fluffy. The sky was a brilliant blue, no sign of bad weather.

"Once we get into the forest the wind won't be so bad," Warkan stated as another gust blasted him in the face. The others nodded.

"Yeah," Hazerk joked. "You're such a light weight, we were afraid of you blowing away on us." Everyone except Warkan laughed.

While waiting, Bryan sat alone facing the forest, resting his hands on the pommel of his saddle. He was deep in thought, far away from the bantering company. He sensed another ride up beside him. Looking over, he straightened himself as Warrior Eelyne hesitantly approached him on his sorrel. Eelyne halted his warhorse next to Dragon. The two horses briefly touched noses. Dragon snorted and arched his neck arrogantly. Eelyne stole a wary glance at the Head-Master Sword, who had returned to staring pensively off into the woods. "What is it Warrior Eelyne? Something on your mind?" Bryan looked over to the young man and smiled. He watched as some of the uneasiness apparent in Eelyne dissipated.

"Master Sword?" he said diffidently.

"Yes."

"I was wondering, well I know it's a lot to ask, especially from a man like yourself, but I was wondering if you could coach me in some swordplay tactics?" Eelyne said.

Alexa, noting the conversation, curiously rode up within hearing range.

Bryan looked thoughtfully over to Eelyne. "How old are

you?"

"Eighteen, Master Sword."

"Just call me Sword Bryan."

"Eighteen, Sword Bryan."

"Well, Warrior Eelyne, you're old enough to already have completed your basic training. At this age, you should already be good at sword handling, if you listened to your instructors."

"Yes I know. My swordsmanship is good enough, I guess," he piped up. "But your sword tactics are a legend in the camp and all over Eetharum, too. I've heard you could beat Galefen. Just a couple of tips from the greatest swordsman would last me a lifetime."

Alexa stared stunned at Bryan, unable to believe that he was a legend. She had no idea. She had never heard of him before, at least she thought she hadn't.

The Master Sword leaned back in his saddle and smiled knowingly, though not arrogantly. He rubbed his unshaven chin with his fingertips. "First off, Eelyne, let me straighten something out." Eelyne gulped. Alexa stared wide-eyed. "I don't believe a man can be legend if he's never proven himself where it counts. I've only ever been in contests. Yeah, I won from the west coast to the east," he grinned a bit conceitedly, "but I believe that to use the word great it has to be something deeper than a mere contest. No matter how trying a match is. And Galefen earned that by courage and selflessness. Never forget a war hero for who he is and what he stands for."

"Yes, Master Sword," Eelyne said with understanding.

Alexa continued to stare dumbfounded at Bryan. She was still unable to recall ever hearing his name in contests. She was certain she and her brothers had attended a highly anticipated sword match in Sansdella several years back...

"Does that mean—" Eelyne began a little disappointedly.

"No." Bryan smiled, "I would enjoy very much to give you pointers during our travels, whenever we have time." Eelyne grinned from ear to ear and patted his sorrel enthusiastically. The Master Sword turned to the eavesdropping Alexa, who was biting her thumbnail lost in thought, "And, you." He startled her out of her reverie. She jerked to attention. "I got you something."

"Me?" she asked incredulously.

Bryan shifted in his saddle to untie the slender package he had brought the day before from the town. He guided Dragon over to Zhan and handed it to her. She took it, unsure how to react. "You need to tame some of that spitfire and learn better sword fighting yourself." He cleared his throat, "Um, because you're in dire need of it." Alexa narrowed her eyes indignantly at him as she unwrapped the slender weapon. "I'll teach you both. You can practice with each other."

Eelyne could barely contain his excitement. "This is great. Thank you, Master Sword."

Alexa calmly tore the cloth packaging away and looked the weapon over. It was simply made, but perfect. She pulled the long, slender blade from the sheath. A sweet ringing sound issued forth as she drew it. She held it upright in front of her, the silver blade flashing in the sunlight. The sword was lightweight and straight, woman-like in its appearance. The hilt was plain, but beautiful in its simplicity. Alexa lightly ran her fingers over it, careful not to slice them. *It's beautiful.* She felt a warmth grow inside of her. She placed the sword horizontal just below the hilt on her fingers. It balanced out perfectly.

"Crafted excellently," Bryan stated.

"Yes," Alexa answered awestruck. Her fingers were almost caressing the weapon when she stopped abruptly at seeing a recognizable insignia engraved on the hilt. She looked up to Bryan astounded. "This is a Galeon sword," she said shocked.

"Yep." Bryan shifted in his saddle. "Don't get too excited. It wasn't the most expensive, but Galeonics never make cheap weapons. Besides, I figured you'd need one. All you have is that bow. What would you've done in close contact battles?"

"My dagger."

"Not good enough." Bryan turned and gestured at Eelyne, "You'll need a Galeon sword to match his when you practice. Isn't that right, Warrior Eelyne? Your sword should be Galeon made. That's all Shelkite outfits its warriors with. Nothing better."

"Right," Eelyne confirmed.

"Thank you." Alexa stumbled over the words.

Bryan raised an eyebrow and bumped Dragon, circling the black warhorse to face the other direction. "Oh, don't thank me. I expect to be repaid in full." He clucked to Dragon, and the horse trotted over to Alkin who was now conversing with Apollos who had reappeared.

Alkin gestured for the group to gather before the forest road entrance. Everyone assembled in a semi-circle facing Apollos. The unicorn stood proudly. The gusty winds played almost passionately with his iridescent mane and tail. The sun ever-so-slightly shone through his prismatic horn causing small color spots to dance across the waving grasses. His fine angular face was held high, his copper hooves were set square and his deep chocolate eyes studied the group intently. The sight of such a magnificent creature rendered them all speechless.

"Just a word of caution before we go," the unicorn began. He waited for a reaction from anyone. When no one stirred, he continued, "Everyone should be aware and on guard while we go through Charad. The main road we'll be using is well traveled and relatively safe," he paused, and a disgusted look came over his equine features, "except, of course, for the occasional human scum that pillage travelers." He tossed his mane in his indignation, "But I know you're all good enough warriors to deal with that. We're more in danger from creatures that have siphoned over from Carthorn. Since Charad Forest connects to Carthorn in the east, some strange creatures may be lurking about. And I'm not talking about a panther. Although Carthorn is a wondrous place, it has its dark side. And more often than not that's what likes to pay travelers a visit. So, just be vigilant. That's all." He stopped abruptly and turned away as if there was no need for any response. He began trotting gracefully toward the forest road.

Alexa looked over at her companions. Eelyne and the Prince showed no reaction, albeit Eelyne looked a little pale. Sword Bryan actually smiled at her. Although Alexa felt it was more of a smirk. Maybe he was hoping she would be eaten by something. She watched the three follow after Apollos. She glanced over at Warkan in nervous hesitation.

The brawny man rolled his eyes. Kicking his horse into a trot, he stated skeptically as he passed her, "I wouldn't worry too much about it, sweetheart."

Hazerk followed close behind. He was grinning. "It'd be amazing if we saw a griffin or something wouldn't it?" He motioned for Alexa to follow.

Alexa watched apprehensively as the others entered into the forest and began to disappear down the furrowed path. Getting a sick feeling in the pit of her gut, she sighed. She let the air puff out her cheeks and let it escape slowly. She wasn't sure if she was ready for this. She didn't feel as confident as she had been. She hated to admit she was nervous. Despite her reluctant feelings, she squeezed Zhan's sides. The horse followed eagerly.

They traveled along the wagon-rutted road all afternoon and well into dusk, progressing deeper and deeper into the heart of the ancient forest. They rode in relative silence. Each held their own awes of the forest to themselves. That is until something caught their eye and their excitement seemed to overtake them. They would then break the silence with a gasp, point and exclaim their wonder.

The trees were tall and their girths thick with age. The monstrous plants towered high over the travelers. Their tops swayed wildly in the roaring wind, but never hazardously. The comforting smells of the wood were enchanting. The coalescence of cedars, pines, ferns and wild flowers made an aroma as calming as a lover's touch.

Pretty song birds twittered and flitted around them. Apollos' presence seemed to have an unearthly effect on the forest and its residents. The wildlife was unable to avoid investigating the unicorn. Handsome foxes paused for a long look. Curious bunnies, deer and a bobcat all chanced a glance. Even once, from atop a branch, a yellowed-eyed panther gazed mildly down at them. And Hazerk swore he saw a phoenix fly low through the trees—the others ridiculed him and told him it was just an eagle. The forest's beasts weren't the only creatures engrossed by Apollos. Even the trees seemed to pause their wild wind dancing so they could have a chance to caress the unicorn's snowy white coat as he passed.

Only once in the late afternoon did they come upon other travelers making their way north. It was a single wagon pulled by two stocky oxen. A heavy-set man was walking alongside the beasts carrying a walking stick, a peddler no doubt. His young, plain looking daughter rode in the front of the wagon. The two passed the company with no words, just a good-day nod from the man and a smile accompanied with a friendly blown kiss—directed at the blushing Eelyne—from the maiden.

In order to have gotten by without any questions, Sword Bryan had ordered the Prince and Alexa to put their hoods up and chins down. He didn't feel it necessary for Alkin to show his face in case he was recognized. He felt to be on the safe side and hide Alexa, too, for it might look a little suspicious to see a young woman riding alone with a group of men.

Apollos had given them advanced notice of the on-coming wagon. His unicorn senses allowed him so. He then made sure he was unseen. Invisible was not quite the word. He could have easily slipped into the woods and waited until they had passed, but he preferred to stay close. So, with just a blue tinted glint from his horn and a slight flicker he blended into the background of the forest. He simply faded from sight, taking on the shapes and hues of the objects he passed.

Alexa couldn't outright distinguish him, but if she looked closely she could see his ever-so-slight movement. Of course, it could have just been the breeze blowing through the forest.

After dusk, Sword Bryan decided by the aching in his legs and back that it was time to call it a day. Apollos had gone deeper into the woods off the road and found a small clearing that would suffice for the night. They followed his lead and everyone dismounted with a groan.

"Ahh," Hazerk sighed, cracking his stiff back. "Let's get a fire going, my bum's numb." He and Eelyne set to work, while Warkan took care of the horses, un-tacking, rubbing down and graining them.

After looking after Zhan, Alexa plopped down next to the fire, stretching gratefully. "Ah, not so fast, Sand Queen." The Master Sword came to stand over her shoulder. "I think you and

Eelyne have your first lesson to get started with."

Alexa stared at him a little disbelievingly, and then shrugged, "All right." She hopped up a little over enthusiastically and went to retrieve her new weapon. "I'm thirsty. Would it be all right if I had a drink first, sir?" she asked a bit mockingly, as if she were a humble student asking a huge favor of a reverend master, which actually *was* the case, although it didn't occur to her just then.

"There's a small creek down the way. Alkin and I will get water," Apollos spoke up. He and Alkin, carrying the water pouches, set off into the dark, the unicorn's natural glow slowly fading into the night.

"All right, pupils!" Bryan clapped his hands together devilishly as Alexa and Eelyne faced him with slightly anxious looks in their eyes. "Let's get started! No mercy!" He threw his head back and laughed, "This is going to be fun."

So they began. And Sword Bryan indeed proved himself to be unmerciful. They practiced hard, though they were tortured by the smell of dinner cooking and hot tea wafting through their little harbor in the woods. They practiced long after Apollos and Alkin had returned from the creek. Alexa chanced a curious glance toward Apollos to watch the unicorn graciously dip his horn into the water to purify it. But her peeping proved to be disastrous. She was struck hard on the thigh by the flat of Eelyne's sword. And when the others began to eat, Sword Bryan still didn't stop drilling them until he felt his own stomach give a loud protest.

"All right!" He lowered his sword. "That's enough. I'm getting grouchy. Need to eat," he grunted. He stalked over to the fire and sat, the lesson ending abruptly.

"Humph, getting grouchy?" Alexa mumbled, but no one heard her. She went and sat alongside Eelyne by the crackling fire.

As everyone was hungrily shoving the heavily salted meat into their mouths, Warkan looked up from his meal. "Well, by the looks of things I certainly hope she doesn't have to face one on one combat with this wizard," he commented flatly.

"What exactly is that supposed to mean?" Alexa said icily, almost choking on her dinner. Everyone paused their eating to stare at Warkan.

"What? I was just saying she's not…well…she's not exactly a seasoned swordsman," he stammered.

"She's not *that* bad, Warrior Warkan," Sword Bryan rolled his eyes, but his voice held a slight reprimand, which Alexa was grateful for. Though she didn't think of it at the time, later when she thought back, she felt flattered to receive such praise from the Master Sword.

"Uncalled for," Alkin stated.

"Sorry, Master Sword, my prince, Alexandra. I spoke out of place," Warkan apologized, returning to his plate.

"Also, I want you all to choose carefully what you say from now on. I mean about the mission, because even some trees have ears. Let's not say 'wizard' anymore as to not prick any unwanted attentions," Alkin stated with authority.

Once again Warkan looked up from his meal, this time with disbelief in his eyes, staring at Alkin. "Pish!" he snorted, laughing slightly. "Forgive me, my prince, but what do you mean *ears?* You must mean the lumbermen are hiding and listening."

Alkin stopped chewing. "No, the trees. They can hear," he stated through a mouthful of meat.

Warkan burst with sudden laughter, his face red and eyes squinty. He giggled almost girlish-like. "Forgive me," he wheezed, "Old fairy tales, that's all that is." He chuckled some more and wiped his eyes.

"No! It's true," Eelyne said.

"Whatever, youngin'." Warkan disregarded him.

"I believe it," Hazerk commented.

"Yeah, you would," Warkan mumbled. Hazerk ignored him.

"I heard a tale once of how the trees murdered a man," Bryan simply stated, snatching everyone's attention.

"Trees murdering? They were pulling' your leg." Warkan cleared his throat adding, "Um, Master Sword."

"Oh," Hazerk clapped Warkan on the shoulder, "have a little imagination. Head-Master Sword, I could do for a little story." He looked to his superior expectantly. Bryan ignored him.

"Tree spirits are very old. Some say not very wise, but I knew a few in the old days. They're called dryads," Apollos said. He was lying comfortably in a bed of leaves between Alexa and Alkin.

"What? You believe in tree spirits, too?" Warkan was incredulous.

Apollos' eyes glimmered mischievously, "You're asking a unicorn?" Now it was everyone else's turn to laugh.

"Well, that's different." Warkan attempted to save himself. "You're living, breathing. You have blood flowing through your veins." He turned to rap on the tree he was leaning on, "Trees don't. They have roots and leaves."

"You're probably safe saying that here. But I warn you, don't go doing that if you're ever in Carthorn. Most of the trees in Charad have been harvested and planted. So spirits don't reside in them. They only live in the trees born at the beginning of time. What's left of them are in Carthorn," Apollos said.

Warkan scratched his head, "Well, I don't intend to be waltzing through Carthorn any time soon."

"Apollos?" Alexa broke in.

"Yes."

"How old are you? Do you remember the old time with the magic?"

"Oh," the unicorn sighed, his equine features thoughtful. "Too old to count or maybe I've forgotten. Even in my lifetime, I haven't known the wonders of the ancient world. When I was a colt, I knew only a few other mystic creatures," he answered a little wistfully.

"Do you know my father? He's at least two-hundred-years-old," Alexa asked the unicorn.

"No, I'm sorry to say I've never had the pleasure of meeting your father. I try to steer clear of wiz—I mean magic men, good or bad. Sorry." The unicorn's chocolate eyes sparkled. Alexa smiled fondly at him.

"Why've you never found a female unicorn to keep your race alive," Alexa suddenly, blatantly asked.

"Unicorns mate for life. I've just never found the right

filly." He flipped his silky mane. A playful twinkle was in his eye. "That's due to the fact that unicorns are rare. I've lived in Shelkite for centuries. But, I suppose, if I went looking I might find another. Just never have. I've friends in Shelkite. It's hard to be devoted to two things."

"I know this sounds odd," Hazerk spoke up, "but could I touch your coat? It's very intriguing. I mean how it glows and all."

"I could let you, but then I'd have to kill you," Apollos stated bluntly.

Hazerk let out a hesitant chuckle, and then seeing Apollos' level gaze, he abruptly stopped. "You're joking right?" He eyed the unicorn dubiously.

Apollos snorted; a mischievous look was in his chocolate-colored eyes. "Only partially," he snickered. Hazerk made a surprised face as the unicorn continued, "I would just require some of your blood for retribution." He lowered his muzzle to rub it on his hoof casually, as if this was the most normal thing to say. He closed his eyes in satisfaction as he scratched. "Actually," he went on, feeding their curiosity, "there are only two of you here that could actually touch me and no harm would come to you."

"I don't understand." Warkan looked confused and slightly exasperated.

Apollos let them all ponder in silence for a moment, enjoying their puzzlement.

"A virtuous person," Eelyne suddenly said. Everyone's heads popped up out of thought. They all looked surprised except for Alkin, who just smiled knowingly. "Only the innocent can touch you. They can ride you, too. Because you're a creature so pure nothing soiled can touch you without penalty," Eelyne said with growing confidence. "I've read it somewhere. I specialized in magical history and beings at school."

"Right. You know unicorns," Apollos praised him.

"Ha! Well, I guess we all know who those two are," Warkan snickered.

"Oh, I think the answer might surprise you, Warrior Warkan," the unicorn stated slyly.

"Well, I know it's not me." Hazerk laughed, and then

stopped abruptly adding, "Although, it's been awhile." The others stared at him with shocked grins. "Anyway…" His laugh faltered.

Apollos tossed his shimmering mane, his horn catching a blinding light from the dancing flames of the fire and laughed. "Ah, humans! I'll never understand them." He moved on, directing the conversation away from the improper path it was taking. "But unicorns can be foolish when it comes to the innocent. I know of a time in the past when innocents were used against us. This was far before my time, I might add. But a magic user would use a young girl to convince a unicorn to follow her into a trap. The magic user would then chop off the unicorn's horn and harvest its magical blood. That's the tale anyhow. Because of it I've always been leery of little girls." Apollos chuckled. He looked at Alexa, "And that gives you the reason why I'm not too fond of magic wielders. Except you of course."

Alexa smiled sadly, ashamed for the first time ever of her heritage.

"Anyways, anyways," Hazerk said, waving a hand trying to change the subject. "Come on, Sword Bryan, tell us that tree story." He turned to Warkan and added, "Just sit back and shut up, you might like it."

"Who said I wanted to tell it?" Bryan protested. "I can't tell stories. Apollos I'm sure knows it. Let him tell it." The unicorn stared at him expectantly, playing that he had no idea about the story. "Oh, all right," Bryan grumbled. "But don't blame me if I get it all mixed up." Everyone nodded and looked at him eagerly. Bryan took a sip of his tea and began, "Okay, there was this tree—no there was this *man* once very long ago that—"

"Does he have a name?" Alexa interrupted.

"Yeah, you have to give him a name," Hazerk agreed.

"All right, I'll start over. Apollos, what was the man's name?"

Apollos raised his head looking surprised, "What? I don't know the story." He stared at Bryan a little devilishly.

"Okay. Well once upon a time, long ago, when the forests were still very populated with tree nymphs. There was this young man by the name of DeSont who lived in a cabin by the woods with his family."

"Try Thankeil," Apollos broke in. Bryan glared at him and the unicorn added quickly, "It just sounds better is all." He then started to nonchalantly lip up a mash that had been prepared for him.

Bryan cleared his throat and started once more, "Well, *Thankeil* lived in a cabin by the woods. And he would often go walking into the forest on long summer days. It gave him serenity. He loved the trees and flowers. He loved nature. Well, one spring day while Thankeil was enjoying a walk through the paths in the woods he so adored, he came upon a beautiful maiden who had fallen asleep under a willow tree. But she was like no other maiden he'd ever seen before. Thankeil stopped, entranced. The young maiden was curled up at the trunk, sleeping ever-so peacefully. Her skin was light bronze and looked as soft as silk, her body willowy and her face so radiant it almost hurt him to look at her. She wore a slender dress of sparkling emerald and her long, beautiful, wavy locks of hair shimmered a dark green. Thankeil, completely mesmerized, reached out a hand to touch her, but she started awake. Her emerald eyes opened wide in shock, she gave a yelp, leapt up, and vanished into the tree. Thankeil was left there stunned. A dryad! Humans rarely saw nymphs; they usually shied from them. But Thankeil had fallen in love with the maiden. So, he stayed and pleaded endlessly to the tall willow for the maiden to come out and speak with him. But it was to no avail. Day after day, Thankeil would leave his duties to go and plead for the dryad to come out and see him. He told her how beautiful she was and how he longed to speak with her, that he would not harm her. He'd bring her gifts and leave them at the base of the tree. And always the next day, when he'd return, they'd be gone. He felt it would only be a matter of time when he would see the maiden again."

Then, one day, while he was leaning lazily against the trunk, rambling on about his ambitions and himself, like he had so many days, a figure appeared around the corner of the tree. The dryad had come out. Thankeil leapt up, speechless. The dryad smiled and placed a soft hand over Thankeil's heart and said, 'You are beautiful, too, human.' She reached up and touched a yellow lock of Thankeil's hair. 'You are beautiful outside as well as inside. I have listened to all you've said these past months. So kind, adventurous and wishful, unlike other humans I see tramping through the woods, always with their axes looking for a tree to destroy. Come, I'll show you the wonders of the forest as a dryad knows it.'"

She took Thankeil by the hand and they spent their time speaking with one another while they walked the golden woods. Thankeil returned day after day to see her. He called her Willa, for she was the spirit of the great willow tree. The two soon fell in love. Thankeil told his family of Willa. Strange as they thought it was, they accepted her. Willa even braved a meeting with his family at the edge of the forest."

Thankeil and Willa spent much of their time with one another, and Thankeil promised her he'd protect her tree from any lumbermen, and they'd build a house of stone in a clearing near her tree."

Willa loved Thankeil dearly and feared the day when his human life would come to an end. For she would live on, at least until her tree finally withered and died. For the spirit trees born at the beginning of time live to be very old. Thankeil and Willa knew the danger and hurt that was possible in their future, but they risked it so they could love each other devotedly while they had the chance."

One night, as they were walking under the canopy of trees by the sparkle of starlight, they heard music and laughter coming from within the forest. Willa paused, a smile spread across her features. She took Thankeil by the hands and said excitedly, 'It's the trees; they are dancing merrily, having a Star-Gathering Party. Come, I'll introduce you to the others. They surely will love you as I do.' So, they quickly ran hand in hand to find the gathering of tree spirits. They came upon a clearing in the forest to see many tree spirits dancing and singing in their other worldly ways. Willa and Thankeil paused at the edge of the party to watch. It was the most wondrous thing Thankeil had ever seen. Suddenly, Willa grasped his hands and pulled him into the dance among the others. The dancing went on, Thankeil's presence gone unnoticed for a while."

Then a dryad stopped and pointed, staring widely at Thankeil, 'A human!' she screeched. The music, the dancing, the laughing, all stopped immediately. Thankeil stared fearfully at the dryad who had spotted him. She was still pointing a slender, pale finger at him. She was the birch's spirit, her skin alabaster and her hair long, straight and rich brown."

Willa clutched onto Thankeil protectively. 'He's with me. He'll do you no harm, I promise,' Willa said a little shakily. All the spirits gathered around to stare at the human. But one tall, male broke through the whispering crowd. A staff with oak leaves sprouting atop of it was held in his hand. He was broad, old he looked, but his bushy beard and shaggy hair were still a deep brown with leaves and vines intertwined in them. He stared at Willa accusingly."

'How dare you bring a human among us!' He said.

'I tell you, Oak, he is a friend. His name is Thankeil. He loves the forest,' Willa replied, still clutching Thankeil tightly."

The oak's spirit snorted, 'Ha! He is a human, a vile creature that allows and creates the destruction of trees!'"

'He's promised to protect my tree home. I am sure he'd do the same for you all. He can speak to the other humans!' Willa answered."

Then Birch called out again, pointing her finger, 'I've seen them together many times. They spend almost every day together.'

Oak glared at Willa, 'Tell me this isn't true. You know you're not supposed to be in contact with humans! We forbid it.'"

'It is true. We love each other,' Willa said angrily. The tree spirits began to mumble and speak amongst themselves. Thankeil and Willa retreated farther from the grumbling, unhappy crowd, afraid to leave. Willa huddled up next to Thankeil. And Thankeil, fearing for his life, wrapped his arms tightly around her."

Finally, Oak broke from the crowd, pounding his staff on the ground, he stated, 'We've decided we won't allow this relationship to go any further.'"

'Well, you can't stop us!' Willa called back."

'Yes, we can.' Then Oak, quick as lightning, reached out

112

and grabbed Thankeil, ripping him and Willa apart. He threw him to the other male spirits who restrained him."

'No! You can't!' Willa screamed."

'We've decided,' Oak said arrogantly, 'that this man is going to pay for the evil deeds that his kind has done upon trees.' Thankeil was then taken away, struggling and calling out for mercy. Willa was restrained by the other dryads. She cursed them to bring him back and screamed for Thankeil. They ignored her. The tree spirits took Thankeil and mercilessly threw him over a cliff."

Willa never got over the pre-mature death of her lover. She cursed the others and secluded herself and cried relentlessly. She never stopped mourning Thankeil. And even at Star-Gathering Parties, which happened each year at midsummer, Willa would sit out from the dancing and playing, solemn tears rolling silently down her face. She soon earned the name Weeping Willow from the others. But they still showed no remorse or sympathy for what they had done."

Bryan leaned back on his elbows and took a sip from his tea. "There you go." He sighed.

Alexa snorted out a laugh, "Where did you hear a sappy story like that? You surprise me, Sword Bryan."

Bryan glared at her from over the fire. "Heard it at the Blue Mermaid. The bard that told it said it was true. I don't know if it is or not."

"I thought it was good. Interesting…" Hazerk stated, but he seemed a little irresolute. "I liked the detail you put into it… and the animation of the voices. You could be one of those traveling storytellers." He laughed, albeit a little nervously for poking fun at his superior.

Bryan grunted, "See if I ever tell another tale."

"Tale? So, it's not true," Warkan chimed in.

"Yes, it is true." Apollos looked up from his dinner, his muzzle covered with sweet mash. "So they say. Every legend is based on some sort of fact." He returned hungrily to his mash.

"Well, I believe it," Alkin stated.

"Me, too," Eelyne quickly agreed.

113

"Anyway." Bryan stood, brushing his pants off. "I'll take first watch. The rest of you should get some sleep."

Chapter 13

The heavily cloaked man was indeed very much out of place. But no one seemed to notice him as he slowly made his way about the busy main street of Yilvana Port. It was mid-morning, and the trading boats had docked and the uncouth sailors had begun to unload their goods. The streets were packed with traders' tables and tents and the buyers bustled in every direction. Horses and carts were jammed in the heavy traffic and livestock were periodically herded through the throng.

Yilvana was a tropical paradise. The locals dressed lightly in flowing vibrant colors. The children ran dirty, barefooted and merrily through the streets. Yilvana was the largest trading seaport in all of Eetharum. The goods brought to Yoldor from oversea continents were known throughout the world, even as far to the north as the vast country of Sushron, which was out of the boundaries of the allied countries.

Sushron, the subarctic and mountainous north, was where the cloaked man had traveled from. It had been where his abode had been for the majority of his life. But if anyone ever asked, he always blatantly stated that it wasn't his home.

His thick, black cloak was beginning to weigh him down. The heat from the incessant days of summer was breaching him, but he dared not remove his cloak—his sanctuary. No matter how warm it got, he dared not remove the hood in which his marred face hid.

Although he was feeling rather warm, he couldn't remember a time when he had been happier. He had hope again. He was free. He was starting over. This was as far as he was going. He had picked this place as his new home in hopes to find a familiar, lost face among the people. He had brought with him only a small pack of his belongings and a sturdy mare that had traveled with him all the hundreds of miles and, of course, his trusty weapon. When he had left, he couldn't bring himself to part with it. No matter what blood had tainted its name.

Coming out of the busy main street, he paused at the start of another. It was lined with two story apartments. It was clean and well kept. He smiled in the shadows of his hood. His coffee-colored eyes sparkling for the first time in literally centuries. "Well, Blize, this is as good a place as any," he said to his mare. "I'll board at one of these inns until I can find a small place of my own. Hopefully out of town…secluded. No one will bother us and you'll have plenty of room to run."

The grulla colored mare, Blize, snorted and bobbed her head, pulling gently at the reins held in her owner's hand. She eyed him fondly before nuzzling his shoulder. The black cloaked man smiled once more and fondly clucked to his only friend in the world and began to lead her down the road.

*****

"I wasn't saying you were a terrible swordsman…woman, whatever. I was just saying you might need a little more practice," Warkan was saying the next morning. He was trying to reconcile himself to Alexa as she coldly regarded him from astride Zhan.

"Well," she began arrogantly, "let's just say I'd take you on in an archery match any day. If you feel so inclined."

"Oh, you think you're that good?" Warkan stared at her in ridiculing doubt.

Sword Bryan, riding abreast with Alkin at the head of the company, had to crack a slight smile. He'd been keeping his eyes on the road, pretending not to eavesdrop. Obviously, Warkan's apology the night before wasn't enough to soothe Alexa's wounded pride. The two traveling companions had been going back and forth about their many achievements for at least a half an hour. Alexa boasted of her archery skills and Warkan boasted of specializing in combat and winning honors. Frankly, Bryan was getting a little sick of hearing how great they were at this and at that. *Can't really call it eavesdropping anyhow.* He twisted his lips wryly. They weren't exactly being secretive; they were the only ones talking besides the birds.

The Master Sword had awakened and packed up the camp early so they could get moving before the sunrise. He was intent on getting as quickly as he could out of the wretched forest. It made him uneasy for reasons he couldn't explain. He loved trees, but he loved wide-open fields more. The company had been trotting along at a clipping pace, enough to satisfy Bryan's hurry. But for the

116

meantime, they'd relaxed their pace to rest the horses. Consequently, the slower gait initiated Alexa and Warkan's discussion.

"Well, how about I just show you," Alexa declared, her tone assured but not arrogant. Bryan heard the girl shifting in her saddle. He didn't need to look to know she was taking out her bow and an arrow. He huffed out a quiet sigh and made an exasperated grimace. Stealing a glance at Alkin, Bryan noted with surprise that he seemed utterly oblivious to the conversation going on behind them. The young prince was busy looking at the trees and wild life, softly humming to himself.

"Alexa," Hazerk spoke up, riding up between Warkan and her. "We all believe you. Just pleeease give it a rest. Warkan was just being a pig," he said turning to the stony warrior and giving him a scowl. Warkan glared vehemently back.

"No. It's fine," she pepped. "I want to settle this."

"Didn't you hear me, you silly girl. You—don't—have—to—prove any—thing," he stated slowly as if he were speaking to a dim-witted person. Alexa smiled, shrugging her shoulders. "Listen—"

"For the love of Shelkite!" Bryan suddenly blurted, cutting off Hazerk's lecture. He halted Dragon, causing the whole company to come to a complete stop. He spun the black stallion around on his haunches to face them. Prince Alkin came back to reality and did the same with Sapharan. The three warriors and Alexa were staring at him in surprise at his sudden outburst and emergence from his usual silent guidance. Bryan quickly regained his composure and cleared his throat. "We will all halt. We will all watch. So that we may go on," he stated curtly, and then looked to Alkin for his input.

"Yes, please do. If that'll appease you," Alkin sighed, looking at Alexa and Warkan wearily.

Alexa smiled widely, her sapphire eyes glittering happily, her pleased countenance having a strange, perhaps magical effect on all of them. "Thank you." She shifted in her saddle, staring up into the trees searching for a target. "Okay, see that dragonfly way up there. I'll bet you, I'll get that little guy square and dead."

Everyone turned their heads to look up. Bryan squinted, barely seeing a little flicker of movement at the top of an enormous maple tree that was several yards in front of them.

"Ah, Miss Alexandra," Eelyne started.

"Huh?" Alexa set her bow and aimed.

"I don't know if it's a good idea killing things we're not needing to." Eelyne looked at Sword Bryan apprehensively.

"You know, he may have a point," Alkin said. But Alexa's arrow was already whizzing over their heads.

"Yeah," Bryan agreed as he watched the arrow.

"It's just a dragonfly," she said, waiting eagerly.

Right on target, the arrow shuddered then stopped. The glittering wings of the dragonfly tensed and then went limp. The arrow and the quarry began to fall rapidly to the earth. They fell to the base of the maple with a small plop.

"Good shot!" Hazerk praised the grinning Alexa. He was thoroughly impressed. "Wow, but that was a large dragonfly," he said squinting over at it. Everyone nodded their heads in agreement, all still a little stunned from the incident.

"Well? See?" Alexa smirked at Warkan.

Warkan shrugged and grunted. "Good shot," he simply said.

"You know—" Bryan hesitantly began to comment on the peculiar bug, but was cut off by a sudden loud buzzing noise. It was coming from above their heads. Everyone looked up perplexed. "What the—" Bryan shaded his eyes from the sunbeams streaming through the branches. There seemed to be a tuft of cloud hovering over their heads a hundred feet or more.

"What is that?" Alexa asked. Everyone shook their heads, wordlessly watching the rippling, noisy haze. Then, suddenly the cloud seemed to swarm, maddening like a hive of angry bees. An obnoxious ringing noise was emanating from it. Realization that they were in trouble took effect on all of their faces.

"Pixies!" Eelyne broke the confused silence, his face fearful. "You killed a pixie!"

"What?" Alexa said, unable to believe. She was stricken with fright.

Warkan gave out a loud boisterous laugh, and then stopped short when he saw a wary Eelyne quickly advance back down the road at a good clip, pulling the pack mule right along with him. "You've done it now. They're mad," the young man called back.

By that time, Sword Bryan and Prince Alkin had dismounted and walked over to investigate the fallen creature. "Yep, it's a pixie," Bryan stated a matter-of-fact, turning the dead woodland creature over with his boot. "Hmm, this can't be good," he said aside to Alkin. The Prince nodded his head in grave agreement.

"Ahh! Help! Help!"

The two men turned their heads to see a swarm of angry pixies attacking Alexa's head. Warkan had withdrawn himself and his horse. He was standing next to Eelyne farther back down the road. Alexa was futilely swatting at the irate pixies. Hazerk had stayed to help, but the pixies didn't seem to be interested in him, all their efforts were in attacking Alexa. Hazerk fiercely swung at the ones swarming Alexa yelling, "Get away, you demons! Get back!"

The Master Sword and the Prince looked at each other horrified. Alexa yelped out some foul curses and covered her head with her hands. She attempted to kick Zhan forward, but the pixies would have none of it. They followed, attacking the horse. Zhan reared and the distracted Alexa was quickly unseated. The pixies buzzed to the ground with her.

"Get Apollos!" Alkin ordered Bryan as he swiftly snatched the terrified Zhan's reins as the horse attempted to bolt past. Bryan hastily leapt onto Dragon and galloped up the road calling out for the unicorn.

Hazerk was now down on the ground calling the pixies every foul name he knew. He thrashed them mercilessly with his broad arms, sending hoards of them falling at a time. They started attacking him fiercely.

All Alexa could make out were tiny green clad bodies, with iridescent wings buzzing all around her. There appeared to be both genders present, but it was hard for her to tell. They were screeching angrily at her, though she had no idea what they were saying. They tore at her face, hair and any part of her they could get to. And, as if it were not bad enough, some of the little beasts had knives. She felt sharp pricks all over her skin. Beads of blood sprouted to the surface. She could only cry out, "Help! Stop! I'm sorry! I didn't mean to! I didn't know! You blasted creatures!"

Bryan found Apollos up the road. He could hear the unicorn's voice answering him before he could see him. Then suddenly the unicorn materialized out of the air, galloping toward him. Dragon only gave a slight start at his appearance. Bryan pulled the stallion to a skidding halt. The unicorn met them, worry evident on his features. "Pixies. Attacking," Bryan simply explained. The unicorn nodded, and then was off galloping toward the catastrophe.

When Apollos reached the dilemma, he found both Hazerk and Alexa sitting in the rutted road endeavoring to defend themselves. A very angry Hazerk swatted at the pixies like they were bees and Alexa sat huddled and cursing.

He stopped in front of the two struggling people. He coolly lowered his prismatic horn, aiming at the irate pixies. There was a moment of pure palpable magic in the air surrounding him as he drew forth his power. His beautiful horn took on hues of sparkling pink like flavored sugar crystals. His coat fluffed like soft velvet and emitted a stunning white glow. The observers' breaths were taken at his glorious manifestation of magic.

Small tendrils of translucent, pink hued lights grew forth from the tip of Apollos' horn. They spewed out, thousands of clear, pink, glowing strands, all connecting to a pixie and encircling them like a soap bubble. The pixies abruptly stopped their attack. The awful sound abated. They were encased in a prison. Bound by the magical web, their angry faces scowled, their mouths threw soundless insults and their hands beat against the webs threateningly.

Connected to them by the streams of gleaming threads, Apollos lifted his head and slowly moved the pixies away from Alexa and Hazerk. Hazerk was staring mouth slacked at the unicorn and his cords of light, binding and surrounding the little human-like bodies. Feeling the assault stop, Alexa raised her head and looked hazily around.

Apollos turned and guided the spellbound pixies over their heads to the sky above the treetops, directing them with his horn. With a gusto shake of his head the glimmering threads broke free from his horn and wafted away on the breeze. The pixies stayed encased in the magical nets. Apollos allowed himself a few moments of pleasure in watching the pink clouds enveloping the pixies float out of sight, his chocolate eyes holding an amused twinkle.

Snorting wryly, he turned his attention to the two on the forest floor. Alexa, having quickly recovered her awe at the unicorn's demonstration of magic, was grumbling curses under her breath as she searched out all the stinging pricks on her flesh. Hazerk, on the other hand, was staring mouth agape at the sky, his eyes searching for the lost pixie clouds. Apollos let out a musical laugh, bringing them all back to the present.

"Are you just going to leave them trapped?" Hazerk asked, astonished.

Apollos tossed his mane, a neutral look in his eyes. "They'll get out of it. We should be on our way, out of their territory, lest they should come after us again."

Alexa and Hazerk stood, brushing themselves off. The others started to regroup. Zhan nervously came up beside Alexa. She gave him a reassuring pat and whispered soothing words.

"What little demons! That's not at all what I thought pixies were like," Hazerk commented irritably. "I thought they were giggly, friendly and airy like." He flitted his hands around merrily, but his eyes held snapping flames.

"Well, she *did* kill one of them. What would you expect?" Eelyne stated as he rode up. Alexa gave him a sour look.

"At least you weren't pixilated," Apollos said.

"Pixilated?" Alexa said, the irritation apparent in her voice and gestures. "*Pixilated!*" she repeated bitterly. "I think my skin is shredded like meat in a butcher's shop." She pushed up the sleeve of her slashed cloak and held up her arm for them to observe. Her normally smooth skin was inflamed. Her forearm was slashed in all different directions, some cuts so deep that she had carefully folded the skin back over the wounds.

"I'm sure you've got something in that miraculous pack of herbs you carry that's a cure-all," Bryan stated wryly as he mounted.

Alexa turned to him, "As a matter of fact—" she started to say smartly, but then stopped mid-sentence, her mouth open as if she had suddenly forgot what she was going to say. A puzzled look came over her features. Bryan stared at her expectantly. She slapped her hand over her mouth and straightened her stance, seemingly surprised with herself.

"Well?" Bryan prompted. He was actually kind of curious what it was she had. But then it was his turn to stare at her puzzled. She shook her head; and a lost look glazed over her eyes. Then a very girly giggle escaped her. Bryan was shocked. He couldn't help but let a small, perplexed smile escape him. He wasn't the only one to notice her uncharacteristic laugh. Everyone in the company paused what they were doing and turned to look at her, everyone but Hazerk.

"Ha!" She belted out suddenly, removing her hand from her mouth and pointing at Bryan like something was his fault. "I forgot what I was saying!" She let out another giggle that sounded more on the side of insanity.

"Are you all right?" Bryan asked, bewildered at her sudden personality change.

"Uh-huh, yes." She stumbled, turning to put her foot in Zhan's stirrup. Missing it completely, she began to laugh hysterically. Zhan eyed her skeptically. Everyone stared wide-eyed at her. Worry bordering on alarm was evident on their faces.

"What's wrong with her?" Warkan blurted.

"She's pixilated," Eelyne said pointedly.

"Pixilated? I am not!" Alexa giggled and dropped to the ground on her backside. Bryan jumped down from his mount and held out his hand to her. "Who are *you*?" she demanded, looking up at him a little dubious, like he was trying to pull a quick one on her. Bryan laughed.

"Yep, pixilated," Apollos agreed. "It will wear off in several hours. The pixies excrete the dust to confuse whoever gets in their way. They think it's funny. But it's just a pure inconvenience when you're trying to travel and then forget where you are and where you're going, let alone *who* you are."

"She doesn't know who she is?" the Sword looked up, a rare, playful glint in his eye.

"Oh, I do to. But I can't think of it right at the moment…" Alexa stated, flopping back to lie on the ground, outstretched. "Let's lie here and wait for the stars." She closed her eyes for a second, and then popped them open. "By the way, where am I?"

"A haunted forest. Now, up you go. We've *got* to go." Bryan offered his hand to her.

"No joke!" She stared around the woods, aghast.

"Come on, I'll help you mount; and we can be on our way," Bryan said a little impatiently. The others were all mounted, except Hazerk who was digging around in his saddle packs. They were watching patiently, amused by her antics.

"I'm not going anywhere with you. I don't know you," she said point blank.

"I'm your knight in shining armor. I've come to take you home."

"You don't look very shiny." She studied him over thoroughly. "In fact, you look grimy," she said. "But, actually, I *guess* you're not *that* hard on the eyes." She nodded her head approvingly, a sincere look in her eyes. "I'm sure that under all that dirt you have the potential to be rather handsome…"

"I'm glad you think so," he said amused. "You could use a bath as well." He held out his hand once more. She took it, hopping up to her feet.

"I didn't realize I was waiting for a knight…" She pondered while Bryan guided her over to Zhan. "But then again— wow! What an exquisite animal!" Her round eyes sparkled a dazzling sky blue as she looked over Zhan as if for the first time ever. She went to his head, and he nuzzled her outstretched palm.

"Yes, so you've told us many times. Come on, girl, up you go."

"I don't see how I could. I've never seen him before."

"Do you really think she should be riding in this state?"

Alkin inched forward on his mount to stand in front of them.

"Well, hello!" Alexa held out her hand in greeting, smiling cordially. "It's so nice to meet you. Is this knight escorting you also?"

"Ah…I ah…"

"No bother. I can ride, for sure. At least I think I can…or I thought I could…" She looked away wistfully for a second. Finally, she turned to Bryan and he assisted her in the saddle. At first she perched a little wobbly, and then she settled in hesitantly. Grasping the reins loosely and clasping the pommel of the saddle like a child, she looked around to them, an excited look on her face. "Ready," she announced.

"Okay." Bryan sighed as he mounted. "Are we ready? Let's go. Move out!" He started forward. They began to depart the pixies' territory when they heard a call from behind.

"Wait! Wait, gentlemen and fine lady!"

They halted and turned around to see Hazerk quickly stuffing something into his saddlebags. "I'm coming, too! I don't know my way out of this haunted woodland," he called. He hastily tried to mount as his warhorse began to move forward. He jerkily swung his leg up and over the saddle as his horse began to trot. He exerted much more power than needed; and they watched in stunned astonishment as he heaved himself up and clear over his huge chestnut mount. He landed in a heavy heap on the other side, looking flabbergasted. The sane people in the group stared at each other speechless. The unicorn snorted amusedly.

"Great," Bryan breathed through his clenched teeth. Alkin laughed. Eelyne finally let out the stifled laugh he'd been holding back; it came out as a snort. Warkan rolled his eyes.

For the next several hours of traveling, which led them well into dark, Sword Bryan, Prince Alkin, Apollos, Eelyne and Warkan had to endure Alexa's and Hazerk's total confounded state of minds.

The two ambled in the back of the company laughing loudly—both in untypical Alexa and Hazerk laughs—at anything and everything. They would constantly whisper and snicker behind the others' backs. Which they would cease immediately, both smirking sheepishly, if anyone turned around suspicious of being a target.

When they would tire of jokes, the two would belt out songs. Any songs they knew and even ones they had made up on the spot. They were usually about things they passed by or about the others, particularly Warkan, who was never happy when they targeted him. Their songs were never sensible, but no one could deny that listening to them sing nonsense helped pass the time.

Chapter 14

By the next morning Alexa and Hazerk had returned to their normal mind-sets, feeling only slightly light-headed. They didn't remember anything while they had been pixilated, except that they had felt extremely content the previous afternoon.

The company had rose at dawn and was preparing to set out for another long day of riding.

"You know." Bryan overheard Hazerk telling Apollos as they were gathering up the gear, "Pixies were *just not* what I had in mind when you gave us that warning of certain *risky* things siphoning over." The unicorn flicked his tail and tossed his head, letting out a chuckle.

The Master Sword was on a mission. He pressed the group as fast as he dared, only taking into consideration the horses' welfare. As they moved farther south over the next few days, he noticed a temperature change in the forest. It was warmer, considerably warm for early summer. The horses were sweating visibly, and the company had taken to rolling up their cloaks and stowing them away after sunrise.

As they traveled in silence, the forest's ancient trees became sparser, and tiny, well-kept homesteads popped up along the road. They passed small villages. And any villagers they happened upon were friendly and asked no questions, which contented Bryan.

There was a noticeable change in the vegetation also. The evergreens and massive deciduous trees were replaced with palm trees and citrus trees of various kinds. Beautiful hanging vines began to appear, along with ferns, cactuses, shrubbery, banana trees and even cocoa trees.

The company soon discovered Prince Alkin had a special interest in horticulture. He couldn't contain his thrill at seeing the land transform into a paradise. He gladly pointed out and named many plants and trees. He had a surplus of information about them, as well as the country they were traveling through.

"You know the indigenous people of Yoldor discovered how to make chocolate hundreds of years before now. We've just only persuaded them to give us trading rights for it," he stated as

126

he plucked an orchid and handed it to a smiling Alexa.

"I've never had chocolate," Alexa said as she fondly examined the flower.

"It's good," Eelyne inserted.

"Well, you can thank Prince Alkin for that," Sword Bryan stated. "He's the one who convinced Chief Bahjahn not to hoard it. Shelkite now has trading rights with every country in Eetharum for *every* good." The others made the correct sounds that implied they were impressed.

"Yes, if I may say so, I'm very happy with my dealings with the chief. We get on quite well. It's a huge benefit to Shelkite. All our fruits, pearls and chocolate come strictly from Yoldor. We also get first rights to other goods brought into Yilvana Port from other continents." Alkin grinned, apparently pleased with himself.

Soon, the woods came to an end. They entered into a pleasant rural area. They pressed on, their pace as sure and as quick as ever. The Master Sword kept them on the main road, which headed straight south and into Yilvana Port on the coast. In a lagoon not far from there was where the merpeople were rumored to have dwelled. At least that is what the ancient records had said. The current map they carried made no indication of it.

The company traveled this route for a few days, building camp inconspicuously off the road alongside other travelers. The Master Sword figured if they kept to themselves, but didn't seem shady, the citizens and guards of Yoldor would overlook them as mere travelers who had come to buy goods, and they would not be bothered. Apollos kept himself constantly invisible, knowing he would attract unwanted attention.

At sunset, several days after crossing the border, they crested a large hill. The sight rendered them all speechless. Even Bryan had to pause and appreciate the beauty of the vale below. On the horizon Yilvana Port rose before them, a massive bustling city even in the growing darkness. And beyond the grand labyrinth of buildings and homes and streets that weaved serpentine-like through them, was the Elendace Sea. To their far right was the setting sun. Its rays glistened a dazzling orange on the harbor waters, where countless ships sat docked and bobbing in the placid waves.

"What a beautiful city. I would love to have a warm bath right now and sleep in a bed," Alexa said wishfully.

"Well, you're just going to have to bypass that wish," Bryan said, without taking his eyes from the glowing city. "We head that direction." He pointed to the southeast toward a shore in the distance. "That's where the merpeople are, in a lagoon a couple days east of the city. We'll camp just outside the city, on the shore tonight."

"But—"

The Sword shook his head, his expression firm.

"You know, I was thinking that perhaps we should go through the city," Prince Alkin spoke up. "It wouldn't hurt to have a nice rest in an inn just for one night. Plus, it'll give us a chance to scope things out. Just to see or hear of any evidence of corruption among the people."

"You want to chance that, my prince?" Bryan asked. "Some of the higher ranking guards may recognize you. And what if the chief himself decides to take a jaunt through the city? You'll be hard pressed to explain why you are wandering around his city in disguise and unannounced. If he is corrupt, then it may turn out to be difficult to leave. I say leave the investigating to your trained spies and the talking to your emissaries. They may be here already."

"Oh, come on, Bry—Master Sword," Alexa pleaded, quickly correcting herself after the displeased look he shot her.

There was a moment of tense silence as Bryan considered. He looked around to the other three men, seeing hopeful looks in their eyes. "All right, fine," he resigned. The others' faces split into wide grins. "One night. And we have to be careful."

They started down the hill, riding along the winding road that led to the city's North Gate.

"Good. I'm dying for a hardy meal," Hazerk said happily to the agreeing Warkan and Eelyne.

It was past dark once they were safely past the guardians of the North Gate and on their way to an inn. They found one immediately. The Master Sword didn't feel it necessary to be picky. His first concern was to find a place with good stables and care for the horses.

With the animals attended to, they easily found enough rooms to accommodate them. The Prince paid the tab. In the tavern they ate a decent meal with their ears pricked for anything odd spoken by the patrons. Nothing out of the ordinary caught their attentions.

While dining, Alexa and Hazerk found it hard to contain their mirth over the natives' peculiar accents. In play Alexa, rudely, but discreetly mimicked the bizarre speech, getting it perfect. Her growing, meaningless impressions sent Hazerk into fits of wheezing, suppressed laughter, and caused Eelyne to have a huge grin plastered permanently across his features. The other occupants of the tavern seemed oblivious to their growing racket.

As the night wore on, and they consumed more drinks while joking and talking nonsense, Alexa became sillier. Thanks to growing up with eleven older brothers she was quick witted and blatant. One of her sarcastic jokes caused Prince Alkin to snort his drink out his nose, and she even elicited a glimmer of a smile from Sword Bryan. Surprisingly, Warkan also seemed to be enjoying himself. He didn't look aggravated once and he even refrained from rolling his eyes.

Back in their rooms, Alexa, after succumbing to the fact that she had to share an adjoining room with Sword Bryan, took a long, hot, oiled bath. She took care to scrub herself squeaky clean from head to toe with the supplied bar of lilac scented soap. The others did the like in their own rooms.

As she lay in the steaming waters, feeling quite relaxed and tranquil, she looked down to the pendant resting lightly on her chest from its gold chain. She lifted the chain and let the key-shaped charm dangle in front of her eyes. Staring at it glistening from the moisture, a distant thought occurred to her. Contemplatively, she took the chain off over her head. Holding it in her hand, she turned it over and examined it for really the first time. The chain was fine and normal. The pendant was small, not even as wide or long as her baby finger. The key was shaped like any normal skeleton key. Nothing was engraved on it, and as far as she could tell there was absolutely no authentic value to the piece of jewelry. She raised it to her mouth and bit into it hard.

"Ouch!" She yelped rubbing her tooth. Almost immediately she heard Sword Bryan's footsteps in the next room walk to the adjoining closed door.

"Okay in there?" he hollered through the door.

"Yeah, of course…just stubbed my toe," she called back still rubbing her sore mouth. The footsteps retreated. "Guess I shouldn't have bit so hard," she whispered to herself, staring perplexed down at the key. The spot where her teeth had made contact had chipped off. A black surface was showing through. "Humph," she pondered, "just a hunk of metal." She closed her wet hand around it tightly and held it up to her ear as if listening to it. Closing her eyes, she attempted to use her senses to see if the charm revealed anything to her. It started in her gut, a slight humming of magic and a feeling of vibrations. It moved through her viscera and spread to her limbs. She felt herself slip into a trance.

There was a loud knock on her door, causing her to startle back to consciousness. "Are you still lounging in that bath? Get to bed. We're not lollygagging in the morning. This isn't your holiday," Bryan demanded through the door.

"All right, all right." She dropped the chain and charm to the floor and took one more dunk under the water. She slipped her head all the way to the bottom of the tub, staying there until she could stand it no longer. Emerging, she sucked in deeply, exhaling long, savoring the air and the warmth of the water. She climbed out of the tub and dried herself with a towel heated from the fire. She stared warily down at the necklace. *It's giving off vibrations. Strange ones, not bad perhaps, but definitely unfamiliar.* She pressed her lips together in thought. She turned to dress for bed, leaving the pendant in a heap on the floor.

The next morning, Alexa sleepily stumbled out of her room into the hallway of the second floor of the inn. Rubbing her eyes, she looked up to see a clean-shaven Master Sword standing beside her, locking his door.

"Good Morning," he said in an abnormally cheerful voice.

"Morning?" she mumbled back, "It's still night." She glanced down to the end of the hall to a window that still showed the impenetrable blackness of night.

Bryan smiled, "It'll get light soon enough."

The door to Alexa's left opened and Hazerk stepped out, still buckling his sword around his waist. She noted his unshaved whiskers were still in full effect. She raised an inquisitive eyebrow.

"Oh, I know." Hazerk rubbed his hand over his rust-colored stubble, "I'm going to grow it out."

At that moment, the sound of boots scuffing across the floor filled the soft silence and Eelyne, Warkan and Alkin came around the curve in the hall from the other end of the building. They were also clean-shaven. Warkan was sporting a few cuts and looked murderous if anyone dared to mention it.

"All right. We're all here, let's head out. I want to be at the lagoon in under sufficient time," Bryan said in an authoritative tone.

They all shifted for the stairwell, and Alexa suddenly blurted, "Wait! I forgot something."

"What?" Bryan said wearily as she turned and disappeared back into her room.

Alexa stepped and paused in front of the tub she had bathed in the previous night and looked down to where the mysterious necklace still lay. She bent over and picked it up. Her fingers prickled slightly at its touch as if it were charged with some kind of energy. Her senses were now more in tuned with the pendant's curious vibrations since she had opened that door the night before. She momentarily considered whether or not she should wear it, at least until she had more time to examine it closer. Outside, she could hear Sword Bryan's muffled call for her to hurry. Making her decision, she clasped the chain in her hand and turned to leave. It was enchanted to protect her; of course it would give off some sort of vibration.

In the hall, the men waited a little impatiently. Finally, a few minutes later, Alexa appeared, tucking a necklace gently down the front of her shirt. "Ready." She smiled.

Bryan looked at her suspiciously, "You better not be

131

stealing anything, or I'll cut your hands off myself."

Alexa glared at him exasperated, "I don't steal."

Hazerk laughed, "What are you saying? Of course, you do."

Everyone stared at him shocked, Alexa more than anyone, her eyes rapidly changing to a blaze of defense. "What do you—"

Hazerk's grin broadened and he threw his arm around her shoulders, giving her a squeeze. "You stole my heart a while back, my love," he said as if he couldn't believe she didn't know. Alexa's face relaxed back into a smile. Bryan snorted dryly and turned for the stairs along with Warkan. The others grinned and slowly followed suit.

After gathering their gear and tacking the horses, the pink morning light started to pierce the inky sky. Yilvana Port was awakening around them. Booths of baubles, food, weapons, fabrics and anything else one could imagine were opening and the people were beginning to start their daily routines.

Sword Bryan led the small company toward the East Gate, straight down the main business strip. This, he soon discovered, was a bad idea. He kept losing Alexa along the way to each weaponry booth that was set up. Whenever he sent someone back to fetch her, they, too, became enticed. By the third time around Bryan stomped back to retrieve her himself, dragging poor Dragon behind.

Standing at the largest, thus far, of the weaponry booths, Alexa appeared transfixed by a strange, vile looking weapon she was examining in her hands. Zhan was curiously peering over her shoulder as if he was also interested in what the dealer was explaining.

As Bryan approached, Alexa glanced up, her eyes a brilliant sky blue. She held up the evil looking weapon for him to see. "Look at this! Isn't this amazing? It's from Alidon. It was used in their civil war three hundred years ago. Look what it does." She started to demonstrate, but before she could Bryan snatched it from her, eliciting an annoyed glare from the merchant. Holding it in his hands, Bryan's mind stopped briefly to wonder how it actually *did* work. Alexa noted his fleeting curious look and smiled. "Neat, huh? I'm going to get it." Yielding, he shrugged. Alexa pulled out her moneybag and plunked down the amount. The merchant grinned and thanked them in his heavy accent as they turned to leave. "Can you believe it?" Alexa said as they weaved their way back to the rest of the company. "It's a weapon made from across the ocean."

"Yes, I know where Alidon is. I've been there once. Come on." Bryan hastened.

"I wish I could someday see the different lands. Alidon sounds wonderful," she said, her heart almost bursting from longing.

Bryan turned to regard her, giving her a puzzled look at her enthusiastic display. It was as if she had not heard of Alidon before. It was part of a larger continent than Eetharum and Sushron together. Then, much to his surprise, she blushed. "What is it?" he asked.

"I know. I'm a bit sheltered. Living in the desert does have its disadvantages. My father does it to protect us." She lowered her eyes. Unsure about her sudden, rare self-consciousness, Bryan didn't answer. "I'm just a commoner. A lot of people think of me as only a dirty shepherdess. New places intrigue me, unlike those of…higher classes."

The Master Sword took pity. He had never thought of her as *below* him. He shook his head. "Different lands and cultures have always fascinated me, too. That's why I took to traveling when I was younger, sword fighting competitively and seeing new places. It was great…most of the time." His eyes darkened to deep cobalt, clouded by a dark memory.

He could feel her mysterious, enchanting eyes on him, making him feel strangely awkward. But he was unable to look at her straight on, being self-conscious of his own reassuring words. He chanced a glance from the corner of his eye as they walked. His pace quickened subconsciously. He caught a small smile from her. He could have even sworn it was slightly bound with shyness. Muscles in his body he hadn't known were tense relaxed. He let himself crack a small, crooked smile.

Coming up on the awaiting warriors and prince, he was

saved from any further uncomfortable conversation. *Thank the High Power.* He rolled his eyes upward. Re-grouping, he discovered that Hazerk had gone off to a booth and was in a flirtatious conversation with a native woman. She was dressed in flowing vibrant hues. Her brown skin showing a little more scandalously than the women of Shelkite usually preferred, but it was common here among the women to show a little more of their figures. She was indeed lovely. "Warrior Hazerk!" Sword Bryan grabbed his warrior's attention quickly. "If you remember, I believe you're already faint with love for Alexandra. Let's get a move on."

"Yes, Master Sword." He promptly stood at attention. As Bryan turned his back to take up Dragon's reins, Hazerk flashed the woman a boyish grin and shrugged. She smiled, her black eyes glittering. She turned away, flipping her long, glossy hair.

The company continued on to the gate, bypassing all the beautiful sites Alexa was yearning to see.

Chapter 15

Off the shores of the Elendace Sea the black cloaked man sat in a grove before the sandy beach. He sat on a rock thoughtfully smoking a pipe, watching the tide and Blize roaming nearby, munching on salty sea grasses.

For the few weeks that Kheane had attempted to live in Yilvana Port his presence hadn't gone unnoticed by the town's guards. Whenever he had decided to venture out of his small apartment he was under the close surveillance of at least three Yoldor guards. Although they thought they were completely concealed, Kheane always knew exactly where they were.

How had he thought he would be able to escape his past occupation undetected? His body and soul held shadows of ghosts that exposed too much to the world.

The guards had no idea who he really was, but judging by his clandestine appearance, they had targeted him as some kind of menace. So Kheane decided to leave Yilvana Port. He settled a few miles east of the city in a crude cabin he had built in a grove off the coast. Blize stayed nearby in her own shelter and never wandered far, unwilling to leave her companion.

Lowering his cumbersome hood was a rare pleasure Kheane got to enjoy. But here in the woods with just the animals and the sea for company he reveled in that pleasure more than he had in at least two hundred years.

He puffed out a cloud of smoke and side glanced at his weapon leaning on the door of his home; his ears alert for anything unusual. He heard birds twittering and Blize a few yards away by the stream pawing at the stones and noisily slurping up the cool, fresh water. But there was something else. He couldn't figure it out. The sound was just hanging there, undetectable to all but him. The years in his previous profession had tuned his senses better than any human; they were almost as keen as a wolf's.

Although he was supposedly retired, he couldn't help being leery. There were many searching for his blood. He peered through the trees. And finally, way off to his right, he saw a small company making their way across the beach from the west, the city. They were only specks in the distance, but Kheane eyed them carefully, his mind calculating subconsciously like it had done so many times.

He lowered his pipe and put it out. He then let out a low, musical birdcall to Blize. The mare raised her head from the stream and silently crept to him. As she came to stand by his side, she raised her head and pricked her ears as she too spotted the unexpected party. Kheane placed his hood back over his dark hair, hiding his maimed face. Only the glisten of his dark, coffee-colored eyes could be seen as they peered carefully out to the beach as the group came closer and closer.

After a while Kheane relaxed, noting they weren't trying to move stealthily. In fact, they were being rather loud. He moved closer to the edge of the woods, but not so close he would be seen. Blize followed. He watched. The party consisted of mostly men, men from a country other than Yoldor, and one woman from yet another country. She looked vaguely familiar.

There were five men, four of which Kheane could tell were warriors. The man at the head of the party rode skillfully and assertively, with one hand on the hilt of his sword. Kheane didn't have to see to know he had many other knives hidden on his person. The man that rode next had his face hidden by a hooded cloak. He was quiet and didn't present himself like the other warriors. Next came a stern looking man, and following him came a blazing redheaded warrior, who was laughing and joking with the two walking behind. The redhead led both their horses and the pack mule tied in a mini caravan.

The two walking were lagging behind. They were both younger, perhaps the same age. And one of the two was the only female. The tall skinny warrior and willowy young woman were practicing the sword as they traveled along. The girl would let out a whoop and holler and the young warrior would grin devilishly as he landed a play strike. The young woman moved with ease, but was a little choppy with the weapon she held in her hand.

Kheane smiled as he watched the girl try to land a blow on the young fellow, her long, braided raven hair swinging to and fro, her stance strong, but not guarded. The young warrior was going easy on her. He had some potential. Kheane let out a small breath.

They were of no harm to him; still something else pricked his conscious. He could see no more than what was before him, but he sensed another's presence. It only bothered him for a fraction of a second before he decided it was none of his business. They weren't out to find him. It would have to go uninvestigated. He needed to move on and leave his old ways of life behind. But what had become his natural nature was having trouble letting go. He hadn't been once known as the Cold Wolf for nothing.

Kheane rested a reassuring hand on Blize's shoulder, the signal to show there was nothing to fear. She turned and left to return to the sweeter grasses by the stream. Kheane began to turn and forget about the company as well, but when he threw one last glance at the man riding second, the one who didn't appear to be a warrior, he caught a glimpse of his face as he turned back from watching the young woman. Kheane stopped in his tracks. He turned and stared hard at the man's features; his dark eyes wide with shock. It couldn't be who he thought it was? What was he doing here? Kheane quickly and stealthily moved to a tree that was closer. He crouched and watched. The company was so close he could now hear their voices clearly. The man was talking to the leading warrior. It was the Prince of Shelkite. Kheane's brow furrowed and he thought hard and fast as was his usual way of thought. He looked back to his small home and to Blize. He had nothing here. He hadn't been able to escape his past and he hadn't found the person or the hope he had been looking for. He needed to investigate. Just a traveling company was one thing, but a company with the Prince of Shelkite was another.

He moved quickly back to his cabin and began packing his few possessions and food. Blize, noting his haste, stood by her tack and waited patiently as he saddled and bridled her. Grabbing his weapon, he mounted and began to ride through the woods unseen, following the company as they moved east.

*****

"He ain't pretty! His face is chiseled from stone! He hates ditties and is married to an old crone!" Hazerk sang at the top of his lungs about Warkan. He then fell into a boisterous laughing fit along with Alexa and Eelyne. "Ha, ha! This is too much fun."

137

Hazerk rode up alongside Warkan, who was looking rather annoyed. Hazerk gave him a friendly slap on the shoulder, "Just in fun, buddy." He grinned deviously.

"Humph!" Warkan grunted, and then turned in his saddle to glare at Eelyne. Eelyne looked sheepishly back. "I wish you'd never told them about their little sonnets they made up while they were pixilated."

"Oh, I'm glad he did. Thanks Eelyne!" Alexa replied devilishly.

"Me too," Hazerk enthusiastically agreed. Eelyne shrugged, unable to hide a smirk.

"Okay, guys!" Sword Bryan called back and halted the company. He couldn't contain the smile appearing across his features that the songs had triggered. "It's fun, but enough singing. We're getting close to the lagoon," he said in a business manner. He then pulled out the map from his overcoat's inner pocket and studied it. "It seems that as soon as we crest this last dune, we should be able to see the merpeople's lagoon. We'll make camp a half a mile off the shore. I don't want to impose on their space. Then Alexa, I and Prince Alkin will travel to the sea's edge tomorrow morning to see if we can make contact. It's getting too late to try anything tonight. Agreed?" he said. Alkin, who was leaning over and studying the map from atop Sapharan, nodded. The others murmured their agreement. Bryan was about to advance the company one more time for the day, when a voice came out of thin air right next to him, startling him.

"Sword Bryan? Prince Alkin? Could I have a private word with you?" Apollos inquired.

"Yes, of course."

They retreated a little ways from the once again bantering company. Standing on the sea's edge, their horses' hooves being wetted by the salty waters, Apollos voiced his concern. "I just wanted to inform you that we're being followed."

Bryan and Alkin stared shocked into the air they thought was Apollos.

"What do you mean? I've been doing my best on keeping an eye out for that," Bryan stated. He was unable to keep the alarm he felt out of his voice.

"You?" Apollos said, alarm now apparent in his voice. "I didn't even notice this person as quickly as I should have. And *I* have magical senses. Alexa obviously didn't notice either. He is good, whoever he is. I dared not to go too close to him, because strangely enough I think he somehow knows I'm here."

"How? You've been invisible the whole time," Bryan asked.

"Does he know magic?" Alkin inquired.

"No. I don't believe so. He's just a man, a very skilled one at keeping quiet and hidden. His horse must be trained as well."

Bryan looked up and around, careful to not look like he was searching, lest he be seen. Setting his jaw, he contemplated as he stared out over the rippling sea. The water's coloring changed from shades of jade to deep cobalt the farther it was from the shore. The waves were small and the tide was gentle. Bryan looked to the horizon in the west. The orange sun was beginning to sink into the land, sending its colorful rays of pink and lavender skyward. "Well," he broke his reverie, "if he's this good at being unseen, then he must be decent at killing, too." Alkin looked apprehensively at the Master Sword. Apollos did also, though they couldn't see his features. Bryan sighed.

"Let's not worry about him right now," Apollos finally stated. "I'll keep an eye on him. I must say that, so far, he's not giving off vibrations that tell me he wants to do us harm."

"Is he from Yoldor, Apollos?" Alkin asked.

"No. I don't think so."

The Prince seemed to relax a bit. "That doesn't tell us much, though. Let's just keep moving. If he wants to show himself, we'll permit him. If he won't, then by the end of our stay we'll have to confront him. We just have to make sure he doesn't go anywhere with any information. We don't have much now, but we could."

"Right." Apollos and Bryan both agreed.

"Let's go." Bryan maneuvered Dragon from the water's edge and back to the company. Alexa, Hazerk and Eelyne were now practicing their sword fighting two on one, while Warkan looked on.

"Okay, mount up. I want to make camp before dark," Bryan announced. "And, maybe we can get in another lesson, too."

After taking a quick glance at the silent lagoon, the company moved inland. It was dusk when they set up camp in a small alcove in the trees. With Warkan tending to the animals and Alkin and Hazerk tending to the freshly caught rabbit roasting over the fire, Bryan gave another lesson to Eelyne and Alexa.

To the sound of the crackling of the fire and swordplay, Alexa watched, sword in hand, as Eelyne took a bout with Bryan. The two men moved swiftly and easily, their attacks administered precisely and their guards never down. At watching them, Alexa felt somewhat useless. She could *maybe* someday be as good as Eelyne, with lots of practice. But, she realized, she could never, no matter how hard she tried, be as good as the Master Sword. If she was asked to explain how he sword fought, she wouldn't even be able to find the right words. His footwork was flawless, as was his strategy. He could most definitely keep his opponent on their toes, never knowing what move he would make next. He was too quick, too cunning, and he did it all gracefully. Alexa clenched her teeth in frustration. She felt defeated before she even started. She stared at the ground, where the scuffed footprints of the match were.

"Hello? Sand Queen? Your turn now." Bryan waved a hand in front of her to get her attention. He wasn't even out of breath. Eelyne was leaning on a nearby tree huffing slightly. She picked up her sword and Bryan gave her a pragmatic look. "If I'm not mistaken, I think this is the first time I've ever seen you look so beaten. Like you actually believe you *can't* do something," he said, snagging the attentions of everyone.

"So?" she shot back. "Maybe I can't do this."

The Master Sword sighed, "Yes, you can. I don't want that attitude while I teach you."

"Warkan's right. My sword tactics are nonexistent. I only know the bow and arrow and some dagger throwing," Alexa stated, looking at her sword with wide unguarded eyes, as if she were scared of it.

"Oh, just shut up and fight me, girl!" Exasperated, Bryan

raised his sword. Alexa reluctantly found her stance. "I'll teach you enough. Contrary to what I think sometimes, you're not dim-witted. You *will* learn. I just want you to be able to stay alive. You don't have to know how to take out a whole regiment single handedly. Stay tough! Don't fall out on me already."

Getting a determined look in her eye, Alexa went to strike at him. But before she thought she even thought about moving her sword, Sword Bryan had his blade at her throat. She clenched her jaw and glared at no one in particular.

"Look," Bryan lowered his sword. "You don't protect yourself. You're too worried about trying to figure out how to attack. There has to be an even balance between the two. You can't leave yourself unguarded. You've got to be quicker. At least quicker than your opponent. However, it goes both ways. You can't always be on the run from your enemy either. If you're going to attack, attack! And keep on attacking." Bryan paused for a minute and stared thoughtfully at Alexa. She now looked rather aggravated. "You need to be in better shape. I should start making you all run instead of ride."

"What? I ain't gonna run. It took me a long time to earn Red Man. I'm gonna ride him," Hazerk piped up, sounding a little vexed.

"Red Man? That's your mount's name? Red Man?" Warkan asked derisively. Hazerk shot him a glare.

"Be quiet," Bryan snapped. "You'll all do what I tell you."

"Oh, yeah," Alexa suddenly said accusingly. "I almost forgot. What was it you were discussing down on the beach earlier today? I thought it was a deal I could know and have final input on everything."

Bryan whipped around and gave Alexa his most menacing glower yet. Alkin even looked up from attending the fire with an indignant look in his eyes.

"We were planning on discussing this with you all later. Now is not the time," Bryan said harshly as if he were speaking to a child. He walked over to Alexa, his body quivering and towering over her. She held her stance, but suddenly for the first time, she felt small in his presence. "And for future reference, I'd suggest that you don't speak accusingly to us again," he said, his azure eyes spitting bright flames.

"And," Alkin stood and came closer to Alexa, reining in his irritation, "just so you know. Everything we ever have or ever will discuss has been and will always be for the best of this company. And, as I did promise, any major issues will be settled by all of us. And your say, Alexa, will be vital in everything. But, as Sword Bryan already explained, we can't discuss it here. Let me just say this, keep close to the camp and don't speak of our mission." He went back and sat down.

Everyone in the camp was tense, even the horses shifted uneasily. Alexa let out a huge, pent up breath. Her face relaxed and she looked Sword Bryan and Prince Alkin straight on and said, "I'm sorry. I have a temper like my father. It won't happen again. I promise."

There was a moment of silence.

"Good," Bryan stated shortly, and Alkin nodded his acceptance. "Now let's practice. I'll teach you strategy so it's like a second nature to you." Bryan took up his sword and Alexa followed suit. Everyone went about their business once again.

That night Bryan took the first watch. Apollos was away keeping an eye on the intruder in his own camp. The Sword felt primed, but not afraid or even uneasy. He knew the unicorn would spear the mystery man through before he could try anything.

As Bryan surveyed the camp expertly, he found himself catching eyes with someone, even though it was way past dark. It was Alexa. She was lying awake watching him. Bryan gave her a questioning and penetrating stare that asked 'what's wrong?' Holding his eyes for a second longer the girl shrugged and turned over to face the darkened woods. The Head-Master Sword brushed it off. Everyone slept safely and soundly for the remainder of the night.

The next morning, Alkin, Bryan and Alexa made the short trek to the lagoon. When they came to the water's edge Apollos met up with them, coming out of the woods from their right.

The lagoon was deep cobalt. The placid waves gently lapped up on the white sandy beach. The companions could tell just by looking that the lagoon was practically bottomless, probably filled with caverns and many underwater tunnels.

As the others surveyed the area, Alexa shut her eyes and breathed in the salty air. She listened to the world around her with her senses. She could feel the soft pulse of magic. It was very subtle. The earth around her was distressed because of magic's absence; the land was desperately hanging on to every last remnant. It yearned for it; so it clung to the pieces that were still there: the merpeople. It was like a widower smelling the leftover perfume of his dead wife. It subtly lingered, painfully reminding him that magic once dwelled here.

"They're still here," Alexa said quietly, almost reverently.

"Yes, I feel the vibration as well." Apollos stood facing the tranquil waters of the lagoon; the breeze lifted his iridescent mane.

"How do we call them?" Alkin whispered.

Apollos and Alexa looked at one another in thought. Bryan watched them curiously, patiently waiting to see what they would decide.

"Well, I could swim out to the center and dive down to see if I could find anything and then maybe I could beckon them to the surface," Alexa suggested feebly.

"Hmm, something tells me that won't work. Besides, I don't want you to drown, or worse, get eaten by something," Bryan stated.

"That would probably relieve you," she said dryly.

Bryan grunted a garbled response and shifted his thoughtful gaze back over the water.

"Well…." The unicorn began to pace up and down the beach at the water's edge. He lowered his muzzle and sniffed the seawater as the others looked on, lost on what to do.

"Even if we alert them to our presence, which we might have already, we'll probably have a hard time to get them to come out and speak with us. They won't want to be bothered," Alkin said desolately. "You have no intuition clues, Alexa?"

The young woman shook her head regretfully and followed the unicorn down the beach, kicking a seashell as she went.

Bryan and Alkin watched silently as their two companions

143

slowly circled around to the other side of the lagoon. The morning sun was getting warmer and Bryan was starting to sweat. *Just great, we'll never figure out how to fish them out. Maybe some fish bait....* He amused himself inwardly.

When Alexa and Apollos reached the other side, Bryan allowed himself to admire the pretty picture they made while they contemplated.

The slender, raven-haired young woman looked almost like a fierce warrior as she gazed out over the cobalt waters. Her stance was strong; a thoughtful scowl set across her features, bow and quiver slung over her back. And then there was the unicorn, representing the opposite; the epitome of innocence, with his pure white, satiny coat and blazing iridescent mane and tail blowing in the wind. His horn shattered the light across the lagoon. The two figures standing between the vibrant jade forest and cobalt waters looked breathtaking. As the Sword gazed, a harsh voice crushed his picture.

"I'm going in!" Alexa shouted across to them.

"We don't know what's in there!" Alkin shouted back.

"I don't feel anything evil," she said and then started running back around the lagoon's edge toward them. She reached them a little breathless with Apollos cantering at her heels.

"Then, I'm going in with you," Bryan stated.

"No, I don't want to anger them."

"Can you swim?"

"Of course."

"How long can you hold your breath?"

"Ah…"

"See? It's not a good idea. What if something drug you under? I won't let you," Bryan said firmly.

"Wait! I have an idea," Apollos said, a light in his eyes. They turned to him. "I don't know why I didn't think of this right away."

"What?" they said eagerly.

"I'll just lower my horn in the water and give off magical vibrations. That's got to make them curious, and they'll have to come investigate."

"That sounds like the best yet," Bryan said, and then mumbled, "I feel like an idiot that we can't figure out how to communicate. I even studied earth cultures and relations as one of my specialized classes."

Alkin and Apollos looked at the Master Sword remorsefully.

"It wasn't concerning magical beings, though. This is entirely different. Don't worry. I'll handle it," Alexa stated. "Okay, Apollos, let's try it."

The unicorn lowered his horn into the lapping waters. They all felt a slight tremor in the air as he displayed his magic. His horn lit green and he sent forth silent vibrations that would reach into the bottomless lagoon.

The four of them stared hard at the center of the lagoon, the unicorn watching eagerly as he continued to send forth the call.

They stood there for agonizing minutes. They were beginning to lose hope when Alkin looked up and out to open sea, rubbing his neck and sighing. His quick intake of breath caused them all to jerk their heads up. "Look!" he said in a hushed, excited whisper.

Past the lagoon, way out to sea was a rock. Although most likely the whole of the rock was under water, extending down to the depths, the tip stuck above the waves. On top of that smoothened tip, sat a figure.

Even from a distance, they could see the figure was foreboding. The figure's upper body was broad and well-muscled. The lower half was a great glittering fish tail wrapped around the rock. His face was young, and his features were set sternly as he looked on them inquiringly. He had a mane of blonde hair that fell to his shoulders. In his hands he held an enormous spear.

Feeling choked, the companions moved along the edge of the lagoon to pause at the rim of the Elendace Sea. Bryan was the first to find his voice. "Hello! We come to you in peace!" he called out to him.

"That's what your Relations studies taught you?" Alexa whispered jeeringly out of the corner of her mouth.

"What do you suggest?" he looked down at her, his features

tense.

She smiled, her eyes sparkling a bright sky blue. "I was just teasing. Relax; the hard part is over."

After being the subject of her bewitching smile, the Sword breathed more easily. They stared anxiously as the figure continued to gaze at them in silent austerity. "We only wish a word with you! If you permit!" Bryan persisted. "We apologize for intruding!"

The merman seemed to consider this, and then he raised his hand in acceptance and called out, "We will speak only to the girl! No weapons!" His voice was powerful. He beckoned to Alexa.

"He wants her to swim out," Alkin said a little shocked.

"Right," Bryan said through a set jaw, his eyes beginning to spark a flame of irritation.

"What's the matter?" Alexa was hurriedly taking off her dagger, bow and quiver.

Apollos answered her. "They're asking to speak with the one they think is the weakest and least likely to do harm out of the party."

"What?" Alexa said indignantly, pausing her undressing.

"Right," Bryan repeated tersely.

"I don't like him being armed and not her," Alkin said.

"That wouldn't matter, anyhow. He's asking her to *swim* out to him. What could she do if they decided to attack?" Bryan said.

"Speak to him," Apollos urged.

"We don't want to cause any harm! Will she be safe?" Bryan hollered out to him.

"No harm will come to her if she is honest!" the merman answered.

"I'll be fine. I'll take my dagger." Alexa stated, gazing eagerly out to sea.

The others looked at her. Bryan received a slap of shock upon seeing her half undressed. He almost reacted by respectfully turning around, but he quickly told himself to grow up.

Alexa stepped to the water's edge. Apollos came to stand beside her. "Be careful," he simply said. He gave her a reassuring nudge on the arm.

"Thank you, Apollos." She kissed his soft muzzle and grinned. The unicorn bobbed his head. She waded out to her knees. The cool, emerald water swirled around her legs and the soft sand squeezed up between her toes.

"Alexa!"

She turned to see Prince Alkin looking apprehensive and Sword Bryan looking as apprehensive as he would ever. He was giving the impression of having stepped on a thorn.

"We'll be here if you need us," Alkin said.

"I know."

"Tell us everything."

"I will." She then waded out past her waist and dove into the water and began to swim vigorously toward the fierce looking merman.

Chapter 16

Alexa swam determinedly toward the merman, her strong strokes slicing her way through the water. He looked on motionless, watching her austerely with his hard eyes and pursed lips. Alexa, feeling winded, kept her eyes on the bizarre figure and forced her heart to calm its anxious pounding. She swallowed a gulp of green salty water on accident; she choked it down.

The merman was sitting on the right side of the boulder. His magnificent fishtail wrapped around the rock toward the rear. As Alexa neared, she saw that the tail was larger than her whole body. It looked extremely powerful, as did the merman's upper body. He was much larger than Alexa had anticipated. His naked chest was broad and robust. His muscles were intense and flexed with his slightest movement.

Alexa swam toward the middle of the rock, far enough not to invade his space. No matter how she looked at it she was at his mercy. With the ocean surrounding her and who knew what creatures swimming beneath, she was trapped. She clambered up onto the rock, glancing to shore, her eyes showing the slightest need for support from her companions. She spotted their distant shapes: Alkin's slightly lanky physique, Bryan's tall and strong body, and the elegant equine silhouette of Apollos. This encouraged her, and she focused on her present task. She raised her head determinedly and locked eyes with the merman for the first time.

Alexa drew in a breath. Aside from Apollos, he was the most beautiful creature she had ever seen. His face was an otherworldly handsome. It had an ancient and strange beauty that looked as old as Time itself would look, but he was young in appearance. His skin was a soft, sandy brown. His tail, a brilliant blue-green, glistened with droplets of water. He had strong well-set features with a mane of sandy blonde hair that fell down to his shoulders. His eyes were captivating. They, too, were an extravagant color, changing from blue to green, looking as deep and watery as the ocean he lived in. He gazed at her, holding a cold looking spear upright.

Alexa couldn't speak, and he was waiting. She sat there

dripping wet on the warm rock as the sun's rays danced on the glassy water. A slight breeze wafted by and chilled her; it brought her mind to life. "Hello, sir. I'm Alexandra." She bowed her head, attempting to be formal. "It's gracious of you to speak with me." The merman acknowledged her with a slight nod, and continued to stare penetratingly at her. "It's very important that I talk with your people. Please, if you consent." Alexa tried her best to act courteous, but she felt out of rhythm. She was half dressed, wet, and having trouble using her own powers on this wholly magical creature.

"People? There's not many left of my kind, Alexandra," the merman finally spoke, his voice curt and strong. He cocked his head and scrutinized her. "I allow you to speak with me solely because you have a unicorn in your company. My people are and always have been friends with unicorns. Any other creatures, aside from naiads, we don't wish to associate with. We wish to be left alone. What is it you have to say? Why have you brought me out of the sheltered depths? We're a dying race, and I don't desire to speak with a human or half human, as it is, for any length time."

Alexa closed her eyes and took in a breath to relax herself. She began to speak, but the merman broke in first.

"There's no need to worry. I will listen to your words. Whatever you have to say must be important for you to risk your life to say it. You're a half witch are you not?" he asked. Alexa nodded her head. "Go on," he said.

Alexa felt her courage return. She was part of his world, too, even if it was just partially. She smiled, subconsciously hoping to impress the handsome creature. Then she burst into a succinct explanation of Eetharum's predicament. The merman, to her surprise, turned out to be an immersed and concerned listener.

When she had finished, he leaned back, laying the spear over his lap. He heaved a sigh and said, "In the past this could've been a problem for the merpeople. If there were more than just three of us I would say this would be a problem worth our power and time to help those above waters. But, as it is, I cannot see how the wizard would even be concerned with us, or how he could even use us. We are practically extinct. We're best left in hiding, not provoking his attention. There isn't much three of us could do. I'm sorry for your trouble, but the merpeople are powerless and best left alone."

Alexa looked cress fallen, and the merman gazed at her with sad eyes. "That's what you have to say? Eetharum will become under the tyranny of a cruel man—even worse, a wizard. He's recruiting horrid creatures and wicked men as we speak. He's already killed and tortured, and will do more. We need all the *good* magical power on our side we can get to stop him. Don't you hear me? We can stop him before he reaches further! You won't even give me advice? My father told me you are a wise people and have powers that most magical creatures on land don't possess. I was summoned to help by a power higher than me, and then sent to you. Don't tell me I've already failed? Or am I following an evil power? Is that all that's left?" Alexa was desperate, and it showed fervently on her features.

The merman smiled for the first time, albeit it was intertwined with sadness. Right then, despite her indignation, Alexa would have dove into the water and gladly lived with him forever. She struggled for control of herself. Some ancient magic was at work.

"My child," he said with care.

"I'm not a child. I'm a woman, a sorceress," she stated curtly.

The merman smiled again, "You say that only because my presence has a draw on your human blood. Focus on your magic and listen to me and listen well," he commanded, but not unkindly.

Alexa shut her eyes and felt around for the magic pieces inside of her. She found them and gathered them up. And then, to her great relief, she felt in control again. Her deceptive longing for him dissipated.

It was from an old curse. The merpeople couldn't control it. If a human looked a merperson in the eyes it caused them to yearn greatly for them. It was what had eventually destroyed the merpeople as a race, humans desiring them, taking them and ultimately killing them. The sort of craving was different for each human; greed, admiration, the want for blood. For Alexa's half human heart it was lust.

"The naiad who gave your name is not omniscient. She is only a messenger from the High Power, which is far from evil. Aside from my people there are still many good powers left. They are in hiding and must be sought. You are expected to help if it truly was the naiad who gave your name. Even though you had a choice not to accept, it is honorable you did. The High Power does not expect you to do this alone. The help you seek will be sent."

"Right! That's why I came to you," Alexa broke in exasperatedly.

"Listen! You say your witch intuition sent you to us. I don't know of this intuition. But the merpeople can do nothing. If the wizard knows we still exist, we may be in some danger. But there is too few of us. He knows we wouldn't be able to do any harm; and any power we have would be of no value to him. He would leave us alone. Please don't cause the premature death of the last of my kind."

"You just keep repeating that you want to be left alone so that no harm will come to you. How selfish. All I ask is for advice at the least. You're right, I am *only* a girl. But how am *I* supposed to know what to do to defeat an intelligent wizard? I can't ask my father to do it. He's bound by an oath to never do magic. My brothers don't know magic. The others I travel with are more than willing to help, but they don't know any more than I. So, that leaves me and this counter magic to save Eetharum. It leaves *me,* because I'm the *only* sorceress left, the last witch. That's why the naiad spoke my name. It's because magic is needed. But *you* being a magical creature won't help. Even when on that shore stand men with no magic of their own to save them, nothing but their own intellect and brute strength to use, and probably the last unicorn in the world, who are all willing to give their lives because it's *needed.* This world will keep going on when you and I die. But I won't hand it over to be consumed by evil if there is something I can do now that will secure the futures of innocent others. I want to help. And you *know* you must help in some way, even if it's just one thing. My intuition says so. And, let me tell you this. If there is something you have that Ret wants, he'll come and get it and kill

151

you anyway, even if I hadn't brought his attention to you. Now you can be at least warned and prepared. But please tell me there's something you can do." Alexa had spoken forcefully in her desperation. Oh, how she wished she had been right in believing the merpeople would lead her to the counter magic. What a waste! What would the others think?

The merman gazed at Alexa sorrowfully and thoughtfully. He didn't rebuke her for speaking to him in such a way, which in old times would have been considered extremely disrespectful on her part. She waited anxiously for him to speak as she searched his features hopefully. She now fully understood what her father had meant by the merpeople being reclusive and not liking to be bothered.

"Alexandra," the merman said.

"Yes."

"You must come back tomorrow at the same hour. I'll take you to see my father. He's much wiser and knows more of these things. We may be able to help, but I cannot promise anything."

Alexa's face cracked a smile so fast her cheeks hurt. She had to restrain herself from jumping over and hugging him. "Thank you so much! We're sincerely grateful. I'll come back."

The merman smiled warmly, his brilliant eyes rippling happily like waves. "You're welcome. And please bring the unicorn in the morning, too."

"Yes," she breathed. She began to slide off the rock, but the merman caught her hand and Alexa looked surprisingly back.

"I will guide you to shore. There is a bad spot I don't wish you to swim across alone."

"Oh…" she said a little shocked and curious. But she decided not to question what he meant by 'bad spot' nor why he had not offered to guide her in over it.

"Come." He released her hand and they dove in. She began to swim, the merman close at hand. His fishtail churned the water powerfully. Alexa guessed he was probably not moving as fast as he was capable. She couldn't help but steal a few glances his way. It was amazing to see him swim. When they reached shallow water, he left her with a good bye smile. Then he was gone from her sight instantly.

Bryan, Alkin and Apollos were waiting a ways up the shore watching, looking as if their eyes would pop out of their heads. As she waded out of the shallow waters, they came to her, their faces expressing anxious anticipation.

Apollos reached her first. He stepped in front of her blocking the breeze, letting the warmth of his body warm Alexa's chilled one. His chocolate eyes twinkled as he looked at her. Alexa smiled, resting a hand on his smooth neck. "How did it go?" he asked.

"Well, I think." She shivered from the breeze. The day was warm, but she felt chilled from nervousness. Bryan and Alkin reached them and waited before them, squinting in the sun, their hair tousled by the wind.

Alkin removed his lightweight overcoat and stepped around the unicorn to place it on her shoulders. "Here. Keep this until you dry," he said. "So, what did he say?" he asked.

"Well…" Alexa started, watching their expressions carefully. "We have to come back tomorrow." The others waited for her to go on, their faces wondering. "He would only speak to me because Apollos was with us. He said at first that they were powerless and would rather be left alone."

"Humph," Bryan grunted, but let her continue.

"He says that his father might be able to help, but he couldn't promise anything. It took convincing on my part to get him to just say that." She paused, and then added, "He wants Apollos to come tomorrow, too."

"We noticed it looked like you were having a hard time," Alkin said.

"Why?" she asked puzzled.

Bryan answered, "We heard your raised voice, and noted the desperate hand gestures." He grinned.

Alexa laughed incredulously. "I was yelling at him?"

"You did just fine." Alkin smiled.

"You got us a second meeting," Bryan added.

"And whatever you said pressed him out of his unwise choice of ignoring the problem," Apollos praised.

Alexa sighed and looked back to the rock where she had sat with the merman. "I just hope there is something they can do. There are only three of them left, you know."

"We'll see what tomorrow brings," Bryan said. He then motioned for them to head back to camp. "Let's see if our new mysterious neighbor has shown up on our doorstep with a pie."

He and the Prince had told the others about their follower earlier that morning, knowing Apollos was guarding the man a distance away.

They began to trek back inland to the camp. Reaching the woods, Apollos flicked his tail and gave a small supportive nuzzle in Alexa's hand before he split off to continue his surveillance of the mystery man. The three companions entered into the shade of the trees with Alkin leading the way a few paces ahead. Alexa fell into step with Bryan.

"Listen," she half whispered, slightly nervous about what she wanted to say. It was outside of her usual nature, and she felt strange.

Bryan looked down at her, waiting for her to continue. He was curious as to what she wanted to say. The girl fidgeted, shifting her bundle of dry clothes to under her other arm and pulled Alkin's overcoat tighter around herself. He had to force his eyes to veer in another direction from where they were mindlessly wandering—down the neck of the overcoat.

Alexa waited for the Sword to say something that might show his exasperation with her. But he just stared at her, his bright azure eyes wide and curious. "Ah, about last night," she said.

His brow furrowed. And he gazed at her with his undivided attention. "What about it?" he asked in his normal tones. "Why are you whispering?"

Alexa snorted and continued in a hushed voice, "I just wanted to apologize."

"For what?"

"For losing my temper."

"You already did. Forget about it." He brushed it off and began walking faster.

"Wait…ouch!"

"What is it?" His voice now sounded slightly exasperated. He stopped and looked back at her to see her picking a small thorn out of her foot. "For the love of—here!" He stalked back and dropped her boots, which he had been carrying, at her feet. "You're dry now, hurry and get dressed. Hey! Hold up, Alkin," Bryan hollered up to the Prince, forgetting to address his old friend properly. Alkin stopped and peered back at them. Realizing the situation, he nodded his head. He came to take his overcoat back and wait for her to dress, so they wouldn't become separated.

When they were on their way again, Alexa attempted to smooth down her escaped hairs from her braid, and caught up with the Master Sword, who was now leading.

He didn't look at her, but merely said, "Yes?"

"I just wanted to say I'm sorry I broke our pact. And I promise on my life that I won't act that way again. I want to be as helpful as I can from here on out. I've acted wrongly toward you." She had no idea why she was pressing this issue, nor why she felt nervous. For some unknown reason it seemed crucial to make *him* understand she was sorry, and to have *his* sanction.

"All right." He smiled down at her; although to Alexa his smile looked a little dubious and mischievous. "Is that *all* you were up pondering about last night when you were watching me on my guard?" he added, with a boyish twinkle in his eye.

Alexa narrowed her eyes. "Yes. That's all, Master Sword, you can let the Prince know," she replied curtly, and then stomped up ahead, feeling embarrassed.

Behind her she heard Alkin say to Bryan, "What's wrong with her?"

On returning to camp, they explained the situation to the others. The warriors also reported there had been no sign of their anonymous shadow. Then Alexa and Eelyne had a quick combat lesson. After, they all ate a tasty meal, consisting of more fresh rabbit—a complement of Warkan's hunting. They turned in early for the night, each wishing that both morning and answers would come sooner.

Chapter 17

The next morning they dined on fresh fruit from nearby trees. The fruit was so scrumptious Sword Bryan had the warriors gather up more for later while he, Apollos, the Prince and Alexa trekked back to the sea.

They reached the shore a little earlier than they had the day before. They waited, Alexa anxiously looking out to sea. A breeze blew across the turquoise waters. It carried a wet-sand fragrance with a potent salty smell of marine life.

Bryan broke the silence, "I think someone needs to accompany her out today."

"I agree," Alkin replied. His brow furrowed as he gazed at the waves rising and falling more enthusiastically today.

"I'll go. Since he did say to bring me along," Apollos said. He came to stand gallantly beside Alexa.

"Yes. He seemed more at ease seeing you with us," Alexa said, shading her eyes from the sun as she regarded the unicorn.

"Let's go. Take a hold of my mane," Apollos instructed.

Without glancing at the Prince or Sword, Alexa gently entwined her fingers in the silky, iridescent tendrils of the unicorn's mane. He waded into the whooshing, jade-colored shallows. Alexa followed closely, feeling strength and power emanate from the unicorn. It vaguely crossed her mind that she was allowing her companions to know she could touch the unicorn without retribution.

Soon they were up over their heads. Alexa was being pulled through the water by the unicorn. She felt his legs vigorously churning water beneath her. She was careful not to interfere with his slashing hooves. "Something lurks," Apollos whispered. Alexa glanced down into the depths. Her heart skipped a half a beat upon seeing a blurry, but large shadow moving below. She raised her eyes deciding not to dwell on it.

"I can't sense it...you can?" she asked, perplexed.

"Yes. My powers can sense a bit beyond the stifling water. Water masks your senses, not completely, but enough. Beware of that in the future," the unicorn advised.

Alexa nodded her understanding. She had never realized

this. She wondered if she could even sense anything at all in the water, since she was only a half-blood. She bit her lips in thought, tasting the bitterness of the sea.

Apollos guided her safely to the rock. He helped her climb onto it by hoisting her up with his nose. Then he gracefully leapt onto it and shook himself, sending sparkling water droplets flying.

Alexa looked down at her attire. She was once again in her undergarments. She had removed her pendent as she had the day before, but as always her hair was still corralled in its snug braid. Her mother would be horrified if she knew she was strutting around barely clothed in front of two men. She glanced at the shore to see Alkin and Bryan standing there, shading their eyes, staring out to her and Apollos. There wasn't a doubt in her mind they took the situation serious. *Besides, they've probably seen a woman's body before now;* she had to be realistic. She knew she wasn't anything extraordinary to look at—as far as her figure anyhow. She didn't think her face completely ugly. But she was skinny and had a humble chest. Her older brothers' constant teasing of her looks had always kept her vanity well reined in.

"Here he comes." Apollos interrupted her thoughts. At that moment the merman from the previous day leapt onto the rock.

"Alexandra," he greeted her, "and noble unicorn." He inclined his head in greeting to Apollos. Apollos lowered his finely shaped head in acknowledgement.

"My name is Apollos. What do you call yourself, honorable merman?" he politely inquired.

"You can call me Nereus. It's a version of my name," he answered.

"That's fine," Apollos consented. Alexa nodded in accord, her eyes unmoving from the merman's captivating features.

"Come, let's not waste time. I'll take you to my father, Glyndwr." Nereus then turned to dive into the azure waves.

"Wait!" Alexa called, puzzled. "How can we follow? Are you swimming deep?"

Nereus looked back at her and Apollos, and smiled apologetically. "Excuse me. I'd momentarily forgotten you can't breathe under water."

"I can, Nereus, but Alexa can't," Apollos spoke up. Alexa glanced at the unicorn quizzically. "My horn empowers me to do so," he replied to her silent question.

"Oh," Alexa breathed out, her eyebrows rising. At his comment something in her mind seemed to open, and she wondered about Apollos' powers and how extensive and potent they were…

"Here, come stand beside me." Nereus held out his hand for Alexa. She came to the exquisite man's side at the rock's edge—if she could even call him a man—and tentatively took his hand.

Nereus, looking significantly at Alexa, raised the massive spear in his hands for her to see. "This spear isn't only used for hunting; it contains its own magic. Hold on to it tight and don't let go. It will allow you to breath and speak in my world."

Eyes sparkling with a touch of adventure and apprehension, Alexa regarded the spear with awe. It looked cold to touch. But when she wrapped her fingers around it, it felt warm, and Alexa could feel the magic flow into her. She took in a breath and suddenly felt like she had awakened from a deep sleep. She looked up and reveled in the bright indigo sky. The world was spinning haphazardly about her. She was drunk with the pulsing, foreign magic. Then, suddenly, something felt as if it had pierced her windpipe and she couldn't breathe. Her hand went to her throat, and panic fled into her eyes. She gasped for air, and found she couldn't speak.

"Come." Nereus quickly took her other hand and jerked her into the crashing waves.

On the shore, Prince Alkin and Sword Bryan viewed the meeting with bated breath. They watched stiffly as the merman quickly disappeared into the sea, jerking an unnerved Alexa with him. Bryan's tense features became hard; and he let out a tetchy mumble.

"Apollos will protect her," Alkin whispered earnestly.

"Yeah…but that's my responsibility," he retorted.

Anxious and holding her breath out of habit, Alexa glanced over her shoulder as she was towed down into the cool waters. She saw Apollos leap into the water after them, diving down to swim beside her. She relaxed. Though she was mostly confident, she was hesitant in going to the unknown depths of the sea alone. Discovering the spear was lighter when in water, she held it closer to her body. Closing her eyes for courage, she took a deep breath of…Water? It silkily gushed into her mouth and nose. She could breath. She opened her eyes and looked around. She could see clearly. Her full confidence flooded back.

They swam out and down, the merman dragging her swiftly along. Alexa, wide eyed, gazed at the sights around her. Having thought it was going to be dark and dreary below the sea like the deep river near her home, she was thrilled to be assaulted by vibrant colors. There was an array of brightly colored fish, and a brilliant reef filled with all kinds of plant life and creatures. The sandy bottom was white, the coral a milky cream color. It was a whole new realm. And Alexa intended to ingrain the images in her mind for forever. It was magnificent.

They swam over the reef and down into a wide crevice, going deeper into the sea. It wasn't dark or scary. They took a few turns swimming through tunnels consisting of bluish rocks smoothened by years of water brushing them sleek. They swam by more un-frightened fish. Alexa noted plants and sea urchins that were arranged decoratively around cave entrances carved into rock façades that looked suspiciously like doorways. They were swimming along an underwater street.

On they swam. The street occasionally opened into beautiful expansive areas that could be nothing other than an underwater park or valley. Alexa couldn't stop her eyes from drinking in all the wonder. There were whales, dolphins, seahorses, and brightly colored sea flowers everywhere.

Finally the merman slowed his pace, and they turned into a short pathway that led into an underwater town or what used to be. Homes of all kinds of designs lined the street along with shops and diners, all carved from rock. They were all vacant and lonesome. A purplish light from some kind of stone brightened their path, shinning from lamp posts along the way. Alexa imagined a million merpeople thronging in the streets, going about their business, much the same as those above the waters did.

Nereus took her to a beautifully carved rock that looked much like a palace above waters would, except it was smaller. The doorway was embellished with a purple blazing stone and plants on either side that swayed gently back and forth with the current. A menacing looking fish guarded the threshold.

"Move aside, Sunshine," Nereus addressed the yellow fish that was roughly the size of a dog. It immediately stopped baring its crooked, sharp teeth that were jutting out from its under bite, and put a congenial, almost fond look on its face as Nereus stroked him gently down his back. It gave a warning look at Alexa and Apollos, and then swam off at a zippy pace.

Still holding Alexa's hand, Nereus guided her through the door, beckoning to Apollos. He paused just past the doorway in what was a large, domed receiving hall, letting her hand go.

Alexa looked around. They were swimming above a beautifully polished floor. The room was fashionably decorated with flowers and various aquatic, homey objects hung on the walls. A smooth pathway—a ramp—sloped up out of the circular room to a balcony above and the second floor. A railing, carved up from the floor, ran up the side of it. Three doorways led out of the room in various directions.

"Wait here. My sister will attend you. My father is out back in the garden. I'll let him know you've arrived," Nereus said with a hospitable smile. He swam out of the doorway opposite them.

After surveying the unusual room, Alexa looked over to Apollos bobbing in the water next to her. He was investigating a large pink and white flower in a pearl vase sitting just inside the entryway on a round table carved from out of the stone floor. His muzzle was nestled in the blossom as if he were smelling it. Alexa smiled at the beautiful unicorn, so strangely out of place in this water land.

She decided she would try out her voice to see how it worked under the spear's magic. "Can you understand him clearly like I can, Apollos?" Her voice sounded odd to her, garbled, and bubbles sprang haphazardly out of her mouth. But Apollos seemed to understand her completely well.

He turned from the flower, his mane and tail floating in

billows around him, and said, "Yeah." His voice sounded the same as it did above water.

A few moments later a slender and beautiful mermaid swam into the room, greeting them with a pearly smile, "Hello, friends. Welcome."

"Thank you," they said in unison, Alexa's mouth sprouting bubbles.

"You can call me Vailea," she said. She had the same sandy blonde locks as Nereus, but they were much longer, falling down past her back. They flowed elegantly about her pretty angular face, rising, falling and waving with her every move. Her almond shaped eyes were a vibrant violet and sparkled with life and gentleness. She had long slender arms, fingers and torso. Her chest was uncovered, though obscured by her long locks. And, unlike her brother's sandy brown skin, her skin was a soft alabaster. Her cheeks were rosy, her lips full and red. Her fins were a different color than Nereus'. Instead of fading in and out from blue to green, her fins glistened violet and scarlet.

Apollos swam to meet her, lowering his head in respect, "I'm Apollos of Shelkite, and this is Alexandra of Kaltraz." He gestured with his horn to Alexa floating nearby, still gripping the spear tightly. "I presume you already know our business?" he asked.

The mermaid smiled and nodded, "Yes, my brother filled us in yesterday. And I'm happy to say we might be able to help."

Alexa and Apollos shared a quick relieved glance. Alexa's heart lightened a great deal. Her magical intuition had been right after all! She had been worried she had led the company wrong already.

"Come, I'll take you to my father and brother. They're waiting in the garden. There isn't time to waste if the shores are in as much need as you say." She raised her arm and gestured toward the door opposite them. "Follow me." She swam through. Alexa and Apollos hastened to follow.

Vailea guided them through a wonderful collection of underwater trees, plants and flowers, all growing tall and swaying gently in the current. If Alexa and Apollos were not careful they could have easily got lost in the vast forest. The mermaid led them through a path that wound its way deeper into the garden's heart. The underwater trees were as tall as trees on land; Alexa paused momentarily to touch the bark. It was smooth.

Seeing Apollos' tail flip around a sharp bend to the right, Alexa quickly swam as fast as her legs could paddle to catch up. She looked around, still completely awed at this new world. Fish of all kinds brushed up against her skin as if they were as curious of her as she was of them. She swam over a bed of sea clovers, and a herd of seahorses scattered out, swimming up the trail. She followed in the small herd's wake.

They came into a clearing where Alexa found the others gathered around a beautiful collection of pearls. Thousands of pearls varying in sizes from tiny to gigantic were lying all around them. Their white beauty shed a strange light into the alcove.

"Alexandra, Apollos, this is my father, Glyndwr," Nereus introduced an older merman.

The unicorn and girl acknowledged the old merman by bowing their heads. When she raised her face, Alexa carefully studied him. He appeared younger than he was, but he was by no accounts young. He had a shock of long stringy white hair and a beard just as white and long. He had gentle gray eyes and wrinkled skin. His fins were a subdued blue.

He held out his hands in a welcoming gesture, and said to Apollos, "Many years have gone by since we have last seen your kind. We had feared the upper world had lost one of its most beautiful assets—the unicorns."

"No, not completely; albeit I'm probably the last," Apollos replied sadly.

The old merman's face looked troubled. "The shores will be more than a little darker when the magic of the last unicorn passes."

"I could say the same of the merpeople," Apollos said a little accusingly.

Alexa was puzzled at Apollos' tone, but she said nothing. Did Apollos think they could preserve their race whereas he couldn't his own?

Glyndwr smiled knowingly, but turned to Alexa to speak, "My son says there is a war coming to your lands. You have asked for our help because it's not just a war between men, but of magic."

"Yes," she said, her eyes pleading.

"As you know we can't do much, being only three of us, but we have a way to give you information. This will give you knowledge, and knowledge is a weighty key. If one knows of his enemies plans, then he can learn how he can destroy them."

The old merman looked into Alexa's eyes, seeming to try and detect her reaction. She held her gaze fast, feeling a hot remark bubbling to the surface. Didn't they understand her? "Yes, but we have our own spies who have told us of his doings. We know he plans to crown himself emperor over all the countries of Eetharum. He plans to enslave the land and force the people to swear piety to the Demon. He's gathered an army of beings and humans. We know this *already*. What we need is good magic to counter his."

The three merpeople stared at her. Alexa couldn't read their expressions. She glanced at Apollos. He turned away from her, although he didn't look angry, but rather amused by her sudden outburst. Feeling remorseful inside, Alexa heaved a sigh or what would have been one above waters.

"I see you have inherited the hot blood of your wizard father," Glyndwr said, but he smiled widely and forgivingly. "You are a very determined girl. Stubborn and brave, perhaps a little bit reckless. I also sense a bit of vanity. No wonder you've been chosen by the High Power for this job. You'll need to learn to control that temper and pride of yours better, as well as learn to trust."

Glyndwr studied her carefully. Alexa felt like he could see into the very depths of her heart. *Brave? The other words seem to describe me well enough, even reckless, or so Sword Bryan would say. But, not brave.* She felt humbled as well as chagrined by the merman's brutal scrutiny. "The High Power?" she questioned. It still perplexed her how she was chosen for this extreme task.

"Yes. You do believe in the High Power, don't you? The Master of the Sea? The two are the same. Us sea creatures just

163

refer to the High Power as the Master of the Sea," Glyndwr said.

"Well, yes, of course. But I've never really thought about how it pertains to this," she answered, then added quickly, "Other than the naiad's calling."

"If Apollos gained your name from the naiad, then it was the High Power who sent for you. The Master of the Sea has his own reasons for naming you in particular. Only you may someday know the answer to that. The purpose may not be what you think it is now. But you would do well to acknowledge the call and this chance you've been given to be an instrument. You always have a choice, of course. But it is easier to ride the tide, than swim against it. However, I see you've already made the choice of acceptance. That's good. Since you've been given this puzzle to solve, I'll help in ways I can, for my people are faithful to the Master of the Sea," Glyndwr explained, looking at her in a significant way. "But you must understand what I mean by knowledge. You have come to the merpeople looking for some kind of magical weapon we can hand over so that you can fight this wizard. We don't have magic like that. And the war has not yet reached the waters where we live, so we can literally do nothing physically. But, I can give you a vision."

"A vision?" she repeated quizzically, imploring he continue.

"Yes, through this." He gestured toward a shell lying open on a bed of flowers in the center of the garden. Pearls were arranged decoratively around it. They swam to make a circle around it. The inside of the shell was glimmering milky colors of blue, silver and green—mother of pearl.

Alexa looked at it curiously. Apollos did the same. He had kept a respectful silence, but now he stated, "This is much like the Guidance Naiad is above waters isn't it? One beseeches her presence and asks her a question. Then, if she thinks you're worthy, she gives you answers. Although they're usually a bit elusive, they're trustworthy."

"Yes, Apollos, it's much like that. This shell is the only one like it in all the sea, just like there is only one Guidance Naiad. They're both blessed by the Master of the Sea—vessels. But, this is a little more complicated. It gives you visions of your answers. And sometimes they're much harder to decipher than the mystifying words the naiad gives you. The Mother of Pearl will sometimes show what *could* happen in the future, based on a given person's current path. And I emphasize *could*, Alexa." He turned to her and gave her a hard look, "For the future can change its path as easily as an air bubble. Don't make the mistake in believing what you will see is final. Because I'm positive what the Mother of Pearl will show you is not going to be all sunbeams."

Alexa made a move to touch the seashell, but Glyndwr stopped her, "You must also know that you have only one chance to ask it the right question. Choose your words carefully, because if you do not, you may not get the answer you need. You're allowed only one question ever." Alexa nodded solemnly and glanced at Apollos. He gazed at her encouragingly. He nudged her toward the shell. Alexa's mind was working fervently to come up with the perfect words for her question. "You must place your hand on the Mother of Pearl and ask it loud and clearly what you need," Glyndwr instructed, his gray eyes alight, staring into the glimmering shell. "Apollos, make sure you can see also. Four eyes and two minds are better. You can help her puzzle this through. We will watch, too."

Apollos moved closer to the shell. Alexa looked anxiously around to the faces in her company. She saw the ethereal beauty of Vailea, the handsome Nereus, the lovely grandfather face of the old merman, and the always breathtaking, kindly unicorn. She gathered her courage. Apollos' chocolate eyes implored her to carry on. Alexa placed her spear-free hand into the center of Mother of Pearl and said loudly and clearly, emphasizing each syllable deftly, "Show me what I need to know to understand how to defeat Ret the wizard in Zelka."

Instantly, a light glowed from the shell, illuminating their eager faces. Alexa's hand warmed uncomfortably on the shell, but she didn't remove it. Then the light began to swirl like a storm cloud. They leaned forward to peer into the silvery surface. Alexa's eyes widened as a picture appeared. It was of a man…someone very familiar to her. He looked identical to her father. But this man was not her father. This man's eyes held a malice that Alexa had never known her father to show. He had an angular face that narrowed to a sharp chin, and pale skin with the luminous sapphire eyes that belonged to all of Alexa's wizard-blooded family. He had lanky black hair. He wore upon his hand what Alexa guessed to be the deceased King of Zelka's ring. The wizard Ret. The image changed.

Alexa saw her homeland, the desert in all its glory in its own beautiful way. She saw her family. Her heart gave a jolt, anticipating fearful images, for she saw her mother, father, herself and her brothers. And then to her horror, but not completely to her surprise, she saw her family being kidnapped by evil beings—goblins, harpies and changers. The pictures changed to images of war on civilians, an infantry of fiends riding on black, tainted unicorns. They rode slaying anyone in their path, and made bloody sacrifices of innocent people. There was a man controlling a dragon that was mercilessly spewing fire down on the earth. A man, on foot, wearing a dark cloak, killed several at a time.

Alexa saw faces she knew. She saw a careworn Sword Bryan with an image of herself by his side, peering through a thicket, dirt smudging her face. She saw a tired Apollos hanging his head as a thick, scarlet liquid dripped from his horn. She saw Prince Alkin beaten and bloodied, chained in a cold murky place. She saw Lady Adama holding the necklace she had given Alexa. She saw Lady Dorsa standing in a frozen landscape, her eyes full of tears. She wore a brilliant emerald necklace. A sad looking man Alexa didn't recognize stood nearby beckoning to her. He wore clothes that separated him as royalty, but blood dripped from his mouth.

Then, to Alexa's surprise, she saw merpeople, thousands of merpeople all swimming in the dark cold waters of the north. Their skin pale as the moon and their hair as dark as night, their eyes like piercing swords. The vision changed, and she saw Sword Bryan with his weapon drawn and his face distorted with rage as he charged at a horde of hellhounds and the dark unicorns. She saw a fierce Lady Evelyn sitting on a rearing horse. Goblins wielding maces swarmed all around her as she tried to cut them down with

166

her sword. She saw Hazerk and Warkan fighting and tending to the wounded, and thousands of other warriors from all countries fighting and dying. The image changed, and Alexa saw herself. She was lying on a bed made up in black. She was pale and deathlike. Alexa saw Ret standing over her smiling satisfied.

The next images she could barely stand to watch, but Apollos moved closer to her, his soft body brushing against her. She focused all her attention. She must understand. She watched as the wizard revealed his full plan. She saw her brothers being used and corrupted through their blood to create more wizards, full-blooded wizards…and she was to be the shell to harbor the abominations. She could see inside her womb children growing. Her lifeless form on the black bed grew and grew over again and again with child. She saw wizards, female and male, growing. Their innate evil was encouraged and nurtured in their veins by Ret. Ret then sent them out and they covered Eetharum with blood from wars that saturated the dirt and spilled into the sea, drowning land and sea creatures in its wake. They ruled the lands: minions, under the mighty emperor. Alexa saw red ships set sail, and the lands over the ocean were saturated with war's blood.

The images went white. Then she saw water, pure, beautiful water. It was dripping like teardrops into her cupped hands; her companions stood around her. There was a beautiful verdant valley in a forest. The trees were in full-bloom with apple blossoms. Alexa saw herself pick a ruby-red apple. Bryan was by her side, his sword drawn protectively. She then saw flames lick the sky, bursting forth out of a fountain of fire. Eelyne shielded her from the flames as she reached her hand out toward it. She saw wind swirling above a desert plateau. She stood bravely alone while the wind caressed her face and hair. The image changed, and Alexa saw a peaceful summer night. The sky was dark blue and dotted with thousands of twinkling stars. She stood in a field, and the stars fell from the sky upon her, coming down like fiery rain to her awaiting open hands. Apollos stood nearby, gazing into the heavens.

The images changed again, and Alexa saw a beautiful, but terrifying woman she didn't recognize wield a spear of flame from the sky. Then she caused a river to rise and flood. A wind storm of ice and rain was guided by her fingers. The earth trembled and broke open at her command. Then it ended.

They found they were staring blankly into the silvery bottom of the Mother of Pearl. They were speechless as they let the images sink in. Alexa was trying to embed them in her memory. She shut her eyes and struggled, fearing she might forget them. She didn't feel any better about the situation. The magical shell hadn't shown her how to defeat the wizard. Her heart sank. She saw the dreadful plans Ret had in store for her, her family and the world. But what good would that do if she still didn't know how to stop them? All this had done was to make her more fearful of her task. So much weight was on her shoulders. If she failed, blood would saturate the land. She would become the mother to horrific abominations. *She* would be used to help Ret take over.

"I-I don't understand what I'm supposed to do!" she suddenly cried out. The horrendous images had disturbed her greatly. Some were strangely similar to her dream she had had weeks ago while she slept on the ground passing out of Shelkite.

"Yes. Those were unkind images the Mother of Pearl showed," Glyndwr said gravely. Unkind was hardly the word Alexa was thinking. "I see now the greatness of it all," Glyndwr continued. "Didn't you see the last images?"

"What? The terrifying woman? Yes, but who is she?" Alexa asked desperately.

"No, of the elements?" Glyndwr said calmly.

"Elements?" Alexa repeated, her mind's eye straining to remember.

"Yes!" Apollos spoke up, a light in his always gentle face. "The water, the apple trees, the fountain of flame, the wind storm, the stars."

"Correct. I understand what you must do. And I understand what I have to do to help you," Glyndwr stated. He swam from the rim of the Mother of Pearl, and guided the others away to speak. "In ancient times it was said that if one could gather the purest form of all the elements; earth, fire, water, wind and starlight, then that person would be extremely formidable. However, only wizards or witches could ever have had enough strength to be able to wield a power so great. Any human would die if they tried. Elemental usage has been heard of in the past, but I don't believe any have succeeded in wielding all of them combined. You see, first one must gather the elements. But it cannot be just the element; it has to be the element in its pristine form. It must come from a source that still exists from the beginning of time. From when the Master of the Sea created the world and magic was at its pinnacle. The elements are protected by Keepers. The Keepers were set to guard the untainted elements from unfriendly hands, mostly wizards and witches. Because as we all know, wizards first came into being when demons reproduced with humans." He paused at seeing Alexa's tense face. He smiled and quickly added, "It doesn't mean they are all evil. Wizards and witches began to have children with their own kind as well as humans, and the demon blood lessoned over time. And some, like your father, turned away from that path. But the point is, wizards and witches are the only beings powerful enough to control the elements if they ever got their hands on them. In the hands of an evil sorcerer the elemental power is a dangerous weapon indeed. The Keepers are expecting and prepared to see wizards come searching for the elements. The Keepers have never been known to give up their element easily. The few searchers that managed to gather some of the elements were never able to find all of them in their purest form. But it seems to me you're to go and gather this power, half-blood or not. For the images showed exactly where they are."

"Exactly? I don't know these places," Alexa said abrasively with clenched teeth.

"You will know. How did you know to come to us? Something is guiding you, and I advise you to listen to it every time it requests. Obey even if your path ahead is dark. That's how you will succeed; have faith. Just be cautious, know yourself, your friends and the Master of the Sea, because there are outside, wicked powers that will penetrate you and fool you into thinking they are good, and will beckon you to follow them. It's to your advantage that you're willing to do this task, and will be on guard against wicked powers."

169

"Who is to wield this power then? That woman wasn't me," Alexa questioned.

Apollos snorted, and bubbles sprang from his nose, "Ah! Even I could tell that, Alexa."

"Who then? We have to find her. I collect the elements, and she has to wield them. She must be some great sorceress I haven't heard of. I'd thought my family was the last bit of wizard blood left in the world, and I the only woman…" Alexa stated, wonderingly.

"I've already found her," Apollos stated. Alexa stared at him in puzzlement.

"The woman was you, Alexa," Nereus said pointedly.

"Me?"

"Yes," Apollos answered, "You didn't recognize yourself because the elemental power had changed you to your own eyes. But, it was you. You're the one to wield the counter magic as we've called it in the past."

Alexa looked to Glyndwr as if she didn't believe what his son or Apollos were saying. "How can I…I don't…" She let the question hang. It all seemed so far above her. How was *she* to do it?

"It was you, though you're not meant to do it all on your own," Glyndwr confirmed, and Vailea nodded in agreement.

Then it hit Alexa, an understanding, and she suddenly felt calmer. She was called. She was asked. She answered, and now she must be a tool to defeat Ret. She shouldn't worry about doing this herself. She had a greater power on her side as well as her friends. Then, just as suddenly, new fears surfaced. "Right. The elements are the counter magic the naiad spoke about. That makes sense. We have to find them. Okay, but what of the other images?" she asked. She feared the worst; most of them contained her friends and family suffering. She didn't want to mention aloud she was related to Ret, but somehow she knew the others knew. And, they had decided there was no need to speak of it.

"The unclear future. Like I said, this is what the wizard has planned. It doesn't mean it will happen. I can't explain all the images. And I am sure neither my son nor daughter nor Apollos can either. You must keep these images in mind throughout your journey and deal with them as you know and as they come. Always deal with the present, with a regard to the future. It's never good to dwell too much on the future or the past for that matter. It causes needless worry."

"All right…." Alexa said with a troubled brow.

"You aren't alone, remember that," Vailea empathized. "You have your human companions and Apollos to help you." The mermaid smiled, seeming to connect to Alexa's fears in a way only another woman could understand. "Stay close to them…your friends. You aren't meant to fail, and the Master of the Sea is wise. You just have to trust and obey."

"Now, I've helped you. I've shared my knowledge with you, but there's one more thing that I must do," Glyndwr said.

"What is that? Do you know who the guardians are?" Alexa asked.

"I don't know who guards them all, but I do know who the guardian of water is."

"It's you isn't it?" Alexa said with sudden realization.

"Yes. We are called the Water-Keepers. It's a secret among the merpeople. Our tears are the purest form of water. We are an ancient race, so our tears date back to the beginning. And normally we would never give up such a precious thing so easily, but we see the great need and we will help you," Glyndwr said. He then turned to his daughter, and said, "Vailea, would you please fetch me the pearl vial." The mermaid nodded, and then with a swish of her tail she quickly swam away down the forest path to the house, leaving a trail of bubbles.

"I have one question to ask you myself, Glyndwr," Apollos stated. He had a dark glint in his eyes that held accusations once again.

"What is it, my friend?"

"You say you are the only merpeople left; and that you can't save your race. Yet the visions showed otherwise. And, I also know of another sea that harbors merpeople. It's far to the north in the cold waters of the Nortarwin Sea. Why don't you seek them out and come together?" Apollos said. "It would be wise to combine your strength so you're not alone. And, you could keep growing as a people."

"We don't speak of our brothers to the north. They're not a part of us. They're different, a more dubious people. We don't commune with them."

"They're prone to wickedness?" Apollos inquired.

"I wouldn't rightly use the word wicked. They're a more self-seeking and mischievous people," Glyndwr corrected.

"Don't you think it would be sensible to go to them before the enemy does and confirm their alliance?" Apollos suggested.

"Yes, I suppose. But, it's a long and dangerous sea to travel between here and there. I don't know—"

"Does it look like our path will be out of harm's way? Does it look like Alexa will have an easy time? Do you think Ret will stop at the shores? If he is intent on creating havoc, he'll not be satiated until everything is entrapped. He'll come sooner or later. You are or will be a part of this whether you want to be or not. You have to do your part to protect yourselves and your future," Apollos said with a flare.

Glyndwr gazed at the unicorn impassively.

Apollos had stated his opinion with such firmness and authority Alexa wasn't sure if it was proper to speak to the old merman in such a way. But then she realized Apollos was old, too, and wise. Perhaps he was a higher rank in the magical world. The merpeople did seem to place his kind up on a pedestal.

At that time Vailea returned with a small vial, disrupting the ambiance. She handed it to Alexa. Alexa turned the vial over in her hand. It fit snuggly in her palm. It was carved from one pearl. No ornate designs embellished it, its surface smooth. One small cap snapped shut over the opening.

"A pearl is the only substance that can hold all the elements. You must collect them and hold them in this vial. And, when the time comes…you will drink the elements," Glyndwr stated.

"Drink them? How can I contain fire? Or wind? I don't understand," Alexa pleaded, frustrated.

"You will. The elements in their purest form are

different…magical," Glyndwr explained.

"Where—"

"Do not ask me where the other elements can be found." He cut her off. "I honestly do not know. I am sorry. The Elemental-Keepers all have their own secrets; and for extra protection we don't know much of each other, just of the elemental legend. That's all," Glyndwr said curtly.

"Don't worry, Alexa. We'll help you," Apollos encouraged. He, of course, was speaking of her companions waiting above the waters. "But we should hurry. The others are probably anxious."

"The vial is already partially filled with mermaid tears. Just add the other elements. Be careful not to lose it. Guard it closely against evil. Don't open it once you have them all, at least until you are ready to use it," Glyndwr said fearfully.

"Of course, and thank you." Alexa said, feeling slightly heartened at receiving the first key.

"You're welcome. And, now you must go. Nereus won't accompany you to shore; I've decided we must begin our own mission as Apollos suggested. He's right. It's not right for us to stay here and do nothing. We'll go to the merpeople in the Nortarwin Sea and convince them to join us, come here and flourish and fight if we must."

"You surprise me, Glyndwr, knowing your kind. But that's a wise decision. You won't regret it. I thank you with my whole heart," Apollos said approvingly, a sparkle in his milky chocolate eyes.

"You don't know what it means to me to hear you say that. Thank you, noble unicorn." Glyndwr bowed low to Apollos. When he straightened, his eyes held a hurriedness that wasn't there before. "Now, go. You'll be safe on your travels to the surface; nothing that could harm you is in the vicinity. Apollos take her straight to the surface. You'll find you're in familiar territory. Nereus, give Alexandra air so she can make it to the surface. Apollos you must swim fast." Glyndwr spoke emphatically.

Suddenly Alexa felt in a rush to get to the surface. It was time to get moving. She was in a hurry to begin the mission. She had more knowledge now, and she knew what she had to do. She was *going* to stop those wicked images from coming true.

Apollos swam up alongside Alexa. "Get on my back. They have things to attend to. They can't waste time if they're to convince the northern merpeople." Alexa slid onto the unicorn's back. She felt his legs churning the water around them. His hide was as soft as satin even in the water. Nereus swam up to Alexa's side and her gaze fell in lock with his beautiful eyes. He placed his hand on her forearm and leaned nearer to her so that they were inches apart.

"Good luck, Alexandra, may the Master of the Sea guide you. Our thoughts will be with you. And know that we will be helping you," Nereus said with affection. Alexa's heart skipped a beat as the merman leaned in and placed his mouth softly on hers. He exhaled long, filling her lungs, giving her air. He then leaned away, taking his spear from a dazed Alexa. He kissed her cheek and said farewell to Apollos.

Apollos rose and climbed through the water. Alexa held on tight, being able to breathe only because of Nereus's magical kiss. As the unicorn ascended, she smiled and waved good bye to the merpeople, wishing them luck in her heart.

Soon they were out of sight. Before them was only the great vastness of water. Gradually through the obscurity came dim light. Alexa had seized Apollos' mane, and her legs were wrapped snuggly around his barrel. He was swimming nearly vertical. They traveled as if they climbed a steep mountain. She felt the unicorn's muscles contract and expand beneath her legs over and over again. Then suddenly she couldn't breathe. Apollos felt her body go taut with fear and heard her choke. "Hold your breath, were almost to the surface!" He encouraged.

Time passed, and Alexa felt she might pass out. The water was pressing heavily all around her. She tried to speak, but nothing but garbled mumbles came out. She struggled to fight the instinct to gasp for air. Her underwater vision became blurry. She squeezed her eyes shut. "Hold on. We're almost there!" Apollos called fearfully. He swam yet harder, straining his body against his own fatigue. And then, finally, the sun's rays shone brightly. They sliced through the jade-colored waters like dreams slipping into reality. Apollos surfaced with gusto. Alexa sucked in as much air as she could possibility attain, and never had she been so thankful for it.

Chapter 18

Prince Alkin and Sword Bryan paced the white sandy beach in disquiet. They had been waiting for well over an hour in the hot sun. The jade-colored waves of the Elendace Sea crashed on the shore in a soothing, rhythmic manner, but neither man found it calming.

Alkin had finally retreated to the shade of the trees, and now sat examining the sharpened blade of his beloved Sword of Shelkite. He glanced up to see his friend still pacing restively near the water's edge, looking out to open sea. *It's not like him to act so unsettled*, Alkin mused. He stood and shaded his eyes against the glaring sun, sheathing his sword. He strode over to the Master Sword, who was staring severely at the sea as if it had done him some sort of wrong. "I hope they're not down there much longer," Alkin said, looking the waves over.

"Yeah," Bryan said edgily.

At that moment something burst out of the lagoon directly to their left. Both men turned and saw the snowy white head of Apollos, and a gasping, drenched Alexa emerge from the depths. They ran to them.

"You all right?" Alkin asked anxiously upon seeing Alexa's pale face as Apollos slowly made his way to the bank, dragging the slender girl with him. She hung weakly onto his mane, her body floating out behind her.

The Prince held out his hand. Alexa seized it gratefully, giving an affirming jerk of her head. Alkin heaved her out of the water; and Bryan quickly threw a blanket around the girl's shoulders. Apollos stumbled feebly onto the shore, snorting and shaking his head to clear his nostrils and ears. Alkin made a movement to touch the unicorn and steady him, but quickly withdrew his hand when the unicorn peered at him skeptically from the corner of his eye. "I'm okay, friend," Apollos assured the Prince. Then he promptly dropped to his knees and rolled in the warm sand, grunting with pleasure.

Alkin smiled briefly at the unicorn, and then quickly turned his attention to Alexa. Bryan had wrapped her so tightly in the blanket her arms were plastered down at her sides. But the color in her cheeks was returning, and she gave him a meager half smile. She opened her mouth as if to speak, but Alkin held up a hand and said, "It can wait. Rest for a bit."

They trekked to the shade of the waving palm trees and plopped down, all feeling a great amount of relief in some way or another. Apollos joined them and layed down, tucking his legs up comfortably. His velvety coat had dried, and it shone pleasantly in the sunshine.

Leaning against the tree, Alexa extracted her arms from the blanket and started undoing her braid to run her fingers through her hair and quickly re-braid it again. She sighed as she stared out over the water pensively.

Bryan studied Alexa's angular features, noting her sapphire eyes were gazing worlds away. They had an uncomforting look about them. He glanced at the unicorn; he was closely watching Alexa, too. Now that the girl was back under his vigilant eye, Bryan's anxiety was gone and his curiosity was piqued. What had happened down there?

He didn't have to wait long to find out, a few quiet minutes later Alexa burst forth, spewing everything. She rarely paused for a breath and didn't look at anyone, except Apollos to confirm facts here and there. She told them of Nereus, Vailea and Glyndwr, their world, the Mother of Pearl, the visions she saw, the elements, and of what they had been appealed to do.

Alexa didn't dare look at the Prince or Sword during her explanation. She was waiting to sense out the men's reactions to not ever telling them that Ret was her uncle. She explained that Ret was her father's twin and of what he had planned. Though, she didn't tell them of her uncle's plans for her personally. Apollos nodded approvingly. He didn't protest when she left out that detail.

Alexa paused for a breath, stopping her report. She tore her eyes from the sea and looked at Prince Alkin. He showed no surprise at this last bit of information. He was lost in despondent thoughts. With downcast eyes he absently brushed sand off his black boots. Coming to, he lifted his hazel eyes and met hers with a look of concern. Alexa relaxed. He wasn't angry with her for withholding her relation to Ret.

On the other hand, she didn't have to look at Sword Bryan to know he was shocked. She sensed once again an unease and distrust of her flow through him. She could feel the Sword clamming up and becoming tense. She couldn't say why, but it distressed her greatly.

Alkin spoke, disrupting her senses, "Evelyn and I suspected this. In fact, we were pretty sure you must be related to Ret, considering the rarity of magical-blooded people nowadays. Don't worry. It doesn't matter."

Beside her, Bryan clenched his jaw and said roughly, "Why didn't you tell us?"

Alexa turned to him, her eyes flashing in defense. "You already distrusted me, thinking me a spy. Do you think I wanted to reveal to you that this man was a close relative of mine?" The Master Sword didn't answer, but his features looked resigned. Alkin rubbed his forehead tensely with his fingertips, looking out over the sea in thought.

"But if you'd been straight forward from the beginning we would've trusted you more," Bryan finally stated, his voice was firm, but not harsh.

Alexa rolled her eyes. "You're Right. I'm sorry," she said begrudgingly.

Fighting his bitter impulse to mistrust, Bryan raised an amused eyebrow, gazing wryly at her.

Alexa took this as a sign of forgiveness. She decided she would explain her past more, hoping it would rectify herself. "My father, Erec, or Erecin in full, trained me and my brothers only a little in magic. He always said it was dangerous and not something we should let overpower us. We were taught to control our so-called evil blood. My Uncle Ret, or actually Retsin is his full name, is rarely spoken of in our family. My father acts as if he doesn't exist, although he does know of my uncle's whereabouts. He knew he was a counselor on the king's court in Zelka. Just before my father married my mother, my uncle and he had a disagreement over something. He's never said what about. They'd been traveling with each other their whole lives. They moved from place to place, never staying anywhere long, doing magic for a living in circuses and things like that: harmless things. My uncle wanted more. He moved to Zelka to elevate his status and become a counselor. My father thought he may have studied and delved into the darker kinds of magic; I guess he was right. But, my father didn't want that kind of power. He wanted a family, and that's when he renounced being a wizard."

Alexa looked at the Prince. He nodded mutely, his hazel eyes troubled. Then she glanced at the silent Sword. He showed no emotion, but just stared at her attentively. Alexa felt strangely heartened that he didn't scathe her for being her anymore. For some unknown reason it seemed vital he shouldn't think ill of her.

"I wonder what they argued about," Alkin finally said.

"Yeah, I wonder that myself now, too," Alexa replied.

"I wonder if he knew something bad was brewing in that brain of his brother's," Bryan added cynically.

"I think he may have," Apollos said. "But there's nothing we can do about that now," he added in a practical tone. He stood up and shook himself, ending the conversation abruptly. "Let's get back. We're rested now, and the others have to know all this, too."

"Wait, Apollos," Alkin called to the departing unicorn, and then turned to Alexa who was brushing herself off. She wrapped the blanket snuggly around herself, suddenly feeling self-conscious as the Prince gazed into her face kindly. "You told us some startling things. Are *you* all right?" he inquired.

Alexa lowered her eyes to the ground and shifted her feet bracingly. She *must* tell them about Ret's plans for her, but for some reason she couldn't just now. It was too horrifying, degrading…personal. It choked her to just think about it. "Yeah," she merely said. She looked up bravely to give the Prince a forced smile. He smiled back and patted her shoulder awkwardly.

Bryan was standing beyond the Prince waiting to leave with Apollos. Alexa met eyes with him; and for once the Master Sword didn't look away. He clenched his jaw and gave her the slightest of encouraging nods, and then turned on his heel to follow the unicorn.

When she reached the cover of the forest, Alexa ducked behind a tree to quickly pull on her shirt, trousers and boots.

179

Apollos appeared at her side. She gave a startled jump. "Don't sneak up like that! You scared me," she scolded as she pulled on her boot, balancing on one foot.

"Sorry, didn't mean to." He reached out his muzzle and steadied her on her foot.

"Thanks." Finishing, Alexa paused and looked at the unicorn who was gazing at her strangely. "Do you think I should have told them about...." She pursed her lips.

"No," the unicorn cut in gently. "Honestly, I wasn't expecting you to tell them right away. That was hard medicine to swallow—to see yourself so. You wait until you're ready to tell them. It's not imperative right now."

Alexa gazed into the unicorn's kind, chocolate eyes. They were so gentle and wise, and yet formidable, too. She nodded. Apollos bobbed his head, sending his silky mane flipping to the other side of his sleek neck. Alexa smiled.

"Just remember." Apollos began walking down the forest path toward their camp. Alexa followed closely by his shoulder. "What you saw in the Mother of Pearl was *not* the future. It was only Ret's plans for the future. Don't think about it too much. That's why we're here together. You, me, Alkin, Bryan, and the others, we're to stop that from being the future."

Alexa nodded glumly. She reached her hand over to him. She couldn't resist the urge any longer to touch the unicorn's glossy mane and run her fingers through it. She scratched behind his ears; and he tossed his head in delight. "Right. I know," she said compliantly.

"I know for a fact that Prince Alkin and Sword Bryan intend to see you through until this is finished. And, the same goes for me. The others I'm sure feel the same; they're noble Shelkiten warriors. The Power will take care of us." The unicorn's eyes glittered with confidence.

"I know," was her distracted answer.

A few minutes later, when they could see the backs of Bryan and Alkin ahead of them again, Alexa brought up something that had been troubling her since she saw the visions. "Apollos?"

"Yes."

"I had a dream, if you could call it a dream, it just seemed so real, when we were traveling through Shelkite's fields. It was…very similar to parts of what I saw in the Mother of Pearl. It can't be a coincidence."

The unicorn raised his nose in the air, his eyes thoughtful. "Have you had dreams like this before?"

"No."

"Hmm… I don't think you're prescient. It could have been caused by something magical invading you. It might've given you a glimpse of its origin or something of that nature."

"Like you mean my blood, since I'm related to Ret. By that connection I could have seen what he has planned for me. Does that mean my brothers may have gotten the same warning, too?"

"I don't know," he said uncertainly. "I'll have to think it over." He looked at her fallen countenance. "It might not have been something bad invading you. There's no sense in worrying yourself silly about your family. We're doing everything we know of right now to solve this."

"My brothers don't know of any of this; and my mother is only human…defenseless."

"Right, but they have your father. I'm sure he's a clever man. Worrying does no good. Prince Alkin and Lady Evelyn, along with the country of Galeon are doing and will do all they can to stop any more bad from happening to the people of Eetharum," Apollos reassured.

"I know," she acknowledged fretfully.

Chapter 19

When they reached the camp, they found the others gathered around a crackling fire while they roasted something delicious smelling. "Lunch?" Hazerk beamed and held up the game. They nodded and sunk down around the fire, careful not to sit too close in such warm weather. "I could camp like this forever." Hazerk grinned as he offered out the meat.

"So, what happened? You look a little shaken up, girl," Warkan said bluntly. Bryan threw him a scowl, but took a seat opposite the stern warrior.

Alexa sighed and dove into an explanation again. By the time she had finished they had all eaten their food. The men sat staring mutely at her as if they hadn't expected their mission to amount to such a big issue.

This time Prince Alkin noted Alexa's slight hesitance in explaining certain parts of the vision. He stole a questioning glance at Bryan. The Master Sword merely raised a wary eyebrow. He had caught it, too. They would confront her and Apollos later about it.

The others started voicing their concerns. "So, what's this going to do to you? Being only a half-blood?" Hazerk asked worriedly. "That, ah…Glendywere merman said the elemental power would kill humans if they attempted to use it."

Alexa shrugged, "I don't know."

"Humph," grunted Warkan.

"It could weaken her a great deal," Eelyne added.

"What do you know?" Warkan said critically.

"I specialized in magical beings, remember?" he retorted. He pulled from his sack a fat book and started flipping through it hurriedly.

"You brought a book with you?" Hazerk laughed incredulously.

"Books," mumbled a distracted Eelyne.

Warkan stared, flabbergasted. The others smiled.

"Good, I'm glad he did. Because everyone obviously knows that I don't know much!" Alexa stated in his defense.

"Don't worry. I'll try to find something for you, Alexa,"

Eelyne said emphatically.

Alexa made a mental note to ask him in private if he could find anything about evil magic invading dreams.

The rest of the afternoon was filled with assumptions, worries and tentative plans. Alexa voted to go straight through Carthorn and into Kaltraz where she could meet up with her father so they all could have a conference. Eelyne supported her enthusiastically, knowing Carthorn still held magic he could witness; it would bring his studies to life. Warkan was cynical. He claimed he never heard of anyone coming out of Carthorn alive—until Apollos spoke up and said he had. Hazerk candidly announced he would go anywhere, as long as there was food and a potential good fight.

Close to supper time, Alkin, Alexa, Apollos and Bryan consulted this proposal in private. The unicorn supported the plan, claiming if there was anywhere the magical elements might be Carthorn was the place to start looking. Both Alkin and Bryan agreed. It was settled. They would begin their march to Carthorn in the morning.

Just before dusk, Bryan had Alexa and Eelyne train with the sword two on one. "Eventually I'll have you fight up to four on one, and in teams. But let's not get ahead of ourselves," he said cheerfully.

It was fun when Eelyne was the one defending himself. Alexa's spirits rose to the clouds while she and the Master Sword were a team. She felt as if it really were possible for her to be a good swordswoman. However, her elated feeling didn't last long. Her spirits went crashing to the ground when it was her turn to be on her own. She could sense Eelyne and Bryan's delight in giving her a killing blow every time she turned around. She growled and kept pushing to do her best, but the two men seemed to be enjoying hassling her too much.

"Ha! Don't look so foul, Alexa!" Eelyne laughed when they had finished their bout. Bryan was grinning devilishly at her. She merely grunted and kept her face screwed up.

"Okay, now you two against me. Work together," Bryan ordered. And they did, but to no avail. Bryan couldn't help himself from laughing at their growing frustration. "Okay, we're done," he said finally with a chuckle. The two pupils voiced their relief and went over to the fire, feeling defeated.

As the company sat eating their supper and trying to forget all the pending troubles, Apollos perked his ears in alarm.

"What is it?" Alkin asked, shushing the others.

"Our shadow is approaching," Apollos whispered. His eyes and ears were attentive. His head was held high, his tail arched. At that moment, if it wasn't for his horn and the obvious intelligent look in his eyes, he would have looked like a wild horse sniffing the breeze, catching a predator's scent.

Bryan rose slowly from his spot and quietly drew his sword. Warkan followed suit, silently taking up the battle-ax he carried strapped across his back. The Prince, Eelyne and Hazerk took out their weapons. They stood in a half circle facing the shadowy woods where Apollos stared alertly. The silence was tense as they waited. Apollos had sensed the man in ample time.

"He's close." The unicorn lowered his head, trying to decipher the visitor. The others braced themselves.

"I feel him now, too," Alexa whispered.

Bryan was suddenly aware she stood at the opposite end of their half circle, farthest away from him. He clenched his teeth; his charge needed to be right next to him. But he dared not ask her to move.

"He means no harm," Alexa said in relief as if the man had told her himself.

"How do you know?" growled Warkan.

Bryan moved infinitesimally toward Alexa; as if somehow it would stop her from doing something stupid. He glared at her from out of the corner of his eye, but she was paying him no heed. She was looking into the dark forest with interest. *Great!* He was suddenly in a sour mood.

"She's right, let him approach," Apollos confirmed, he bobbed his head in reassurance. But the others kept their guards up until they saw a dark shape emerge from the shadows.

The tall figure paused just beyond the fire's full light. The fire flickered and danced around his black cloak. The man had the hood drawn over his head, shielding his face in its depths. In the shadows of his hood, his dark eyes glistened from the fire's reflection. He did not speak.

"Who are you to follow us?" Prince Alkin suddenly demanded, his voice was crisp and to the point, so unlike his usual congenial demeanor.

"Ah, a unicorn. So, that's what I felt," a raspy voice said from within the hood.

The companions looked at each other uneasily. "Answer my question," Alkin pressed.

Alexa thought that no one in their right mind would dare disobey the Prince's authority at this second harsh command. But the visitor merely laughed heartily with his hoarse sounding voice. *How arrogant.* Alexa was slightly amused. His husky voice sent shivers down her spine, though it was strangely alluring. It sounded as if his vocal cords had been scrubbed across coral, as if he had used his voice far too much, or that he hadn't spoken aloud in a long time. Alexa settled with the latter explanation.

Alexa wasn't the only one receiving shivers down their spine upon hearing the stranger's voice. Alkin had, too, but it wasn't for the same reason. It wasn't alluring at all. It was a sudden jolt of fear. He had heard this voice before. But he couldn't bring to mind who it was or when it was. Whenever it was, it hadn't been a pleasant meeting.

"Don't get all up in arms, gentlemen, my lady," the stranger said with a smile in his voice. He slowly approached the fire.

Bryan watched carefully as the flickering light illuminated parts of the man's hidden face. There was no outward show of weapons, his hands were empty, but the Master Sword was intelligent enough to know he had more than one weapon hidden on his person.

"Why are you following us? We don't want to do you any harm. How'd you know about the unicorn? You don't have magical blood. " Alkin pushed on bravely.

"No." The stranger sat down at the fire. The companions didn't move. They still stood facing him menacingly. "I don't need

185

magic to sense him. I've been around long enough to know these things—I'm sorry, can I sit at your fire and talk business?" he asked condescendingly, peering up at them.

"Of course." Alkin sat down sophisticatedly, his royal manners coming back. The others followed suit. Apollos continued to stand protectively, but at ease. There was a moment of silence, and then Alkin asked, "Tell us your name, so we can get acquainted."

The shadowy figure turned his head to look behind him into the forest, seemingly ignoring the Prince again. He whistled. Out came a sturdy mare, colored a mousy black-blue. She stood by her master, fully tacked and obedient. She nuzzled his shoulder. "This is Blize," he said. After patting his mare he regarded the company again. "I'm called many things, but Kheane has been my rightful name for many years."

Bryan narrowed his eyes; he didn't like this man's patronizing air. The Master Sword had marked him from the beginning as an exceedingly dangerous person. He wasn't far off his assessment. Bryan glanced at the Prince. Alkin seemed unsettled, but only Bryan, being his Sword, would have noticed, although the stranger seemed to have caught this, too. Bryan then stole a glance at Alexa. The girl was practically gawking at the stranger—Kheane, whatever his name was.

Alkin was about to introduce the others, but Kheane broke in before he could speak. He didn't seem to care to know their names, unless it was that he knew them already. "I was living in a cabin off the coast when I saw your company pass. I came from the north. I'd decided I wanted to retire from my wretched work and pursue unfinished business. But when I saw your company, I couldn't help but wonder what the Prince of Shelkite was doing traveling covertly. And, that perhaps this trip you are all on ties to me in some way. I think I can help. I want to help. Let me come with you. I can't run from my past anymore, and the unfinished business will have to stay unfinished."

"How do you know the Prince?" Bryan demanded. His voice was much more daunting then even Alkin's was. The Sword did not like this visitor at all. He didn't trust him and he didn't want him coming with them.

"Let's just say I'm well-traveled," Kheane said.

Ignoring his comment, Alkin asked, "What do you know of our trip, as you call it?"

"More than you think, I think," Kheane answered coyly.

"If you want to join us, you'd better start answering questions openly," Bryan growled.

"Relax, Master Sword, I respect you. You *are* very good at what you do," he replied portentously. Not realizing this was an enormously good compliment, especially coming from the man sitting in front of him, Bryan glowered all the more. "Look," Kheane started diplomatically, "How about we talk this over in the morning. Let's leave on this note. You all know I'm not trying to do you any harm. And I know you're not trying to do me any harm. You know that I know about your trip. You know I want to help. Hopefully in the morning we'll all warm up to the idea a little more."

At this he stood. No one stopped him. Bending at the waist in a slight bow, he smiled, his eyes did anyway. He then turned to his horse. "Come, Blize." The mare turned and followed him happily. "I'll see you all in the morning. Sleep well!" he called over his shoulder, "Don't leave without me." With that he disappeared into the dark forest.

After his departure, Alexa made a noise as if to speak, but Bryan didn't let her get as far as to say she wanted to add the man to their company. "No," he said resolutely.

"Hey—" she shot back indignantly.

"Stop," Prince Alkin said sternly. He held up a hand and looked firmly at the two of them. The others stared at each other blankly, not sure what to think of their visitor Kheane. "We will decide on this together," Alkin stated calmly. He waited until both Alexa and the Sword nodded in agreement, albeit it looked as if they both had to break their necks to make the gesture.

Alexa wanted to blurt out that it had been decided at the castle she could make important decisions. This, she was certain, was important, and she knew they must agree to take Kheane on. However, Bryan looked relentless and Alkin looked doubtful. She bit back the thought. She had also agreed things would be talked over civilly. She calmed herself.

They talked into the night. Bryan graciously heard Alexa out, and Alexa graciously heard the others out. Bryan didn't like the man's manner. To him it boded ill, and he felt he was deceiving them. And, he said furthermore, that the name Kheane had an all too familiar ring to it. Not a nice one either. Strangely, both Alkin and Eelyne agreed on that point.

Warkan didn't think one man against the six—he corrected himself at Alexa's evil eye—the *seven* of them was any match. And he would agree to have Kheane join, but he also thought they should watch him closely. Hazerk was completely undecided. He also didn't like the atmosphere about Kheane, but, kind hearted as he was, felt they should believe him. Alkin still couldn't get over his uneasiness of recognizing that recognizable voice. He told the others of this concern. Nevertheless, he desperately wanted to trust Alexa and ended up supporting her.

Eelyne, being a fan of Alexa's witch senses supported her, but said he would research the name Kheane in his books. This caused him to swallow huge criticism from Warkan again. Who asked sneeringly why a man alive today would be in a history book. However, it didn't deter Eelyne. He was going on the implication of what Kheane had so blatantly stated—that he had been around long enough to be able to notice an invisible unicorn when there was one. And this, to Eelyne, was evidence enough to research.

"All right, all right," Bryan held up his hands in defeat. "We'll talk to him tomorrow morning. If you all still think we should trust him, then I'd be stupid to go against the majority." He looked specifically at Alexa. Her bewitching sapphire eyes sparkled a happy sky blue. He then regarded Apollos, who had been silent throughout the whole discussion, "I value your opinion," he simply stated.

The unicorn tossed his mane, his chocolate eyes glittering audaciously, "Let's trust him. I felt no ill will in him."

"Okay, it's settled then. All agreed?" the Sword inquired. Everyone mumbled and nodded in agreement.

They headed to their blankets in a foggy mindset. No one had much sleep that night, and Bryan didn't get any. He volunteered to stay up for the rest of the night in watch. Apollos kept the Master Sword company on and off as the unicorn didn't need as much sleep as the humans.

During one of Apollos' awake moments Bryan asked the unicorn what Alexa had hesitated in telling them earlier in her report. He didn't ask this accusingly, just curiously. The unicorn studied the Master Sword non-judgmentally for a moment before saying what she had withheld was a personal and painful shock to her. And, that it was of no detriment to the company right now. She would tell them in due time.

"Alexa's stronger than you give her credit for, Master Sword," Apollos said. Bryan knew that. And the unicorn knew that he knew that. But Apollos went out on a limb and pressed another issue before drifting off to sleep, "You know, I've watched you two. True, you're her guardian, and she needs you, but despite what you may think now, you need her, too. Don't shut yourself away from her just because of your past. She could become a great friend…all other things aside…" Apollos then, with a big yawn, fell asleep, seemingly knowing the stir he had caused in Bryan's chest.

Sitting wide awake beside the snoring unicorn, Bryan pondered out some things. He *was* bitter. Alexa had been right in her assessment upon meeting him that he was bitter. As the handsome Apollos snored softly on, the Master Sword felt something creep into his chest—dread. Dread on Alexa's behalf. Had she seen her own death? He glanced over at the slumbering girl and remembered the look in her eyes that night in her chamber, after the council, when she had told him she wanted him to be her Sword-Guard. They had had the darkness of loss in their pretty midnight colored depths. He didn't want anything bad to happen to her. The Sword's body and senses gave a resentful twitch at the foreign feeling stealing over him. It wasn't because he was merely her Sword-Guard that he felt this way. It was because *he*, himself, didn't want anything to happen to her.

Sighing, he looked up to the pale moon and thought what a

189

wonderful story it could tell if only it could speak. There in the sky it had seen so many things from the start of time. It had seen the beginning of troubles as well as the solutions; if there were any. It was a faithful witness at all times. If only it could give him advice. But perhaps it would be better if he should again put his trust in what he had been taught to as a child; the High Power. Bryan stayed awake pondering all this with a heavy heart in the darkness until the morning sun sifted through the trees and melted the feelings away.

Chapter 20

The Master Sword woke the others early. The sun had just lit the woods enough to see their camp clearly when he went around and kicked the bottoms of everyone's feet. "Come on guys, get up!"

There were a few resistant groans, but everyone got up and around. By the time they had their horses tacked and were ready for departure, Kheane appeared from the same spot he had emerged from the night before. Blize was tacked and ready. He still wore the obscuring black cloak and hood shielding his face. His coffee-colored eyes still held the same aplomb.

"Well? Do I travel with you?" said Kheane in his raspy voice.

"Maybe," Bryan said covertly.

"Yes," Alkin intervened, "we've decided to trust you. But, give us your word that you're here only to help."

"Good. I give my word. I'll be useful in a fight," Kheane declared, his dark eyes glinting.

"What makes you think we're going to be in a fight?" Warkan broke in.

Kheane turned his attention to the warrior and said knowingly, "It's not hard to tell." He turned to Blize and prepared to mount up, but Alkin stopped him.

"First, we have to tell you that it concerns us you know about our undertaking; we'd thought it was confidential. Tell us what you know and how," Alkin said diplomatically. Kheane stepped down from his stirrup and gave them a scrutinizing look. Alkin added, "We won't ask to know any more about you personally…right now."

Kheane nodded understandably. "I recognize this girl you have with you. At first I didn't. She looked vaguely familiar to me, but I know now that she's the only niece of the wizard Ret you're trying to stop. I know you, prince, merely because of the old occupation I held; I was required to know the influential by face."

Alexa butted in, "How do you know Ret?"

"Alexa!" Bryan reprimanded.

But Kheane regarded her and answered solemnly. "He

191

asked me for my help once…I refused. I'm sure he hunts me, now."

"Who are you?" Alexa asked eagerly.

"I'm Kheane. You all have nothing to fear from me. Though, my past does have a way of popping up from time to time to haunt me. But, I want nothing to do with it anymore. All I want now is quiet and the chance to find someone I lost. I can help you. And I'm hoping you'll help me when the need arises."

"If you want quiet why do you ask to travel with warriors?" Bryan asked curtly. He was slowly warming up to the stranger, very slowly.

Kheane looked at him sharp, his eyes blazing, and said, "Because to have quiet, a person must work for it first. *You* know that, Master Sword."

"Who have you lost? A woman?" Alexa asked. Bryan and Alkin gave her a warning look. But she kept her eyes on Kheane who regarded her coolly.

"Maybe," Kheane said, "but it's in vain. The individual is more than likely dead. That's why I ask to come with you. I don't have anything left for me to do."

"Find your quiet," Alexa answered softy. Kheane's eyes smiled amusedly at her. Bryan scowled.

"All right." Bryan cleared his throat, and glared at the apparently smitten Alexa. "Let's head out. I want to reach Carthorn as soon as we can."

They traveled north from the sea's edge. Carthorn was the northeastern country bordering the peninsula that made up Yoldor. Departing from the sea, they all felt a small loss somewhere in their souls. The waves seemed to say, *stay, stay*, every time they tumbled onto the shore. But slowly, as the company went, they heard less and less of the sea beckoning to them, and their minds turned to the path ahead.

They traveled quickly through the lightly wooded area they had sheltered in. They then crossed a stretch of sand dunes, having to dismount on a couple occasions to ease the chore for their mounts. Later, in a more rocky terrain, they passed by an ominous, grumbling and sputtering volcano. As they ogled it, the thought crossed their minds that it could be the fire element. But Alexa assured them it couldn't be. It didn't feel right and nothing was guarding it as far as she could sense. Apollos agreed.

Kheane fell into the company's rhythm easily. He seemed to belong, so Alexa felt. He traveled silently at the rear, his hard, black eyes forever scanning the vicinity. He never once removed the hood hiding his features. It piqued Alexa's curiosity almost to a point of distress. She wondered dreadfully about this strange man. What did he do? Where did he come from? Why did he hide his face and wear a cloak in the heat of day? Who had he been looking for? How did he know Ret and her?

Bryan rode at the head of the company with Alkin and Apollos, while Alexa rode just a few paces behind where he could get to her easily enough if need be. To Bryan's satisfaction, Kheane followed his orders without question. In fact, Kheane hardly said a word even if he was spoken to. And if he couldn't get around answering he would merely reply with a short, curt remark.

The Master Sword would every now and then turn in his saddle to survey the company. He would see Eelyne awkwardly trying to peruse his books astride his sorrel. Hazerk would be staring ahead, giving him a nod of 'all's well'. Warkan would be scowling around at the scenery, and Kheane was always on high alert. To a tiny bit of Bryan's annoyance, he noted that Alexa was constantly craning her neck around to watch the shady man.

They paused sparingly throughout the days they traveled. It was hot and cloudless. The red, glaring sun was merciless.

A few days travel from the sea, after dusk, when the gray moon was high in the purple sky, they could see on the horizon the mysterious forest of Carthorn looming. On its outskirts a lit village lay peacefully and dreamlike to their sun worn eyes. Perhaps they could find lodging one last night before braving the strange forest, Bryan thought. But he feared it would be a stretch to find a place to accommodate them all in such a small village.

They rode down the main street. Some curious children ran to the street to investigate; even some adults stopped their evening chores to look up. They were friendly and greeted the company pleasantly, and then went about their business. The company could smell food cooking as they passed the lit homes. A twinge of homesickness pricked Alexa's heart.

A little boy, desperate for a bath and comb, trotted up to them. "Are ya headed fer an inn, mister?" He came to Sapharan's side. The boy's head barely reached the warhorse's shoulder.

"Yes, do you have a suggestion?" Alkin said with a warm smile.

"Sure do! My father's an innkeeper. He'll take ya all. We've hadn't a group this large in a long time. It'll be good fer us! It's straight up there to the left. Brant's Tavern is across the way. Ya all can grab somethin there to eat and drink while we get yer rooms ready." With that, he took off up the street calling to his father happily.

Alkin laughed, "Well that was easy enough."

"After the trek we've had a couple of pints sounds good," Hazerk announced.

"It certainly does," Bryan answered, spitting some sandy grit out of his mouth.

"I don't think my eyes will ever be the same after all the squinting," Eelyne said, rubbing his achy eyes.

"I think I'm sunburned," Hazerk replied, gently patting his tender, pink cheeks. "I don't think my face has been this red since my mother smacked me for using dirty language when I was a boy. This fine alabaster skin is not meant for the sun." He grinned.

"Humph," Warkan commented, his own face was more than a little pink.

Alexa just smiled. Her skin was used to the heat, and she glowed prettily from being in her beloved sun all day once again.

They halted and stiffly dismounted at the tavern. The little boy appeared at Alkin's side again. "Ya all go in. We'll tend to yer horses," he said excitedly.

Alkin handed Sapharan's reins to the boy's eager hands, "Thank you, young man."

"Many thanks to ya." The boy grinned and gestured to his pals to come and get the other horses and mule.

As they headed up the rickety tavern stairs, Kheane spoke

up, his peculiar, raspy voice cutting the air, "I'll stay with the horses, just bring me something out."

Bryan paused on the stair step. The idea of Kheane not being watched still troubled him. He raised an eyebrow at Alkin; the Prince shrugged his shoulders.

"You don't want to be seen?" Alkin questioned.

"That's right," he answered.

Alexa, noting the Prince's hesitance, piped up "I'll stay with him; just bring me something, too." Her sparkling eyes and rosy cheeks made for a handsome countenance, and caused a few blind eyes amongst the men to open.

"No, you won't," Bryan said firmly, coming off the stairway to stand next to her almost possessively. Alexa scowled at him. He glared back. He would be gutted first before leaving her alone in this man's company. Why was she so eager? Why could she never use her brain?

"She'll be quite safe in my care, Master Sword, no need to worry," Kheane said in an annoyingly patronizing way.

"No, Warrior Warkan can stay," Bryan decided gruffly.

"Come in with us, Kheane. It's likely you won't be recognized here. And if you are, we'll take the repercussions; since I said it would be safe," Alkin said sincerely.

Kheane shrugged his shoulders; his coffee-colored eyes glinted amiably in the half light. "All right," he consented. The problem solved, they all strode happily up the stairs toward their dinner. "It has been a while since I enjoyed a drink with company," Kheane stated as they entered the noisy tavern.

"Good, I'm glad we can assist." Alkin smiled.

By the next morning they were rested, packed, mounted and ready to head down the road to the forest. The previous night they had all enjoyed a delicious meal with a drink or two for each. The men had split two rooms between them. Alexa had enjoyed a room to herself, albeit it was adjoined with Bryan's.

The innkeeper's wife had packed them plenty of fresh food and was seeing them off. Her heavy set form bustled around the big warhorses making sure everything was packed especially well in all the saddlebags. "I still think yer all bordering on crazy to enter that uncanny wood," she said for the hundredth time. She was double checking Hazerk's saddle bag. "The men don't even hunt in there it's so peculiar, too many strange creatures and things happening. Jest be real careful. Hope ya make it to the other side. Ya know it's no trouble at all to go around the worst of it. It's not that far out of the way."

"Yes, but we're in a hurry," Alkin persisted. He had been trying to convince her since the evening before that they were in their right minds, without betraying their mission. It was proving difficult.

"Can't see why is all…jest can't. There's no reason to go in there. We've got roads headed toward Kaltraz. Jest travel a bit to the west, then north is all. *Around* Carthorn," she went on.

"Yes, we do thank you for your advice and most especially for the lodging, the horse care and the food. It's greatly appreciated. You needn't worry. We'll make it through," Alkin said as the stout woman paused at Sapharan's muzzle.

"We thank you, sir! Ya've help us out very much." She gave the horse a pat and grinned up at the Prince. The innkeepers didn't know he was the Prince of Shelkite. They were under the impression he was a wealthy merchant on business. Alkin had paid them well over what the expense was. The family was pleased.

"All right, we should be off," Bryan said with authority, although, he was smiling at the kind woman.

"Yeah, well if I can't convince ya not to go that direction, then ya must know that there have been rumors of a strange woman that lives in there. Jest be careful. They say she knows magic and has two demon dogs to defend her. Don't want ya all to be waylaid by some witch." With that, the innkeeper's wife smiled and clasped her hands together expectantly. She was apparently done trying to dissuade.

At the mention of a witch the men looked at Alexa with sheepish grins. However, her eyes were dancing and she smiled widely, showing her set of nice teeth as she regarded the woman.

The innkeeper's wife didn't seem to notice the significant smiles amongst them. She glanced at the grinning Alexa, and said, "Ya *are* jest the prettiest thing ever; so slender with ya long raven hair and starry blue eyes. I wish I had a girl of me own." She sighed longingly.

"Women must be scarce around here then?" Hazerk asked gravely.

"No," the woman said puzzled, not comprehending the joke at first. Then she suddenly scowled at the men's chuckles and Alexa's rolled eyes. "Ah! Now that was unkind!" she scolded Hazerk, shaking a finger at him and the others for laughing.

"Aw, it's all right. Alexa knows I'm joking. She's like the little sister I never wanted." He looked fondly at Alexa with bright eyes.

"Right! As if I need another brother," Alexa laughed.

"Well, good luck to ya all. And watch yerself, lassie, with all these men." The innkeeper's wife smiled and waved as they reined their mounts around and headed north. They said their farewells and set to traveling again.

They met up with Apollos at the forest's perimeter. The unicorn was looking lively and well rested. He held his head high and his tail at an arch, his horn twinkled mysteriously in the early morning light. Tossing his head vigorously and snorting in the wind, he greeted them merrily. "All well, humans?" he asked with a mischievous glint in his eyes.

"As well as we can be, considering we're about to march into that," Bryan stated as he looked venturesomely through the dark trees of Carthorn.

"Are you going to give us another speech before we go in, Apollos?" Hazerk inquired, "Because as long as there is nothing worse than a hoard of pixies in there, I think we can handle it." He ended with a throaty laugh.

"I guess there's nothing more to say then. Although, I can assure you there *are* things much worse than some stupid pixies. But I spent almost two years in this forest, and I got out alive. I know its surprises well enough, I hope. But I'm sure it can still pull a good one on us if it wants," Apollos said.

"Two years! Why?" Eelyne asked astounded.

"He came here to see the Guidance Naiad," Alkin answered for the unicorn.

197

"It took me to wait patiently by the shores of the Faded Sea two years for the naiad to finally answer my call," Apollos said with a snort of displeasure at the memory.

"You never found another unicorn in all that time?" Alexa asked.

"Not one. But I didn't dare wander far from the sea. I didn't want to miss my chance. I kept safe in a soft bed of moss beneath a hollowed willow at night, and stood at the shores by day; waiting, that was the price. Nothing much happened really to tell of. I did get a visit from a hungry sea-creature once. *That* was a surprise!" the unicorn said with wide eyes.

"All right, enough talk. Let's get a move on." Bryan roused his company and put a stopper on any more time consuming questions. "You guys can talk as we go."

They inched toward the forest, searching for a path. There was none. "I'll lead the way," Apollos volunteered.

"Right. Prince Alkin you ride next. Then I and Alexa will follow. Then Kheane and Warrior Eelyne you ride after Alexa. Then Warrior Hazerk and Warrior Warkan will guard the rear of the company," the Master Sword ordered out.

"Well, I guess someone has to watch the butt of this outfit. It might as well be Warkan. Better to lose him than the prince or the lady, huh?" Hazerk smiled impishly over at his fellow warrior.

Warkan grunted. "Yeah, it takes real skill to defend you all. You're all in deep trouble if you get ambushed by an army of pixies again, aren't you?"

"Oohoo," Hazerk hollered up to the others, whom were just breaching the forest. "I think Warkan made a joke! I'm not entirely sure it was a success, though. I have to think it out..." he taunted good-naturedly. The others cracked a grin and a small snicker. They were too busy concentrating on finding a path around the dense branches. Warkan didn't answer. "I'm just joking, Warkan. We need your expertise." Hazerk changed his tune as him and Warkan entered the dim woods. "You *did* specialize in weaponry," he said, eyeing Warkan's big pole ax strapped to his warhorse's saddle and the battle ax across the big man's back. "Me, I was one of the first to graduate from the medical school. And you see how much of my skill I've used on this jaunt so far…humph," Hazerk ended thoughtfully. Warkan looked pleased, but said nothing.

Apollos soon found a path to lead them by. Although it wasn't a legitimate one, it worked since they had no specific direction they were headed for, except for north to Kaltraz eventually.

The atmosphere of the forest was strange. It emitted the sense of deception at every bend. Yet, it was a glorious wonder. Its sour-sweet life sounded out loudly to the travelers. It was beautiful and sinister. The trees towered above them, blocking most of the sun's rays; although there was enough light to see by. Moss blanketed the buttress-rooted ground, and all kinds of verdant plant life flourished everywhere. Thick vines hung from the trees and all colors of fungi and mosses grew on the massive trunks.

Odd, unfamiliar noises hounded the company's ears. They knew they weren't passing by unnoticed. Creatures from the trees watched; creatures along the ground watched. Brightly colored birds flew about squawking, and monkeys hung from trees chattering. Even a couple of lazy tigers lounging on low branches watched warily with their big amber eyes as the company rode by.

The weather was unusual. One moment it was dry and the sun's rays tried desperately to pierce through the canopy of the broad-leafed trees, and then the next minute it was raining a warm, soft drizzle.

The horses were uneasy, but having their own history of grueling war training they stayed calm at their master's touch. Zhan, having been trained by Alexa since he was a foal, trusted his mistress readily. The constant comforting murmurs from the riders to the horses were the only sounds the company made for a long while as they went.

"Easy, Lord." Warkan patted his slate gray's sweaty neck. The horse tossed his nose and snorted nervously.

Hazerk's neck snapped around to face Warkan. "What did you just call him?"

"His name is Granite Lord," Warkan replied, giving his burly horse another hard pat.

"Ha! And you made fun of my Man's name," Hazerk

scoffed.

"Red Man is a child's name," Warkan said loftily. "Granite Lord is noble. Besides his coat is the color of granite. It's unique."

"Yeah, if you haven't notice, Red Man's coat is a sizzling red; more so than the normal chestnut I might add, matches my hair. We're a team through and through aren't we, big fella?" Hazerk said proudly. He gave Red Man a firm pat. The warhorse pulled at the reins impatiently and noisily chomped his bit, rolling his brown eyes back to show the whites in excitement.

"You guys both named your horses for the color of their coat; it's the same difference," Eelyne laughed.

"Does that make sense?" Hazerk asked.

"Why? What's your mount's name?" Warkan interjected.

Eelyne's warhorse was a shiny sorrel, a light chestnut coat with a flaxen mane. "I call him Swift Phoenix." The two men couldn't argue with that.

Up toward the front of the company, Alkin turned around to regard the silent Alexa. "Do you have any witch intuition pertaining to the direction we should go?" he asked a little distraughtly. He didn't need to hear her answer; he could see it in her troubled eyes.

Alexa shook her head unhappily, her lips pursed. The Prince gave her a weak smile and turned back around, speaking soothingly to Sapharan. Alexa sighed and clenched her jaw in frustration. Her eyes darted around the forest as if she thought she might see a sign or find an answer. However, she felt nothing. It seemed from the moment she stepped into this mystical wood her senses had plugged. Was it from the strange, wet mist creeping around them? Or was her own slight fear of the unknown masking it? Maybe there was magic hanging heavily in the air, hounding her from all sides and she wasn't skilled enough to block it out. Alexa felt like something had been cut off from her. Like someone was striving to suffocate her magical senses. She would speak to Apollos about it later. Hopefully by then the foggy feeling would clear up. It was an alien sensation to her; to not be able to sense the things she normally could. She looked over to Sword Bryan, who was riding alongside her. He rode coolly, looking warily ahead.

She couldn't even decipher what mood he was in. How strange!

Bryan glanced over at Alexa to see her watching at him. He was almost startled by the look in her eyes. Her sapphire eyes were darkened to midnight blue and disturbed; they didn't glitter like usual. Her normally shapely lips were pursed white. His brow furrowed as she looked away without a word. "We'll figure it out," he suddenly found himself saying to her.

She regarded him again, an eyebrow raised curiously. She didn't say anything, but gave him a weak, wry smile. Bryan found he was unable to stop himself from admiring her lips. They were attractive. They were full and perfectly shaped. He then realized he was gawking, and he felt quite ashamed he was unable to control his thoughts in the path they were headed. He was the Head-Master Sword and this was his charge; he couldn't be thinking that way. Not to mention that it was Alexa! He clenched his teeth and glared straight ahead, but not after giving her a foul look as if it were her fault he was fond of her lips.

Chapter 21

That evening they stopped earlier than usual. Bryan was aware his company was feeling stressed; a little extra down time would do them good. However, he wasn't about to waste the time. He intended to train Alexa and Eelyne tonight. He hoped it would take the troubles off Alexa's mind.

Alexa felt frazzled on the inside. She sweated anxiously for not having any magical senses. She wished she could take a walk in the forest by herself just to get her senses back in order and calm down. But there was no chance that would ever happen. Lately Sword Bryan had been watching her like a hawk. She was relieved when he decided to stop early. It was even relieving to hear him announce that she and Eelyne were going to have a lesson. She hoped the physical work out might clear her mind.

They found a spacious grove of trees seemingly without anything lurking around. They un-tacked and rubbed down the tired horses. Hazerk and Warkan prepared a fire and began fixing the meal. Alkin plopped down at the foot of a robust broad-leafed tree. Resting his head against the bark he contemplatively gazed up to the bits of the dusky, purple sky peeking through the forest's canopy.

To both Alexa and Eelyne's delight Bryan let them sit down and relax for a bit. Kheane sat at the fire silently watching the company. The blue-black Blize stood lazily over his shoulder with a hind hoof cocked.

Alexa had remembered to ask Eelyne about the possibility of evil magic invading her dreams and eliciting visions. He had been diligently trying to find an answer for her since.

As he leafed through one of his books, Alexa sat cross-legged next to him and peered over to the text. Apollos stood above the young warrior's shoulder so he, too, could read the words. The three of them quietly discussed Alexa's dream as they perused.

"There isn't any way it's your blood connection to Ret that gave you your vision. I'm sure of it. It'd be more fitting happening to your father than you. Him being his twin," Eelyne whispered earnestly.

Alexa narrowed her eyes and scanned the page. There were many things on precinct and visions, but nothing sounded similar to what she had experienced. There was no chance she was precinct. She had never had visions before; and to discredit the claim that her powers might be blossoming, she hadn't had any since.

Eelyne continued quietly, "The only thing I can figure is that some magical object with an intimate connection with Ret gave you the vision, like somehow it passed on its history to you. If it belonged to Ret it would be able to expose his plans. And since you're sensitive to those kinds of things you got the story loud and clear."

"That makes sense," Apollos said, "But, Alexa, you've never met Ret. Do you have anything that might have belonged to him at one time? A family heirloom?" he inquired.

"No," she said despairingly. There was a pause, and then she remembered something. Eelyne and the unicorn were surprised to see her morose countenance change so quickly to realization and excitement.

"What?" Eelyne asked.

"This is a far stretch, but…." She pulled out the necklace that Lady Adama had given her. She held it in her hand for them to see. It glinted in the flicking light of the fire. They stared at it thoughtfully.

Apollos snorted disdainfully, "That reeks of magic. And I can tell you it's not pleasant. Where'd you get it?"

Alexa's eyes deepened to a midnight blue. "I thought I felt something, but I'm not experienced enough to tell if it is good or bad."

"You should be able to tell with that. It bodes evil." The unicorn was alarmed.

Alexa's brow furrowed. She leaned in to whisper, "Lady Adama gave it to me. She said it was given to her by the only wizard she ever knew." Alexa growled and clenched her teeth. "I should have realized! How could I be so stupid? My father and Ret are the only two wizards left she could have possibility known …at least in Eetharum. It couldn't have been my father; he's never

203

spoken of knowing her."

"That's interesting…." Apollos said emphatically.

"Come to think of it, I think I was bewitched not to feel the evil magic in this thing," she said in an excited whisper. "When I stepped into her room I *felt* something evil. In fact, I'd been feeling something bad in the air since I had entered the castle, but not after my meeting with Lady Adama. She had a fire going in the hearth; Ret could have sent her something to burn to mask my senses," she said philosophically, a glitter in her eyes.

"You are speculating a lot," Apollos said. He was reluctant to blame Alkin's mother of being a trader. Alexa stared at him. Coming quickly back from her theory, she suddenly realized she was accusing a person of royalty, which could possibly mean her death.

"Yes, but…." she faltered.

Eelyne just stared at her, not daring to utter a word, lest the Prince should hear.

"This is what I figure," Apollos said gravely, "that thing is responsible for your dream. Maybe Lady Adama knows of its origin and maybe she doesn't, but at any rate it's been in Ret's care at one time. And now it's found its way to you and it has either done its job by warning you or it has another more sinister job we can't openly see. I can't imagine Ret would go through the trouble of cursing an object and making sure it gets to your hands just to warn you of what he's up to. It doesn't make any sense. In fact, I'm sure he probably wasn't planning to warn you. The vision was just a side effect of what it may have done to you."

Alexa stared blankly at the unicorn. "Done to me…"

"I wish you'd shown me that necklace earlier. Get rid of it. I'm afraid it may have done its damage already, but we can't be too sure," Apollos said earnestly, fear was evident in his normally serene chocolate eyes.

Alexa threw the pendant to the ground like it had turned into a snake. The three of them stared at it; and Apollos ground it into the earth with his hoof as far as he could. Alexa stared silently at the patch of dirt where the necklace had disappeared into, her eyes wide with disbelief.

"What about Lady Adama?" she whispered hesitantly.

"Don't worry of that now," Apollos said grimly. "I'm reluctant to believe she has done this knowingly. And if she has, then we have an even graver problem than I thought. It means we have a trader, and the Prince, his sister and Shelkite are in more danger than originally thought. But let's not think of it. We have to work on stopping Ret in the only way we know how right now," the unicorn said almost desperately.

The three of them sat in a bleak silence, their eyes miles away in pensive thought. Alexa was now glad she had been smart enough to have asked Melea to watch over Shelkite's castle. There was definitely need of it.

Bryan had been watching the discussion between Eelyne, Alexa and Apollos with curiosity. The conversation looked like a serious one, judging by all their faces. He watched from the corner of his eye as Alexa threw a piece of jewelry to the ground as if it had bit her, and then Apollos menacingly grind it into the soft earth. Eelyne looked on speechless.

The Master Sword stole a glance at the Prince. He appeared not to know of the anxious, whispered conversation only yards away from where he was sitting. But Bryan knew Alkin was good at pretending. When one was sure he was paying no attention, the Prince was actually listening with rapt ears.

The others paid no heed; all but Kheane, Bryan noted. This caused a twist in Bryan's gut. This man was hanging around and gathering a ton of information on them. He was always listening and watching, never saying a word, never really proving his allegiance. He was still too shady for the Master Sword's comfort. The interest Alexa showed in the dark man and the idea that Kheane seemed to have knowledge of her bothered Bryan all the more. He was sincerely hoping Kheane didn't mean her or them any harm. Unless he got more answers from the shady man he wasn't going to trust him alone with even Dragon.

Bryan was agitated with all the secrets. For some reason it was bothering him a great deal that Alexa was hiding something from him, more than the whole Kheane situation. What had she held back in her story from him and the Prince? What was she whispering about so candidly with Apollos and Eelyne now?

These boiling questions came to the surface in a hot, annoyed temper. He stood abruptly and ordered brusquely for Eelyne and her to get their swords.

The two popped up out of their conversation and hurried to attention for practice.

He had them fight each other one on one for a warm-up. Then he joined in for the two on one routine. At this point, he decided he wanted to make them really work hard, forgetting about his earlier plan of just working them to clear their thoughts.

"Okay, now you're going to have to put in some effort," he stated austerely. "Warrior Warkan! Get over here and fight on Warrior Eelyne's side with your ax. Alexa and I'll be a team. Then we'll switch."

Warkan snapped out of his lazy position around the fire. He looked devilishly at them. He was apparently in a good mood and happy the Master Sword was using him as a teacher.

Bryan could smell Alexa and feel the heat of her as she worked relentlessly beside him. She was still a little feeble at her swordsmanship, but she was getting better every time. Her confidence was certainly better. Bryan let them go around this way for a while. He noticed they were getting tired. Eelyne and Warkan were sweating and Alexa was groaning every time she blocked a heavy blow from Warkan's ax. Her advances and attacks were also getting weaker.

"Okay, stop. Let's switch," he ordered.

They switched to where Eelyne and Alexa were a team. They found Warkan and the Master Sword were quite a tough team to hold off.

Soon, Alexa stopped abruptly. Resting her sword tip on the ground, she leaned wearily on its hilt. "I need a break!" She glared at Bryan with snapping eyes. Why was he making her suffer when she was sure he knew her mind was already overworked with worries?

The others stopped, too, grateful for Alexa voicing their thoughts, but not wanting the Master Sword to know.

Bryan stared back at her with his own pair of blazing eyes.

He clenched his jaw and eyed her as she breathed heavily, bent over her sword. "All right, just a quick one," he consented. What was he planning? To work her to death to get her to reveal her secrets? He scolded himself. But still in a temper, he said despite his thoughts, "In battle there won't be any breaks you know." He stalked over and plopped down by the fire across from Kheane, wiping his sweaty forehead. He glared into the flames, unaware of Kheane's perceptive eyes on him.

Alexa and the two men reluctantly came over and sat down. Alexa sat on the far side, giving her satchel an angry shove. It turned over and the Alidonian weapon toppled out. She snatched it up to store it back in the bag, but Kheane broke the tense silence with his coarse voice.

"You know how to use that?" he asked, gesturing at the oddly shaped weapon.

The whole of the company looked up at his voice, curious. Bryan's clear blue eyes eyed Kheane harshly.

"Well…I've never used it. I bought it in Yilvana Port. It's Alidonian. Why? Do you?" she said, still breathing heavily from her exertion.

Kheane's dark coffee-colored eyes smiled in the low light. The majority of his face still hid in shadows of his hood. He reached inside his cloak and pulled a weapon out that was the exact make of the one she held in her hand.

Alexa's eyes widened and an excited look came over her face. "You have one, too! Can you show me how to use it?"

Kheane chuckled, it was low and raspy. "Of course," he said with a slight condescending glance at the Master Sword, who stared back with a lofty raised eyebrow. Kheane stood up and walked to the clearing where they had just practiced their bouts. Alexa rose and hastily followed him. "Not tired?" Kheane asked.

"Nope," she answered breathless.

"All right, watch." And he bent his arm back and flung the weapon. It whizzed over the others' heads, causing them to duck automatically. It turned and came back to its master's hand.

Alexa stared agape. She looked down to the instrument in her hand. It was a bent blade. The hilt was just big enough to wrap one hand around and the blade was broad and extremely sharp. Sharp enough to slice through a man's neck and still travel back to its thrower's hand.

Alexa bent her arm back to have a go, but a chorus of exclamations from the suddenly fearful company stopped her abruptly.

"Not over here!"

"Are you trying to behead us?" Hazerk cried with wide eyes.

"Do it that way!" Bryan hollered, amused now and forgetting his anger.

"Oh, sorry." Alexa grinned sheepishly and turned to toss the weapon in the opposite direction. It didn't come back.

"Humph...." Grunting, Alexa moved to go retrieve it, but Kheane put out a stern hand to stop her from marching into the forest.

"I'll get it."

He came back a moment later and demonstrated once more how to throw it. To the company's fearful annoyance and a little bit to their amusement he sent it whizzing over their heads again.

"Will you stop?" Warkan said icily.

Kheane just chuckled, and to the company's delight demonstrated a few times more in another direction.

"Wait a minute," Bryan suddenly said with realization in a tone that stopped all action. He was looking at Kheane frostily. The others stopped their excited chatter over Kheane's talent.

The Master Sword marched over to Kheane and faced him. "Hold out your left arm," he ordered starkly. For a moment Kheane just stared at him unfalteringly. It seemed he wasn't going to obey. But a yielding look came into his eyes and he held up his forearm. Bryan shoved back the sleeve of Kheane's cloak and revealed a marking on his skin of a black wolf's head. Blood dripped from its snarling fangs. "That looks familiar," Bryan said triumphantly holding up Kheane's arm for the others to see.

"Yeah!" Eelyne stated and dove for one of his books.

"You need to tell us who you are." Bryan regarded the dark, silent man again. "This is too dangerous for us to let you to continue traveling with us. Your name sounds familiar, you know of our task, you've spoken to Ret, you know Alexa; and you're obviously a very good killer."

Silently, Alkin rose and came to stand with them. "I promise we will consider everything before turning you away, but we need to know the truth," he said.

Kheane didn't speak, but eyed the company discerningly.

Then Eelyne spoke up excitedly, "Look, I've found it! I thought the marking looked familiar. It's in this text."

Bryan and the others hastened to look at the picture. There, mid-way through a page, the exact drawing of the wolf baring bloodied teeth was.

"I thought it looked familiar. I'm a history addict." Bryan smiled at his finding, "I saw it on his arm when he raised his hand to throw the weapon."

Eelyne summarized the passage with enthusiasm, "It says here the man bearing this symbol is called the Cold Wolf, a lurid assassin from the northern country of Sushron, a man of old Alidonian blood. He rose up two hundred years after the Lost War, when restructuring of the allied countries was still in process. It says he was trained by an infamous assassin's order, but broke loose and took jobs on himself, becoming the most feared and deadliest man in Eetharum. It says that people, not knowing his real name, named him the Keen Wolf or more commonly, the Cold Wolf, for his cruel and callous killings. His taken name, Kheane, derives from the theory he's as keen as a hunting wolf. His blood is sought in Sushron and almost every country in Eetharum, but he's also worked for many Eetharum royals surreptitiously." Eelyne stopped emphatically and stared up at the man known as the Cold Wolf speechless.

Chapter 22

"I…I don't understand…"Alexa faltered, apparently upset this man was not the person she was hoping he was. "The Lost War ended over five hundred years ago…that would make you over three hundred years old. Only wizards live to be that old. You don't look a day past forty," she ended perplexedly.

Bryan didn't wait for Kheane to answer, but stated knowledgably, "He's of old Alidonian blood. They're the only race in the entire world other than wizards to have long lives like that. But they are dying out fast. If there are any left, they are all in hiding like Kheane. In Alidon, about three hundred years ago, there was a brutal civil war. The old Alidonians, the long-lived ones, had been in slavery for many years by a new breed of Alidonians that could trace their ancestry back to foreign regions. There was a rebellion and many of the old race were killed."

"Yes," Kheane suddenly spoke, his raspy voice catching all the company's rapt attentions. "I was only sixteen when the war broke out. I was a slave to a wealthy family. The land was in chaos. I've never seen so much gore and hate as I did in that war, even now with all my years of shedding blood and dealing revenge. If you must know, in order to trust me, I'll tell you about myself."

Alkin and Bryan looked at each other significantly and nodded their heads. The others settled down around the fire to hear Kheane's tale.

"The family I was owned by was killed. I woke one night to find the slave homes ablaze and the family strung up by their necks and burning. I decided at that point I was going to escape Alidon. I wanted no part of the war. I wanted freedom, but I wanted it in another world far away from the wretched land that was only a sad remnant of my ancestors' home. Many of my fellow slaves went to war, but I had no family and no ties. I went to the shore to find the merchant ships docked at port. I had many times wandered past them on some errand or other dreaming that someday I could sail away on them to a new world. But the merchants would have nothing of me sailing with them, though I begged them. They didn't want any part of the war and they certainly didn't want to be caught with a slave aboard their ships. I hid by the bay watching the ships for days, contriving my plan. There I met a girl scheming to do the same."

Kheane paused. His black eyes glittered in the low firelight at the memory and he smiled in the depths of his hood. Alexa noted his eyes were worlds away, centuries away, and she wondered if they were seeing the only beautiful memory in his dark life.

"She was the same age as me and also a slave. Her owners had been killed along with her family. Since we were both orphans we bonded quickly. We made plans to stowaway on one of the ships. And that's exactly what we did. It took months to travel to Eetharum from Alidon. But, in my three hundred years I have to say it was the best three months of my life. Though we both were always in a state of fear for being discovered, we made plans for the future. We planned to stay together and help each other out. When our journey came close to an end and we were days from docking safely at Yilvana Port, there was a violent storm. The ship was wrecked and we were separated in the storm. I grabbed some scrap to float on. And although I called and searched the waters, I never could find her. Many of the men lived from the wreck and I was sure, and still hope, that she survived. She was strong and smart. It could be that she had only been blown away from the rest of us. Well, I and the rest of the men floated to shore. In Yilvana Port I was taken under the wing of a man who worked for the assassin's order in Sushron. I was forced to leave my lost companion behind. There I worked and trained for many, many years. I was renamed from my birth name to Kheane. And I earned that reputation you just so rightly read out of that history book.

Eventually, I wanted to be on my own and I broke away from the Order at a hard cost. I was the best assassin in the Order, the best in the world. With my weapon I had brought with me from Alidon I was unstoppable. I took jobs I only wanted to. I did many things I would like to forget. I mostly killed the not-so-innocent…but sometimes the innocent, if necessary. I told myself it was all only to survive at first, but over the years it became who I was. I helped out a lot with the reconstruction of Eetharum, doing in people and royals that were still trying to cause problems after the Lost War. That's its rightful name, too. Everyone, blinded by hate, had lost the real reason they were fighting about. It ended in a stalemate. The land went into a dark recession for two hundred years. Eetharum was badly wounded from it. So, hunting down one assassin wasn't enough for the rulers to focus their attentions on during that time. I became very good at not being found and doing my jobs quietly."

Kheane paused and waited to hear if his listeners had anything to say. They all waited patiently, completely immersed in the tale, even the Master Sword. "Well, I can't go through every bit of my history. That would take three hundred years." His voice smiled. "But I will tell you, that finally one day I had had enough. And it is true; I don't want to be an assassin any more. I'm done killing for an occupation. I just want to look for the girl that came over with me. I've kept a vigilant eye out for her all these years during my travels, but I've found nothing. I came to Yoldor in hope to find some evidence of her. But I'm afraid it's in vain. And it seems my past has a way of stamping me as a menace. I can't go anywhere without suspicious eyes prying. But, yes, I was offered a job by Ret at a good price. I thought, even though at the time I had already decided to retire, that it may be worth my while to go and check it out. I traveled secretly to Zelka and met with the wizard. He told me of his plan. He was sure a vile creature such as me would join him. Well, let's say I did agree and I went to Kaltraz to scout out this young witch I was to capture and bring to him."

Alexa stared open-mouthed at Kheane. The dark man continued regardless of the frosty reactions he was now receiving from the company.

"I watched you for days, Alexa. I saw you racing around on your horse and being harassed by your brothers. I watched you shoot your bow, and I saw you with your family in your home. I decided then and there I wasn't going to be a catalyst of a war. I was on the verge of working for the wrong side. And as funny as this sounds, when I was my own master, I only took missions I thought worthy and this was not one. So, I ran. I ran to Shelkite, the place where my second mission was to take place, given to me by Ret. I was to assassinate the Prince of Shelkite."

At this, Alkin perked up, understanding and recognition was evident all over his features. He stood regarding Kheane forebodingly. "It was you! You threatened me. You came into my room that night."

Kheane's eyes smiled slyly.

Bryan abruptly stood and drew his sword, gazing at Kheane with flaming eyes. *Curse the cold-blooded murder to hell, anyway!*

Kheane threw his head back and laughed condescendingly, eyeing the sword Bryan held at his throat. "No offence, Master Sword, but if I wanted to, I could have severed your throat before you even drew your sword. I know you're good. I've watched you, but you are no match for me. I've been killing men for three hundred years. I'm sure I could take on all of you."

"Don't be so proud, Kheane, you'll fall into your own pit." Bryan seethed. "So you're the one who put all this into play. You threatened Prince Alkin; and then I was ordered to become a Master Sword, while Apollos was sent for answers. And now Alexa's in danger...." Bryan faltered, lowering his sword, suddenly aware, "but...it was all necessary." Hearing himself recount everything, he understood Kheane's perspective.

"Yes, wisely stated, Master Sword. Forgive my arrogance. You must understand my background has called for it many times for survival. But, don't you see? I was sent to murder your prince, and instead I threatened his life giving him a warning to save his own life, forcing him to take action. And now look, we're all out to stop Ret. If I had just killed you, prince," Kheane regarded the shocked Alkin, "It would've been all over. Ret would be one more step ahead. I did it that way to save myself and prevent an outright war."

"I don't understand. Why me? Solely, I'm unimportant to Ret's plans. How'd you breach my castle walls and get past my guards? And I finally know why at hearing your voice it made me shudder. You came to my chamber during the night, cloaked and hooded in black and said some horrid things."

"Yes, to save you. I warned you of the wizard in an indistinct way, to scare you into looking into his affairs. Do you understand my reasoning? I want to help. I want to see quiet amongst people. My whole life has been surrounded by nothing but hatred and bloodshed. I'm done. I want to live in as much peace as possible. To know that life can be kind. But first, more blood must be taken to end the trouble Ret is causing.

You are an important piece. Ret wants all the countries under his control. Shelkite is a strong country. He felt you were his biggest threat. Dispatching you would leave the country without an heir. It would have caused discord—an easy in for him. And, as for how I breached your castle, that is centuries of experience. I'll tell you, though, if it had been a hundred years ago when I was desperate and didn't care if I lived and when I hated others for loving and living happily, I wouldn't have spared a single man in your castle or you. I would have soaked your warm, lovemaking sheets with the blood of you and the lovely woman I caught in your arms. I could have, but I didn't." Kheane ended smugly.

The others looked at Alkin with curious eyes. Surprisingly, Alkin blushed under their stares, but the shadows from the fire hid him.

"What woman?" Hazerk openly teased, momentarily forgetting Alkin was his prince, "I didn't know there was a potential Princess of Shelkite about."

"I don't…" Alkin hesitated, "She…I…it can't ever work out for political reasons." Alkin looked wryly away from the company's interested eyes. *I'm the Prince of Shelkite, what am I doing explaining myself?*

Bryan knew; it had just come to him. The woman was a pretty, cow-eyed brunette with silky, bouncy curls. And she held strong ties with the country of Zelka. He was sure of it. However, he didn't say a word. Alkin's business was his business.

"None-the-less," Kheane started again with amusement at his purposely placed controversial statement. "I've changed. I'm not so much begrudging of others. It took years to change, by the way. And now I want to live happily, if I can, with your help." He ended his speech there. He had shown a much more sensitive side than he had intended to, but he was desperate to help and be a part of this company. He needed human contact and companionship.

He had been alone, friendless and hateful for so many years. He was tired of it. After a moment of silence, Kheane looked around to all the company's thoughtful faces. Had they understood his logic behind everything? Did they believe he meant them no harm and was giving up being an assassin? They did; he could tell. "So, do I stay?" he asked.

"Yes," Alkin answered immediately. "You saved my life and another's, not to mention you didn't take Alexa to Ret. Now that we know about you, Kheane, I trust you. You're here to stay and help the company. And we'll protect you because of it. Do you all agree?" He turned and addressed the others for their input. They nodded in consent, even Sword Bryan, who was still smarting from Kheane's earlier remark on his skills.

Kheane regarded Bryan, noting that he still didn't wholly trust him, but was willing to accept the others' decisions. "Do you trust now that I could watch out for Alexa by myself?"

Bryan narrowed his eyes and said dryly, "Yes, but don't ask to again."

"I won't unless you say so," Kheane answered. And then he added with a sly grin that reached his eyes, "Just so you know, you are the best swordsman I've seen in a couple of centuries, other than myself, of course."

The Master Sword raised a wry eyebrow, but nodded curtly in thanks.

"Kheane," Alexa perked up, "What's your real name? The one you came over to Eetharum with."

"It has no meaning anymore. I'm not the same person," he stated in a curt close-ended way.

This didn't deter Alexa, "The orphan girl is the reason you keep going, isn't she? What does she look like? We all will keep an eye out for her."

"She used to be. But, like I said, it's useless. She's probably dead," he answered in a sour-realistic way.

"Can we see your face?" she pried on.

"Alexa, stop it," Bryan scolded, "You have the strangest notions, girl. Leave the man alone."

"I've been burning to ask these questions forever," she

stated pointedly.

"Well, if you must." Kheane reached up and pulled down the hood obscuring his face. They all stared wide-eyed as the reason for the hood was revealed. A long, raised, purple scar was seared across Kheane's face. It started at the corner of his right eye and ran down to his lips where the corner of his mouth was deformed. The scar then disappeared down over his chin to his neck and down into his shirt. On the left side of his face, he had red and purple scars slashed across his cheek as if a beast had swiped at him with claws. His nose looked as if it had been broken a few times over and had been badly set back.

"I stand out too much with a mess of a face like this. And if you think this is bad, you should see the rest of me…not the soft flesh of a babe." At this he gave out a hoarse, sardonic laugh.

The company was speechless as Kheane silently placed the hood back over his ruthlessly scarred head. The scars seemed to have reached down past his skin and into the very flesh of his torn soul.

Alexa felt a powerful surge of pity for Kheane. She was completely awed at him, his whole story. It was so exotic, callous and romantic all together. At hearing his story, Alexa couldn't stop her womanly romantic heart from coming to the surface, an innate sensitivity she had no control over. She usually hated it so much, but this time she didn't fight the feeling. She desperately wished Kheane could have all the happiness in the world and even secretly envisioned herself with him.

"Alexa," Bryan's voice shot sharply through her imaginings. "I think Kheane's a little too old for you, considering you're seventeen and he's three hundred."

The company all laughed, including Kheane in his luring, cold voice. Alexa started and blushed, and gave her Sword-Guard a deadly glare.

Bryan had been watching her closely. He noted the change in her face, seeing a starry frost come over her eyes. He had to put a stop to it. Although, he didn't like the guilty feeling he had acquired from embarrassing her.

"Who said I was interested? I'm not seventeen anyway. I'm

over eighteen." She stood up with as much dignity as she could muster, brushed off her pants and stalked over to pet Zhan, away from the men's teasing stares, where she could blush crimson all by herself.

"When did that happen? You were only seventeen when we called for you?" Alkin said, in good spirits. He had gotten over his shock quickly and had forgiven Kheane fully. He planned to help the tortured man anyway he could by clearing his name.

"The day of my birth past while I was traveling to Shelkite," she said, feeding Zhan a piece of dried apple.

"Humph, anyway." Alkin turned to Kheane and said, "Before we turn in for the night, what is it you want from us? You said you wanted our help?"

"Just for your royal protection, if you deem it worthy," he answered.

"Right, and you will have it. When this is over I will make sure you have a safe place to live and your peace," the Prince stated sincerely. Kheane nodded gratefully.

They ate their supper in a comfortable silence. Everyone felt better since Kheane's clandestine life was revealed. Kheane himself actually felt better than he had in a long time. It was a good comfort to have others in his confidence. It was a like a wet, suffocating veil had been peeled off his face. He ate his food in a contented state.

The only person feeling a qualm was Alexa. She munched on her food with an unsteady sensation pulsing through her veins. She had come to the point where she felt she needed to tell everyone the purpose Ret intended for her. She also felt it was direly important everyone should know about the pendant, that it might have altered her. This was extremely important. This was *her* company. She didn't want to put them in any harm, especially if it ended up being her doing the harm. Besides, she remembered, it was *her* who had let her temper go because Prince Alkin and Sword Bryan were having a private conversation without her.

The notion further bothered her because she had felt Bryan's curious and irritated eyes on her all evening, not to mention the Prince was throwing her suspicious glances, too. She knew they knew she was holding something back from them. They were uneasy about it. Apollos had said it was fine; so they had accepted her silence. But Alexa realized she was being unfair to them. They needed her to be honest. They were here to help her. She shouldn't keep anything from them so they could help her. She would tell them everything, even if it meant the Prince would have her hung for heresy.

Alexa swallowed her food and cleared her throat, looking out around the fire to all their faces. Everyone looked up expectantly. Apollos recognized what she was doing and bobbed his head with encouragement, his eyes alight with comfort.

"I…um…haven't told you all the reason Ret wants me. I know why Kheane was to take me to him," she said hesitantly, and then added to Kheane, "Do you know why?"

"No. But, I'm sure it wasn't for a family reunion. I do know, though, that he's paranoid of wizards becoming extinct. He's obsessed with finding full-bloods." Kheane said.

"Yes, partly. I think he believes he can use me to right that problem," she replied.

"Go ahead, Alexa," Alkin prompted gently.

She looked at all of their anticipating faces and landed on the handsome Sword's. He was watching her attentively with his shiny azure eyes. His face held no irritation now, but strangely enough he looked slightly compassionate. Alexa locked eyes with him; he didn't turn away.

She then told them everything as she gazed into Bryan's encouraging face. She explained of Ret's plan to use her body as a shell to harbor creatures and bring them into the world. She told them of how Ret was planning to use her brothers and her to do this, by siphoning out their magic blood. She explained that he wanted to create his own breed of full-blooded wizards. Ones under his power and that would help conquer the countries.

Then, hesitantly and tactfully, Alexa explained to them about the pendant she was given. She told of how Apollos and Eelyne had recently discovered that whatever the pendant's purpose was it was entirely wicked. She dared not look at the Prince when she revealed this detail. She kept her eyes completely focused on the unwavering and emotionless Master Sword, only briefly flicking her eyes to Apollos for certainty.

By the time she ended her account, she noted with distress she was trembling slightly. Sitting cross-legged on the ground, she quickly tucked her sweaty palms in her lap to steady them. There was a few agonizing moments of silence as everyone digested her words and their food. Hazerk awkwardly stifled a loud belch.

Kheane spoke first, "Prince," he said to Alkin delicately. "I was going to tell you, from what I could gather in my meeting with Ret, I think there is a good chance someone in Fordorn is assisting him. I'm not saying it's your mother, but I'm sure he has an accomplice."

"Alkin, there's a good chance your mother doesn't know about the pendant's origin," Apollos added earnestly.

The Prince was quiet as his hazel eyes thoughtfully followed the colorful, flickering flames of the fire. After a moment the handsome prince sighed and looked up to the anxious faces watching him. "Alexa said she claimed a wizard *gave* it to her. I love my mother dearly, but she has changed strangely over the years. She's different from what I remember as a child," he stated desolately. He regarded Alexa intensely. Alexa was anxious, and sucked in a breath of air. But Alkin merely smiled sadly and said "You're frightened because of what you felt you had to tell me. Don't be. You did the right thing. You told us everything you know. I have no reason to condemn you for your suspicions." He looked thoughtfully away into the fire. "If what you say is true… then, in theory, my people are very much in danger, my home…my sister. I'm positive Dorsa is ignorant to this. She has a heart of gold. I'd thought Shelkite was safe…at least until Ret's armies came for us. But if he has an inside hand, my homeland is in just as much danger as Galeon, maybe more." He groaned and dropped his head into his hands. "What have I done?" he exclaimed to himself, "I've left my castle exposed! My sister is defenseless!"

"Not completely, my prince," Bryan interjected encouragingly, "The warriors are still there, with the guards and a Master Sword. They are all trained well."

"Not if the problem is eating them from the inside. They

will be caught off guard and be unprepared," he lamented.

"There is one watchful eye," Alexa broke in hesitantly. "Before I left, I felt something was amiss. And I asked a trustworthy person to be extra vigilant. I made her vow and I know she'll keep it. I can be very persuasive…it's part of my blood." Alexa smiled slyly, hoping to hearten the distraught prince.

"Her? Who?" Alkin said.

"Melea. One of your servants," Alexa answered.

"Melea, my servant?" Bryan said incredulously.

"Yes. She's smart and good. I sensed it in her. I told her to send for help if anything seemed wrong. *Anything*. She was to send for a Master Sword, or for you Prince Alkin, or she was to ride to Galeon for help."

"She agreed even behind my back?" Alkin asked skeptically.

"Only because she knew it would be protecting you," Alexa replied quickly.

Alkin heaved a sigh and slumped back, "I'm a horrible ruler…I've deserted my people…my sister, perhaps my mother. If only there were a way to see what was happening back home." Sitting up straighter with hope, he asked Alexa, "Is there?"

Alexa shook her head sadly. "I don't know how. I haven't been taught."

"I guess I'll just have to wait until we reach Galeon for news, but that could be months," Alkin said resignedly.

"We could send someone for news, and then rendezvous in Kaltraz," Bryan suggested. "I could go." Alexa's eyes snapped up in alarm to look at him. Bryan gazed at her thoughtfully. He didn't know why he proposed to go. He knew he had a responsibility here. And he knew he didn't want to leave it. "But, I can't. I've pledged to be a Sword-Guard," he said, realizing he was strangely pleased to see Alexa's troubled reaction.

"No, you can't," Alkin agreed.

"I could," Kheane said.

"No. You're needed here." Alkin set his jaw, raising his chin defiantly, "No one will go. Alexa selected this company for a reason; and we're sticking together. I'll have to trust that my land

and people are in good hands. I'll send for word immediately once we get where we can." Alkin glanced around at his surroundings. It was completely dark and the white moon's rays gleamed through the shadowy branches. A light breeze picked up and the company shivered as it whispered eerily through the trees. They were suddenly aware of the strange sounds emitting from around them. "I think we've momentarily forgotten where we are…"Alkin said a little nervously. "Let's get some sleep and start out early. So we can get going and get out of here as soon as we can." He began to unroll his blankets and situate himself.

"Even in all my years," Kheane stated as they all settled in their beds around the still blazing fire, "I've never ventured into Carthorn."

"Yes," Apollos said mysteriously, "we can't forget where we are. This forest will pretend to be your friend, but it always undoubtedly turns its back on you when you least expect it. I'll take the first watch."

Alexa settled in her blanket as close to the fire as she dared to without singeing herself. It was a comfort. Zhan crept up behind her to doze protectively over her shoulder. Bryan settled as near to her as they both felt comfortable with; and Hazerk slept on her opposite side.

Bryan sensed Alexa tossing around. She flipped around to face him. They were feet apart, but it suddenly felt odd, unlike it had even days before. He glanced over to find her long lashes closed quietly over her eyes. She was breathing easily. Bryan smiled inwardly. He was glad she had shared her secrets with them. They weren't what he had expected, but it still made his gut churn at the thought of anything that horrid happening to her. And, although he had vowed to be her Sword-Guard weeks ago in her chamber back in Fordorn, he promised himself over again he wouldn't let her fate be what she feared.

With eyes closed and trying desperately to drift off to sleep, Alexa listened to the forest sounds. They were a bit unsettling, but she knew she was safe with her company, especially with Sword Bryan and now Kheane. She smiled, thinking fondly of the men that slept around her. All of them, even the unicorn, were her closest companions. She wished avidly in her heart that they would be okay in the end.

As she listened to the soft snoring of the company, something pricked Alexa's heart, causing sleep to elude her. It was the idea of something or someone. She couldn't identify it at first. She had been experiencing unfamiliar emotions lately. She had struggled with them. She had tried to snuff them out or hide them away, but they were becoming more untamable. She didn't want to admit to what they might be.

She clenched her jaw and buried her face in her blanket, biting down on the coarse material with her teeth, wanting to shriek in frustration. She realized she was becoming exactly what she detested. She knew Bryan had noted it in her that very night. She had become starry eyed with silly romantic notions.

Alexa had had boys come around asking for her back at home, but her brothers had always kept them away. And the only one they allowed around was one Alexa heartily wished they wouldn't. They did this as a joke, because he was such a nuisance to her. She rolled her eyes at the thought of him.

Alexa had always been satisfied with doing her own thing, not worrying of clothes and pretty things. She had always made sure she was pleasantly presentable, but she had never actively pursued boys like other girls her age did. Sure, she may have kissed at least one handsome young man helping her attend her family's sheep one afternoon just for an experiment…But, now, her own mind was betraying her.

Heart thumping, Alexa decided there under her blankets to just face the fact and get it over with. On her back, staring through the threads of the blanket to the dim world outside, she admitted to herself she found Kheane extremely alluring. He was wrapped in a cloak of mystery and danger any woman would be attracted to. But what Alexa couldn't, wouldn't, admit to was what Sword Bryan's eyes had silently rendered to her, and how she felt tremendously delighted about it.

The Master Sword had treated her differently lately. He was no longer looking at her with disdain. His eyes held more depth now when he gazed at her, alluding to sincerity in some feeling toward her. Albeit, Alexa was still aggravated over his comment he had made earlier about her and Kheane. Not to mention she had never forgotten he had called her a scrawny, little girl and a haughty witch…but it didn't bother her as much as she was trying to make it bother her. He had said or done other small, more significant things that had replaced those mocking comments. She had an inclination his bitter remarks derived from some resentment surfacing from his past; and they really had nothing to do with her whatsoever.

She found herself wanting or needing Bryan's approval more and more each passing day. She couldn't figure why it suddenly seemed so important, until now. The answer was plain and simple. She was fond of him. In fact, she had to admit she was more than just fond of him. She had almost choked when he suggested he should leave the company. In spite of this feeling, she wasn't about to tell him. He may have been treating her nicer lately, and he may have had a few appealing looks in his handsome azure eyes when he was watching her, but that sure didn't mean anything significant. Besides, he was a Master Sword and she was just a commoner. She quickly decided she would ignore the situation. Because more than likely she was only imagining he might be interested in her.

At this resolution, Alexa rolled over and attempted to get some sleep. But Hazerk unexpectedly flung his arm out in his sleep and whacked her hard on the face. She gasped for air and held her smarting nose. Eyes watering, she turned back the other way to face the now slumbering Sword. She sighed desolately at seeing the fire's light dance across his attractive features. How could she possibly ignore it?

She soon fell asleep with the sinking feeling that this was only the beginning of the confused events and emotions she would face in the days to come.

Chapter 23

At dawn the company rose and started out again. Alexa found to her relief that her senses had seemed to unclog over the night. She had asked Apollos about it the evening before; he explained that it was natural for her to feel assaulted at first with all the magic hanging in Carthorn's air.

A huge weight had lifted off the company; everyone was in everyone's confidence. And the travelers' moods had improved a great deal toward each other, especially Sword Bryan and Kheane's feelings toward one another.

They rode in broken silence, ducking hanging vines and low branches, weaving around marshes laced with mist. They traveled over narrow creeks, and around buttress rooted trees, their trunks massive enough for ten men to circle hand to hand. They heard frequent noises from various, unidentified creatures scurrying through the underbrush. However, nothing menacing had reared its head yet.

Alexa was feeling pleased. She had her senses somewhat back and decided to let them wander amongst the group. It occurred to her that this was an invasion of privacy, but what else could she do with all this time?

Sword Bryan was riding next to her. He was relatively content for the moment; just some slight worry was nagging him. Alexa surmised it was merely the normal anxiety derived from leadership. Her senses couldn't discern that he was actually bothered by her disturbing future.

Prince Alkin was tangled in distress. Alexa didn't have to guess why. She knew his thoughts were focused on his mother's questionable allegiance.

Kheane, on the other hand, was emitting an almost joyful vibe. The ex-assassin appeared to be feeling better about his life. He was hopeful. Alexa kept an enthralled eye on him for most of the morning.

When her senses landed on Eelyne, she was surprised to discover the normally cool young warrior was fretting over something. His mind was jumbled with questions, doubts and fears. Alexa could only sense feelings and emotions. She could never pinpoint their origins precisely. It was always an educated guess on her part as to why they were in a particular mood. However, from her experience, the patterns of his emotions hinted that he wasn't thinking about something, but rather someone.

While they were all preoccupied in their thoughts, and Alexa's senses were engaged, the first catastrophe of Carthorn hit them. Unfortunately, neither Apollos nor Kheane sensed it either. Apollos was in a rare moment of deep daydreaming—as unicorns occasionally do; they aren't perfect. And Kheane, feeling content for the first time in centuries, had made the mistake of letting his guard down, something he hadn't done since the beginning days of his assassin training. However, he was the first to utter a snap warning seconds before.

"Something's… Alexa, watch out!" he barked gruffly.

Startled and bewildered, Alexa looked at the ex-assassin. In that moment a gargantuan snake dropped from the branches above. The creature landed with a vile hiss on top of the unsuspecting Alexa and Zhan. Its body was so long only the head and the belly had come down to gather up its prey. Bryan, who had been riding next to Alexa, was hit hard by the descending belly. Disorientated, Dragon stumbled sideways into a tree, smashing Bryan's knee.

Alexa's horrified curses tangled in the atmosphere with Zhan's enraged squeals. The snake opened its massive maw to show them fangs leaking venom, and then hastily wrapped its thick body around the horse and girl.

"Kill it! For the love of Kaltraz, kill the blasted thing!" Alexa screamed over the stunned hollers of the men and horses.

Bryan came out of his shock and quickly drew his sword. He slashed at the swaying serpentine body in front of him. His sword cut into the beast's scales, barely drawing blood. The snake turned abruptly on him and Dragon. It snapped menacingly at their heads, hissing. Bryan dodged; Dragon craned out his neck and took an angry bite out of the creature.

"Apollos!" someone cried.

"Help!" Alexa screamed. Her arms were pinned at her sides. She was utterly defenseless and was beginning to panic. The snake jerkily lifted her and Zhan into the air.

"Get over here!" Bryan roared needlessly at the already attacking warriors.

Kheane had drawn his sword and was cutting gashes in the snake's thick skin. It was scarcely causing damage. Hazerk and Eelyne were slicing relentlessly at the beast's mid-section. The creature dropped down more of its sinewy body, feeling the fight was becoming harder than it had first presumed.

Warkan had out his battle-ax and was whacking at the serpent as if it were a tree trunk. The burly man was only able to hack his way into the fleshy outer layers of the hide before the snake flipped its body and pinned him to a tree.

Kheane, giving up on his sword, took out his Alidonian weapon and whipped it toward the beast. The blade cut into the back of the snake's head and lodged there. Red blood spurted out, raining down on the company with its putrid stink. Alexa caught a gush of it straight on and began to gag. She and Zhan were being squeezed dreadfully; she began to gasp for air. Zhan's terrified squealing turned to a meek grunt.

Apollos raced up from the head of the company with his horn lowered and charged full force toward the snake. He leapt lithely up, a vicious glint in his eye, and rammed his horn deep into its flesh. The great snake twisted its body and thrashed angrily, hissing and snapping with its crushing jaws. Apollos tweaked his horn and pushed it deeper. There was a flash of black when the unicorn let off a deadly vibe of magic into the snake's body. The creature hissed and gave a tremendous shudder. It was weakened, but it wasn't deterred from taking another venomous snap at Bryan, who still had the serpent's head engaged.

Alkin, having slid his blade into its neck, jumped off Sapharan and onto its coils. He began tugging unrelentingly at Alexa's shoulders. "Hold in there!" he encouraged as he strained to pull her out by her underarms.

Alexa winced. Her ribs felt like they would snap any second; her vision turned blotchy. *This is it. I'm going to die…Well, at least Ret won't be able to use me…* She despaired. She couldn't breathe. She saw nothing but a white blur before her eyes. Then, waveringly, the world left her.

Warkan tore loose from the snake's hold, the beast being occupied with the others. The brawny warrior jumped up, snatched his pole ax from his warhorse's saddle, and ran up the snake's back to its head, slipping dangerously in seeping crimson as he went. Balancing on the writhing creature, he took the weapon in his hands and rammed it straight into its skull, bellowing angrily.

The creature shuddered, its head falling to the ground and its body twisting in resistance. Then with several convulsions, the snake stopped moving.

Sweating, Alkin gave a hard tug on the limp body of Alexa. She slipped from the snake's coils and he carefully carried her to the side of the path. He laid her down, gently resting her against the trunk of a tree. He knelt and examined her. Hazerk promptly leapt off the dead serpent and came to her side, earnestly inspecting her health as Alkin carefully wiped blood from her face. Bryan and Eelyne, still trying to catch their breath, rushed over.

Seeing the humans, Zhan gave an indignant squeal for attention. The white horse was still trapped under the snake's body. Warkan and Kheane quickly freed him. He stood and shook himself robustly.

"She'll be fine," Hazerk said breathless from the fight. "Someone get her water," he demanded, still anxiously examining her. He was handed a water pouch; and he gently trickled some on her face.

Alexa's dark lashes fluttered open. Her blue eyes looked hazily up at the men's anxious faces staring down at her. Shaking her head and breathing in deep gulps of air for a few moments, she smiled weakly. "Ugh." She carefully poked her ribs. "It felt like I was going to snap in half," she said hoarsely, then fell into a fit of wheezy coughs.

"You *are* a twig. I think you're okay, though," Hazerk said, feeling around her rib cage for any damage. "Can you stand?"

She nodded and slowly got up, glancing at Zhan, who was nibbling on a patch of grass off the path. Seeing her mount was alive, she asked, "Is everyone okay?"

"Yep. We just have a new pleasant aroma is all," Bryan answered dryly, with a small smile. He was feeling extremely relieved she was all right. He had fought blindly; and with a surprisingly piercing fear they would find Alexa dead.

Taking a moment to let the event sink in and to catch their wits and breath, they looked around to the carnage. The chopped body of the snake lay motionless. The creature's bowels were strewn about, the ground littered with its flesh and soaked with blood. Everyone was completely covered in the snake's putrid reek.

"Well, I guess we learned our lesson," Alkin said, wiping his hands and face on his cloak. "We've got to pay better attention. This forest has a way of tricking you into feeling secure and then shaking you up." They all nodded in glum accord.

Apollos snorted his agreement. "It's part of the magic here."

"Right. We should keep moving. Are you okay to ride on, Alexa?" Bryan asked.

Still feeling slightly shaky, Alexa gazed into the Master Sword's dirty, serious face. His azure eyes were vivid with genuine concern. "Yeah, I'm fine," she managed to say. She pulled away from his stimulating gaze and wiped at her face vigorously, trying frantically to clean the dirt and blood away; as well as the fluttering feeling he had imparted on her…

"All right. Come on," the Sword ordered. "Gather the horses and mount up. And keep your eyes open."

Everyone moved halfheartedly toward their mounts. Alexa fumbled her way to Zhan. Bryan reached out a hand and steadied her, knowing she was pushing herself more than she should. She didn't look at him or say anything to him as he helped her into Zhan's saddle. He looked attentively up into her stoic set face as she gathered her reins.

Brushing away a lock of escaped hair, she peered down at him gravely. "I could have managed, but thanks," she said stiffly.

Feeling choked, Bryan merely nodded and went to catch Dragon. The stallion was wandering dangerously close to Blize, who had laid her ears back at him in warning. The Master Sword quickly swung himself into the saddle and lead the company out, leaving the mess behind them.

The company rode in silent vigilance now. They traveled at an easy, but steady pace. Everyone was watchful of their surroundings as they cut their way through the once again friendly forest. The sun shone through the thick canopy of trees and the colorful birds sang their beautiful serenades.

Several hours after the snake attack, they came to a stream—shallow, cool, and rippling over a bed of smooth stones. As they approached, it looked as if it were materializing from a dream. A light mist swirled around it and among swaying willows, cedars, and ash trees, all leaning over the banks peering at their elegant reflections.

The company came to the edge preparing to cross, but Sword Bryan paused and commanded his weary followers to take a break and clean up. They were thankful; it had been a dreadful several hours they had to endure smelling their own reek.

The company washed up and ate in passive silence. Alexa took to herself and washed her hands and face under the cover of the hanging boughs of a willow over the stream. She knew she was still under the watchful eye of the company so she felt no fear. And, of course, if Bryan had thought her doing anything wrong he would have taken the liberty to say so.

Listening to the rush of water, the bird songs, and the gentle wind blowing through the willow, Alexa could feel the serenity of the forest. She took a seat on the bank and let the clear water rush over her bare feet. She sat and stared contemplatively into the water for a while. Zhan stood by her side, taking long, noisy slurps from the stream, and basking in the tranquility, too.

Alexa's body ached from the morning's adventure, but she was recovering fast, inside and out. The forest seemed to have a strange effect on her, as it did on all of them. She tried to decipher it, but it was complicated far beyond her will to understand. It could easily deal out so much grief, yet it was healing, too. It contradicted itself. It was like it had a life of its own, very unstable, as if it didn't know what it wanted to be. Even the odd assortment of deciduous and tropical trees growing together showed evidence of this. Alexa now understood why it was uninhabited by humans.

A short while later Bryan moved the company out. By that

time they were ready to start again, for the pleasant atmosphere of the stream had changed while they rested. The atmosphere had begun to emit an intense feeling that they were uninvited to stay any longer. It had gotten peculiarly silent; and the breeze seemed to whisper for their departure. The company wondered if there were hidden mystical creatures watching them; and they had the influence to either allow them to stay or not. Perhaps the forest and its creatures remembered the wedge that had been placed between them and humans during the Lost War, and were feeling not so forgiving.

Later that evening, before twilight, the company's ears perked at the sound of water mingled with vague laughter. The watery sound was unmistakably a waterfall's rush. They quickened toward the alluring sound, hoping to see an awe-inspiring sight. They weren't disappointed.

They came to the edge of a steamy pool of azure water. The melodious sounds of the cascading waterfall and joyous birdcalls created an instantly soothing environment. The sight and overtaking mood stole their breath away, rendering them all silent. Not just one mouth was gaping.

A splendid waterfall gushed down into a swirling pool of water. The white water danced, splashed, and tumbled happily down over a stony ridge into a steaming pool. Large boulders blanketed with green, plush moss surrounded the blue water. Willows and cedars stood as sentries. The banks thrived with luxuriant beds of bluebells, lilies and buttercups.

The pool was nearly perfectly round and appeared bottomless. Opposite of the waterfall, the water trickled down a smaller, narrower waterfall to become a gentle flowing brook. The area was warm and intoxicating with the scent of flowers hanging in the air. Misty puffs of warm air sprouted from the pool. It was a warm spring—a haven it seemed.

Arriving at the bank, the company realized they weren't alone. They had accidently crept up on a gathering of unsuspecting nymphs. The beautiful dryads and naiads were enjoying the pleasures of the warm water. They were laughing with otherworldly voices and splashing around in the swirling water.

Some were diving playfully from the ridge while others lounged on the soft moss.

The company took in a breath as one. Everyone's eyes were wide with wonder, trying to take in the stunning sight. The nymphs were far more than stunning. Choking back words, they stared dumbfounded. This act, however, was enough to alarm the jovial beings; with shouts of fear they vanished almost immediately. Some dove into the water and dispersed: the naiads. Others fled into the forest and disappeared: the dryads.

"Wait!" called Apollos. But even a mystical brother couldn't stop the frightened beauties from fleeing.

One, however, did pause, infinitesimally as it was. Her rich, brown, almond-shaped eyes looked piercingly and intriguingly straight at a flabbergasted Alexa. Alexa held her breath as she gazed into the eyes of the earth itself. The dryad had long, nut-brown, wavy hair that flowed around her creamy skin. She wore a sheer, green, shimmering garment that barely covered her pleasing figure. Glancing at Alexa from the corner of her eye, the dryad gave her a slight nod and the smallest of knowing smiles. Then, she bounded lithely over the rocky surface, disappearing into the forest. Alexa stared, mouth agape. Sudden realization took a hold of her.

"Wow!" Hazerk breathed. "I don't think I'll ever be able to make love to a real woman again…"

"Shut up, Hazerk," Bryan commanded exasperatedly. He was glancing from the pool, now empty of nymphs, to Alexa who was apparently meditating on something big. Her sapphire eyes were a bright sky blue; and she chewed her lip fervently as excitement came over her countenance. The others waited patiently, anxious for their next order.

"Prince Alkin, I think you just got your intuition wish," Alexa spoke suddenly, an excited twinge in her voice.

"Yes?" Alkin said eagerly as he moved Sapharan next to Zhan.

Alexa still stared with glittering eyes at the waterfall. Apollos came to her side, an understanding look over his striking equine features. Alexa regarded him and the unicorn nodded approvingly. She moved her eyes from him to the eager Sword and Prince.

"What better creature to be the guardian of the purest form of earth than a nymph? They must be the Earth-Keepers. They're the earth itself."

"Right!" Alkin exclaimed, understanding.

Suddenly everyone's spirits rose. Bryan smiled widely at Alexa, who returned it happily, eyes dancing.

"Good job, Alexa, woohoo!" Hazerk hollered, and pumped a dramatic victorious fist in the air.

"What of the Guidance Naiad?" Eelyne suggested, his face alight. He was thrilled at actually seeing some of the mystical creatures he had always studied so diligently from a book.

"Hmm…I don't know," Alexa contemplated.

"But, it couldn't be her…" Bryan said a little hesitantly, gazing at Alexa for consensus. The others looked at him puzzled and a little skeptical. Alexa was thoughtful, not disregarding as she gazed intently back at Bryan.

"What do you mean? She's a nympiad or whatever you said they were," Warkan commented.

Bryan shrugged, looking away from Alexa's pensive stare. She apparently didn't realize she was making him uncomfortable. Her eyes were awfully captivating….

"He's right. It's probably not her," Apollos suddenly stated, realizing where Bryan was coming from.

"Why not? She's a well-known nymph. Like a queen of sorts, right?" Hazerk questioned.

"Exactly," Kheane interjected huskily, "The Earth-Keeper would *not* be known."

"Besides," Eelyne perked up, "She's a naiad."

"A water nymph," Alkin added.

"And, we already have the water element," Bryan finished what he had begun to put into words.

"Right," Alexa nodded in accord.

"But maybe we should head in that direction. We could speak with her…" Eelyne suggested diffidently, unable to restrain his excitement.

"That took me two years last time. We don't have that kind of time," Apollos said frankly.

"It wouldn't hurt to head that way, though, since we don't have a clue where to find the element anyway. What do you think, Alexa?" Alkin inquired the contemplating girl.

Alexa started out of her thoughts and looked at the Prince, catching his kind, hazel eyes. She grinned at him. "It's definitely a start. Maybe if we camp near here tonight we could try to communicate with the nymphs here. They could tell us something."

"All right, sounds like a plan," Bryan stated. "Let's make camp up a ways on the other side of the pool. It's probably best to not disturb the nymphs' space."

"Good idea," Alkin agreed happily.

"We should take a dip. The water's real warm." Hazerk had dismounted and bent down to touch the steamy water.

Everyone agreed enthusiastically.

"So tempting…we can in the morning before we head off. We've got to make camp now before dark. I don't want any more surprises when were not prepared," the Sword stated wisely.

The company groaned in disappointment, but everyone nodded in reluctant agreement, knowing that was the smart thing. No one wanted to be caught off guard again.

They took up their reins and guided their mounts over the brook. They traveled about a half a mile down the path from the spring. Apparently, it was a popular place for the creatures of Carthorn; there were paths leading to and from it on both sides.

The company made camp in a grove just as the sun disappeared for the night. By that time they had a nice roaring fire. They sat contented around its warmth and comfortable light, eating their dinner and listening to the horses eat their own dinner noisily.

As she ate, Alexa decided she wanted to speak with the nymphs alone. She didn't want the others to know her plan, because they undoubtedly wouldn't approve. She wasn't sure how she was going to do it; she would think it over tonight. Perhaps it would be okay if Apollos went with her. Sword Bryan and Prince Alkin would be all right with that. But no, the nymph had definitely looked at *her*, Alexa concluded. Apollos wouldn't be able to help this time. This was her duty; after all she was the one called for it.

Alexa smiled to herself when she had made up her mind. She would go in the morning, before everyone woke. She would burn some sleeping herbs in order to sneak pass the watch person, and then go to the pool to find the nymphs. She felt delighted with her plan. *Plus, I can get a good bath before the men get there.* Just the thought of swimming in the warm water sent an excited quiver through her body.

"Alexa." Kheane's raspy voice broke her thoughts. She looked at him inquiringly. "Let's practice on your usage of the Alidonian weapon," he stated.

Bryan straightened his posture from his spot at the fireside. "I was going to give her a break tonight, considering what happened this morning," he said a little abrasively. He was still not fond of Kheane butting in; for some reason it was mostly when it pertained to Alexa.

"Have you softened, Master Sword? She has to toughen up if she's to fight Ret and maybe in a battle," Kheane said pointedly.

Bryan cleared his throat; the ex-assassin had a point. And normally he would've made his pupils push on, but for some reason he just didn't feel like making Alexa work tonight. Perhaps he *was* softening toward her. He would have to rein that in. "Right. You work with her tonight. Alexa, work on your dagger throwing, too. I'll give you and Eelyne the night off; unless Eelyne wants to take a bout." Bryan regarded the young warrior, who was leaning lazily against a massive oak.

He grinned sheepishly, "I'll pass tonight, Head-Master Sword."

Bryan shrugged and settled back to watch Kheane coach Alexa on the unusual Alidonian weapon. Alexa was only slightly better than she had been before with her throwing technique. But, Bryan and the others watching the practice session were surprised at how good Alexa was at dagger throwing. She threw each one with speed, agility and confidence, hitting her mark almost every time. The Master Sword was impressed. Kheane was pleased too, and told her so, which made the young woman glow with pride.

Soon the days' earlier troubles were forgotten and a game of competitive dagger throwing started. Everyone participated, even Alkin and Warkan; though Apollos lounged by the fireside. The unicorn watched the boisterous, cheerful company fondly with his glistening, chocolate eyes. However, he did keep vigilant for anything threatening that may have been watching, too. And he had to remind them a few times not to throw the daggers at the trees.

The company played congenially and well into the night before exhaustion overtook them and made them come to their senses. They then settled down and fell into a contented sleep, still jesting with each other as they drifted off one by one to sleep. Eelyne took guard duty.

Chapter 24

Before the first rays of dawn, Alexa woke with a start, her mind filling with the plans she had established the night before. She hoisted herself up on her elbows from the hard ground, leaving her warm bedroll. Scarcely daring to breathe, she surveyed her surroundings. An eerie, warm breeze blew around the dense woods, sending an excited shiver down her spine. The red coals from the fire sizzled comfortingly in the midst of the sleeping company. Even Eelyne who was supposed to be alert was sleeping soundly against a tree. Alexa couldn't believe her luck. She smirked. This was good for her, but he would definitely hear about his mistake later.

Alexa's eyes were alight with mischief as she glanced around to the others. Bryan, lying to her left, had his back toward her and didn't stir. Apollos was curled up like a puppy next to the coals; his soft velvety eyelids closed and his mane glimmering in the low light. Kheane was snoring faintly, his hood drawn down past his face. The horses dozed peacefully at their tethers. They all seemed in an enchanted sleep. Their exhaustion now made her plan of burning sleeping herbs unnecessary.

Alexa rose and quietly slung her sack over her shoulder. Alkin muttered incoherently, and she froze, her heart pounding wildly in her chest. Seeing he was asleep, she relaxed and smiled fondly down at the Prince. As she crept away, she found herself thinking how fine a person Alkin was and how lucky Shelkite was to have him as ruler.

Alexa walked in silence down the rutted path leading to the waterfall. She reassured herself as she went that it was not far and if she needed them they would be there in minutes. Besides, as always, she carried her dagger and bow with her.

As she strode down the mossy path, the forest woke with the morning's first light. The sun's rays came shyly down through the trees to sparkle on the dew drops scattered on the greenery. The birds began to sing softly, cooing and twittering merrily. Alexa could hear the heady sound of the waterfall; it was just around the next bend.

As she nearly skipped with anticipation around the curve,

she came to an abrupt halt upon seeing a white stag crossing the path before her. The magnificent creature paused at seeing the dumbfounded girl. Raising his delicate shaped head, the pale stag pricked his ears toward her. His large, round, black eyes bored unflinchingly into her. He wore a great crown of antlers that many hunters would have sought greedily after.

He gazed at her with his piercing eyes, and Alexa gulped, wide eyed. Her father had told her of the noble white stags. They were said to be unapproachable and untamable, but the wisest creatures the High Power had ever placed on the earth. She had to speak to it. She had to find her voice, but she was entranced beyond words.

The stag had an untamed ere about him, yet he seemed to be waiting on her. He looked at her imploringly as she continued to stare stupidly. But all Alexa could do was think to herself, *oh, I wish you could somehow help.* The splendid creature blinked and lowered his head, his nose almost touching the earth, as if he were bowing to her. He then stepped carefully over the path and into the forest's cover.

A breeze caressed Alexa's face, ruffling her tendrils of escaped hair. A voice deep and soft rode on it. It was not spoken, but it came into her mind gently and affably; *the breath of the world dawns from the soil of your blood.* Long after the stag had disappeared into the forest, Alexa stood gazing into the trees where he had slipped away, silently absorbing the experience.

Coming to and still puzzled over the words, she made her way to the peaceful, azure pool. She was delighted to find the nymphs once again bathing in the steamy waters and basking in the morning light. And once again, before she could utter a word, they screeched and dashed away. "Wait! I have to ask you something!" she called helplessly after them. Yelping, they paid her no heed. "I need your help, Eetharum does. Wait!" she blundered on, rushing toward a dryad leaping from the mossy rocks to the forest floor. "I need to know where the earth element is. It's important! There's an evil wizard. I have to save Eetharum!" But her pleads were futile. The dryads and naiads were gone. Frowning after the departed, finicky creatures, Alexa clenched her jaw. "You stupid, no-brain, frantic beings!" she grumbled. She dropped her sack on a nearby rock covered in plush moss and dainty lilies bowing their heads toward the pool. "You all are perfect examples why men lose their heads!"

Glowering, Alexa looked around the pool. The waterfall was just as enchanting as it had been the day before. Alexa's sapphire eyes glittered as her mind slowly forgot her failed mission. She would like to climb on the rocks behind the waterfall and stand behind the falling sheet of water, but first she would bathe. She dropped her quiver and bow to the rock and unbuckled her dagger. Taking a seat, she quickly pulled off her boots and climbed out of her trousers. After removing her cloak, she slid her lightweight shirt over her head and discarded her undergarments. Sighing with delight, she unbraided her hair, relishing the feeling of it flying loose for once. It fell to her waist in raven colored ripples. Her hair was normally straight and silky, but it had many days of hard riding on it, and not to mention snake innards. It was in dire need of a washing, as was the rest of her. She pulled from her sack a bar of lavender scented soap and leapt into the warm water gleefully.

Surfacing, she thought she couldn't have delighted in it any more. The water temperature was deliciously perfect. She quickly washed herself and her hair, and proceeded to take out her newly sharpened dagger and shave off any undesirable hair on her body. She would need to hurry, lest the others woke and noticed her disappearance. She didn't want to alarm them, yet she had no desire to have to bathe with them either. They would have undoubtedly acted like a bunch of wild stallions, despite what they said. This was much better. She would just swim around a bit more and enjoy herself. She would even wash her clothes and let the warm breeze dry them. She still had plenty of time; the sun was not completely up yet.

Bryan clenched his jaw as he surveyed the camp. He glowered down at Alexa's empty bedroll. At that moment he thought he might explode he was so angry. Where had she gone? Why hadn't he or Kheane or Apollos woken at her departure? Letting out a low growl, he looked over to the snoozing Eelyne.

Pursing his lips, the Master Sword stalked over to the young warrior and kicked the bottoms of his boots hard. Eelyne jerked awake. Instantaneously he was shocked and ashamed at what he had done.

"She's gone," Bryan growled down at him. Eelyne's wide, fearful eyes darted over to Alexa's bedroll. The others stirred awake, mumbling inarticulately.

"I—ah—I," stammered Eelyne.

Bryan didn't wait to listen. He strode back over to his bedroll and began strapping his sword belt on, not removing his ominous glare from the young man. Eelyne looked away, feeling extremely disgraceful and incompetent.

"Wha-what's going on?" Alkin stretched and yawned, standing up from his bedroll.

"Our little lady is missing in action," Bryan seethed.

"Huh?" The others gasped in unison and looked around as if they might see her hiding in the bushes for a prank.

Apollos stood and shook himself. "She can't be far. She probably just wandered to the pool. I can't sense anything evil."

"You all pack up camp and get the horses ready. I'll go get her," Bryan ordered, his tone not any less severe. At that he stomped off down the path, scowling as if he enjoyed it.

Feeling he might overflow with fury, Bryan grumbled and mumbled to himself all the way down the path. How could she be so foolish? Why did she take off without telling them? The insane girl! He would drag her back by that wretched black braid of hers!

He came to a stomping halt on a rock banking the azure pool. He peered down into the water. He could see a slim shadow moving just beneath the rippling, steamy surface. It was her. Bryan relaxed; she was at least still in one piece. But he wasn't going to let her get away with what she had done. He felt like he had somehow failed. He was supposed to be her Sword-Guard, and it infuriated him beyond sanity she had slipped away unknowingly from him. He made sure he had a set scowl on his features when her head broke the surface of the water. As she wiped water away from her eyes with her slender fingers, Bryan continued to glare down at her. When her sight cleared, she started upon spotting him, but she covered her surprise coolly.

"Girl, have you already forgotten what happened yesterday?" Bryan growled at her, his brain hazing over with rage, worry and relief. Alexa merely stared at him placidly with her big, sapphire eyes. "You were almost breakfast for a gigantic snake. Are you so daft that you still run off by yourself?" he finished crossly. She didn't answer him, but continued to stare at him mildly. This aggravated him all the more. "Well, Sand Queen, what do you have to say for yourself?" he pressed impatiently through his clenched teeth.

Alexa blinked at him coyly. "Do you want to take a dip, Master Sword? The water's perfect."

Suddenly the current situation registered. Dazed out of his anger, Bryan took in the whole picture. He gazed down at the girl floating in the azure waters at his feet. She was undoubtedly fully unclothed, but he couldn't distinguish anything past her bare shoulders, which were just peeking out above the swirling waves of the pool. His eyes involuntarily peered deeper to search out the rest of her, but the pool was too shadowy. Bryan felt an unwelcome heat rise up his neck to his face.

Hoping she hadn't noticed his fleeting moment of gawking, Bryan managed to mutter curtly, "You're changing the subject." He shifted his weight awkwardly, still endeavoring not to stare down into the obscure waters. Alexa smirked devilishly at him. Bryan's heart rate increased. He had obviously failed in covering up his display of attraction.

Resigning, Alexa shrugged her shoulders and said, "I thought I'd try to talk to the nymphs myself." She looked guiltily away from his frown.

"And?" Bryan implored tersely. He couldn't help but notice how her eyes seemed to reflect the rippling waters. They glowed such a brilliant azure when they landed on him, making him uncomfortable.

"They ran off before I could say anything," she ended regretfully. She peered up at him with wide innocent eyes, trying her feminine wiles for his forgiveness. Though, she wasn't regretful she had tried; she just craved his approval.

"It was an unnecessary risk and foolish. What if something had happened?" he scolded her sharply, but his tone had less of a sting to it. He was desperately trying not to admire her sun-bronzed, smooth shoulders. The sight of her in this state was softening his cool heart, as was her remorseful countenance.

There was a moment of submissive silence between them. Alexa was gazing thoughtfully away at the cascading waterfall and Bryan took the opportunity to study her, letting his eyes wander and his thoughts ponder. Her long, raven hair was floating silkily around her on the water's surface. He had never seen it down before. He found himself wondering what it would look like; it probably fell to her waist, soft and glossy. He suddenly realized he had been feeling more and more enticed by her each day, even with all the dirt and grime. But right now she appeared more alluring to him than ever. Maybe he hadn't let himself see her as a person before, only an obligation. He had tried so hard to shut her out for stupid, complicated reasons. Apollos *was* right....

"Well?" Alexa's voice cut into his thoughts and his mind quickly came back to the present. "Are you just going to stand there and watch me bathe? It's kind of unsettling," she said bluntly, boring him with reproachful eyes.

His eyes narrowed and he scowled. "Well, hurry up and get out of there. We don't have all day to wait on your girlishness," he snapped.

"Calm your horse, Master Sword. If you'd just give me space I'd be done and I could get dressed," she smiled smugly at him, giving her raven mane a toss.

"Right," he grumbled. "I'll be over there." He jumped down from the rock and crossed over the trickling brook to the other side of the pool. "If you need me, I won't be far," he called over his shoulder.

Alexa swam to the edge, watching him as he made his way into the forest. "I'll be fine and don't look," she hollered affably after him.

"As if I would want to!" he called back, rolling his eyes, but feeling as if he had just told the biggest lie.

Alexa grinned to herself, her heart beating rapidly. She

tried to quell the animated feeling in her chest. He had *without a doubt* looked at her with desire. But it couldn't be true, could it? She smiled happily to herself and dove down into the water, plunging herself to the bottom, enjoying the thrill racing through her body. *He's just denying it.* She was hopeful as she whisked along the sandy floor.

Bryan stomped his way into the forest. He stopped a little way down from the pool, but near enough if something might happen. He plopped down on a fallen tree lying off the beaten path, grumbling inwardly. What was happening to him? For a minute there he felt like he was only sixteen again. She was bewitching him; the little vixen! He rubbed his face vigorously and sighed, resting his chin in his cupped hands. He stared at the ground, trying to clear his mind while he waited. *Ugh, females.* It was unsettling to feel like he was thrown out of his demeanor in his own territory; that would be commanding a company with silly distractions like this!

Bryan sat on the decaying log going over everything, all their conversations and strained encounters and all his confused feelings. The minutes felt like agonizing hours as he finally discovered that he actually felt something rather strong for Alexa. This was hard to admit, considering he wasn't sure if *she* had feelings for him. And considering their situation it was definitely not a good thing. How did he fall into such a pit, especially when he had tried so hard to go around it? He felt bitter. *Well, if she's going to act coquettish with me, I'll just ignore it. It's like a woman to do that anyway…though I didn't think it was like her. But, from how she was looking at Kheane, it's probably him….She doesn't feel anything for me; she's just playing stupid games….*

Finishing her bath and feeling elated, Alexa swam to the rocky edge where the waterfall emerged in a foamy mass into the pool. Alexa ducked under the pounding water and hoisted herself up onto the ledge behind the cascading water where a breezeway connected either side of the pool. Squeezing the water out of her hair, she lost herself in dreamy thoughts initiated by the enchanting echo from the water reverberating off the rock wall.

Alexa tilted her head back and breathed in the moist, warm

air, smiling to herself. Suddenly, her senses latched onto something. A shock of fear sliced through her viscera. Her eyes snapped open and she looked over her shoulder. She was startled to see a poorly clothed, strange man standing directly behind her.

"Nymph!" the man wheezed in a throaty voice and pointed at her. His wide eyes practically bulged out of his head.

Alexa swallowed a gasp and quickly reined in her escaping composure. The man edged cautiously toward her, slightly bent. He was emaciated and his clothes hung on him like rags on a clothesline. His dirty brown hair was a mass of tangles and grease.

Alexa's eyes darted over to her clothes and dagger lying behind the man. Her heart raced at the inconvenience of the situation. Here she sat naked, with her dagger a good ten feet away.

The man paused his advance and studied her with a crazed look. Alexa stared levelly back at him, raising her chin haughtily, assessing how she was going to take him on. He looked weak, but he was in a strange state of mind, he might be stronger than she figured.

"Who are you?" she demanded crossly, forgetting any modesty and standing up to face him as boldly as she could.

The man smiled, showing a mouth of decaying teeth. His eyes glinted wickedly. "You're no nymph. Just a girl." He smirked, giving her a sly look.

Alexa narrowed her eyes and calculated how she could get around him to her weapon. She clenched her jaw and straightened her shoulders, glaring at him suspiciously. "I asked you a question. Who are you? What do you want?" she demanded icily, preparing to leap for her dagger.

The man laughed at her and began walking toward her again, his hand out stretched as if to touch her. He must have gotten lost in the forest and never been able to find his way out, Alexa's mind subconsciously concluded. He didn't answer her, but continued to reach for a lock of her hair draping over her shoulders.

"Stay back!" she growled, her blue eyes spitting flames. But the stranger merely grinned at her and kept advancing.

Right as the man was about to touch her, Alexa dove for her dagger. That same instant, he lunged at her with a snarl, grabbing her hair and yanking her harshly back. Nevertheless, Alexa managed to clutch her fingers around her weapon. She unsheathed her dagger in the flurry of warding him off. He attempted to restrain her.

"Get off me, you vermin!" she growled.

Unheedingly, he groped for the dagger, and they fell into a tangled wrestling match. The man twisted her fingers, wrenched her wrists, and clawed her arms mercilessly. He kneed her hard in the stomach and tried to control her by grabbing her hair and wrenching her head violently. They fell to the ground and the dagger clattered at their side. The stranger snatched it up with surprising speed. Alexa fought the man fiercely; her heart racing in fear as the man pushed her harshly to the ground. She saw stars as her head slammed on the rock and she fell under him.

"Bryan! Bryan!" she yelled as the man tried to pin her arms.

Quietly sitting on the log, Bryan came out of his ponderings at seeing something flit by in his peripheral vision. There was a familiar ringing sound, accompanied by a tinkling laugh. He looked around suspiciously. He turned his head back and found himself staring straight at a pixie flying right in front of his nose. It giggled and tugged at the lock of hair hanging down over his forehead. "Hey! Get!" He swatted at her. This only seemed to entice the pixie and she laughed and buzzed around his head pulling at his face, ears and hair. Annoyed and remembering he was in danger of being pixilated, Bryan stood and began walking away, waving his arms at her. "Get out of here," he snarled, but the little creature followed him down the path toward the pool.

Suddenly, Alexa's crying voice rent the air. The Master Sword's head shot up like an animal spotting danger. He instantly began running as fast as he could toward the warm spring. His mind was suddenly in full gear and his heart raced with fear for her and anger with himself. How could he have been so stupid to leave her alone?

Bryan's throat tightened and he could barely breathe as he

charged down the pathway. The pixie was in hot pursuit thinking it was a game. She laughed and dashed around his head. Ignoring her, Bryan suddenly felt like he was getting light headed. Feeling content, he slowed down and found himself tripping over a root and falling flat on his face. Quickly shaking away the pain and dizziness, he gave the pixie one last angry swat and hastily got back up. He raced toward the pool again, determined not to be pixilated.

Making it soundly to the spring, he scanned the area and saw through the waterfall two figures wrestling. He heard Alexa's fearful voice calling out for him and cursing her attacker. "Bryan, help! Please! Get off me, you scum, get off!" He heard her scream along with an unfamiliar male voice gibbering incoherently.

He dashed around the rocks and to the back of the waterfall to find her being attacked by a terribly thin man. They were rolling around on the ground. The man was biting at her and tearing at her, attempting to stab her and pin her down. But he was having a hard time controlling the feisty girl. She was defending her own skillfully.

At the sight something roared to life in Bryan's chest. He was utterly enraged. He leapt on the stranger with full force and ripped him from atop of Alexa, throwing him violently against the rock wall. The man slammed into it with a sickening thud, his head snapping back. He fell to the ground and didn't move.

Worry and anger renting through his veins, Bryan turned and regarded Alexa with fearful eyes. He was panting and shaking with anger as he assessed her. Alexa had inched away along the ground to rest against the wall. She had grabbed her shirt to cover herself. Beads of sweat and water dripped down her face and her chest rose and fell rapidly with the big gulps of air she sucked shakily in and out. Her normally dazzling eyes held complete horror and relief as they darted from the strange man to the Master Sword.

Trembling, Alexa clutched her stomach and huddled like a child up against the wall, choking back silent sobs. "Th-thank y-you," she gasped.

Bryan came quickly to her side and knelt, "Are you all

right?" he asked with a catch in his voice. His hands trembled slightly as he brushed back black locks of hair obscuring her face.

Alexa nodded numbly, staring at the stranger lying face down and motionless not three feet away. She grimaced and fought back the stinging tears threatening to take over. She had the most excruciating pain in her stomach. She had never felt such pain before. She didn't think she could bare it. "Is h-he d-dead?" she choked out, weakly eyeing the man.

Bryan glanced at him, "I believe so. If he's not, he's got some explaining to do."

"I th-think he's mad—" she gasped, and then coughed. It racked her body with a horrifying pain and she yelped out loud.

Bryan clutched her shoulders desperately as he saw blood begin to seep through her shirt. "You're hurt!" He went to yank away the garment, but she held on to it tightly, wanting to cover herself.

"Let me see! You're bleeding," Bryan growled at her earnestly. Blood was rapidly soaking her shirt.

"No, I got to get dressed…." She stumbled to stand. Bryan grasped her firmly, helping her. "Help me." She reached for the rest of her clothing with a strained hand, the other clutching her abdomen. Halting and gasping a bit, she gently let off the pressure she was putting on her stomach and lowered her shirt to examine her wound, still concealing the lower half of her body.

A long, deep gash seared across the flesh on her stomach. She gulped and pressed her hand to it, trying to stop the blood flow; the crimson fluid seeped between her fingers. Tears of pain squeezed through her shut eyelids and she started to feel lightheaded.

Stunned, all Bryan could do was stare wide-eyed. He had never seen a wound so ghastly. Alexa looked pleadingly into his alarmed features. He gazed at her as if in a trance, for once he was unsure what to do. The wound was lethal; she would die.

Bryan's eyes frantically took all of her in. Alexa held her scarlet soaked shirt tightly swathed around her waist. Her head was bowed so her long raven locks obscured her face like a curtain and fell down over her shoulders concealing her chest. Her free arm was tenderly wrapped around her stomach, holding her trembling body.

"Master Sword…" she pleaded, raising her face and bringing him back with her frightened eyes.

Bryan jerked back into life and went to gather up her things, but found that she was swaying on her feet. Still clutching her shirt to cover herself, Bryan caught her before she crashed to the ground. He hastily gathered her up in his arms, wincing awkwardly as he felt her hot, wet skin on his bare hands. She stared up at him with dazed eyes, sweat gathering dreadfully at her hairline. Bryan gazed down at her, his eyes wide and unguarded with concern. He was not going to let her die. He grit his teeth with determination.

"Come on," he said gently. He quickly wrapped her in her cloak, picked up her dagger and lifted her carefully back into his arms. Alexa heaved a sigh and fell into semi-unconsciousness, her head falling back onto his shoulder. He hugged her tightly to his chest and quickly made his way back to the camp, his heart pounding. He had failed again and hated himself all the more for it; he had failed her. He had no right to call himself a Sword-Guard, let alone a Master Sword.

Bryan would not, could not let her die. Something at the sound of her voice desperately calling his name had confirmed the resolution he had just discovered sitting on that rotting tree. Alexa's voice and the sight of another hurting her had caused a strange pain and anger in his chest he had never thought possible again. If Alexa died it seemed the world would be a void, cold place without her. He felt that not just the mission would come to a complete and devastating stop, but that life, his life, just wouldn't be whole without her; like trying to play chess with only the king against the rest. But these strong feelings might be caused by his colossal feeling of failure in his duty. Not for her…right?

Bryan's long strides carried them quickly down the beaten path, his breath working hard with worry. He glanced down at her features contorted in pain. Her eyelids flickered uneasily and her lips parted slightly. Bryan pursed his own lips at seeing a small trickle of crimson creeping out of the corner of her mouth. Her chest rose and fell rapidly, her breaths labored and gurgled.

He felt a lump form in his throat, so much so that he thought it would literally choke him. He squeezed her body toward his own more snuggly, and tried to jog down the path. "Hang on, girl. You've got to make it…please," he whispered in her ear.

To his surprise, her eyes fluttered open and she gazed into his face. Her sapphire eyes were the deepest dark blue he had ever seen them. They held an intense, but fading, flicker in them that told him she was fighting.

"Keep awake, Sand Queen. I'll get you help." Bryan managed a tight smile down at her. She only blinked her answer, but her eyes softened before she closed them again. She hacked again and blood came spewing out of her mouth, splattering on his shirt. Bryan felt her body give a massive tremble from the pain shocking through her small frame. His heart went out to her.

As he held her close, he could smell the clean sweetness of her. His senses prickled with unsolicited pleasure. Suddenly, never in all his life had he wanted to be in the company of a particular woman as he did right then. With a twinge of guilt, he found himself vaguely fancying she wasn't wounded. But it was for other reasons far more impractical than simply her safety. Why was he thinking this? Why was he feeling this way about her? He had tried so hard to despise her. Then again, why had he tried to despise her?

Bryan fought a visualization of him and her together on this same path; but instead of running for help they were evading the others so they could be alone. They would find a cozy glade together and huddle under one of the ancient trees. It would umbrella them from the world, a place where they could escape to and explore an island of paradise all their own, where no one could breach the shores.

Bryan shook his head, clearing his thoughts. He was getting too sentimental or maybe just mental. This is what he meant by being thrown out of his element. She was becoming a complete distraction to him. How was he supposed to do his job? He had never had a problem keeping on track before. Besides this was Alexa, the arrogant witch he didn't feel anything for beyond that of his Sword-Guard duty. So he sternly told himself.

Angry with himself and still feeling a large amount of apprehension for Alexa, Bryan came storming into the camp with his face set in a hard scowl. The company rose up in alarm at seeing the two in the awful state.

"Warrior Hazerk, get over here!" Bryan hollered. Hazerk leapt up and came to Alexa's side as Bryan gently laid her down on a blanket and carefully wrapped her in another. The others quickly came and gathered around the injured young woman staring at her in consternation.

"What happened?" Alkin choked, taking in the dreadful bloody sight.

"I found her bathing in the pool. I left her for a few minutes so she could dress, but then I found a man attacking her when I returned," Bryan quickly explained as Hazerk examined her wound. The warrior's brow furrowed in disquiet.

"Here, keep pressure on it," Hazerk ordered the Master Sword, who was the closest at hand. The warrior got up and quickly went to retrieve his pack with his medical supplies in it.

The company all looked on anxiously as Hazerk worked on Alexa. Alexa's head bobbed and lolled as she came in and out of consciousness. Alkin moved around to her side so he could pull her onto his lap and hold her head. Her eyes flickered up at him and he smiled down at her encouragingly, she gave him the weakest of smiles.

Bryan fidgeted on the spot, "Well? Can you help her?" he demanded after a few minutes.

Hazerk sat back on his heels and stopped his working; a look of distressed defeat wreathed his face. "I can't do anything," he said sorrowfully.

"What do you mean? Didn't you learn anything at the medical school?" Bryan growled, his eyes flashing. The others stared blankly, wondering if the Master Sword was going to punch Hazerk squarely in the face.

"I can't do anything," the warrior said dejectedly with more force. "The wound is too deep and badly placed. She's lost too much blood." Hazerk backed away from the vile look on the

Master Sword's face.

Bryan was about to retort, but Apollos suddenly appeared over everyone's shoulder and looked calmly down at the girl laying in agony. "I told her to watch out for water. They mask her senses. She must not have felt him approaching," the unicorn said with sad eyes. "I didn't sense him either."

"Apollos, can you do anything?" Alkin asked. His voice held a crack.

"I can try."

"Well, do then," Bryan said impatiently. Alkin gave him a reproachful look. "Please," the Sword-Guard added.

"Alexa?" Apollos addressed her. Alexa looked up at him as if through a haze. "I'm going to try and heal you, but brace yourself it's going to be painful. Are you ready?"

Alexa managed to nod her head. She raised her chin boldly, watching the unicorn with rigid eyes. Alkin took a hold of her hand and held it tightly as Apollos raised his head and closed his gentle eyes, calling on his magic. They all watched in hopeful anxiety.

The unicorn lowered his horn, now glowing a brilliant bright white, and opened his eyes looking steadily at the Master Sword and warriors, "Hold her down. This is going to take a few minutes."

They all nodded stiffly. Bryan and Warkan took a hold of her legs. Hazerk and Kheane took a hold of her arms. Alkin held her head gently, speaking encouraging words softly in her ear. Eelyne looked on, too ashamed to say or do anything.

The unicorn lowered his horn to just inches above her wound and Bryan glanced wide-eyed to a now fully conscious Alexa and saw the determined yet fearful look in her eyes light up as the unicorn neared her abdomen with his searing horn. Bryan couldn't help but admire her as the unicorn inserted his burning horn as gently as he could into her open wound. She screamed in pain, despite trying desperately to hold it in.

The men all flinched and watched as the girl ground her teeth and cursed, straining at their hold on her. Her face was deathly pale and sweat poured from her brow and beaded all over her skin making their grips slick. Bryan watched in anguish as her eyes frantically darted around. Her eyes landed on his face and he held her gaze intensely. She didn't look away from him for a long moment, her blue eyes trapped in excruciating pain.

Apollos continued to calmly hold his sizzling horn at one end of the wound. It snapped and hissed fire-like inside her gut. Just as Bryan was feeling the unicorn should be done, Apollos thrust his horn deeper and began moving it up and down the length of the wound. The cove was filled with such a bright, white light they could barely stand to keep their eyes open to watch.

"Please stop!" Alexa screamed and tried to thrash, but the men held her tight. Apollos continued this practice for long, agonizing minutes. Bryan watched on, wishing he could take the pain from her. His jaw was clenched so tight it felt as if it might snap.

Finally, Apollos stopped and gently removed his horn from her stomach. The light and heat from his prismatic horn ebbed away to its normal soft glow.

The company looked down at the pallid girl. Her eyes were shut tightly. Her breath was still labored, but the wound on her stomach looked nothing like it had minutes before. It looked as it would after years of healing. It was merely a slightly raised, white scar across her skin.

All the men waited anxiously for her to wake. They watched in silent relief as the color slowly came back into her cheeks and her breathing slowed to normal. Then, finally, she opened her eyes. They were all relieved to see they held a spark of her fire in them again.

Alexa glanced around to the men and unicorn staring down at her. She cranked her chin down to take a look at her stomach. She removed her hand from Kheane's steady hold and ran her trembling fingers along the scar. Sighing with fatigue, she let her head fall back onto Alkin's lap. A small weak smile spread across her features as she looked at Apollos and his glittering chocolate eyes. "Thank you," she whispered froglike to him. She looked at the Master Sword with appreciative eyes that said the same, but holding so much more.

He grinned down at her feeling so relieved he thought he

might faint, although he would have never admitted it.

Chapter 25

"Who was he, do you think?" Alkin asked. The men were at the warm spring surveying the attack scene. Only Hazerk and Apollos had stayed behind to watch over Alexa. The company was gathered around the dead assailant. The thin man's body lay in awkward angles and motionless on the ground.

"Who knows?" Kheane answered while bending down and examining the corpse. "He has nothing to identify him…no markings."

Sword Bryan gazed a little unnerved down at the body at his feet. He had never killed a man before. It was a strange and unsettling feeling to know he had taken life away from another human being. A person only got to live once…

Kheane looked up to the frowning Master Sword standing silently over him. Bryan returned Kheane's stare. It was hard to read the ex-assassin's face since it was obscured by his hood. But his hard, coffee-colored eyes held an understanding the Master Sword wasn't sure if he found comforting or not. "You'll get used to it," Kheane said in his strange, raspy voice. The Master Sword's eyes studied the Alidonian's confident face and raised a skeptic eyebrow, his frown deepening. "He was trying to kill her, wasn't he?" Kheane said pointedly. Bryan shrugged coolly; he had a good point. "Besides, who knows what else he had in mind for her. From the way he looks, he was probably deprived of more than just food. She probably looked appealing having just bathed. He was undoubtedly planning on stabbing her in more than one way," Kheane stated blatantly, his tone dryly amused.

Bryan's face contorted into a disgusted glare at the ex-assassin. But he said nothing knowing it to be true. Although, hearing the truth out loud brought another wave of anger over him. It caused his former uneasiness for killing the stranger to dissipate. He didn't want to dive too far into this new, unwanted feeling he had obtained from his desire to protect Alexa's virtue…well, except maybe from himself. He gave his head a stiff jerk to clear his thoughts. Kheane's black eyes watched the Master Sword shrewdly. Bryan nodded curtly and turned away to investigate what the Prince, Eelyne and Warkan were now discussing over on the mossy rock where Alexa's quiver still laid.

They were debating on what should be done with the body. They could just unceremoniously dump it in the woods, or make a pyre, or bury it. They had no idea what the man's origin was, so therefore they didn't know what his tradition was. "Does it really matter?" Warkan asked bluntly.

"No, but—" Alkin hesitated. His good manners were giving him qualms over being so insensitive toward another's customs.

"My prince, there's no way to find out what his custom is. Let's just cover the body and leave it in the woods and move on. Nature will take its course," Warkan pressed.

Bryan joined them. He bent to gather up Alexa's quiver full of her black arrows and her well-made bow. As he straightened, he stated, "He's a murderer. He doesn't deserve much of a funeral. Let's bury the body and get out of here." Warkan shrugged, honestly not caring what they did. Alkin finally nodded in agreement, realizing they didn't have much of a choice considering the situation. "Okay, well, let's get this done." Sword Bryan looked to his men. Through the whole conversation Eelyne was silent and pointedly diverted his gaze from the Master Sword. But he jumped to the orders enthusiastically. "The sooner we get this done, the sooner we can clean up and get moving," Bryan stated in a close-ended way.

After the men had taken care of the body, they indulged themselves in a quick washing in the pool. All clean, they headed back to the camp. They found Hazerk with the camp packed up and Alexa roused and extinguishing the fire. She was fully dressed in her now washed and dried clothes, although her shirt still had remnants of the bloodstain across it. She moved about the camp a bit shakily, but in better health.

"What are you doing up?" Alkin demanded solicitously. He came to her and looked into her face imploringly. She gazed back at him with an appreciative sparkle in her eye. "Well, you have your color back. Do you feel better?"

"Yes. Hazerk is an excellent caretaker and Apollos, of course, is watchful. I'm fine, really," she stated as robustly as her still waxing strength would allow.

"Well, that's a relief to hear," Alkin smiled, giving her a brief and friendly kiss on the cheek. "Don't scare us like that again," he said and then took up Sapharan's lead to begin tacking him.

Alexa grinned from ear to ear at the Prince's sentiment. Turning, she caught eyes with the Master Sword, who was watching her and the Prince with a keen, conflicted gaze. Her grin faded, but she gave the Sword a small, timid smile, diverting her eyes slightly in shame over what she had done. Surprisingly, Bryan returned her smile with a small nod, and she knew she had been forgiven.

"Alexa, I'm glad you're okay." Eelyne approached her, severing the gaze between guardian and guarded. "I blame myself completely for disregarding my duty."

Alexa smiled reassuringly, "How is it your fault? I'm the one who ran off." Eelyne shrugged unconvinced and went to tack up Phoenix.

Alexa moved feebly to her bedroll, bending over carefully, holding her tender stomach and hoping no one spotted her acting in this pathetic manner. Sitting on her heels, she slowly rolled up her blankets and packed her things. At hearing the crunch of boots on the ground, she looked over to see the black, tall boots of the Master Sword. Alexa let her eyes follow them up over his form to his face. Her handsome Sword-Guard was holding her quiver and bow, and looking at her smugly with a raised eyebrow. Alexa went to stand abruptly, but the sudden movement sent a shock of pain through her body, causing her head to swim. She crumpled back to the ground. Bryan shot out his hand and steadied her. Alexa straightened slowly with his help. Embarrassed, her eyes flashed sourly and she said haughtily, "Come to tell me, 'told you so'?"

"Do I need to?" Bryan looked at her amusedly. Alexa lowered her gaze. "Though, I'm not completely blameless either," he added. Alexa raised her chin, her blue eyes widening with wonder. "I shouldn't have left you," he continued with perfect poise. "Here are your things." He handed over her quiver and bow.

"Thank you," she replied softly. She turned to finish her

packing, but Bryan stopped her.

"Are you well enough to travel? I would like to get moving, but if you're not feeling well…" he let the sentence hang awkwardly.

"Yes, Master Sword, I'm sure I can manage to at least stay in the saddle," she said levelly, her usual confidence returning rapidly.

"All right," he replied in a happy tone. He then fidgeted on the spot wondering whether or not he should help her pack her things. He decided she would rather not have his help, lest it should hinder her pride. He turned to Hazerk, who was stuffing his things into his saddlebag, and said, "If you and Apollos want to wash up in the spring go ahead, but we'll be heading out as soon as you've finished."

"Great. I'll be on my way," he said enthusiastically, but then stopped when he remembered his patient. He looked over to Alexa, who was moving with care around Zhan. His brow furrowed.

"She'll be fine. I'll make sure of it," Bryan assured.

Hazerk nodded, but approached Alexa. "Okay, Lil' Sis'?" he said in her ear, his hand gently resting on her shoulder. She nodded in reply with a brave smile. This seemed to appease him and he hollered to Apollos, "Ready for a dip, pal?" Apollos bobbed his head, and the two made their way down the path.

In a short time they were back on the trail again, headed to an uncertain place, but at least they were moving forward, which seemed to quench their anxiety. They pressed on for uncomfortable hour after uncomfortable hour, and rested for fewer hours than wished.

A couple arduous days later, Alexa rode near the front of the company with the Prince, Master Sword and Apollos leading the way. She was uncomfortable. She shifted and jostled in her saddle. Zhan turned a confused ear back every now and again, no doubt wondering what the matter with his mistress was. Alexa rolled her neck and winced. Looking upward between the heavy swaying branches to the small patch of sky above, she felt a sense of vertigo. She pressed her hand on her stomach where the wound had been. It seemed to alleviate the ache. Apollos had saved her life, but the pain hadn't ebbed.

Kheane, who was riding alongside her, looked over at her with a thoughtful eye. Her body had just experienced a killing blow and then it had been quickly healed in a most unnatural way. She was bound to be uncomfortable, he reflected. Plus, to his mind, she must be feeling stressed because of the nasty scar now imbedded in her skin forever. For a woman, he figured, this must be a difficult thing to accept. He felt he had to say something to console her, although he had never done such a thing for anyone in his whole life. "Well, Alexandra, we're bonded souls now," he said. His voice came out harsh and raw sounding to his own ears.

"Why do you say that?" She looked over at him, making a wincing face, holding her stomach.

"You're an initiated warrior now. You've scars to prove it and be proud of," he replied. Alexa gave the ex-assassin a weak smile, appreciating his attempt at cheering her. Having the scar didn't bother her, just the pain did.

"More like scars of stupidity." Warkan's wry voice came up from behind.

Kheane turned in his saddle and gave him one of his unsettling stares. "In my experience, sometimes a little stupidity turns out to be a good teacher, and therefore turns out a better warrior. Only of course, if one lives through it," Kheane stated. Alexa gave Kheane a glowing smile.

The Master Sword, listening to the conversation from ahead, suddenly felt his annoyance with Kheane rear its ugly head again. Not because of what he had said, but because he was trying to bond with Alexa. Bryan forced the feeling away and thought of what Kheane was saying instead. The Master Sword could remember quite a few stupid things he had done when he first began as a warrior. And, yes, the hard lessons he had learned from them hadn't been forgotten. Perhaps this incident would turn out to be a good thing for her.

"So, change of subject," Hazerk spoke up. He rode Red Man up to Alexa's other side. "Eelyne and I were wondering, Alexa, why you don't, or maybe you can't do all the fancy magic we always hear about in the tales of witches and wizards, like in the Lost War."

Alexa smiled. "Ah, yeah, well, I believe a lot of that is legend and a bit exaggerated."

"Oh, you mean like sorcerers tricking unicorns and then sawing off their horns and using their blood for spells. Or cutting out dragons' hearts, or turning people into animals, moving things without touching them, or blowing things up with fire, stuff like that," he said, and then hollered up to Apollos, "Sorry, Apollos, no offense meant!"

"None taken," the unicorn replied.

"Well, some of it is…but," she started slowly, realizing they were all straining to hear what she had to say. Perhaps they wanted to see how powerful she was and how leery they should be of her. "You see, my magic has been dormant, like my brothers', ever since I was born. My father made it so. He just recently started to teach me how to awaken it and use it for good only. I suppose it's because I'm more spoiled than the rest." She grinned sheepishly. The men all laughed wryly.

"Well, that explains a lot," Bryan said lightly, grinning.

Alexa tossed her head with poise, carelessly brushing off the snickers. "It could also be that I'm the last witch in the world—or at least in Eetharum. But if I practice, I'll eventually get better and seem more *magical* like you say. But not in the way you say, especially since I'm half human. My blood is diluted too much. I'll never be able to create grandiose magic. And what power I have is all about control. I'm still learning to control it. My magic is more apparent when my emotions are intense. Sometimes I don't create magic deliberately, especially if I'm angry. I need to learn to channel that intensity at my will in order to use the power better. The strongest magic I have control over now is my senses. I can sense things, people's feelings and intentions. And, of course, there's my witch intuition. There are many things I'm sure I'll be able to do, but nothing extravagant. I'm not sure of all the powers I'll have. I guess I'll find out as I learn. It's a gradual process. Most of the showy things you hear told in tales that sorcerers do are for evil purposes and take evil magic as a means to gain what they want. For instance, like Ret wanting to harvest the magic out of me and my brothers' blood to create a more pure, powerful magic. I know it's in my heritage to have a dark nature, but I was taught and I feel that it's not right. So I won't have those powers nor ever be that powerful. I choose not to be evil. Do you understand?"

"Yes, Lil' Sis', don't worry. We were just curious. We don't think you're a demon." Hazerk laughed.

Alexa smiled, her pain momentarily forgotten. "Oh, yes, and I can be awfully persuasive if I want to be."

"Well, any woman can do that if she wants," Prince Alkin laughed.

"Yes, but it's different." Alexa smiled mysteriously.

"Now you have us all scared," Alkin added with a worried brow, but a wry smile was across his lips.

"Don't worry. I haven't bewitched any of you into doing anything. Or doing something my way…I promised," Alexa reassured the men, now all staring with wondering eyes at her.

The men returned her grin with slightly uneasy smiles. Each remembering strange feelings they had acquired upon looking in her sapphire eyes at some point during their trip.

"Speaking of sensing things…" Apollos said from the head of the company. He stopped, and they all halted behind him, suddenly attentive to him and their surroundings, which, at the moment, seemed normal for the wood.

The unicorn looked curiously around the forest floor. Then he raised his head to peer above them. They all followed suit. A dense, gray fog seemed to be seeping down among the branches over their heads. "That's strange for midday," Alkin deduced. "The sun is out. I can see it and the blue sky through the trees."

"That isn't fog," Alexa said detached, as if she were listening for something or feeling out something without the use of her physical senses. Her head was cocked to one side, much like a dog listening for something in the distance.

"Great. What now?" Warkan grunted from the back of the party.

"Quick! We have to move fast," Apollos ordered, his voice

urgent but reserved. He took off at a canter, crashing through low hanging branches and underbrush.

"What is it?" More than one company member demanded as they all urged their mounts into as fast as a gait as they felt was safe for the footing.

"If it descends on us, and you inhale it, you'll hallucinate your own deaths. Hurry, it's looking for prey!" Apollos hollered in answer.

At that explanation, the company asked their horses for a higher and more dangerous speed. The warhorses' snorts and the thumping of their hooves on the ground were the only sounds among the harried companions as they fled the black air pursuing them. They flew over fallen trees and through a shallow creek and under a garden of low hanging vines before it caught them.

Realizing their hopeless capture, Apollos skidded to a stop, whipped around to face the company, and managed to shout out before it descended on them, "Keep your eyes on me and think of nothing but something worth living for. I'll get you through this. Remember!" The fear he injected into their minds showed on all their faces and was something Apollos would never forget. There as an infinitesimal moment filled with pure fright between Apollos' words and when the black air seeped into their midst. The company heard one more command from Apollos before they were all completely lost to their own uninvited imaginations, "Follow me. Don't stop."

The next thing Alexa comprehended was the complete muted silence all around her. It was as if someone had stuffed cloth in her ears. She rubbed her eyes trying to clear away the black patches forming in front of her eyes, but the act was futile. The black air thirstily sucked up every ray of light and coated the company with its toxin. The afternoon had suddenly changed to as if it were the hour right before dawn: the darkest part of the day. Alexa struggled to hold her breath against the oncoming surge, but that proved to be futile also. She had to breathe and she did. The horses did, too. The black air gleefully slithered into all their nostrils, mouths and pores.

At first, Alexa was surprised. Nothing happened. She

opened her tightly shut eyes. Then she started hearing things. The horses began to snort and dance restively. They arched their necks and pulled against their masters' hold. Alexa heard murmuring. It was the men. She looked around, but was unable to decipher much in the darkness. She could see shadowy silhouettes of the men and horses, but no more. The murmuring turned to fearful mumbles of plea. The horses began to grunt and squeal and toss their heads. Some jerked around wildly and tried to rear. The mumbles turned to shouts and calls for mercy and pleas for help and crying out in pain or fear. It was the worst sound Alexa had ever heard in her life. It spilled chill after chill down her spine and raised all the hair on her body.

Then, suddenly, Zhan threw up his head in fright, almost knocking her in the nose and whinnied in a horrid, frenzied pitch. Alexa did her best to calm the horse, but he began flinging his body around and twisted in every direction. She had no control of him. Zhan reared straight up and pawed the air screaming in panic, his eyes rolling. All the horses were caught in the web of their own hallucinations. Alexa looked desperately around. She saw the half conscious warriors and prince barely hanging on to the beasts as they too thrashed and groaned in their own worlds. "Apollos! Where are you?" she cried out frantically. The company had come to a halt on their path, but they were writhing like a dying snake.

"I'm here, Alexa, I'm here. Look at me! Do as I say and trust the Power!"

Then, Alexa saw a light beat back the dark and a white shape appeared. It was Apollos. He was glowing as if he were the moon. A gentle, but bright light emanated from him. Out of his, oh so wonderful, horn came waves of iridescent shimmering light. It was attempting to beat back the black air, but the air was pressing ever harder on it as if it had a life of its own.

Alexa watched with hopeful eyes as she saw wave after shimmering wave pulse from the unicorn's horn. He spoke words of comfort to the company and to the horses in their own tongue as his magic slowly filed into the darkness. He was like a creature of heaven, an angel. Alexa kept her eyes on him, but her lips were close to Zhan's ears, murmuring words of encouragement, love and trust.

Then, she heard it, a voice in her mind's ear. The black air had been struggling to break through the natural barrier set up by her magical blood, and it had discovered that all it could do was speak its toxin to her. It was a quiet voice. It hissed in her ear, speaking ever-so slyly to her, taunting her with words, cruel laughs and snickers. She would fail, it said. She would die, it said. Many other frightful things it whispered; all seemingly entwined in raw truth.

Alexa shut her eyes and mind from it. This was something she thought she could handle. *It lies*, she told herself. She had to concentrate on staying aboard the whirlwind Zhan and will the voice away. But the voice was relentless. She spoke to it, imploring it to stop. Nevertheless, it continued. She started to feel panicky. It would soon take over completely and utterly corrupt her mentality. It seemed to know her intimately, her most inner-fears. She couldn't block it.

Then, she remembered what Apollos had said. She opened her eyes and focused them determinedly on the unicorn attempting to fight the black air. As difficult as it was, she endeavored to trust that the High Power was in control. She focused on things she lived for, her family and home, and of the company…of Bryrunan.

The cruel voice weakened.

With time Apollos' iridescent weapon slowly filled the area and blocked out the dark air. The blackness didn't leave without a fight; it roiled and moved like a thunder cloud. But eventually it lifted to high above the trees and drifted away with an unnatural speed for just plain air. The horrific sounds of cries of fright and pain died down and the company slumped with exhaustion.

The warriors and prince fumbled to dismount, essentially falling off their warhorses. They hit the ground struggling to stand on their wobbling legs. The horses had calmed. They stood with their heads hanging low, their noses brushing the ground and their eyes dull.

Alexa sat astride the now settled Zhan, watching the company collect itself. Apollos stood silently by her side, waiting.

"That was the Arch Demon himself," Hazerk managed to

finally say hoarsely.

"Derived from him no doubt and only defeated by faith and goodness," Apollos answered.

"Tell me that really wasn't happening," Eelyne gasped.

"That was really not happening…but it would've killed you," Apollos replied.

"That was the worst thing I've ever experienced," Hazerk said.

"Pretty close for me, too," Kheane added, bending over to catch his breath.

"That must be saying a lot from you," the Prince breathed.

"All the snow is gone…" Eelyne said looking around perplexed. Everyone stared at him apprehensively.

"What snow, Warrior Eelyne?" Sword Bryan asked hesitantly.

"Wasn't there a blizzard? I was freezing. I thought I'd die. I couldn't feel my body," Eelyne stated, rubbing his hands together and pulling his cloak around himself tighter.

"No," Bryan answered.

"There were flames everywhere," Hazerk looked up, his eyes recalling his vivid hallucination. "I was burning alive."

No one spoke.

"The forest flooded from the sea. And I was struggling in a maelstrom. I swallowed gallons of water. I was drowning," Alkin said, his voice and eyes unsettled. "I can still taste the salt water in my mouth." He spat on the ground.

"I was being disemboweled alive. The pain was…unbearable," Warkan said emphatically, he placed a hand on his midsection.

"It was the same for me," Bryan said. "Very real. I could feel myself being hacked into and saw my intestines unraveling." He gave a shudder.

There was a moment of silence and then Eelyne said, "What about you, Kheane?"

Kheane gave a wry smile. "I was utterly forsaken. Then the earth cracked, swallowing me in a chasm. I fell continuously."

"You, Alexa?" Eelyne pressed.

Alexa saw all the men's faces turn toward her. Now becoming habit, she glanced at the Master Sword and held his sturdy gaze intensely. "I was protected…somewhat, by my magic. I heard voices," she said trying to lock the slippery voice far away from her memory forever. They all nodded in silence.

" Let's keep moving. You all rested enough?" Apollos disturbed the unsettling thoughts of the company. They all nodded and began collecting themselves, mounting up.

"I wonder what the horses' hallucinations were," Eelyne said as they started to move forward again.

"You spoke to them, Apollos. What did they feel?" Alexa asked, pricking the curiosity of all the company.

Apollos' eyes sparkled, "I can't exchange communication between humans and animals. It's forbidden. Humans were not meant to speak in that way with horses, so that is how it must be."

"Who forbids it? Come on, Apollos, tell us," Alexa pleaded, the others advocated her plea.

"I can't," he laughed, "Forget it."

They all fell silent as they trekked down the forest path, but it lasted only for mere moments before they came to a stop and looked cautiously on two large, black wolves blocking the way with bared teeth and raised hackles.

"What now? Just chase them off, or shoot them with your arrows, Alexa," Warkan said impatiently.

They received agitated, low growls from the wolves. The animals stood as still as statues, their amber eyes locking in on each one of the humans. The company's horses pranced in place restively, pulling at their bits.

Apollos stood at the head of the company, his head lowered and his horn pointing at the beasts defensively. His muzzle brushed the ground. His eyes were focused on the wolves as if he were communicating with them.

Warkan, who was slightly behind Alexa, reached stealthily for her bow and arrows.

"No. Don't hurt them!" She angrily snatched her weapons from his reach. He gave her an annoyed glare.

"What shall we do, Apollos?" Alkin asked.

"Wait. They're not possessed, or evil in nature. They're guardians," he answered.

As if it were meant to happen right at the moment Apollos finished speaking, a human came out of the woods to stand behind the wolves. "Easy, boys," she said to the dogs.

Chapter 26

It was a woman, a wild looking woman. She was dressed in thick animal skins. She wore knee-high leather moccasins strapped on by strings of leather winding all the way up her calves. Her hands were covered up to her elbows with leather gloves. Her pale face was smudged with dirt and her gray eyes were piercing. Her hair was flaming red, tangled and frizzed in all directions with bits of leaves and twigs twisted amongst the locks. In her arms she carried a stack of dry wood. She studied the company with a mixed expression of surprise and suspicion.

"My name is Levaun." Her voice was deep for a woman, but not masculine. She had an unfamiliar accent. "How did a large company like you make it this deep into the forest? I'm surprised. What do you want?" She peppered off the demanding questions so fast the company didn't have time to recover from taking in her eccentric appearance.

Alkin was the first to find his voice, "We wish you no harm, Levaun. We're just passing through and wish to keep our business to ourselves. I'm Alkin a merchant from the city of Shelport in western Shelkite. These are my traveling companions." Alkin then named off each one of the company members including Apollos, who hadn't made himself invisible.

"I didn't know it was common to have a unicorn as a counterpart in mercantile," she said curtly, but continued before Alkin could answer, "You can't expect me to believe you've come to Carthorn for trade. And it's much too far out of your way and dangerous for you to just be passing through." Her gray eyes narrowed as she stared levelly at the Prince. "I'm not a fool, my good man." She smiled slyly.

The company was all stunned by her attitude with Alkin; though they knew she didn't know he was a prince. The Prince smiled guilefully at her and bowed his head. "Too true. But as I said, we wish to keep our business to ourselves. But, would you be so kind as to lend us some help?"

Levaun shifted the pile of wood in her arms to a more comfortable position before she answered; her eyes never left the Prince's. She smiled. "I can't see why not," she concluded. "I haven't seen a soul in ages. It might do some good to have some company for once. How about this? No questions asked, you all come to my cabin by the lake and have some dinner. It's safe and not far from here. By the looks of you all, you could use a break. This forest has a way of breaking a person down."

"Would that lake happen to be the Faded Sea?" Alkin asked. She nodded. "Okay then, lead the way."

"Good. This way." She turned on her heel and started down the path at a surprising clip calling to the wolves, "Come, boys." The two black wolves bobbed on their legs and playfully nipped at each other before charging happily down the lane after her.

Prince Alkin looked over at Sword Bryan for affirmation. The Master Sword nodded and led the way after the eccentric woman.

Keeping a considerable distance from Levaun, but enough to see where she was headed, the company whispered fervently among themselves. "Just be careful. We don't know if we can trust her or not. It's strange she has survived by herself in this forest..." Bryan told them.

"I didn't feel any magic or an evil in her...she's just a hermit more than likely. But, still, keep a watchful eye," Apollos added.

Alexa was reminded of tales of lost children being mothered by a kind old woman befriending them in the woods, only to find she was leading them into a vicious trap.

"She's the most beautiful creature I've ever seen," Hazerk breathed.

Everyone turned to stare disbelieving at the warrior. He had a starry, glazed look in his eyes as he looked ahead to Levaun.

"You've got to be joking! Creature is for sure...." Warkan sneered.

"Nope. She's absolutely intriguing," Hazerk stated, clearly smitten.

"She's not attractive at all. She's clothed in animal skins!" the clearly disturbed Warkan exclaimed quietly, and then continued in disgust, "Her hair needs a desperate brushing. And, yuck, bright red hair and pale, freckled skin—"

267

"What's wrong with freckles?" Alexa interjected huffily.

"She looks scary, Hazerk." Warkan shuddered.

"Does not," Hazerk retorted.

"Now that we all know how Warrior Warkan feels…." Bryan said dryly.

Alkin leaned over and whispered in Alexa's ear with a grin, "Don't worry. Your freckles are very striking." Alexa smiled gratefully back, feeling warmth in her cheeks.

"I admit she seems a little rough around the edges, but that's what I like," Hazerk stated.

"Eeek," was all Eelyne could say as he stared incredulously at his fellow warrior.

"Okay, then, are you all in agreement she is nothing you desire?" he asked. Everyone agreed. "Good. I won't have any competition," Hazerk declared happily.

"She kind of reminds me of Alexa," Sword Bryan said attempting to sound serious, but he gave a roguish glance at Alexa.

"Hey!" she hollered indignantly. "I *don't* take that as a compliment." Everyone laughed.

"Okay, okay," Bryan laughed as she glared at him with her eyes spitting sapphire flames. "You're not that bad, but I'd say you aren't too far off from becoming that," he teased her playfully.

"I am not like that at all," she stated firmly, a disgusted look on her face; but her lips quirked into a half-smile at the Master Sword's attention.

"You are a bit manly…." Warkan laughed.

Alexa narrowed her eyes at him, and then regarded Kheane in mock offense, "You're just going to let them harass me like that?" Kheane merely continued to ride in his silent manner, but appeased her when he looked at her with his black twinkling eyes.

"Well the only girls you like, Warkan, are the ones you pay time for anyway," Hazerk shot at the burly warrior.

Eelyne turned in his saddle and gave Warkan a horrified look, "Really?"

Warkan looked as if he could wallop Hazerk's head off with his ax. "Don't believe a word that red-headed idiot says," he growled.

"I intend to put a stop to that business one of these days," Alkin inserted thoughtfully.

"Well, what kind of women to do you like? We've been all over the place and I've never heard you once say that you liked any of them," Hazerk continued snidely.

Warkan made an annoyed face and snorted, "I just like women a little more dignified and feminine."

"Oh, the ones that don't know how to enjoy life…well for you, that makes sense," Hazerk asserted. Warkan just scowled.

"Kheane, what kind of women interest you? It seems you'd like the rough type?" Hazerk pried.

"Dead ones," he simply replied. The company's conversation came to a shocked halt at his curt answer. Hazerk chuckled nervously. After a moment Kheane broke out in a boisterous laugh. His voice cords sounded as if they had never laughed. It was a harsh and unpleasant sound, making the company nervous, and leaving them wondering whether or not they really believed him joking. "I'm kidding," he stated brusquely.

"Oh. Well?"

"I haven't thought much about it…I mostly think of the girl, the orphan girl. I would like a woman like her, at least what I think she'd be like as a woman," he groused.

"What about you, Master Sword?" Hazerk turned his attention elsewhere.

Bryan just shrugged, seeming uninterested in the conversation. He didn't know Alexa's insides had done a complete flip at the idea of learning what he desired in a woman. Her heart beat faster. She willed the feeling to stop and go away. This infatuation was getting out of hand, she thought vaguely, as she strained to hear what he had to say. However, he didn't appease them with an answer at all.

"The Master Sword likes his women dainty and feminine, the all-around damsel in distress type. Very dignified. Isn't that right, Sword Bryan? You absolutely love dancing with the ladies at the balls." Prince Alkin smiled devilishly.

Alexa cocked her head to get a better look at the Master Sword. She regarded him curiously, wondering if it were true. If it was, she was nothing like that. But the Master Sword gave no indication it was true or not. He just smiled mysteriously and shook his head, disregarding his friend.

"And what about you, my prince, if you don't mind me asking?" Hazerk asked the Prince.

Alkin sighed as he thought. "I suppose I don't have a certain type. I like them pretty strong-willed and intelligent." He smiled.

"What about you, Alexa? What kind of women do you like?" Hazerk asked.

"Ha, ha, very smart of you." She smirked.

"What about me?" Eelyne perked up, not wanting to be left out.

"You couldn't get a girl if you wanted to," Warkan jeered.

Eelyne was about to retort when Alexa cut in for him. "Warkan, you're such a bully. Of course, he could. He's smart, handsome, thoughtful, and athletic." The words were out before she realized her mistake. All the men turned and looked at her smugly, all except Sword Bryan who simply stared at her with an inquisitive brow.

"Hmm, I think we'd better keep Eelyne and Alexa's bed rolls on opposite sides of the fire tonight," Hazerk snickered.

"Hang on now, that's not exactly how I meant it. I was just defending you, Eelyne, you know that," she quickly pleaded for Eelyne's support.

He smiled boyishly, "I know."

"Looks as if we're here," Apollos announced, putting a stop to all the human chattering he could never bring himself to understand.

They came into a small, circular clearing. It was far enough off the shore of the Faded Sea they couldn't see it, but they could smell the watery atmosphere. There was a one room, log cabin built there. Smoke drifted pleasantly from the chimney and the scent of pine wafted on the air. A small campfire out front had a spit on it with a fresh rabbit cooking. The only other structure in the clearing was a small shelter containing firewood. Encircling the grove were torches ablaze and set high on stakes every five feet.

The sight was inviting to the homesick company.

Turning to face them, Levaun said, "Welcome to my home."

"You live here? Alone?" Alkin inquired in astonishment.

"Yes," she said brightly. "I can't stand people." She smiled apologetically. "I'm originally from a small town on the edge of the forest. The citizens there and I never got on well after I lost my parents. So I decided to move. I came here. If you're wondering how I've survived, I owe it mostly to my wolves. They are great protectors. My parents also taught me a lot in survival."

"We've a unicorn. How have you protected yourself from the magical elements?" Sword Bryan asked, impressed by her courage.

"There are other forms of protection from them." She smiled secretively.

"You must be the so-called witch the townsfolk were speaking of. One we were to be careful of," Prince Alkin said, suddenly remembering.

Levaun laughed loudly, her deep voice melodious. "No, I'm no witch, just very determined to live here. They're a superstitious crowd. I enjoy being on my own. But you're welcome at my fire. At least until you're rested. Come on, un-tack the horses and we will eat and talk some more." She gestured for them to come and prepare for the evening.

Later when the sun had set and the stars were boldly shining in all their glory, the company sat in the clearing drinking in the sight above the treetops. The inky, dark blue sky was a brilliant background for the millions of sparkling specks of light. It was breathtaking. There seemed to be more stars here under the wing of Carthorn. But that couldn't be, could it?

"My cabin is located on the north side of the Faded Sea. It's less than a mile from here. I'll take you there if that's where you all are headed." Levaun said as they sat around the campfire eating the delectable rabbit she had prepared.

"Apollos, where was it you stayed when you were by the sea?" Alkin asked the unicorn, who was not joining the others in the rabbit dinner. Considering he didn't have a taste for meat, he was enjoying another one of his warm mashes.

"The southwestern side," he mumbled through a mouth full.

"The lake is vast. We would have never crossed each other's paths, although if we had, it would've been shocking to me. I've lived here fifteen years and I have not once seen a white unicorn among all the creatures," Levaun said. "If I may ask, was it the Guidance Naiad you searched for then?"

There was a pause in the atmosphere and the company all eyed each other apprehensively. They were still unsure whether or not they could trust her with any amount of information.

The long pause was enough to make Levaun retract her question, "I apologize. We did agree on no questions." She stood and stoked the fire, causing the hot coals to spit, fizzle and burn more brightly.

After another minute of silent eating, Prince Alkin leaned forward to speak to Levaun. He had a curious and confused look in his hazel eyes, "Why did you say specifically a white unicorn. I've only ever known there to be white unicorns. Isn't that right, Apollos?" Alkin directed the last part to the mystical creature. Apollos nodded his head and made a gesture equal to a human shrugging their shoulders.

Levaun swallowed her mouthful of food and licked her lips as she thought, seeming as if she were contemplating on whether or not she could trust them. "Well, you see, I thought the same thing, too, up until a few years ago." She took another bite of her food, giving no inclination to continue her explanation.

This snagged the company's attention immediately. They all waited impatiently for her to explain. "What do you mean? Are you saying there are other unicorn's still alive out there? I'm not the last one?" Apollos inquired earnestly.

Levaun wiped her mouth on her arm and looked at Apollos meaningfully. "The forest has been changing more than usual these last few years. And with that I've notice a few new creatures that weren't here before. Or rather, I don't even think they existed before…I don't know how to explain it. But Carthorn has become even shadier than I think it ever was or is supposed to be."

Apollos and the company passed apprehensive looks around to each other.

"It's all rather fishy and I don't like it. Maybe something greater is working here. But it's definitely not something good. The unicorns I've seen, if that's what you could even call them, look exactly like Apollos, except for a few different traits. They are dark. Really dark, a black you almost get lost in when you see them. When they're around, your eyes play tricks on you. Their horns are ebony, solid and shiny. Their hooves are the same. They have black eyes, showing red where the whites should be. And the strangest thing, they have sharp teeth, like as if they were meat eaters. Oh, but they're beautiful, too. So beautiful. That's how they draw their prey in. I've named them the darkhorns. I've seen several of them. They haven't tried to harm me or the wolves, but I've seen them act violently. The last time I saw them was a few weeks ago. A herd of them was traveling north." Levaun paused to gaze at the company's shocked, pallid faces. Alkin went to speak, but she silenced the Prince with a raised hand. "There's more. I've seen a higher number of goblins. Before they mostly hid in their caves and kept to themselves. But they've been out doing wicked things. A few months back I was hunting and saw them with captives they must have gotten from a village on the outskirts of the forest."

"That's probably where Alexa's attacker came from," Bryan broke in.

"Yes. He must have escaped from them," Alkin agreed. The others agreed.

Levaun nodded, "And that's *still* not all. I've spotted manticores. They were extremely rare before, but now I seem to be dodging them more often. You'll need to watch out for them; they're vicious. And, I had a run in with a changer the other day. It had me tricked into thinking it was an overly curious and playful monkey. If it hadn't been for my wolves it would have captured me…and probably stripped me of my flesh." She shuddered.

"Well, it seems meeting you was meant to be, Levaun," Alkin said sincerely. "You've already been a great help to us. You've provided us with vital information and food. We thank

273

you."

"I have more to tell if you wish to hear it. And if I can help in any way in getting you safely through the forest, I will. I may not be fond of human company for long periods of time, but I definitely don't wish you all harm."

"Yes, by all means, if there is more, please tell us. Although, I'm already worried by what you've told me. I hate to think there's more," Alkin said despondently.

"Well, I've ran into hatchlings…."

"What kind of hatchlings?"

"Dragon."

Bryan's mount lifted his head from his grazing and nickered at the sound of his name. The Master Sword couldn't help but let a small, amused smile escape him. He turned and gently hushed his friend. The warhorse went back to eating contently.

"How would dragon eggs get here without a grown adult?" Hazerk asked.

"Exactly. They couldn't. That means there must be a full grown female around somewhere," Levaun answered. "I haven't seen one, though. The thought had crossed my mind to just kill the hatchlings. Since it was still within my power to do so at the time, but I didn't know what the consequences of that would be. If it meant that an irate female dragon was going to track me down, I decided it wasn't worth it. I've survived here this long, but I'm afraid I have no clue how to fend off a dragon, unless, of course, I had a dragon whisperer. And as far as I know *I* don't have any dragon whispering talents!"

"What in the demon's name is a dragon whisperer?" Warkan said a little jeeringly.

"Oh, come on, Warkan! Be realistic. You can't tell me you don't believe in the famed dragon whisperers? After all that you've seen now?" Eelyne burst out. The burly warrior frowned at being chided by his younger counterpart.

"Dragon whisperers were only among certain blood-lines in men. It's said that the men who possessed this innate talent could understand the dragons' language and have them do their bidding. The dragons would do it willingly. It wasn't as if they were slaves.

274

Dragons are fickle creatures by nature. And depending on their master they could be used for good or evil. In our history records many battles are recorded where there are dragons on both sides," Eelyne gladly explained to the whole group.

"So, you're saying dragons have been extinct, and now they are suddenly turning up again?" Hazerk inquired directly to Levaun.

"I don't think they've been extinct exactly, but dragons have definitely not been seen for hundreds of years, as well as dragon whisperers," Eelyne answered for Levaun. Hazerk gave him a look that told him to back off. Eelyne shrugged.

"Well, this is interesting news," Alkin concluded.

"I know I'm not to ask questions of you, but out of curiosity, are you searching for the Guidance Naiad? Is that why you've traveled to the Faded Sea?" Levaun asked changing the subject.

"We actually aren't looking for Guidance Naiad exactly. But if we happen to meet her that would be good, because we could use a few answers. However, I know she can be very difficult to contact. So we're not too hopeful," Alkin admitted.

Levaun suddenly looked forlorn, "I'm sorry to disappoint you, but it seems you are out of luck anyhow. The Guidance Naiad has left," she said sadly.

"What do you mean left? She usually comes and goes as she pleases," Alkin said.

"No, I mean she's gone for good," Levaun said.

"What do you mean? This *is* sad news," Alkin said hastily.

Levaun's gloomy gray eyes focused on each one of the company's members before she continued. Her pale face, from being under the forest's cover for so many years, shone shockingly in the firelight and her hundreds of freckles seemed to glow in the low light. "At first I just felt it happening. A few months ago there was a palpable presence missing here. I've lived so close to the Faded Sea for so long I sensed it right away. It was like someone had sucked away a piece of heaven. I felt it in my heart, you know, the part that's still attached to that place where all our souls long to be. I felt sad and lost. But it passed, and then she came to me in a dream. I had never seen her before, but I knew it was her. She told me she was leaving Eetharum forever. She was going home now, and I was to tell anyone searching for her that they must not rely on her for guidance anymore. They were to believe and search for their answers in the High Power. She departed saying one last thing. She said the Mother of Pearl will soon no longer be a portal for answers either. I was so shocked, I didn't say a word. I don't know what she means by Mother of Pearl. I've never heard of it." Levaun ended here with a dejected sigh.

The company passed meaningful looks to one another. "Well, we do. Thank you, Levaun, for your information. It's much appreciated," Alkin said. "As you must have already figured out we aren't just merely passing through. We're on a mission. And it does have a great deal to do with everything you've seen changing around here. We're attempting to find some answers in how to stop something terrible that's happening in Eetharum," Alkin explained, deciding it was safe to at least give her some information. "I strongly urge you to come with us, Levaun."

The company all passed surprised looks. But, after a moment of considering the situation, each one quickly supported the Prince's proposition, pleading with Levaun not to stay in the treacherous forest.

Levaun looked extremely hesitant. "I don't know…" She glanced over to the cozy home she had made and down to the wolves curled up at her feet.

"It's become far too dangerous for you to live here and survive on your own, even with the wolves," Alkin pressed.

"Yes. And the wolves would be more than welcome in our company," Hazerk added. Levaun gave him a small, sad smile. She reached down to stroke the sleek hair of the wolf closest.

"You could find a nice secluded place and settle there for as long as you wish. You'd only have to put up with us long enough to get out of the forest. What do you say?" Alkin beseeched.

They all waited in anxious silence for her answer. Levaun continued to stroke the wolf. "My place is here," she finally said, looking up. "I will take you to the Faded Sea if that's where you still want to go. And I will help you in every way that I can, but I can't leave here."

"I see. Well, I hope you'll reconsider before we leave," Alkin said reluctantly. With that, he stood. "We should rest. We've had a long few days and have our work cut out for us," he said, giving Alexa a depressed, knowing glance. She nodded her head grudgingly and stood to make up her bed roll. "I'll take first watch," Alkin offered.

Chapter 27

The company decided to rest only one day at Levaun's cabin. They couldn't afford to waste any time. They would leave at dawn the next day and head for a nearby valley to the north. The decision to travel to the valley was made by the company on the account Levaun had given them of it. She explained it was a beautiful, verdant valley filled with scores of apple trees. She said it emitted a feeling distinguishing it as old, extremely old. She claimed it might possess magic there. Because, strangely, the trees seemed to always be ripe with apples year round. Levaun had only mentioned the valley in passing among other things she had discovered in Carthorn; she still didn't know of their mission. In private, Alexa and Apollos reminded the others of the vision of the apple trees in the Mother of Pearl. To everyone the orchard seemed like an apt place to checkout.

The company took their time off to reorganize their things and give their mounts a little extra resting time. They gave their horses special attention, grooming them until their coats shone, and feeding them fresh carrots they had dug up from Levaun's garden with her permission. They also spent the day listening intently to all Levaun's stories and information she could offer. And, of course, Sword Bryan spent a good part of the day drilling Alexa and Eelyne in their swordplay.

Mid-morning, Levaun took the Master Sword, Prince Alkin and Apollos to see the nest of hatchlings by the shore of the Faded Sea. Sheltered behind underbrush, the four watched the playful dragonlings in astonishment. Levaun commented that the group of five babies had indeed grown a lot since she last saw them. The little dragonlings seemed oblivious to their watchers. They played with each other much like puppies would play with one another. They yelped, growled, rolled, and snapped at each other. The only difference was their whole area of play was scorched and smoldering, the effects of their playful spits of fire.

The day turned out to be hot and humid. Alexa could feel the sweat rolling down her back and trickling down between her breasts. Her arms and back ached, as did her still tender scar. She had insisted she was well enough to swordfight, so the Master

Sword had continued on with his usual merciless drilling. Though, now, she was second thinking her choice. Nonetheless, she was resolved to push through the pain.

Eelyne and she had been practicing for what felt like endless hours. She paused her attack on Eelyne and made a gesture that meant for Eelyne to stop. The warrior was just as pleased to get a break. He went over to plop on the ground, drained. Alexa bent over the hilt of her sword and tried to catch her breath. Her chest heaved, and she sucked in thick air brimming with the dampness of promised rain. She placed a gentle palm on her scar. The skin and muscles surrounding it throbbed and burned. "Need a few minutes…." she breathed to Sword Bryan who was standing nearby with his arms crossed, looking exasperated by their unapproved cease in swordplay.

For a moment it looked as if he was going to deny them a quick break, but then he smiled, uncrossing his arms and said, "Okay, take a quick break. Get some water, and then prepare yourselves to go around in a bout one on three and then four. You've done one on two and two on two. It's time for you to move up."

Alexa stared at him with an evil look in her eye, but said nothing. *She* was the dummy who insisted she had felt fine…She straightened determinedly, pushed a sweaty lock of escaped hair out of her face and went to retrieve her water pouch. She took her pouch and went over to stand by Prince Alkin, who was sitting with Levaun on a bench discussing pathways out of the forest.

"I also found that not far from Orchard Valley is a section in the forest that seems to be impenetrable. It's a wall made of thick brush and trees. I've never been able to go around it or through it. It goes for miles and miles east and north. I suggest you pass by it. Just go straight north. Don't try to breach it. I don't know what's beyond it."

"Thank you. I assure you, we'll take your advice in account when we get on the move," Alkin replied.

"You're welcome to all the advice I can think of to tell you. I wish you could tell me more of your reasoning for this absurd traveling route. I can guess it's much more than you are letting on.

But again, it is none of my business…and maybe I don't want to know," Levaun stated.

Alkin patted the woman's hand, which was resting in her lap. "You're correct. But, if you still refuse to travel with us, I'm afraid I can't tell you anymore than you already know. Just remember to take careful care of yourself from here on out." She nodded her head understandably.

"Okay, Sand Queen, Warrior Eelyne! Break's over," Bryan's voice cut through the conversation. He spun around to regard the rest of the group, "I need a few volunteers," he said, smiling impishly. He was answered by silence. "Okay, you all—" he started.

"I'll go a round," Alkin cut him off.

Everyone was stunned and completely mute, except for the Master Sword who didn't act fazed at all. He grinned. "Great," he said. He looked around to the rest of them expecting others to volunteer.

"You don't expect to us to actually swordfight with our prince? Do you? What if we accidentally injure him?" Hazerk blurted, aghast.

"Prince! You're a prince?" Levaun suddenly exclaimed, jumping up from beside Alkin and staring unbelieving at him with a trace of fear in her eyes.

The whole company simultaneously glared at Hazerk who was looking rather sheepish.

Alkin looked up at Levaun. He nonchalantly raised an eyebrow; a reticent look laced his features, "In a matter of speaking…perhaps." He then jumped up and said enthusiastically, "Let's forget what was just said and go around a few bouts. Come on, Warrior Hazerk and Warrior Eelyne, you side with me against Alexa. Warrior Warkan, you come in after a few minutes and join us. And then Alexa and Warrior Eelyne will switch places. The Master Sword will oversee our moves."

They all jumped to action at the Prince's command. Alexa took her stance. She held the hilt of her still sheathed sword, earnestly waiting for the first attack blow from one of the three males now encircling her. She disregarded her throbbing wound.

Drawing her sword, Alexa looked straight in Alkin's eyes. They were kindly as usual, but they had a playful, competitive glint that Alexa found alluring. She gave the smug looking prince a sly, half smile. He gave her a slight nod. He was standing to her left. Hazerk was to her right. She could sense Eelyne standing directly behind her. Her skin prickled with anticipation. She closed her senses to all else around her and focused on the armed men around her, trying to feel out their first move so she would not be caught off guard and struck down instantly.

Hazerk was the first to strike. Alkin thrust immediately after. She parried the first and dodged the second, spinning to block a blow from Eelyne. Hazerk swung his large double-handed sword. Alexa twisted to block the blow, her arm feeling the force and smarting from the strength behind it. A mere infinitesimal second later, Alkin took a mean swipe at her ankles. She leapt, almost losing her balance, crying out in the unfairness of the action. She was only answered with a roguish laugh from the Prince, and a few more hard to block blows from Hazerk and Eelyne.

The foursome went around like this for several minutes. Alexa only had time to parry or dodge. She didn't land a single blow on her adversaries. Her frustration showed clearly on her face. Near the end of the bout, Hazerk swiped at her knees. She leaped high in the air as if she were a school girl playing jump rope with her friends. She would have landed squarely if it hadn't been for Alkin sending a hard blow at her while she was in mid-air, which caused her to twist and block it, sending her whole body sprawling in the air off balance. She landed in a heavy heap on her backside. The three males' blades went straight to her throat. All three men grinned. Alexa clenched her jaw, glaring at each one from her humble spot in the dirt.

"Good job. Alexa, we'll have to work some more on that, but not bad. Okay, Warrior Eelyne, your turn to be on your own. Get up, Alexa. Stop pouting and try to not hold anything against your new partners. You're on the same side now," Bryan said from the sidelines.

Pushing aside her pride, Alexa allowed Alkin to give her a

hand in standing. Sighing loudly and attempting to put aside her agitated feeling, she took her stance beside the Prince. Getting back into focus, she prepared for her first move against Eelyne.

Standing a hair's width from Alkin, the Prince gave her a nudge. She looked over at him to find him grinning at her. To her surprise, her insides melted completely. Her posture relaxed. She smiled bashfully back; but at that same moment she was blindsided by a blow from Eelyne. The hit knocked her off her feet and back on the ground where she had been moments before. Her body stung from the impact.

There was a scramble amongst the sword fighters to see if their counterpart was okay. They all shoved at each other to reach her.

"Are you all right?" Eelyne exclaimed, "You're lucky I hit you with the side of my sword. I hope I didn't hurt you."

Pushing the men's helping hands away, she slammed her palms down and stood abruptly. "I'm fine!" she growled. The men, as well as everyone else in the camp, watched in amused silence as she quickly brushed herself off. She took her stance again, acting as if nothing ever happened.

Sword Bryan cleared his throat, "Okay. Now, try not to get distracted this time, Alexa."

Alexa looked over and met eyes with the Master Sword. He was looking rather amused, but grumpy all the same. She nodded her head curtly. He turned away from her. She then set to work on the task ahead of her.

As they teamed up against Eelyne, Alexa often found herself fighting shoulder to shoulder and back to back with the Prince. The brush of his body on hers sent shivers down her spine, which she tried to ignore. But, it was hard. Especially since he kept sending roguish grins her way any chance he got. Alexa found herself looking away, realizing she was entering a dangerous zone here, finding herself attracted to and flirting with a prince. It didn't help either that he was excellent at his swordplay. Something she seemed to find irresistible, considering it was one of the things she found pleasing in the Master Sword, too.

Several minutes into the bout, Sword Bryan ordered

Warrior Warkan to join on their side against Eelyne. It went rather well considering everyone was dodging Warkan's wide swings with his battle ax. After a while at this pace, Bryan announced, "Okay. That's good for today. Alexa, we'll work more on your three on one practice and then maybe on team practices before adding a hazard such as Warrior Warkan to fight against solely you." Warkan laughed boisterously, while the rest of them laughed a little nervously.

"Thank you," Alexa said breathlessly. Looking glum, Bryan shrugged carelessly and turned curtly from her gaze. His indifference gave a strange jolt to Alexa's heart. She shook her head. Why should she care what he thought of her? Had she not decided that he didn't care anything for her and was way out of her reach anyhow?

A bit later, as the evening hours arrived, Levaun prepared a delicious meal for the company. They all sat and conversed pleasantly around the fire. The always silent observer Kheane caught Alexa's attention and said, "Would you like to work on your skills with the Alidonian weapon again tonight?"

Alexa perked up, happy to have something divert her thoughts from the Master Sword and now the Prince. "Yes," she answered.

"Wait," Hazerk spoke up, a wily smile on his face. "Today we all got to see for the first time…*Master* Alkin's sword fighting skills—and if I might say, it was rather awesome. I'd like to be entertained even further and see Kheane go up against Master Sword Bryan. If you both don't mind? And if Alexa doesn't mind missing a lesson with Kheane."

At this suggestion, everyone in the camp expressed their pleasure at the idea. All except the Master Sword and Kheane, whom both just stared at each other. Noting their reluctant silence, everyone pleaded to them to do it. Finally, both men seemed to decide at the same time without a word to each other. They stood and went to a spot where they had plenty of room to bout and faced each other.

All the company and Levaun watched intently and anxiously. Hazerk moved over to sit by Levaun and whispered in her ear, making her smile. Alexa grinned at him and shook her head. She was sitting next to the Prince. She glanced at him to find him gazing at her. He smiled softly, a fond look in his eyes. Alexa couldn't bring herself to look away. But the Prince gestured for her to watch the commencing bout.

She looked over to the two men facing one another. Her stomach gave a flutter at seeing the look on the Master Sword's face. She found him so handsome, intriguing, proud and puzzling. His face was stern and focused. His perfectly formed body flexed a display of the power beneath. He drew his sword fluidly. It came out with a pleasant sing-song sound.

Kheane was just as daunting and captivating in all his clandestine darkness. His hand was inside his cloak; the observers could barely hear him draw his sword. He held it out. It was long and slender. A split second later the two men clashed into the throes of the match.

True to Hazerk's guess, it was quite something to behold. Not all the competitive matches in the world set up for the entertainment of the public could compare to the match taking place here. It was a beautiful dance of death. Each man was precise in every move, in every thought and motive. The two were not just playing around either, the spectators feared for the men's lives as the match progressed.

Alexa watched as if she were in a trance. Something new arose inside her and came to life, something foreign, but not unpleasant or unsolicited. For as long as she could remember she had never desired something as badly as she did at that moment. Every move he made, every face he made, every sound escaping his lips, was like air to her. She needed it. She longed for it. And she breathed it. She drank it up like water to quench a lethal thirst. It took every ember in her being and self-control not to run to him, pull him away from his match and take him away to give all of herself to him. Seeing him now dissipated all girlish affections she had felt for the Prince, and for Kheane. Her eyes locked on every move the Master Sword made only to confirm and forward all her feelings toward him. If only he could see how she felt. How she wished the pairing was even possible! Her feelings were nearing a dangerous infatuation, way beyond just a mere fondness for him now....

Alexa tore her eyes from the two men, desperately trying to redirect her thoughts. She pretended to watch the match along with the others, but her eyes were looking over their heads off into the distant woods. And that is where she kept them until the wonderful match was completely over; until she could trust herself to look upon the Master Sword like a normal person again.

Kheane and he were laughing and shaking hands. It had ended with Kheane the victor. Bryan took his defeat gracefully, saying casually, "Can't win them all."

The ex-assassin merely replied, "You did well."

They came to sit around the fire and talk merrily with the others, exclaiming over the intense match. Alexa couldn't help but watch the features of the happy Master Sword. He was smiling and laughing loudly, something she rarely saw him do. Her insides jumped when he briefly glanced and smiled widely at her. She grinned back, albeit it was cloaked with a yearning she couldn't conceal any longer. He gave her a puzzled, thoughtful look at her strange display before turning to laugh again with Kheane, whose coarse voice sounded so strange laughing as it never had before.

At twilight, the company refreshed themselves in the warm waters of the Faded Sea. They washed away the stickiness and sweat the hot and humid day had left them. Levaun had wished to stay back to prepare and pack food for the company's departure in the morning.

Alexa sat on an elevated bank overlooking the waters of the lake, where the white half-moon shone brilliantly. Surrounding the lake were grassy rolling knolls, stretching far from the bank to meet the thick, encompassing forest. A light mist appeared and undulated around them. It swam over the knolls, gently creeping over the quiet waters to kiss the half clothed bodies of the men. The air had distinctly cooled from the earlier mugginess. And Alexa longed to jump in the warm water and join her company. However, she thought it best she stay put where she was and enjoy the nice scenery the men were providing.

She gazed silently down on the company from atop her

pedestal of rock and dirt. A small smile tugged her lips as she watched Apollos roll in the shallow water and leap up to playfully paw in it. She eyeballed the men as they waded around with bare chests, their trouser legs rolled up. They refreshed themselves by splashing water on their arms, chests and faces and wetting their hair.

Alexa openly admired the naked chests of her company. Every one of the men looked as if they could have been the subject of a sculpture to depict one of the gods of old. Their strong, well-muscled torsos flexed pleasingly to the eye as they moved about. Even Kheane's heavily scarred chest was taunt and nicely chiseled. If Alexa had ran into him in the dark, she would have been frightened to death, for he had removed his cloak and all the horror of his scarred face and torso stood out menacingly. But, now, to her, he seemed as gentle and kind as a kitten.

The leaner builds of the Prince and Eelyne were just as pleasing. Although they were more slender than the two other warriors and Master Sword, their muscles were well formed, too.

Deciding to speak, she said with wry satisfaction, "Ahh, I feel like I'm surrounded by the gods." She said this in play, but Alexa was having serious trouble tearing her eyes away, especially from the Master Sword's tall, broad body. The tantalizing Sword, however, was apparently ignoring her. While the others chuckled merrily and perhaps a tad vainly at her comment, he showed no sign of hearing her. He merely kept scrubbing his grime away.

Grinning, Hazerk waded over to her. He placed a hand on her bare foot where it was dangling down from atop her perch and gave it a playful tug. "You have it all wrong, Lil' Sis'. I'm afraid we're just the mere attendants of a goddess." Alexa threw her head back and laughed, most enchantingly with the moonlight on her dark hair.

"Too true," Prince Alkin chuckled, admiring her pretty silhouette openly.

"Maybe the goddess of war," Warkan said with an attempt at being funny.

Bryan's head shot up amusedly along with all the others to peer at Alexa's reaction to this jab. Everyone knew that the goddess of war was the least beautiful of the goddesses. The men snickered, waiting for her to explode.

She simply said with a laugh, "I'll take that as a complement from you, Warkan." The men smiled. Warkan shrugged with a lazy grin across his lips. Alexa studied Warkan's stature. He was by far the biggest of all the men. He was broader, stronger and taller and also looked rather disproportioned. Then, knowing full well he could crush her between his thumb and finger if he wanted, she said, "At least my head isn't freakishly too small for my body." Everyone burst out laughing. Even Warkan cracked a grin. He turned and splashed a heap of water at her. Alexa laughed openly, surprised at his uncharacteristic show of playfulness.

The group quieted down. And after watching the Master Sword for a moment longer, Alexa stood and turned away. She needed a change of scenery. Her thoughts were tormenting her with visions of herself entwined in his capable arms and snuggled tenderly against his strong chest. She yearned to touch his skin with her fingertips. How would his kisses feel on her lips? And, what of that intriguing trail of hair starting at the bottom of his belly and disappearing into his trousers…?

So annoyingly tantalizing! She clenched her teeth sourly. She had to leave.

"Okay, Alexa, it's your turn! Come on, strip down. Get cleaned up." Hazerk's mischievous voice cut into her fancies.

She turned back to face them and grinned knowingly, "Nah-ah." She shook her head and looked at all their impish faces skeptically. "The last time I stripped down a crazy man attacked me. I'm not about to be caught in that situation again." She laughed.

"Wow, Master Sword! I didn't realize you felt so strongly about Alexa," Hazerk teased, giving his superior a playful nudge with his elbow.

"Ha!" Bryan snorted with a wry scoff.

"You're going to get pretty rank smelling if you don't," Eelyne jumped in playfully, hoping to persuade her. They all gave her a boyish smile. Kheane even had a small grin across his always sober features.

"Nice try. At least my stench will keep all you wild stallions at bay. Now, stop trying to convince me to undress in front of you. I'm not a show girl for your entertainment."

"I'm sure your stench isn't the only reason men stay away," Warkan added as one last good-natured jeer when she turned her back. She chuckled and waved his comment away.

"He's insulted you twice now! I'll take him out for you if you want," Hazerk called, as he made a playful combative move in Warkan's direction.

She shook her head, smiling. When she went to turn away again, she was stopped short by the Master Sword's firm voice. "Alexa, Don't you walk away alone, again," he called. "Sit back down and wait until we can go with you."

She sighed reluctantly. Oh, why did his voice bring chills to her like a god whispering her name? Even when he was being contrary…. Well, she decided, if she was going to have to endure his presence she would at least clean up, fully dressed, of course. She would just wash up the best she could amid all the distractions. She slowly made her way down the steep bank and joined the now cat-calling males.

*****

Early the next morning, they said their goodbyes to Levaun. She still continued to stubbornly turn down all of Prince Alkin's beseeching for her to accompany them. She did, however, generously help them prepare to leave. She also drew up a crude map of where the apple orchard was located. The company was grateful for all the assistance and information she had provided. They told her so, though no one more so than Hazerk. He had scarcely left her side since they had arrived. And now he whispered in her ear, eliciting a smile from her before he mounted Red Man to leave.

Having the company all mounted and ready to begin their journey to the orchard, Sword Bryan knelt down and gave the two wolves an affectionate pat goodbye. Wagging their tails in delight, the animals bounced on their front paws pushing each other out of the way, each envious for attention. The Master Sword smiled fondly at them, remembering his childhood dog, his best friend. With one last nod at Levaun, and a quick glance around at his company to ensure its order, he mounted Dragon. Then, once again, they promptly set off down one of Carthorn's many mysterious paths.

The path Levaun sent them on was steep, narrow and full of roots emerging from the ground and low hanging branches. The roots threatened to trip the horses. The branches threatened to unseat the riders. And the journey threatened everyone's peace of mind. Nevertheless, the company had no other troubles then those minute obstacles in reaching the apple orchard. They reached the bottom and end of the path by midmorning, unscathed save for a few scratches. The thick woods came to a sudden stop and opened into a great vale before them. They blinked from the bright sunshine until their eyes adjusted from the gloominess of the forest. The company filed from the narrow path onto the lush, grassy terrain. They drank in the beauty around them.

The vibrant colors and overall loveliness of the valley was a pleasure to their senses. The forest set a circumferential boundary around the expanse of valley. The valley possessed hundreds of fruitful apple trees. All were filled with red, succulent, plump apples. The green of the trees' leaves were as vivid as the red of their apples. Their trunks were stout, gnarled and ancient. But one only had to look to know they were strong.

Weaving between the trees, northeast to southwest, was a rushing, glossy river. Its breadth was not narrow or too broad. Its depth was about waist deep. The emerald grass was thick and smoothly blanketed the small dips and rises of the valley terrain. It was highly tempting to the horses. A sweet, apple scented breeze wafted gently at their faces, causing stomachs to grumble with hunger and tongues to water with craving.

Looking farther into the center of the valley, Alexa spotted the tallest and oldest looking apple tree. The magic in her core hummed in recognition. She pointed at the tree, breaking the company's fervent observation of the valley and said, "That's where we have to go."

Chapter 28

As the company slowly made their way farther into the valley, they sniffed the apple perfumed breeze appreciatively. They were headed in the straightest fashion toward the large, gnarled apple tree. Alexa was leading the company with Sword Bryan and the Prince directly behind her. She rode with poise, her face set resolutely.

"Mmm, I have to one of those." Hazerk went to grab at one of the scarlet apples dangling from the nearest tree.

Apollos suddenly appeared next to him and whispered fretfully, "Don't touch those!"

Hazerk snapped his hand back as if the apple had bit him. "How come?"

The unicorn tossed his nose in the air. "We don't want to risk anything until we have what we need," he whispered.

"Huh?"

"Shhh!" Alexa hissed, twisting in her saddle to scowl at Hazerk with her fiery, sapphire eyes.

"Yes," Apollos said quietly. "We have to be quiet. We can't scare the trees."

"You mean the dryads, right?"

Apollos sniffed and flicked his tail, "Yes."

The company made their way quietly across the valley. They traveled up and down the small knolls, forded the crystal river and headed up one last hill toward the tree. The trees around them appeared to have noticed their presence for they began moving more in the soft breeze, their plump apples hanging precariously on their branches. The sunlight streaming through the leaves made shadows and light dance all around the company. The horses seemed to have picked up on their riders' carefulness. They stepped more surefoot and softer, their heads low, eyes alert and ears swiveling for sounds.

Once they neared the ancient apple tree, they dismounted a couple hundred feet away and paused to gaze at it. It was a gnarled looking tree. But it was abundant with scarlet, luscious looking apples and vibrant green leaves. Despite its awkward form, it waved elegantly in the wind.

290

Gazing stoically ahead, Alexa handed her reins unknowingly off to the Prince, who had been standing closest to her. With her dagger strapped on her right thigh, her bow and quiver across her back, and her hand on the hilt of her sword belted at her waist, she strode with confidence toward the tree. The Master Sword was quick on her heels, his features austere. She glanced back at him, said nothing, but looked to Apollos and motioned for him to come also. The unicorn swiftly came up beside the Master Sword, giving Alexa the lead. The others hung back, watching earnestly and silently.

Alexa marched straight up to the tree's nearest branch hanging just above her head. Pursing her lips, she contemplated for a moment. She looked over her shoulder to the Master Sword and Apollos. Bryan had his hand gripped tightly on the hilt of his sword, his features set intensely. Apollos looked on encouragingly, imploring her to take an apple. Alexa flashed them a quick, brave grin, knowing it was now or never, and then reached up to grip a plump apple.

Suddenly, the scenery transformed before all their eyes. Just as Alexa's fingertips brushed the red skin of the apple, the apple, as well as all the apples on every tree in the valley, shrunk down and transformed back into bright pink and white blossoms. The valley was instantly changed from a vibrant red, to a soft, delicate pink.

Flabbergasted, Alexa spun around, her mouth agape, and took in the transformed valley. The apple blossoms danced in the breeze, releasing a euphoric aroma. The company all gazed in wonder. The Head-Master Sword diverted his attention for but a second. When he turned back to Alexa, he saw something beyond her taking form from out of the tree's trunk. Hastily he drew his sword and called, "Alexa! Look!" His azure eyes were avid and his features taut.

Alexa spun, her hand going to her hilt. A creature emerged from within the tree and walked fearlessly toward her. It was undeniably a dryad. Alexa stared astounded, unable to speak. The dryad was so remarkably beautiful that Alexa doubted her own eyes. The being had long, straight, shiny, bark-brown hair. Her lips were as scarlet as an apple's skin. Her eyes were almond-shaped and a dark fathomless brown. Her skin was creamy, tinted the palest rose, and the blush of her cheeks were a dark crimson. She wore a shimmering, vivid red dress that flowed down her slender figure to trail behind her on the plush, emerald grass. She came to stop in front of Alexa and smiled. Alexa released the death grip on her hilt. The Master Sword kept his blade drawn, but stood at ease as he watched the exchange.

"Why do you come to this tree and pick one of my apples?" the dryad asked. Her voice was sweet, and Alexa could smell the scent of apples on her.

"We're searching for the Earth-Keeper. We're in need of the pure elemental power that lies within the earth. Do you know what I speak of, blessed dryad?" Alexa replied as politely as she could.

The dryad didn't speak, but moved toward Alexa and placed a soft palm on Alexa's cheek. Looking into her eyes, the dryad said, "You are a witch by half your blood, are you not?"

Alexa looked solemn, "Yes. My name is Alexandra."

The Dryad studied her face astutely, though nonjudgmental. Then stepping back, she gestured toward her tree behind her. "This tree is from the start of time. It has grown since the day the soil was first born from the Master of the Earth. I have been its caretaker since that time. I guard and protect the power it holds. I am the Earth-Keeper. Why have you sought me?"

Alexa felt such a flood of relief and happiness come over her she nearly shouted out in glee. She restrained herself, however, allowing herself to only grin wildly. She was so thankful.

"You understand I cannot just give away this power to anyone?"

"We don't seek the power selfishly. We desperately need it to stop evil from destroying Eetharum. The High Power has asked me to do this," Alexa answered urgently.

"I know of this evil you speak of," the dryad said sorrowfully.

"You do?" Alexa said, perplexed.

"The earth whispers and cries many things in my ear," she

said. Then she looked away from Alexa to Sword Bryan and Apollos, who were standing with tense hope. "You have a great ally, I see," she said of Apollos, then added, "You, too, have your own keeper. The Master of the Earth is wise." She smiled brightly at Bryan. The Master Sword acknowledged the dryad and bowed his head reverently, his heart greatly pleased.

The dryad motioned for the Master Sword and Apollos to come and stand with them. Alexa looked on her with awe. The dryad was so much more than just the Earth-Keeper. She was certain. This creature was connected intricately with the High Power. There was no doubt in Alexa's mind.

Once the four of them were all standing beneath the boughs of the apple tree, the dryad reached up and touched a blossom, which suddenly was no longer a blossom. The whole tree, along with the rest of the valley, changed back into its original state of plump, scarlet apples. The dryad picked the apple. "Here." She gave the fruit to Alexa.

Alexa took it in astonishment. "You're giving this to me freely?"

"I have no doubt, you who keep company with a unicorn, your blood is not evil, no matter its origin. I've heard the earth's pains and I feel the Master of the Earth is with us. It's my responsibility to tell you to simply believe he is with you and will not forsake you." She smiled fondly at the stunned group. Then seeing Alexa's confused expression while staring at the apple in her hand, she said, "Eat the apple to its core and take one seed and combine it with the other elements."

"Now?"

"Yes. It won't harm you. It'll only make your stomach feel pleasantly full for hours to come."

Alexa bit the apple. Her teeth broke the scarlet skin easily. Succulent, sweet, sticky juice ran down her chin. "This is delicious! I can't describe it," she exclaimed. She quickly devoured the whole thing. While she ate, the others spoke of simple things with the dryad. Strangely it came natural, as if they were speaking to a dear friend of the weather.

Finishing the apple, Alexa plucked the seeds from the core.

She took one seed and placed it in the vial with the mermaid tears. The other seeds she gathered and dropped them carefully into the opened palm of the dryad. They all smiled at each other as the task was done and Apollos tossed his head gleefully.

"Alexandra, once you have this power, you must do a favor for me," the dryad said.

"Anything."

"Will you promise me that wherever you go, you will grow life there? The kind that is indigenous to the land."

"I'll be able to do that?"

The dryad chuckled merrily, "You'll be able to do many things."

"Then, of course, I'd be pleased to," Alexa promised. Then looking solemn again, she added, "You are a very exquisite being, next to Apollos. What's your name?"

The dryad smiled reticently and began to move away from them, "You may call me Apple if you wish."

"Please, before you go, could you tell us where the other Elemental Keepers are," Alexa pleaded after her anxiously, for the dryad was becoming quickly aloof and had her hand on the trunk of her tree.

"Good luck, dear Alexandra. Good luck to you as well, her brave keeper, and you, beloved unicorn. If you're meant to find the elements they'll be revealed to you." With that, she melded into the trunk of the apple tree and disappeared.

The three companions turned and looked at each other happily. Sword Bryan smiled widely, his clear blue eyes twinkling, "Good job, Sand Queen. We're another step closer."

"I couldn't have done better myself," Apollos praised, butting a grinning Alexa affectionately on the arm. She gave the unicorn a tight hug around his neck as they made their way back to the others waiting anxiously for the news.

"She knew everything already. I just got lucky," Alexa said merrily.

"I think it was more than just luck," Sword Bryan commented with a smiled.

"Right." Alexa pondered cheerfully. Right, because *she*

was the key that was turned to open the door. And after all, a key cannot turn itself.

They reached the others and quickly told them the good news. They all expressed their delight enthusiastically.

"Well, all I want to know is if we can eat these apples now?" Warrior Hazerk said good-naturedly, as they all prepared to mount up.

"I don't see why not. I'd like one, too," Apollos answered.

"Great!" Eelyne added.

Selecting trees other than Apple's tree, they all gleefully picked several apples for themselves. They collected enough for now and later and also gathered some for their horses, Eelyne picking some for the pack mule. Then the company sprawled out on the grass before they reentered the perilous forest and enjoyed the fruit that had been tempting them since they had stepped foot in the valley.

Chapter 29

"Two keys down and three to go."

"Ugh, don't remind me."

"We've been gone a long time and we still have three elements to find. And they could quite possibly be in another country far from here. Who knows what's going on in the world? Ret could've taken over completely by now."

"Don't be so positive, Warkan, you're making me giddy with hope," Hazerk shot sarcastically back to the stoic faced warrior bringing up the rear of the company.

"Well, I was just pointing out—"

"Don't forget that part of our mission was to figure out what the keys were. This is just going to take time." Prince Alkin sighed, sounding as if he were trying to convince himself. "I have complete faith in my Shelkite warriors, the Galeon warriors *and* Lady Evelyn," he added confidently.

It had been a few days since they had left the orchard. The company was making their way north through the forest, traveling toward the Kaltraz and Carthorn border. Apollos, as usual, was leading the way down a narrow path among the thick trees, vines and soft moss. This part of the forest was dense, and Apollos' prismatic horn shimmered with a light that both comforted and guided the companions.

The company kept up a casual conversation to help ease the apprehension the forest pressed on them as they trekked through its heart. The wood was unusually quiet. As if it wanted to listen to their very thoughts. The company was vigilant of their surroundings; on the keen lookout for some of the creatures Levaun had warned them about.

"Have any intuition clues, Alexa?" Eelyne asked hopefully.

Alexa turned to look nonchalantly at the warrior, "Nope." She wasn't about to let her once again lack of direction affect the elated feeling she had been nurturing since she had acquired the earth element. Alexa could sense the disappointment in all of the company as she answered. She knew, however, they hadn't had their hopes up too high anyway.

The afternoon passed and turned into evening without a

single sight of any creature aside from the colorful birds watching from the branches above. Right before dusk Alexa felt something collide with her senses. It was something magical, several strong magical things. She tried to puzzle it out for a few minutes before saying, "Wait a moment." She broke the sleepy silence of the companions. They halted at her command, noting the familiar discerning countenance and fervent sparkle in her eyes. They knew she was on to something. They waited anxiously. "Apollos, do you sense that? It's magic," she said.

"Yes, I do. I've been trying to decide the direction it's coming from," the unicorn answered. He held his head high, his eyes wide and ears pricked. His nose was pointed into the light breeze, his nostrils flaring. "This way," he said absently and turned east off the narrow path. He silently slid through the thick branches; the company seemingly crashed along behind him. He paused at a hedge-like wall. The company eyed it. It ran north for a long distance and gradually turned east.

"This is the wall Levaun spoke of," Alkin said, dismounting. He walked to the wall with Apollos and attempted to feel inside the thick vines and branches. The unicorn stuck his nose in and sniffed.

"The magic is coming from the other side of the wall," Alexa said, looking up and over to the dark blue sky above. The hedge rose to about thirty feet.

"Yes," Apollos agreed.

"Do you think the next element is behind there?" Hazerk asked.

Alexa was craning her neck about her, trying with all her might to sense out the area. As always, to her frustration, the forest seemed to press in on her senses and clog them. "I can't tell."

"Well, let's see. I can climb that easily," Sword Bryan stated and dismounted. He strode over to the wall and scrutinized it. Just as he placed his foot in one of the vines, using it as a foot hold and hoisted himself up, they were all alerted to heavy hoof beats pounding toward them. Everyone's head shot up defensively, the Master Sword leapt down. They alertly looked around for the cause of the hoof beats, pulling out their weapons.

From the north, in the clearing alongside the wall, came a figure riding at a gallop toward them. As it neared, they could tell the rider held a crossbow. The warriors, in intense and focused silence, held their weapons ready to strike. Apollos lowered his horn. Alexa drew her bow. Then they realized the man was not riding the horse. To their astonishment, a large centaur skidded to a halt fifty feet from them.

He was well muscled, both his human half and animal half. His horse body was tall and slender, proportionate in its seamless joining with his regular-sized human torso. His body was chestnut and sleek. His hair was the same coppery coloring, long and flowing. His bare chest was bronzed by the sun. It nearly matched his coat. His eyes were dark and alert. He clenched his square jaw as he studied them severely. The company was stunned, but not put off guard. They held their stance and waited for him to speak. Holding his weapon at the ready, he spoke, "Who are you? What do you want?" he demanded. The company sensed more eyes on them. Twigs snapped as a half a dozen other centaurs came from the woods, surrounding them, all with their crossbows at the ready.

Alkin, with a quick glance at Apollos, took the unicorn's nod as an okay that the centaurs were good. He told the truth, "I'm Prince Alkin of Shelkite and these are my warriors. We sensed magic beyond this wall and were about to investigate. We don't mean any harm."

The centaur eyed them suspiciously. Then glancing at Apollos, he seemed to take Alkin's word for it and lowered his crossbow, the others followed suit. His features still not softening, he said, "I'm Hard Flame, these are *my* warriors." He swept his arm out arrogantly toward the other centaurs. "We're the guardians of the Empress Jadelin and her kingdom."

"Empress?" Alkin looked puzzled. "I don't know of any empress or organized kingdom in Carthorn."

Hard Flame smiled proudly, showing nice, pearly teeth. "That's because it's a secret kingdom."

"Well not anymore…." Hazerk mumbled behind Alexa. She stifled a snicker.

"It's within this wall?" Alkin said. The centaur nodded.

298

"There are other creatures? Magical creatures?"

"Yes. Come. It's a sign you're here. I'll take you there. Empress Jadelin will want to meet you. And your unicorn is especially welcome with great surprise and warmth from us all." He raised his hand to his mouth and whistled loudly to the sky.

The company gazed at each other slightly befuddled at the quick invite, wondering whether it was safe to accept. With a few hasty glances between Apollos, Alkin, Alexa and the Master Sword, the decision was made quickly. They agreed; they needed information.

There was a loud, chilling caw coming from above their heads. The company looked up to see four massive griffins. They carried in their beaks, by hefty ropes, a large wooden platform. They lowered it carefully to the ground between Hard Flame and the company. The creatures' wings caused the wind to stir as they descended. The company looked on them with awe.

Hard Flame mounted the platform as soon as it was grounded. He turned around to beckon the company, his hooves clomping noisily on the wooden floor. "We'll take half up now and immediately return for the remainder of you."

Apollos and Alkin, leading Sapharan, boarded the platform. Alexa waited for Sword Bryan's say. He glanced at her, eyeing her without thought and waved a hand for her to come. The Master Sword looked back to Warrior Warkan and said sternly, "Until we rejoin, you're in charge." The warrior nodded and stayed back with the rest of the company.

The Master Sword and Alexa lead their mounts onto the platform without a problem. Hard Flame gave the signal. The griffins nodded and took flight slowly, carefully lifting the platform. The horses snorted and braced themselves, eyeballing the great creatures and the disappearing ground all at once. Their masters quickly moved to soothe them.

Once in flight, Alkin turned to Hard Flame, "Why do you say it's a sign? And invite us so readily?"

"Because we had thought there was only one unicorn left in this world," he answered pointedly, looking up toward the top of the wall.

Apollos stepped forward eagerly. "There's another of my kind here?" A bright light was in his chocolate eyes.

Hard Flame looked down to the unicorn and smiled. "Yes."

"Oh, Apollos!" Alexa exclaimed, her eyes dancing. She reached out and scratched his withers. Apollos shook his mane elatedly. His eyes gleamed as he looked to the Prince and Bryan. They smiled. The unicorn raised his head proudly and waited expectantly as the platform slowly rose above the wall.

Alexa looked down and into the enclosed area. Her breath caught in her throat. It was painstakingly beautiful. Her eyes darted to behold everything. She barely noticed the light hand suddenly resting on her shoulder. Down below them was a vast yard. It was meticulously groomed. The grass was cut and the bushes trimmed, a garden admirably arranged in paths all around. Lilac trees were everywhere, scenting the air so pleasantly it sent a euphoric sensation through her being. She sighed appreciatively. A small, elegant palace was off in the distance to the northwest. Small cottages, stables and buildings made up a village to the northeast. It went beyond Alexa's eyesight to see the end of the road that led through the town.

"Why is this secret?" Alexa asked, leaning over the edge for a better look below. Zhan whickered nervously at his mistress.

"Be careful," Bryan whispered firmly in her ear, his fingers closing tighter on her shoulder.

Alexa suddenly became aware of his hand and she felt a shiver run through her body. She stepped back from the edge and looked up slightly starry eyed into the Master Sword's face. He was watching her intently, his beautiful azure eyes whisking protectively over her face. Alexa stared at him stupidly, feeling her attraction to him rise up unwillingly. He smiled crookedly at her, removing his hand. She gulped and tore her eyes from him, not understanding nor wanting to see the smirk on his handsome face. She looked over to Hard Flame, who, she just realized, was answering and had been answering her question while she had been momentarily distracted.

"...a haven. After the war, we good creatures wanted a place we would be safe and would not be bothered by humans.

Empress Jadelin came after we had established ourselves. But we wanted a leader, someone who was not biased; because we have so many kinds here. Although Empress Jadelin *is* human, we found her to be just and good hearted. So we set her up as our empress. I'm sure she will be pleased to have visitors of her same kind."

The griffins lowered the platform to land it gently on the grass and waited patiently for them to dismount before briskly taking off again. The occupants filed out onto the grass, looking around them, taking in the sights and charming smells. Alexa looked down the road to the small shops and homes. She noted vegetable gardens behind some of the homes. There was also a wooded area inside the wall where a tiny, wooly creature with huge, round eyes was waddling from, carrying a basket of berries. She smiled.The creature spotted her. Its eyes got even larger. Frightened, it scurried quickly away.

At that moment, another centaur approached them. His whole body, his human half and horse half, was a sleek, dark black. He was just as broad and well-muscled as Hard Flame. His hooves were solid and his fetlocks lightly feathered. He carried a long sword strapped across his girth. His face was more handsome than Hard Flame's, by human standards anyway.

"Night Strider," Hard Flame addressed him. "Tell the empress she has visitors of her kind and of Estella's."

At that, Night Strider was off in a flash, his big hooves kicking up sod as he took off toward the palace. The five of them waited patiently for the griffins to return with the rest of their group. They let their horses crop grass as they waited. Alexa watched Zhan fondly for a second as he happily tore at the juicy bits of grass, stuffing his mouth as full as he could get it. She smiled at the horse and gave him a loving pat. She looked up to see Alkin watching her and grinning. She smiled back. He gave her a wink and looked away on hearing the griffins return.

Alexa looked up to see the platform slowly lowering. She could hear Hazerk's loud, excited voice booming out about something. She chuckled and glanced at the Master Sword standing with his arms crossed. He rolled his eyes good-naturedly and then caught Alexa's gaze. They looked at each other passively for a second, his face showing no emotion. Alexa tossed her senses out and tried to decipher him quickly before she lost the chance. He was content for once. She couldn't feel any sign of bitterness in him at all, albeit she could feel the slight stress and fatigue he was suffering from. But like a good warrior, he never showed it outwardly. Bryan broke her gaze as the others landed and began filing off. Hazerk and Eelyne were exclaiming about everything excitedly. Warkan looked less ornery than usual, and the poor pack mule looked bug-eyed as he drug Eelyne and Swift Phoenix off the platform.

Back together, they mounted up, and Hard Flame led them toward the palace. The trek was a nice one. They rode through nicely manicured grounds and weaved through both gardens of flowers and food, and passed a large open, rolling field with a rushing stream slicing through it. When they reached the palace, their eyes were dazzled, for it looked as if it were made completely out of white marble. At least the front entrance was marble. It was not large by any standards, but it was a palace nonetheless. There were ten marble steps leading to the entrance, with marble pillars lining the front terrace and gently sloping ramps on either end of the terrace presumably for the centaurs' convenience. Alexa looked up to see many windows and a balcony above overlooking the fields. When she returned her eyes to the terrace, a woman was standing in the doorway.

Alexa didn't have to take much of her in to suddenly feel insignificant. If she had to describe her it would be as beautiful. Alexa didn't usually consider people to be beautiful. When she thought of beautiful, she thought of landscape or of a well-bred horse, or of the merman and dryad she had met, but this woman was beautiful. She was tall and stately. Alexa could tell just by glancing that the empress was taller than she was. She was slender, but had a curvy figure. The pink satin dress she wore complimented her greatly. Her skin was like porcelain, no freckles, and had a pink flush to it. Her lips were full and rosy. Her face was not angular, but had soft features that made her look kind. Her eyes were a nice shade of blue topaz. Her hair was sunshine-blonde and laid in long swooping curls and waves down her back.

Alexa heard the men in the company take in a breath in unison, and she suddenly disliked the empress. *Even after they saw the dryad?* She wanted to blurt her bitter comment, feeling possessive of the men, especially one in particular. Although, she knew their reaction was because this was a human woman. It was more natural for them to exhibit this response. Alexa wondered if the Master Sword had been one of them who'd taken in a breath at the sight of the empress. She instantly tried to decipher him again.

Letting her senses loose again, Alexa was hit hard with an intense, jubilant feeling coming from someone else in the group. Surprised and curious, she turned around to try and see who it was.

Prince Alkin stepped forward and introduced himself. The rest of the company moved forward up the stairs, past the frozen Alexa. She was trying desperately hard to feel each person out as they passed her. She stood with one foot on the bottom stair, her head cocked toward each man as he walked by. *It's not the Prince or Bryrunan.* She felt relief. *Not him either, nope, but he's fascinated by her, no....*

The silent and still heavily cloaked and hooded Kheane stalked by Alexa and her heart skipped a beat at the connection. Though the ex-assassin showed not a single sign of it on his face or even in his eyes, it was him emitting the elated feelings she was receiving. Kheane followed the company up to the terrace, standing at the back of them, silent and vigilant as always. Alexa watched the greeting exchange from the bottom of the stairs. She astutely glanced from the ex-assassin to the empress and back again. Narrowing her eyes and brow furrowing, realization dawned on her. This was his lost orphan girl. The woman he was searching for was Jadelin, now an empress. Alexa smiled, her heart happy for him.

"Alexa, stop daydreaming and come say hello to our hostess." Prince Alkin beckoned to her.

Alexa mentally shook her senses free and bounded up the marble stairs to stand next to Kheane in the back. "Hi," she said pceking around the others and raising a hand to the empress. It was rather rude of her to greet an empress this way, but Jadelin didn't seem to mind. She smiled.

"Hello, Alexa, I'm Jadelin."

Her voice was pretty, too. *How unfair*, Alexa groused to herself, but kept a smile on her face. Alexa stole a glance at Kheane as the others spoke easily with the empress. He was already looking at her from the corner of his eye. It startled her to see his dark, coffee-colored eyes discerning her unexpectedly. Alexa pointedly stared back at the ex-assassin, trying to communicate. *He knows I know something. How on earth does he know that without magical senses?* She was flabbergasted. Kheane gave her a curt nod of confirmation, though there was a sparkle in his eye now. She smiled back knowingly, realizing that if any of the other men had any ideas of sweet-talking this lady, they would not get far if Kheane had anything to do with it.

Empress Jadelin was leading them into the main entranceway. The floor was marble also. The room opened up into a large foyer with a curving stairway up the left side of the room and a gently inclined ramp curving up on the right—for the centaurs. There were pots of sweet smelling blossoms about the room. The room had a happy feeling about it. Upstairs, Alexa could see yet another balcony with beautifully carved railings looking down over the foyer. A hallway led both right and left.

Alexa looked over her shoulder to see their mounts being led away to the stable by other centaurs and creatures appearing to be either the grounds keepers or the stable hands. Zhan's comfort was always one of Alexa's first concerns. Once she figured he would be fine she listened to what the empress was saying.

"Estella is in the back courtyard. You have to meet her at once. And please don't call me empress. Jadelin is fine. I'm of no royal blood. My mystical friends persist in calling me their empress. But I only ever promised I'd help dictate if they needed an outside opinion. I don't look on them as my subjects at all. They've been so kind to me all my life. They rescued me, actually," she rattled off incessantly; it was obvious she didn't have company often. "The same as they rescued you, too!" She bent down and lovingly reached out her arms to a long haired, gray cat that had come bounding into the entranceway to see her. She scooped him up in her arms and cuddled him. The cat purred and rubbed his head on her chin. "Hard Flame found this little guy wandering outside one of the villages near Carthorn's edge and brought him to me—another way to spoil me. I love cats." She smiled. "And don't let Hard Flame fool you. He's a big softy." She grinned wider.

Alexa's slight jealously she had felt a bit ago melted quickly at observing the empress. She seemed so innocent and kind; and acted as if she had been planning all week to host a gruff and smelly bunch of warriors for the weekend.

Jadelin led them into a great room with comfortable chairs, settees and chaise lounges. A small library was there, along with a fire ablaze in a hearth. It all looked very inviting to the weary company. To the back of the room two sets of double doors stood open; they could see a pleasant courtyard through them. And there in the courtyard was a unicorn. She was dipping her elegant head into the courtyard's fountain to have a drink. Her crystal horn was sparkling softly from the last rays of the setting sun, pastel color spots danced across the flagged-stoned path. Her iridescent mane shimmered and her hooves glistened a light coppery color. She looked identical to Apollos, although somehow more feminine.

Apollos was rendered still. He looked on her with eyes that held so much depth. Alexa was certain he felt many things at once. He must have been elated to realize he wasn't the last of his kind. He must have wanted to know what other unicorns were like. Did they act the same as him? Would she be the filly for him? He had the look in his eyes as if he had just come home for the first time in years.

The whole company was still and silent as they watched Apollos' reaction. Finally, Estella raised her head and took in the arrivals. She instantly caught eyes with Apollos. Everyone grinned like idiots, glad for this union, including Jadelin. For she was happy her friend finally had one of her kind here, too.

Estella tossed her shimmering mane. Her eyes were alight, and she whinnied a beautiful musical note. Apollos answered her, and Alexa realized she had never heard him whinny before. Estella gave her mane another playful toss, reared up and came galloping into the palace through the open doors to meet him. Her hooves barely made a sound on the marble floors. Apollos moved forward to greet her, his neck outstretched. They touched noses timidly. Then they were talking, but in their own language.

"Let's leave them to get to know one another," Jadelin said happily. "Are you hungry?" she asked eagerly as the two unicorns turned and walked through the doors to the courtyard. The company all agreed to food immediately. "Great! I'll let Morning Breeze know we are having more eating with us tonight. She'll be happy. She loves having guests. You'll love the food, I'm sure."

With that, the empress gently placed the cat on the floor, watched him bound away, and then turned on her heel toward the kitchen supposedly. Then suddenly, she stopped and turned back, "I'm sorry, I'm so rude. Let me show you to your rooms. You'll stay the night, right? It's getting too late to keep traveling. And I would love to talk. We never have visitors. At least all the years I've been here there hasn't been many."

The company agreed happily to stay. Beds sounded heavenly, and maybe they could pick Jadelin's thoughts to see if she could help them find the next element. She smiled at their enthusiastic acceptance and led them back to the foyer and up the marble staircase to the second floor. Down the hall to the left she pointed out small, but elegantly decorated rooms for each and every one of them.

"And don't worry about standing guard at all here. You're safe. Hard Flame always has a couple of his warriors on duty outside the palace and plenty more outside the wall." Jadelin smiled comfortingly, seeming to guess the company was in dire need of a good night's sleep.

The company all sighed simultaneously, totally relieved upon hearing this. Then the empress left them to themselves, saying she would have hot water and supplies sent up for baths. They thanked her graciously.

Chapter 30

"Stop telling us not to call you empress," Prince Alkin gently chided Jadelin later that evening after they had washed up and eaten.

They were sitting relaxed in front of the hearth in the great room. Everyone was spread out in a plush chair or settee while Eelyne nosed through the library. Warkan was bobbing off to sleep in his chair—this was after he had finally stopped ogling Jadelin. Alkin and the empress shared a settee since they were conversing the most. Hazerk sat on the other side of the empress listening politely. The two unicorns were curled up on a soft rug in front of the hearth. Alexa reclined nonchalantly and in silence, day dreaming, on a chaise lounge nearest to Sword Bryan, who sat in a high-backed chair. He had hardly spoken a word all evening. And though he looked comfortable, he sat with his usual stoic poise. He still held his empty mug of ale in his hand. They had all indulged in a drink and felt relaxed for the first time in a while. Among them Kheane was the most aloof of the company. He sat in the farthest chair from the empress, still wrapped in his cloak and never speaking a word to her or anyone else.

"Just plainly your stature, place of residence and the affection your people show you, proves that you are indeed their empress," Alkin finished his mild scolding.

Jadelin shrugged, "I suppose so. I don't feel that way, though." She smiled, gently brushing off the Prince's assertion.

The company had warmed up quickly to Jadelin and her people. They felt welcomed and comfortable with her. They had already revealed parts of their mission to her in hopes her or her subjects had any helpful information. However, unfortunately she couldn't think of anything right off that might help them. Though, she promised she would speak to some of the higher ranking mystical creatures in the morning. She was certain there was something she wasn't thinking of that may be of use to the company. She seemed pleased to be confided in and asked for assistance. She was also horrified at the reason for their mission. Alexa noted she was sincere through and through, a rare and gentle person.

Alexa pondered Kheane while she lounged lazily, her back warmed pleasantly by the coals in the fireplace. Why hadn't he said anything to the empress? He was without a doubt thrilled at the company's serendipitous meeting with his old companion. After all, he had said he was searching for her, wishing to find the woman he loved still alive. And here she was, whole and beautiful beyond what he probably remembered, benevolent and regal. Why didn't he reveal himself? Did he worry she wouldn't remember him? With all the time lost, did he think she now loved another? He couldn't think that. It was apparent that Jadelin didn't have a lover, for she kept too close of a relationship with Estella, always stroking the unicorn's silky mane and patting her fondly. Perhaps she should say something to help push Kheane to reveal himself. Alexa never thought of herself as a match maker of any kind, but this match had already been made centuries before. It just needed a little nudge to start where it had left off. Right? Nevertheless, Alexa thought better of it. Kheane was choosing for some reason not to say anything. The situation was better left up to him, since he was the one involved.

Closing her eyes and leaning back on the chaise lounge, pretending to dose, Alexa sensed out Kheane's mood, hoping to get a grasp on his hesitance. Maybe he was just bidding his time. Her brow furrowed as she caught a hold of his anxious mood. Outside he was calm and as composed as ever, but inside he was a bundle of knotted emotions. He was worried, fearful, regretful, angry and sad, but happy and so full of love for her. Alexa knew he wouldn't be able to keep himself from speaking to her. She decided to leave the situation be. She couldn't bring herself to imagine what the ex-assassin was going through. He had spent centuries in bloodlust, while Jadelin had spent centuries in pure innocence, hidden away here in this paradise. How could they compare? How could they be compatible? Alexa, feeling his pain all too much, detached her senses from the heartbreaking scene taking place inside the always confident Kheane. She opened her eyes and stole a quick glance at the ex-assassin slumped in his chair. His eyes darted over at her knowingly, but Alexa couldn't read his thoughts from the outside. His eyes were keenly guarded.

She looked away feeling empathy.

Uninterested in the conversation taking place Alexa yawned, not bothering to hide it. Bryan looked at her from the corner of his eye, his lips twitching ever-so-slightly in a crooked smile. Alexa stared back at him curiously from the corner of her eye. Then he suddenly broke his silence. "We should get some rest," he rudely interrupted the Prince and Jadelin. They looked at him a bit surprised, but accordingly.

"Yes, well, I suppose I forgot that you all have been traveling a long time and must be frightfully tired. I just got caught up in the pleasure of finally having some company. Please forgive my rudeness!" Jadelin smiled a bit ashamed.

"You have been nothing but kind, dear lady. But my company does have a job they must commit to in the morning. We have to keep plugging forward," the Master Sword said kindly, with a protective glance at Alexa.

Alexa turned away and made a disgruntled face. Bryan was acting more and more like a mother hen to her than anything else. Staring at his handsome features dimly lit in the flickering shadows of the fire, she wondered if he would ever be anything more to her than her Sword-Guard. Or rather that *she would* be anything more to him other than something he was required to watch over. She sighed inwardly and clambered to stand as he stood to leave.

Jadelin broke through Alexa's despondent thoughts as the company gathered into the foyer to go upstairs. She addressed Kheane directly, "You've been silent all night. Is there anything I can get you to make your stay more comfortable?" She stood but a few feet from him, holding her hands out appealingly.

Halting only his step Kheane didn't let a heartbeat go by before he replied huskily. "No, I'm fine."

The empress paused, trying to studying his eyes deep within his hood. "Oh, well then, can I take your cloak? It's Kheane, right? You must be roasting; it isn't really needed." She regarded the rest of the company, "In fact, how about once you all get upstairs, you can layout your clothing and I'll have them washed for you by morning."

"Yes, thank you. That would be kind of you, Jadelin."
Alkin smiled gratefully.

Jadelin followed the company up the stairs, lifting her pink
satin gown ever-so-slightly so she wouldn't trip on the hem as she
ascended the marble stairway. Alexa overheard her whisper to
Alkin, "Your friend Kheane prefers to be alone, doesn't he? He
seems unconcerned with trivial society."

"He likes to keep to himself," Alkin hesitated, looking for
the right words. "He's been self-employed, working alone for
centuries. He's only now joining back into society; well, just our
company. I'm sure there's a lot he must adjust to." They reached
the top of the stairway and stopped in the hall.

"Centuries?" The empress suddenly seemed very
interested, her eyes probing.

"Yes. He's of old Alidonian blood," Alkin replied.

"What? So am I!" She said loudly, excitedly.

Alexa smiled, knowing this was the revealing point. She
glanced back at Kheane as the rest of the company filed
awkwardly around to see why Jadelin was suddenly ecstatic.

"Really?" Alkin replied surprised. "Jadelin is of old
Alidonian blood," he explained to the puzzled company. Alexa
watched as each face in the company turned from puzzled to
surprised and then to awareness. She didn't have to sense out their
feelings to know they were all wondering if this was the woman
Kheane had been searching for.

Kheane peaked the stairs last. He seemed not to be paying
any attention to the fervent conversation taking place. But Alexa
knew better, he wasn't called the Cold Wolf for nothing. He had
heard everything, though he still kept his aloof façade. He looked
up and locked eyes with the empress' eager ones. Her hands were
clasped together like a child waiting for a present. His coffee-
colored eyes held no emotion and were still guarded heavily.

"You're Alidonian?" Jadelin said a light in her eyes.

Alexa's brow wrinkled in puzzlement as she realized
Jadelin yet didn't know who Kheane was. *Maybe she doesn't
remember him!*

"Yes, Jadelin, I am," Kheane merely answered in his low,

raspy tone.

The given empress studied his face longer, lingering on his eyes, trying to imagine the rest of his face within the depths of the hood. Then suddenly, without any apparent cause, the beautiful woman began to tremble from head to toe. Her hands, still clasped, were held tightly in front of her, bobbing with the shudders. Her topaz eyes became full of emotion. Her mouth clenched as if she were in pain. The company was abruptly concerned, all gasping and taking an obliging step toward her. They thought she was having a fit of some sort.

"Jadelin? Jadelin, are you okay?" Prince Alkin was at her side, touching her lightly on the arm as her body trembled violently.

"It-it's y-you," she stuttered through her teeth. The violent shakes of her body were wracking her like she had been left out in a blizzard. Kheane, who was the only one of the company not put at unease by her sudden fit, merely continued to watch her with his intense gaze.

"Yes," he finally said after a moment. The company all looked around slightly confused.

"Are you frightened of him?" Alkin asked. "Do you know what he is?" Alkin was referring to Kheane being an egregious assassin. "He won't hurt you. I promise he's with us."

Jadelin continued to shake, unable to control herself, her long sunshine-blonde curls waving now with the movement, her porcelain skin flushed pink. "No, no." She fought to gain control of herself and waved the Prince's administering hand away, ignoring him. Her eyes were only for Kheane. "Oh, Tol—"

"Jade," Kheane cut her off quietly, "that's no longer my name." He alone seemed to understand the empress' fit and saw that it wasn't fear, but out of utter happiness and shock she shook.

"Oh!" she exclaimed and flung herself across the space between them and into his arms, where he awkwardly held her shaking figure.

The company took in a breath of understanding. No one said a word as Kheane clumsily patted Jadelin's back as she laid her head on his shoulder, clutching him. This was something they weren't a part of. They eyed each other, contemplating.

"We'll leave the two of you. It has been…a long time for you. More than a few life times of ours. You have plenty to talk about I'm certain," Alkin said finally.

Jadelin pulled away, tears streaming down her face and nodded gratefully to the Prince, smiling all the while. "Thank you."

With that, the company left for their rooms. They each paused briefly to watch the two head down the hall side by side toward the door leading onto the balcony.

Alexa stopped at the threshold of her room. She rested her hand on the doorframe, a thoughtful and perhaps wistful look on her face as her eyes followed the two reunited loves. She didn't notice the Master Sword standing but a hair's breadth behind her, watching them as she. After a second she comprehended his close presence. She peeked over her shoulder to peer up at him. He was gazing at her with an unfamiliar look in his eyes. Slightly caught off guard, Alexa couldn't help but let a startled, puzzled look come across her features. Instantly she continued through the door and turned around to study him as he hesitated in the threshold, still watching her in the same way.

She came to a quick conclusion as to what the look was. It was uncertainty, with a vague hint of…aching or longing, maybe? A moment passed and Bryan didn't speak a word. His brow furrowed as if he seemed to be pondering exactly what it was he wanted to say. She waited with her heart in her throat. This look he was bestowing on her was completely new.

"Alexa," he started finally.

"Yes." She looked up expectantly from where she had tried to occupy herself with unbuckling her dagger with fumbling fingers. At her reply, a neutral look stole across the Master Sword's face, confirming a change of mind.

"I'll…be in the room across the hall if you need me. Good night."

"Yes, I know that, Master Sword," Alexa said, trying to conceal her disappointment. He nodded and hurriedly closed the door. "Good night, Bryrunan." Alexa sighed quietly to the shut door. She turned to undress for bed, her heart in her stomach.

*****

Kheane's dark heart had literately almost pumped out of his chest when he had recognized Jadelin on the terrace. It wasn't hard to recognize her; although she was more beautiful than he remembered. How could it be that he could search for her for centuries, only to find her when he had finally given up? She had become such an obsession to him. She was always something there in the back of his mind, never real really. Her memory had kept him going. Somehow he had hung on to the belief she was still alive. At least that's what he had told himself to get through all the horrible, endless, bloody nights and days. The memory of her was something warm and good he could be comforted in. But deep far down he had never really allowed himself to honestly believe she was alive. He realized he had only fooled himself into believing it so he could get through the rest of his days. He had been simply waiting for someone to outsmart him in a fight, or for him to make a fatal wrong move that would end his pathetic existence.

Jadelin had become an unobtainable goddess to him. He held her memory high up on a pedestal, embalming everything good about her in the back of his mind, preserving it so he could take it out every so often and patch up the gaping hole in his black heart. He had told himself she was alive and waiting for him just for comfort. And, yet, here she was. How shocking it had been to see once again the very core of his obsession! She was alive, so beautiful and so innocent....

He was a villain of the worst kind. He had no right to even be in her presence. For he saw that she truly was a goddess in her own way. He had led such a lurid, sinful life. How could she ever accept him? She would be appalled just by his mere appearance. She hadn't changed, not really. Underneath the façade of an empress Kheane could still see the strong, determined orphan girl that had stowed away with him. He found he still loved her; he could never stop loving her. The years apart had deepened his love so beyond its normal boundaries it was unfathomable. But with everything he had done, how could he expect for her to feel the same? If she still loved him, it would be more than he deserved. If she didn't, he would be content in knowing she was alive and happy. Yes, he would. He could die content…fulfilled.

He followed Jadelin out onto the balcony. A warm lilac scented breeze wafted into his hood; his hot face pleasured at the touch. They walked quietly to the balcony's edge. She stopped, placing her hands on the marble railing, looking thoughtfully out at the moonlit rolling fields and the little village snuggled amongst the knolls. Kheane watched her as she composed herself.

"I thought I'd lost you," she finally said.

"And I you," he replied, wishing his voice wasn't so harsh sounding. To him it sounded like a bear struggling to communicate verbally with humans. There was nothing harsh about *her*. She was so elegant and feminine. He admired the way the pale pink, satin gown hugged and flowed silkily down her curves. He noted for the first time that she was barefoot and how delicate her feet and ankles were. She looked over at him with bright eyes, her sunny-blonde curls lifting in the breeze. Kheane could just barely catch the sweet scent of her on the gust.

"I never really gave up hope, though," she said, turning to face him, leaning her hip against the rail casually. Kheane didn't answer. She studied his dark eyes. After a moment she added, "I remember your eyes. They are the same…once I really looked at them, I knew it was you. I've never forgotten them." Kheane blinked, a small smile reaching his eyes. She smiled back, her teeth as beautiful as pearls. "I guess I didn't recognize you at first because of, well, your hood and cloak. And you're so mysterious now, like you'd rather blend into the wall.…But you recognized me right away, didn't you?"

"Yes," he said, inwardly cursing his voice again. She nodded, eyeing him carefully. She didn't speak for a few moments, but just continued to study him. Finally Kheane spoke, "I searched for you. I looked for days. I thought the storm had taken you …."

She leaned against the rail with her back toward the fields. She crossed her arms, her mouth forming a frown. "I tried to stay with you in the storm, but the waves were too strong for me. I found a piece of jetsam and climbed on. I called for you, but it was no use. Eventually I floated to shore. I was sick, barely able to move. That's when Estella found me. I don't know why a unicorn would have mercy on a stranger. But she did. She brought me here. And the rest of the creatures took to me kindly. I was very lucky." She locked eyes with his. "I never forgot you. You were imprinted so deep on my soul. I couldn't forget you. I fretted over losing you, over not knowing if you were alive and okay, over leaving— abandoning you. But the creatures here loved me and claimed I was safer here and the chances of finding you were close to none. I'm sorry I failed you." Her topaz eyes fell to the ground in remorse and she hugged herself as if to comfort a pain she felt inside.

"Don't blame yourself. It was uncontrollable circumstances that took us apart. I thought of you every day. It was good that you were here, safe away from where I was. I haven't led a life I'm proud of. You're better off without that past," Kheane consoled softly.

She looked up, "You say you thought of me."

"Yes. It kept me sane."

"I have waited for you…I have loved you," she whispered fervently. Her eyes holding an intense longing, but it was imprisoned in the pain of all the lonely years. Kheane could see this; he felt it himself. She went to wrap her arms around him saying, "I still love you, my dearest Tol—"

"You shouldn't. Don't call me that," he cut her off, and she stopped, hurt flooding into her eyes.

"You don't love me?" her gentle face was scrunched in pain and misunderstanding.

"I love you." He couldn't lie. She flashed him a brilliant smile, the pain vanishing from her face.

"Then let's not be sad any longer. Come here," she pleaded.

"Jade, I'm not the same person. I've done terrible things. You shouldn't even know of them they are so vile. I'm torn from the inside out, right down to my soul. I don't think there is any way to salvage myself. You couldn't love someone like me."

Jadelin shook her head in disagreement. "You don't believe I should love you, but you still love me. That is something. I don't

315

care what you've done. I will always love you unconditionally."

Kheane shook his head sadly. "You don't—"

She cut him off, an uncharacteristic edge to her voice, "No. *You* don't." Her countenance softened when he looked up to lock eyes with her. She took his hands in hers and said fervently, "If I were in your place and you were in mine, would you care for me any less?"

Kheane smiled, his coffee-colored eyes alight, "No."

She returned his smile. "Let's marry. Tomorrow."

"Okay," he simply replied, but his eyes sparkled with a new hope. His heart felt so light and his soul suddenly felt whole again. The gaping hole in it was being filled in. He looked at her longingly. She reached up and gently touched the tip of the scar at the crease in the corner of his eye. She started to remove his obscuring hood. "I don't know if you want to see what's underneath…" he said.

"I've been longing to see this face for centuries." She pushed his hood down.

Kheane waited for her petrified gasp, but she didn't show any emotion at all, except maybe pain, pain for his pain. Her elegant brow furrowed as she traced the reddish scars seared across his left side of his face. Her fingers gently ran down the large, ugly, purple scar from his right eye to his disfigured lips. Her fingers rested there as she pondered the cause of such a wound. Her eyes lingered on his disfigured nose.

Kheane gently wrapped his fingers around her wrist. She looked back into his eyes, his yearning feelings were mirrored in her face. He hadn't had someone touch him so gently, so lovingly in such a long time. It was an old, comforting feeling, almost nostalgic; one that he longed to never stop. He reached out and touched her soft porcelain skin, taking her face in his calloused hands. Her big topaz-colored eyes beckoned to his heart and tugged at it in a way nothing ever had. Suddenly his lips were on hers. She met him with just as much fervor. Her lips were soft and warm. His must feel so coarse and twisted with scarred tissue, but she didn't seem to mind. He felt complete with her in his arms and he didn't doubt she felt the same. He pulled her toward himself gently by the small of her back. She didn't need much encouragement. She wrapped herself around him as snug, as close as she could possibly get.

"Be near me always," she whispered into his mouth.

He nodded, his mouth busy with the kisses he had longed to give her for centuries. She pulled back all too soon and Kheane reached for her a bit desperately, not wanting her warmth or healing to ever leave him.

"I ache for you, knowing you've been through so much pain." She gently tugged at his cloak.

"It only gets worse." He laughed coarsely. But he removed his cloak and Jadelin took him in with eyes filled with sorrow.

She took his scarred arms in her small hands, turning his left arm around to study the bloodied-mouth wolf tattooed on the inside of his forearm. Kheane watched her fondly as she absent-mindedly traced the lines of the wolf's head with the tips of her fingers, deep in thought, a frown on her pretty face. She took his other arm and studied the burn wounds traveling up from the inside of his elbow and disappearing into his shirt. He watched her reaction, carefully discerning her troubled features. She tugged at his shirt silently. He sighed and removed it reluctantly. She covered her mouth as her fears were confirmed. The scar beginning from his right eye traveled all the way down his chin to his torso where it was only one of many scars seared across his tight, muscled chest. The burn wound crawled up his arm and over his shoulder and covered half his back only to connect to more old wounds twisting around each other to form some sadistic design buried in his skin. They continued down past the waistband of his trousers.

"See?" he commented, noting her horrified face. She was circling him, gently running her hands over his rough skin. She came around to face him, gazing into his eyes sympathetically.

"I wish I could have saved you from all the painful things you've been through," she whispered, tears enhancing her watery blue eyes.

Kheane shook his head and smiled, "You have. The worst pain was only that I couldn't be with you."

"I have scars from that, too," she replied. Their lips met once more and they didn't stop this time.

Chapter 31

It was a good dream. But it was only a dream, too bad, because it was a really good one. One Alexa didn't want to rouse and leave behind to the night. She wanted to keep the story going, it was so pleasant and he was so handsome…But there was this annoying clunking sound that kept interrupting what he was trying to say to her. Every time he opened his mouth to speak, *clunk, clunk*, was his voice. It didn't make sense. What was he trying to say?

Alexa tossed agitatedly in her half-state of sleep, her brow scrunching in frustration as she fought to keep the dream alive a bit longer. *Clunk, clunk.* She groused incoherently in her pillow as she flipped around. *Ah*; the bed was so soft. The softest she had ever had the pleasure of sleeping on. The blankets were so cozy and her toes were toasty warm, unlike so many nights she had spent shivering on the hard ground in the forest. *Clunk, clunk.* She buried her head into the down pillow, finally waking to consciousness. She flipped over on her back and glared at the closed door where the annoying sound was deriving from. What could the Master Sword possibly want at this hour? *I thought we'd be able to sleep in a bit today*. She groaned, turning over. "Go…a…way…Brry-roo-nan," she mumbled into her pillow with no intent for him to hear. The door creaked open; Alexa ignored it. "What is it, Master Sword?" she groused louder this time.

"It's me, dearie," a female voice said. Alexa abruptly sat up and rubbed the sleep from her eyes, peering at the doorway to see the centaur Morning Breeze's head peeking in. "Your Head-Master Sword says it's time to rise!" she said brightly.

"So early?" Alexa attempted to clear the fuzzy sleep from her brain, but was unwilling to forget her dream.

"Early?" Morning Breeze chuckled, "It's mid-day. You were the only one he let sleep in, dear." She laughed again. Her voice was like silver bells; it was pleasant.

Alexa raised her eyebrows in surprise, "Oh." She fumbled with the covers as she rose. Morning Breeze pushed through the door, easily fitting her petite equine body through—it dawned on Alexa that all the palace doorways were built larger to

319

accommodate the centaurs. The centaur was carrying a tray of food. It looked like hotcakes. Alexa's stomach grumbled. "Mmm." She sniffed appreciatively.

"Yes, breakfast. The others have already eaten." She set the tray down at the small desk next to the bed.

Alexa glanced around the room. Pulling at her nightgown, she asked, "Where are my clothes?"

"They're being washed and mended."

"What am I supposed to wear?"

"We have something for you. Don't you worry, dear." Morning Breeze turned her dappled-gray body around, almost swishing her long, silver tail in Alexa's face as she turned for the door. Once she was through the door, she had to turn all the way around again to face Alexa. *How awkward.* Alexa observed briefly as she pulled out the chair to the desk and plopped down. The centaur poked her white-blonde head through the doorway, "Oh, and do hurry with breakfast. We have to get you ready for the wedding. I'm preparing a bath for you."

Alexa gulped a piece of hotcake down. Staring befuddled, she said, "Wedding?"

"Yes, the ceremony starts at twilight. Prince Alkin is marrying Kheane and Empress Jadelin. You're to be an honored guest. Now, hurry dear, we have lots to do. To plan a whole wedding in one day!" The friendly centaur threw up her hands as if exasperated; though she looked excited. "Enjoy." She closed the door.

"Humph," Alexa mumbled thoughtfully to herself as she jammed scrumptious hotcakes in her mouth. So, Kheane and Jadelin were getting married. How nice. She honestly felt happy for them; she was just never one to get overly excited about celebrations such as this. Her main concern was whether or not Kheane would still continue on with the company. She hoped so. They definitely could use him. She would hate to lose him for the missions' sake, and hers; she enjoyed his flinty company. And she couldn't imagine the elegant Jadelin coming along either. Alexa chuckled at the thought.

In just a few minutes there was another knock. Alexa was

just finishing up her hotcakes. She gulped down her orange juice, something she had never had before, but found it delectable. "Yes," she answered.

"It's me again, dear," Morning Breeze said as she opened the door. "Are you ready for your bath? We have to size you for your gown, too."

"Gown?" Alexa looked horrified.

"Yes, come on." The centaur beckoned her.

Alexa poked her head out the door to see if the hall was clear. It was. She skipped out still in her nightgown. Morning Breeze gently grabbed her wrist and practically drug her down the hall to the bathing room. "This is going to be fun," the centaur gloated with a broad smile. Alexa stared dubiously back at her.

Morning Breeze nearly shoved Alexa through the door and followed unnecessarily close behind. Alexa spotted a big tub in the center of the large, circular room, along with two other female centaurs. One was a dark chestnut with long, wavy, strawberry-colored hair tied back from her face. The other was a soft, smoky black, with dark hair and black jeweled eyes. She smiled, her pearly teeth standing out prettily. Like Morning Breeze, all the female centaurs wore corsets to cover their chests. The fashion style was a little racy for Alexa's own personal taste, but the lady centaurs with their elegant human torsos and ample busts pulled it off very lovely. Like all females, they each had their own favorite style of corset and colors they preferred. In fact, the dark chestnut centaur was wearing fingerless gloves that came to her elbows. Oddly, Alexa found herself contemplating centaur fashions. *I wonder what they do for the winter… jackets…or maybe cloaks that fit their human half but also cover their body like a horse blanket….*

"This is Molasses Tang and Thunder Lily." Morning Breeze interrupted her thoughts. "But you can call them Lass and Lily. Lass is going to measure you and Lily will help you with all the beautification." Morning Breeze smiled, giving the frozen Alexa a gentle push on the back toward Lass.

"Hello," Alexa said to Lass as the centaur immediately began measuring her figure. She smiled in response and stared thoughtfully at Alexa's eyes.

"Hmm, what do you think? I say cobalt. A satin A-line, that flows gently down her frame. She is so slender it will complement her perfectly. I think that would be best. Or do you think lavender, Breezie?" Lass asked. Morning Breeze came over to study Alexa's frame, eye and hair color. Alexa stared at them blankly, feeling like a horse at auction. *How ironic.* She joked good-naturedly.

"Hmm, I think you're correct with the blue," Morning Breeze said, "Her eyes will glow."

"Right. I'll get started." Lass gave Alexa a gleeful smile and went directly to a pile of fabric in the corner of the room and began rummaging through it.

Before she could compose her thoughts, Alexa felt someone tugging at her nightgown. Thunder Lily was attempting to undress her. "Hey, um, I can do that myself." She laughed, but there was a hint of appall in her voice she couldn't hide.

"Don't be silly." Lily chuckled.

"Well, I'm off. I have lots to do," Morning Breeze announced and trotted out the door, snapping it shut behind her.

"Come on. Off with it," Lily demanded and tugged the nightdress over Alexa's head. Feeling extremely exposed and slightly embarrassed at the brash immodesty, Alexa attempted to cover herself. "Oh, my!" Lily gasped.

"What?" Alexa said defensively. She tried to hide behind the flimsy fabric of the nightgown.

"What in Carthorn! Were you with child?" Lily exclaimed, catching Lass' abrupt attention. The centaur clopped curiously over.

Alexa stared flabbergasted at the two for a second. Then she realized what they were talking about. "Oh!" She laughed, "No! I had a knife injury." She took down her protective covering and traced the thick, white scar across her abdomen with her fingers, recalling the intense pain. It still ached at times; after all it hadn't happened *that* long ago.

"Oh. Well, it gave me a fright. That must have been painful!" Lily seemed to brush off the shock quickly and began pulling her toward the tub. Lass went back to her sewing.

"I *am* capable of bathing myself," Alexa said as she immersed herself in the warm water. She gave a sigh of pleasure as she sunk up to her neck. Lily was tugging at Alexa's tangled hair, pulling out her long braid and what felt like some hairs, too.

"Yes, yes, of course," Lily merely replied, then poured water on Alexa's head.

Alexa shrugged her shoulders. If they wanted a doll to play with for the day she supposed she could comply. She finally, gladly surrendered to their will and allowed them to tug and pull her around for the rest of the afternoon, cleaning and preening her.

She hoped this whole ordeal was part of the company's plans. She had thought they were supposed to be discussing their next mission. She smiled as she imagined the Master Sword's agitated face as he was forced to take part in this ceremonial event. She sighed despondently at the thought of him. *Somehow* she had to extricate him from her mind. At present, Alexa was sure he felt something for her. His off demeanor last night had proved it. She could tell it, too, by using her senses. His bitterness was gone and she could sense at least a fondness for her. But she couldn't discern more than that. He was a puzzling man, composed, even on the inside. For some reason he was fighting his feelings. Thus, it meant he did not *want* to feel that way for her. So, she had to *not* feel that way for him. It just couldn't be. They were worlds apart. He was the Head-Master Sword of Shelkite, and she was merely a foreign commoner. That was the way it was. Alexa sighed unhappily. Oh, but she was getting out of control of herself! And unfortunately, she knew it wasn't a fleeting, girlish infatuation. At this point, Alexa could admit she was certainly and so very inconveniently in love with the Master Sword….

*****

It was dusk. The stars were just appearing in the smoky gray-blue sky. A silvery-white, crescent moon was rising as the last colorful rays of the sun streaked over the treetops on the horizon. A warm breeze whistled through the branches of the lilac trees, scenting the air pleasantly. The wedding guests were all gathered on the lawn of the palace. The guests, of course, were all the creatures of the kingdom. Excitement buzzed in the atmosphere. The creatures were all happy their empress had found a husband. They were gentle enough to accept him, whoever he was, immediately into their kingdom.

Bryan paced restively, waiting for the ceremony to begin. He and the other warriors were all attired in new suits for the occasion. The centaurs had worked tirelessly all morning and through the afternoon to make sure everything was perfect for their empress' wedding. That included making sure the guests were presentable. The Master Sword never really cared for events like this. But being a Sword he was often required to attend these kinds of things. And here he didn't have much of a choice. He looked over to Prince Alkin who was waiting in front of the crowd under an arbor laced intricately with flowers and ivy. He looked quite happy as usual. He was brought up in this type of lifestyle. It was no bother to him.

Bryan waited at the end of the aisle that had been created through the center of the crowd. It was decorated with white flower petals. The other warriors were already standing by the arbor where the ceremony was to take place. Bryan preferred to wait here for Alexa. He hadn't seen her all day; being parted from his main obligation put his already annoyed nerves on edge. He had to admit he felt kind of useless without her around to protect. He held his hand on the hilt of his sword as he paced back and forth, staring avidly at his shined boots. It suddenly occurred to him, was that *really* the only reason he felt on edge? Or was he just telling himself that? He came to a halt and glared down at the blades of grass.

New excited voices caught his attention and jerked him out of his confused thoughts. He looked up and saw two female centaurs conversing exuberantly and making their way toward the party. He looked beyond and spotted a human figure trailing them slowly. An unexpected smile crept over his lips as he recognized her. He couldn't help but wonder at his increased heart rate; he tried to suppress it.

Alexa was nearing the crowd, walking in her normal Alexa type stride, but she was making an attempt at being more graceful; he could tell. He smiled crookedly at her when she stopped in front of him, giving him a brief, pained look. He raised an eyebrow at her, and she looked smugly back at him for a second before bestowing a radiant smile on him. Bryan felt his breath catch in his throat and he quickly chided himself. He couldn't help himself from admiring her, as breathtaking as she was to him. Why not? What was the harm in only admiring her?

The dress she wore flattered her slender figure. It was a shiny cobalt, made of sinuous satin. It flowed down her body in one long wave, rippling like blue flames when she shifted her weight. The hem kissed the ground and a small train trailed her. The sleeves were capped and off the shoulders with only a touch of ruffle. The bodice of the gown scooped down low, enhancing the hollow between her humble bust. His eyes lingered there for but a mere second before he raised them to admire the rest of her. He vaguely remembered wishing at one time what she would look like with her hair down. He realized he had gotten his wish. Her raven hair fell down to her waist. It was straight and shiny and looked as if it might feel like silk if he were to run his fingers through it. The centaurs had pulled some locks softly away from her face and braided them in small intricate plaits, twisting them around each other in a pleasing design. Snuggled amongst the tiny plaits were small white blossoms; that when she wasn't looking he breathed in the scent and discovered they were lilacs. Finally, he let his eyes wander over her face. Her dainty angular features were rosy, but her cheeks were always rosy. He fondly eyed her light freckles sprinkled across her nose. Her lips were full and pleasingly soft looking as always. Little wisps of hair had loosened and danced around her brow and he found himself resisting the urge to brush them from her eyes. Her eyes, his eyes paused there the longest. They shone like two fiery-blue beacons in the night and sparkled like jewels in the sun. Although, he had been the victim many times of those bewitching sapphire orbs, he actually stopped breathing for a few seconds. He realized it only when he sucked in a breath of much needed oxygen, which in turn made him feel slightly uncomfortable. For she grinned smugly at him, noting his brief ogling he was sure. He cleared his throat and pulled himself together, allowing himself only that mere second to look at her as a woman and not his ward. Everything felt right again, now that she was here back under his watchful eye.

"Ready to get this over with, Sand Queen?" He gestured down the aisle toward the rest of the warriors gazing at her expectantly.

"Sure thing, my dearest Sword-Guard," she said with only the slightest touch of mockery in her voice. It had that bitter chocolate sound to it. Something he found he was partial to. She started down the aisle, smiling widely to the creatures greeting her along the way. He walked just a pace behind her, laying his palm ever-so softly on the small of her back, guiding her down.

"Oh, I almost forgot. I need to tell you that we've an idea where to find the fire element," he said off-handedly. As he expected, she came to a screeching halt and went to turn around to face him. But his hand on the small of her back pressed more firmly, causing her to keep moving toward the front of the crowd full of centaurs, fuzzlewumps, griffins, fauns and the two unicorns.

Only straining from his push for a mere second, she gave in and kept walking, whispering fervently, "When did you discover this?"

"Hard Flame gathered all the inhabitants this morning and we had a conference," he whispered in her ear, bending so close he could smell the intoxicating scent of her. He distantly wished he could just stay there…smelling her forever. How juvenile!

"Without me?" she shot back.

"I thought you could use some extra rest, with everything you've been through…Right? Do you feel better?"

He must have caught her off guard with his unusual consideration, for she paused before answering, "Yeah. It was nice. Thank you…" She trailed off, but then added eagerly, "So? Where is it?"

He didn't answer immediately, and they came to a halt at the front of the crowd, taking their place next to Warkan, Hazerk and Eelyne. Kheane and the Prince were standing under the arbor speaking in low tones; Kheane wasn't wearing his heavy cloak tonight.

The warriors hastily surrounded Alexa, and Bryan rolled

his eyes exasperatedly as they all fought for her attention. "You look beautiful, Alexa!" Eelyne's brown eyes sparkled as he blatantly admired her figure in a friendly way.

"Gorgeous, I say, Lil' Sis'." Hazerk gave her bare shoulders a squeeze and a platonic kiss on her brow. Nonetheless, Alexa blushed at his sentiments.

"Wow! You're a girl?" Warkan said. Alexa laughed and punched him lightly on the arm, the austere-faced warrior actually laughed in return.

Alkin caught her eye and gave her a wink. She smiled shyly back. Bryan watched irritably as the Prince's interested gaze lingered on her longer than necessary.

The crowd hushed as the ceremony was on the verge of starting. But, Alexa's attention wasn't deterred for long. She quickly turned to the Master Sword and said earnestly, "So? Tell me?"

"Well." He tried to control an idiotic grin from forming on his face from having a chance to bend his head closer to her and whisper once more in her ear. "They almost immediately thought of a place only a day's travel from here, luckily. It's an ancient ruin. It's fabled that an eternal flame deriving from the center of the earth comes out there. An old fortress is built around it, from who knows when. The flame is said to be in caverns beneath."

Being as close to her as he was, he could easily sense the tremor of anticipation zip through her body. She hastily turned her head to look at him, almost knocking foreheads with him. She didn't seem to mind the close quarters and the Master Sword didn't feel inclined to back up. They stared at each other's eyes, seeming to dare the other to move back a fraction of an inch.

"And the Keepers?" she whispered, her pretty pink lips barely moving.

"Dragons; supposedly," he replied. He could see the wheels turning beyond her sparkling sapphire eyes as she stared at him, but did not *look* at him; her mind was miles away.

"The plan?" she finally said, now looking at him.

"Working on that one." His brow furrowed. How could they go up against a dragon?

"I say we wing it."

"You *would* just go in head-on." He sighed, fighting the urge to roll his eyes. Her eyes narrowed, but she gave him a crooked smile.

"Well—"

He cut her off with a finger pressed to his lips, signaling that the ceremony had started. The empress was already started down the aisle. Alexa backed away from him as if she suddenly realized there was no reason to be standing so close to him. He suddenly felt colder. Distracting his mind, he turned to watch the pretty Jadelin walk toward Kheane.

She was smiling brilliantly. No one person ever looked so happy. Bryan glanced at Kheane and was almost frightened to see him smiling widely back at her. It was something that was almost discomforting. He couldn't say why. It wasn't because the ex-assassin's face was maimed; it was probably because a smiling assassin just didn't seem to make any sense. Bryan sighed inwardly as the ceremony started. Hopefully it would be short and they could move on to the food and drinks part of this celebration.

Later, Alexa bit on a finger nail as she eyed Jadelin from across the lawn. The formal ceremony was over and all the creatures were mingling, eating and drinking. They had set up tall torches intermittently in the yard to light up the area; it was cozy. They were definitely the most pleasant and accepting group of people Alexa had been around, more so than some humans she had met. Many of the creatures had started several fun games and had beseeched her and the other warriors to join them, but she declined politely, fearing she would make a fool of herself in the silly gown she was sporting tonight. Right now, for some reason, Alexa was more concerned with how beautiful Jadelin was with her long, sunshine-blonde, wavy locks and her elegant, curvy figure, and how plain *she* felt compared to the other woman. But more importantly, why did it matter? Jadelin was married to Kheane and it shouldn't concern her what the other men in her company thought of the dazzling empress; meaning whether or not they found her attractive. Alexa just felt strangely possessive of *her* company, of *her* men. She rolled her eyes at her childish thoughts.

The empress did without a doubt look like the epitome of beauty. She wore a cream satin gown with a short train, longer than the one on Alexa's own dress, but still short. Her hair was down and wavy, much longer than Alexa's hair. She wore a garland of blue flowers in her hair and her eyes were the most unique color of blue topaz. Her soft, pale skin was flushed a pretty attractive pink. Her gown had long sleeves, but was cut low and flattered her ample bosom. Alexa looked down at her own bosom. She had been surprised at how Lass and Lily had somehow boosted her own humble bust up to make it look half-way luscious. Alexa straightened her shoulders and tried to stand up straighter, sticking out her chest. Someone tapped her on the shoulder. Mortified and hoping that whoever it was hadn't seen what she had been doing, she spun around and almost knocked poor Prince Alkin's drink out of his hands.

"Whoa, there. Sorry, didn't mean to startle you," he said, a grin on his face.

She smiled back awkwardly, wondering if he had noticed her girly fussing. "Oh, no, it's fine." She composed herself quickly.

"Take a walk with me." He gestured toward the path twisting through the courtyard.

"Sure." She shrugged. He held out his arm and she took it; well, at least she took it in the way she thought she was supposed to. She had never been taught courtly manners. She was sure the Prince knew this, so she didn't fret over it. He led her down the path and out of the light of the party. They walked silently along the flagged-stoned path for a few minutes before he spoke first.

"The Master Sword tell you of the fire element?" he asked.

"Yes. I've a good feeling."

"A good feeling about dragons?" He laughed, his hazel eyes twinkling.

"Well…I did…." She grinned idiotically back at him; she couldn't help herself. He just drew forth the happiness out of people; it was hard to ignore it. He chuckled at her and glanced over his shoulder to peer at something. Alexa followed his gaze. He was looking at Apollos and Estella. They were playing a game of tag or the like with each other in the open field.

"I'm so happy he's found a mate," Alkin said, but he sounded almost sad.

Alexa turned to study the Prince's handsome face. "You're worried he won't come back to Shelkite?"

Alkin gave her a half-smile, wreathed with gloom. "Yes."

"I can understand the loss. He's an exquisite creature and a good friend. I owe him my life," she replied, suddenly feeling what it would be like to someday be forced to separate from the company and go her own way. She shook her head; she couldn't think of that right now. She was so attached to all of them.

They circled the fountain and began walking toward the front terrace. They ascended the steps and came to the railing to stop and watch the festivities. "Did Apollos ever tell you his story?" Alkin asked.

"No. I guess he hasn't." Alexa suddenly realized.

"Well, I guess there's not much to it. But when he was a colt, he was part of a small herd. He got separated from them one day. He was still young enough that his powers hadn't manifested yet and he was captured. He was forced to be on display in a traveling circus. This was still before he got his powers, mind you, so he wasn't able to help himself escape yet. But one day, a prince of Shelkite came along, my ancestor, and had pity on him and he paid for his freedom. Apollos went to find his herd. But he was unable to find any other unicorn, let alone his herd. They'd been slaughtered. So, he went to Shelkite and made it his home. He's served willfully under Shelkite rule ever since. He's my closest companion. I trust him more than anyone, more than my sister, more than the Head-Master Sword, and I trust them more than myself." He smiled.

Alexa smiled fondly at the Prince, unsure what to say. Then she said softly, "I'm sure he'll be able to balance the time between his new love and his duty." She grinned. Alkin grinned back at her. He leaned casually against the rail, putting aside any princely demeanor. Alexa leaned her elbows on the railing, still smiling at him, unable to remove her eyes from his hazel ones.

"You're a unique, young woman, Alexandra," he stated as

he gazed at her. "I'm glad I've had the pleasure to meet you and travel and work with you."

She smiled even wider at him, soaring gleefully from his praise. "Thanks. Shelkite is a lucky country to have a man such as you to rule," she said in complete honesty. He smiled crookedly at her, his eyes twinkling.

Suddenly, Alexa was very aware of how close he was to her. While they had spoken, they had moved closer, their heads bending toward one another caught up in the conversation. How had she not noticed it two seconds before? She subconsciously leaned away, but Alkin followed her like he was attached to her by a string. She realized immediately what was about to happen, and her heart fluttered in panic. She stiffened in horror as the Prince leaned in and tilted his head toward her face. A couple options raced rapidly through her mind. One, she could back away hastily; two, she could punch him. She rejected both of the options instantaneously. This was a prince! How was she able to turn down a prince without offending him? So, she held stock still as he gently and tenderly placed his lips on hers. His lips were soft and warm and light on her mouth. Should she kiss him back? Wouldn't it give him the opposite impression she wanted? If she didn't, would he be offended? The kiss was over before she had made up her mind. Alkin merely leaned back and smiled fondly. She smiled hesitantly back, her hands fidgeting.

"Come on, let's get back," he finally said. She grinned at him again; mostly relieved she would be leaving this awkward moment. "I think your Sword-Guard is wondering where you are." Alkin gestured to the Master Sword out among the party goers. Even in the dim light, Alexa could see that Sword Bryan was staring straight at them, an impassive expression across his features. Her breath caught in her throat and her heart beat even faster; it felt as if it might come right up her chest through her throat. Had he seen them?

Alkin led her down the stairs back into the boisterous, partying crowd. She followed, feeling rather numb and almost frightened to meet up with her Sword-Guard. Her mind raced as she contemplated making an excuse, claiming she was sick and then running in the opposite direction of the Master Sword. First off, why did she feel this way? It wasn't like Sword Bryan had actually *said* he wanted her himself. There was no way he could be upset with her. *Get a handle on yourself, Alexandra!* She scolded herself as they came closer and closer to the Sword. Besides, she couldn't have turned down the Prince anyway....

Prince Alkin came to a stop next to his friend. They greeted each other casually, but then they both seemed intent on watching a new rowdier game unfold on the field. Alexa fidgeted uncomfortably next to the Prince. The Master Sword was standing on the other side of Alkin; he appeared to be completely oblivious to her presence.

Suddenly, Alkin did the unthinkable and turned to Alexa. "I'm going to speak with Kheane and Jadelin for a bit. Thank you kindly for the walk, Alexandra." He kissed her lightly on the cheek and strode off eloquently toward the newlyweds, leaving her *alone* with the Master Sword.

Alexa's throat constricted and her mouth became dry. She was positive the Sword had seen the happening on the terrace. She didn't want to sense out his feelings. She didn't want to know. An awkward silence stretched between them. Or was it just awkward for her? She desperately needed a drink of water. She couldn't stand the self-inflicted stress anymore. The party was no longer fun. She thought of her soft bed upstairs and longed to remove the wicked, cumbersome gown she wore.

"Um," she said, her voice sounded strange to her ears. Bryan looked over at her for the first time since she had joined him. "I'm tired. I think I'm going to go to bed. Good night." She didn't raise her eyes to look at the Master Sword. She didn't want to wait and hear his response or let alone get a good look at his face. Was she feeling guilty? Nevertheless, she made the mistake of glancing at him before she turned to leave. And there it was; the thing she had been fearing. His bright azure eyes stared at her; they practically burned through her. She stood there stunned for a second. It was not an angry stare; it was far from it. It was not even an accusing stare. She didn't know *what* kind of stare it was. All she knew was that she didn't like it. It made her feel belittled. How had she allowed him to have this kind of power over her? Giving him her best smug look, she smiled vaguely at him and turned on her heel, lifting her train a bit so she wouldn't trip.

"I'll walk you in," he said with a sigh behind her.

She attempted to make her legs move faster to leave him in the dust and forget the whole night, but her gown and her downright ridiculous shoes were not allowing her to do anything of the sort. He caught up with her quickly and easily. She stumbled along in the grass. Twisting her ankle, she cursed quietly as he caught her elbow to steady her.

"All right?" he asked solicitously.

She endeavored to keep walking away, trying to pull her elbow discreetly from his hand. But a shock of pain shot up her calf originating from her ankle. She growled in frustration as she hopped a step, trying to compose herself. Reluctantly, she stopped trying to flee from him and allowed him to steady her, leaning pathetically on his arm. She sighed and rubbed her aching ankle. He stood silently watching her. She glared up at him, not really understanding why. In all honestly, she was really angry with herself for what had happened, even though it was not her fault....

"Why are you being so nice?" she said tersely.

He seemed stunned. His eyes widened in surprise as he gazed into her face. "I didn't realize I was such a brute," he replied curtly. Alexa snorted arrogantly. She carefully tested her weight on her foot. It was sore, but not bad. Though, unfortunately, she might need help getting up the stairs. "It's not very ladylike to snort you know," he stated cynically.

Alexa sighed and tried to stand on her own, leaning her weight off his. "Sorry," she mumbled apologetically, "I'm just tired and I want to get this gown off." She made a face at her own pitiful excuses.

"Well, go to bed then," he retorted, his brow furrowing crossly.

"That's where I'm headed. If you'd let me," she said snappishly and began limping toward the marble stairway leading up to the unmentionable terrace.

She heard him groan aggravated behind her. "Here, I'm

going to have to help you up the stairs, lest you break your leg…or something worse." He rolled his eyes in exasperation.

He followed her and assisted her up the stairway without another word passing between them. Though, Alexa could feel his anger and bitterness growing with each step up they took. She didn't have to use her senses to comprehend that. He became quiet and his square jaw locked as he grit his teeth; and his azure eyes seemed to spit flames. Alexa found herself wondering again why he should care if he had chosen to ignore his feelings for her.

Finally, they made it to her room. It would have made the trip much quicker and easier if he had just picked her up and carried her up the second stairway, but neither of their stubborn minds were going to go allow that.

Alexa gimped through her doorway and turned briskly to shut the door in his face. But to her great surprise, he held it open. Her mouth went dry again. He was staring at her the same way he had been in the field. She stared back more self-assured this time, not willing to allow him to belittle her for this. After all it was none of his business! Or was it?

After an absurdly long moment of staring silently at each other, Alexa finally spoke, clearing her throat and composing herself, "Tomorrow we'll discuss the plans then, I take it?" His bright blue eyes softened, and this worried her. He took a step toward her. *Why won't he leave me be?* She agonized.

"No. We leave for the ruins," he said pointedly.

"What's your plan then?" she replied with less haughtiness.

"I thought you already had one," he stated more quietly and gently.

"Head-on?"

"Has worked so far."

Then to her utter surprise, she said, "As long as you're there to get me out of any scrapes." She was shocked at her own words, but she didn't allow it to show on her face. She set her face to gaze at him stoically, raising her chin haughtily, eyeing him.

He took another step toward her. She held her ground. He stepped once more. He was close enough to her to reach out and grab her if he wanted. Alexa froze and barely breathed. "That's my general plan," he said softy.

The gentle sound of his voice bordering on fondness was so uncharacteristic of him that it jolted Alexa's heart and threw it back into a hammering stampede. She suddenly wanted to blurt out a confession of not desiring to kiss Alkin and what she really desired was *him*. She yearned to throw her arms around his neck and pull him down to her level and bestow blissful, soft kisses on his perfect lips. But she held her composure, uncertain of his intentions.

A pained, unguarded look passed across his features as he gazed at her, but it turned quickly to something else, something more powerful. He stared in her eyes, motionless for a second, studying her frame of mind. She stared back, softening her own eyes, letting all her guards down. She could beseech him easily with her persuasion power, but she would never do such a thing. Seeming to make a decision of his own accord, the Master Sword leaned his upper body toward her as if he were pondering the same thing she was. His eyes slowly watched hers as he came closer and closer. She waited, tilting her chin toward him as an offering, but kept her eyes firmly on his. She could feel the warmth of him and his light breaths on her skin. His fingertips grazed her chin as he was about to take her face gently in his hands. Then, just as she was about to close her eyes, her body quivering, anticipating his touch, something dreadful happened. He suddenly clenched his jaw and a steely look came into his eyes. He backed away. His hand was on the door frame before she could utter imploringly, "Bryrunan."

He turned back to look at her at the sound of the unused version of his name. He didn't look angry for her use of it; his expression looked rather bittersweet. Alexa gazed at him a bit despairingly, trying desperately to keep her poise. She could see a conflict boiling behind his eyes. He looked regretful as he gazed at her. He glanced briefly down the hall. She didn't need him to explain what he was thinking. She could guess a number of reasons for his final resolve to not go through with what he had been about to. She gave him a sad half-smile, feeling like her heart had just literally cracked. He shut his eyes, trying to clear his mind. When he opened them they were heavily guarded once more. He then resolutely clenched his jaw and nodded stiffly to her.

"Good night, Bryrunan," Alexa whispered in finality, the sound of his name seemed to melt off her tongue like sugar.

"Good night, Alexa."

His voice was like a savior's. If only she could wallow in its sound for forever. She closed her eyes in pitiful defeat. He crossed the threshold and shut the door behind him. She could hear his boot falls as he walked back down the hallway. Gone. Her chance for his love was gone.

Alexa turned and sighed a sigh pregnant with sorrow. Her hands were clammy. She rubbed them brusquely on her gown. She would *not* cry. She noted hazily that she was trembling. She began to quickly undress for bed. She tried to occupy her mind with other thoughts as she fought in frustration with the ties on the dress and corset. The soft bed was screaming her name tonight and she couldn't help but think how nice it would have been to snuggle up against his broad chest and fall asleep to his heartbeat. Oh, how she hoped that Bryrunan wouldn't visit her in her dreams tonight. She needed to let go. Her heart felt engulfed in torment. Oh yes, she could easily think of many reasons for him not to kiss her.

Chapter 32

"One…two…three," Alexa counted to herself. It was early morning the day after the ceremony and no one had yet knocked on her door to wake her. However, she had already risen on her own.

She counted while she readied herself. She counted while she washed up and pulled on her form fitting trousers and her light weight top, feeling relieved at their comfort. She counted as she plopped down on the bed and began pulling on her calf-high riding boots. When she tested her tender ankle she was pleased to find it supported nicely. She counted as she buckled on her dagger and strapped her sword on and slid her knife in the flap inside her boot.

"Four…five…six." She continued as she stood to brush her hair and re-braid it into its normal single plait. In the small mirror, she numbly watched her fingers move the locks in and out of each other. "Seven…eight."

She had made it a game this morning to count each foal that had been born at her home the previous spring and carefully envision each one's characteristics. The basic reason for this exercise was to keep her mind occupied, to keep from thinking of the disastrous, previous night. It was the only way she could go down stairs and face the others…to face the Master Sword.

It was a weak solution, but it was working so far. She was staying calm and keeping the memories of the night before at bay. Though, she soon had to stop because there had been only ten foals. So, she began envisioning what each one would look like now. Since she had left months ago they were now older and most assuredly bigger and stronger. It was silly, but it was engaging her mind. And after that, if she had to, she would start to envision all the lambs her family owned. *But that would take ages.* She was sullen.

It may have been silly, but she was now done getting ready for the day. She now had no choice but to leave the room and immerse herself back with the company and all their problems—outward ones and inward ones.

Though she couldn't stop the thoughts flooding into her brain, she felt better composed as she headed down the hall toward the stairway. She primed herself to look in the Master Sword's face and not show any sign of emotion. She knew *he* wouldn't have any problem. She knew Bryan was innately responsible and had such a strong control of his personal emotions no one would ever guess how he felt inwardly. He compartmentalized his feelings very well.

And, if that were not enough, she had to also somehow deal with her pending status concerning Prince Alkin. Had it just been a friendly kiss? Or was he expecting something more from her now? She shook her head, pursing her lips, trying to suppress the complicated thoughts. She had more important things to think about. She shouldn't be thinking about men as she was about to meet a dragon in a day's time!

She reached the bottom of the marble stairs to find the front doors opened. She heard voices outside. Stepping out on the terrace she could see the company along with several centaurs, Estella and Jadelin gathered on the lawn. The company's mounts were tacked up and ready to go, the pack mule loaded up with fresh goods.

She jogged down the steps, being careful of her iffy ankle. Shading her eyes from the brilliant morning sun, she joined the group. She returned their greetings with a confident smile and wave of her hand. She didn't even bother looking at either the Master Sword or the Prince directly.

Searching out Zhan, she took his reins from the waiting Eelyne. Zhan greeted her joyously. He gave his mistress a half-whinny, half-whicker and tossed his mane jubilantly. Alexa smiled, her heart lightening a great deal. "Hey, Pal." She took his muzzle in her hands and looked into his milky, chocolate eyes. He eyed her back curiously. She grinned at his expression and gave him a kiss on his soft nose. He wiggled his muzzle and raised his head to lip her wetly on the nose, flicking his ears forward. She chuckled loudly. Zhan was always good medicine for an unhappy heart. "Well, at least you want to kiss me," she whispered with an ironic giggle. Zhan bobbed his head, flipping his mane. Alexa patted him firmly on the neck. Pulling her attention from her buddy, she glanced up in hope to find what the next form of action was. It just so happened she looked right into Sword Bryan's face, who was standing a few yards away; he had been observing her interaction with Zhan.

Just as she suspected, he stood poised, looking completely impassive as he gazed at her and her horse. After unnervingly locking eyes with her for a brief second, he turned blankly away to speak to Hard Flame, who had been conversing with the Prince.

Alexa took a deep breath, willing her features to look just as impassive. She could do it. She would just ignore the Prince and him as much as possible. She forced her legs to move forward, thinking fretfully that she had no choice but to speak with them to get mission details. However, she changed course upon seeing Kheane and Jadelin.

To her surprise, Jadelin was wearing riding clothes and she held the reins of a chocolate colored mare with a silver mane. Kheane was standing by her, Blize hanging her head fondly over his shoulder. Alexa approached them for information instead. They greeted her happily. "Hi. So, what's the plan?" she asked.

"Since the ruins are only a day from here, Hard Flame suggested he and several of his warriors accompany us. No one knows what to expect, so it's best to have reinforcements," Kheane said.

Alexa regarded Jadelin with a smile, "You joining us?"

"Yes. I know I don't seem cut out for this kind of stuff. But I'm tougher than everyone thinks," she replied with a timid smile.

"Oh, I don't doubt it after hearing your stowaway story." Alexa laughed away the empress trying to defend herself. Jadelin grinned at Kheane; he smiled crookedly back. It brought another thought to Alexa's mind and she addressed Kheane, "I suppose after today you're going to come back to be with Jadelin." Kheane and Jadelin shared a disheartened look and Kheane shook his head solemnly, surprising Alexa. She raised her eyebrows. "No?"

"I started this mission. I'll finish it. I practically begged to join your company. I'll not back out," Kheane answered.

Jadelin added, "He also thinks he needs to do something good to salvage himself. I don't believe in that so much, but I do understand his other reasoning." She sighed and it sounded heavy with frustration.

Alexa stared at the newlyweds perplexed. They had been

apart for centuries, not even knowing if the other was alive, and now that they were finally together they were willingly parting because of Kheane's sense of duty. This was far beyond her comprehension. She had underestimated them in a few ways.

Studying Alexa's baffled reaction, Kheane and Jadelin smiled at her in a way that made her feel naïve and young, albeit their smiles were wreathed with sorrow. Alexa shook her head and sighed on their behalf, "I don't understand it." She gave them a slight encouraging smile.

Within a few minutes, the company, as well as Estella, Jadelin and seven centaur warriors set out for the ruins. The griffins flew them over the wall, dividing them in small groups on the platform. This took some time. But once they were all over, the new, bigger company started making its way northeast, led by Hard Flame. The unicorns followed next in the procession.

Alexa distracted herself by watching the two beautiful creatures. They seemed oblivious to all around them; they chatted happily and played nipping games. Though, Alexa was certain they were still vigilant.

After them, rode the Prince, Jadelin and Kheane. Sword Bryan followed directly behind. Alexa, not being allowed to be a long distance from her Sword-Guard, tried to keep her distance from him nonetheless. She held Zhan back behind Dragon's flank and didn't bother speaking to or looking at the Sword. He didn't bother looking over his shoulder to check on her either, despite that being his normal practice. As usual, the others followed closely behind Alexa. The centaur warriors flanked the whole company and strode silently and stoically, almost blending into the forest.

Even with a larger number, Alexa didn't feel any safer. But it did alleviate the awkwardness she had worried about concerning the Master Sword and the Prince. Alkin had greeted Alexa happily and had spoken a few times with her; but it was nothing out of the ordinary. This confused and relieved her. He didn't seem any more partial to her then he usually did. This had to be a good sign. Maybe it had just been a friendly kiss, or a spur of the moment reaction.

Then a thought occurred to her. Maybe she persuaded him

to kiss her without knowing it. She hadn't remembered turning on the skill she'd often used to get people to do trivial things her way. The persuasion skill had its tight limits; she couldn't *make* someone do something if they really didn't want to. Maybe it was better if she had accidentally persuaded Alkin, because then he wouldn't have been acting completely on his own accord. So there was the chance he would move on without a second thought. Alexa groaned inwardly, scowling at her thoughts. Now she was making excuses! Of course, he had kissed her on his own will.

Alexa had long since gotten bored with watching the playful unicorns and this last train of thought eventually led to another more complex set of estimations. These were the possible explanations for Sword Bryan's odd, but obviously thought out, actions last night. Alexa tried futility to not think about her very confusing interaction with the Master Sword. For she had gone over it and over it last night as she lay in bed unable to fall asleep.

Now staring at his poised back as he rode ahead of her, Alexa found herself counting down the reasons he'd decided at the last minute not to kiss her, therefore crushing all hopes she had had of them being together. Her logic for counting the foals this morning was because she had been trying not to count the reasons Bryan *would not* love her. Because she had come to the conclusion that he definitely felt strongly for her. There was no doubt in her mind about that.

Her reasoning was: One, he was her Sword-Guard and therefore she was his duty and not a lover. It was simple and logical; he was determined not to jeopardize his responsibility. Two, he was a Head-Master Sword and she was merely a commoner. She had thought this many times before, but this argument seemed weak. His personality didn't show he felt superior to her or anyone else. Plus, he had been quite willing to kiss her. If only he was not so stubborn and self-disciplined! Third, some old feelings of betrayal had been aroused by him witnessing Alkin kiss her. So he wasn't willing to let his guard down and allow himself to love her. Lastly, it was Sword Bryan's superior and child-hood best friend that had made the first move for her affections and Bryan now saw her as taboo. From knowing his personality, Alexa knew the Master Sword would never compromise his friend and especially a prince of any country let alone his own. Each of these reasons was probable. Perhaps it was not just one, maybe it was a conglomeration of a few of them.

Sighing agitatedly, Alexa shook the thoughts away. There was no point in lingering on this. She would never know. She tried to sense his feelings out, but all she got was the old, black bog of bitterness he used to have when she'd first met him. She *had* to focus on more important things, like not being the mother to a bunch of abominations created by her uncle. Now that was something to think about! Why was her mind so charged with worries over the Master Sword? He was blatantly ignoring her as much as she was him. The door to that opportunity was locked tight. Something had to be wrong with her brain…

They reached a spacious clearing by dusk. The centaurs quickly set up torches mounted on high stakes surrounding the area. They began unpacking and setting up their tents. The centaurs had graciously supplied tents and cots for the company. Alexa was thankful for this thoughtful gesture. Each member of the company had their own private tent. The tents were not by any means extravagant; they were small, but serviceable. Alexa felt extremely relieved she would have some solitude. She didn't feel like huddling up on the ground next to the Master Sword tonight, or Prince Alkin for that matter, albeit Bryan dutifully and stubbornly set his tent up right next to hers.

The camp was set up quickly and efficiently. Alexa had her tent up and cot out in no time. She had worked side by side with Bryan as he had set up his. Though, they didn't speak a word to each other. Alexa stole covert glances at him, but she found he looked just as impassive as he had earlier. He never once looked at her. This bothered Alexa a great deal. She realized sadly she had become accustomed to his protective glances and it worried her that maybe he had suddenly stopped caring.

She absently fiddled around with fixing her tent, waiting for Bryan to finish his. When he had finally left to join the others, she waited a half a minute before following him. She joined the others by the huge bonfire in the center of the circle of tents. She sat down between Eelyne and Hazerk. The group was preparing for a meal. Alexa stared inattentively into the blazing fire, watching the flames flicker and listening to the wood snap. The heat was immense on her face, but she didn't feel like moving back. Maybe it would burn her freckles off and along with them her feelings for the Master Sword.

Coming out of her sullen reverie, she looked up to see Apollos gazing at her from across the fire. He was curled up on the ground, his legs tucked up beneath him. Estella was curled up next to him and was gazing intently at her, too. Puzzled, Alexa raised her eyebrows quizzically at the two unicorns. They looked suspiciously conniving. Apollos eyed her with his deep, chocolate eyes. Tossing his nose in the air, he gestured toward the Master Sword, who was sitting farther down the circle of warriors in conversation with Hard Flame. Alexa glanced down to the unaware Sword and back to the unicorns. Apollos narrowed his eyes at her, staring at her a little bit chidingly.

Alexa wasn't exactly sure what the clever unicorn was getting at, but she had a good idea he knew something was going on between her and the Master Sword and he wanted her to fix it. Feeling beat, Alexa sighed and nodded her head in acknowledgment. This seemed to appease both unicorns and they turned away to enjoy their dinners. Nothing escaped Apollos' keen observations. He probably had noted instantly that Alexa and Bryan hadn't been interacting today the way they normally did. As she ate her dinner, Alexa vaguely wondered why the unicorn thought it was so important for her and the Master Sword to be on good terms. It wasn't like either of them were slacking on their duties. She shrugged it away and tried to immerse herself in the conversation at hand.

"...the ruins are about two or so miles from here. We picked here because it's a good spot to accommodate us all, and it's far enough away it's safe from piquing the dragon's senses," Hard Flame was explaining to the group.

"You said the legend is that the eternal flame is in caverns beneath the ruins. Is the dragon there, too?" Prince Alkin asked.

"Well, the story claims the fountain of flame is the

dragon's hoard. It protects it viciously. So, my assumption is that if the flame is underground the dragon is very close by."

"Do you or your warriors have any ideas, Hard Flame, as how to breach this?" Alkin asked. The whole group was now paying rapt attention to the conversation.

"I'm afraid I don't have any knowledge of dragon lore. How about you all?" Hard Flame addressed his warriors. They shook their heads in regret. "We'll just be here to help fight, if you need us," Hard Flame said, addressing Prince Alkin again.

"Yes, thank you." Alkin looked grateful, but disappointed. He regarded Alexa, peering around Warrior Hazerk, who sat between them, "Have any intuition clues?" he inquired hopefully.

Alexa suddenly felt sixteen pairs of eyes on her. This didn't bother her so much as knowing the Master Sword was now gazing inquisitively at her, too. She stared blankly for a second at all the eyes glittering expectantly in the firelight. She swallowed. She had been so preoccupied with all her thoughts of Bryan the idea hadn't even crossed her mind to search her senses for some help on the impending matter. How stupid! Perhaps her situation with Bryan *was* making her disregard her duties. "Ah, I…no," she said stupidly, avoiding the Prince's fallen countenance. Then she added, perking up forcefully, "Eelyne, you must know something about dragons that could help us."

"Yeah, sure," he answered, and then he added a little self-consciously, "Well, I know they have an excellent sense of smell and sight. They can spit fire up to about thirty feet. Of course, they can fly, swift and high. And like I said before, they can be finicky and obviously they are quite vicious. Though, I do know they're easily distracted, which could be to our advantage. Also, if they're guarding something, they won't leave it long, or go far from it, which could be helpful, too…That's all I got…sorry," he ended dejectedly. Everyone was silent for a moment as they digested his information. The unspoken defeat everyone was feeling was palpable.

"To help boost my witch intuition I'll need to see the ruins beforehand. I need to know for sure if it's in fact where the fire element is located, and to get a better idea as to how to go about doing this," Alexa stated, finding her confidence. She had half in mind to just say do it head-on, like her and the Master Sword had joked. But now, ironically enough, that seemed almost too private to bring out in the open. As if she were to mention it, it would intimately connect her and her Sword-Guard more than either of them was willing to be connected at the moment. She shook the thought away, squeezing her eyes shut, forcing *him* out of her mind.

"Well then, we shouldn't waste time. Let's scout out the ruins now. That way we can begin right away in the morning," Alkin concluded. The others agreed to this.

"All right," Sword Bryan said authoritatively as he stood. "Just a small group should go. Hard Flame, Apollos, Prince Alkin, Alexa and I will go," he said and then added on thoughtfully, "Kheane and Estella can come, too. We definitely can use your expertise, Kheane, and two unicorns are better than one." Everyone he had listed nodded their heads in acknowledgment and stood to prepare to leave. "Hurry, so we can get back and get some rest," the Master Sword stated as they dispersed to go re-tack their horses.

Alexa felt guilty about having to tack up Zhan again. Since they had ridden all day long, he probably needed a rest. Her animal friend instantly saw her coming over with his tack to retrieve him from his grazing. He merely lifted his muzzle to her ear and gave a resigned huff of sweet horsy breath in her hair. She smiled apologetically at him and patted him lovingly, landing another kiss on his nose. Holding her saddle and bridle, she considered for only a second whether or not to ride him without any tack. She set it down by her tent. She then hugged Zhan tightly around his neck. He nuzzled her neck. Pulling away, she gracefully hopped up onto his sleek back. His spirits seemed to have lifted at realizing she wasn't putting the confining contraptions on him. He danced playfully under her, thinking this was a game. She patted him and then nudged him to join the others. He responded happily.

She waited for the others with Hard Flame and the unicorns. Alkin was the first to join them on Sapharan, the others followed close behind. As he rode up, the Prince eyed Alexa and smiled widely. "You're probably the best female rider I've ever seen," he commented with an admiring twinkle in his eye, obviously noting that Zhan didn't even wear a halter.

"Thanks. You're pretty good yourself." She smiled coquettishly at the Prince, casting a sly glance at the Master Sword in the process. If he was going to ignore her, she would play that she didn't care. Bryan was looking at her austerely; his clear, azure eyes were narrowed irritably. Dragon pulled at his bit grumpily and stomped a hoof. The Sword and his mount seemed to be one entity at times, Alexa thought amusedly. At least Bryan was regarding her now.

Apollos snorted loudly, catching everyone's attention. "Come on, humans, let's go." He motioned for Hard Flame to lead the way and him and Estella followed. The soft glow emanating from the two unicorns' horns lit the path adequately.

The trek was a short one. It was mostly a quiet one, too. Only Prince Alkin and Alexa spoke softly to each other; periodically discussing their theories of horse riding tactics and handling.

Soon through the darkness and trees, they could see the ancient ruins loom before them. The group became silent as each one pondered out ideas in their heads. The ruins were just an old, crumbling stone castle laid amongst overgrown vines, trees and shrubbery. In the dark it looked somewhat foreboding, but if someone happened to cross it in the day, it might seem like a pleasant place to have a picnic.

Alexa let loose her senses; a race of adrenalin zipped through her body as her senses made the familiar connection to something powerful and magical. It took her breath away. "This is definitely it," she whispered.

"Good," Alkin responded pleased.

"There's more than one dragon in the caverns," Apollos asserted, his eyes far away as he too sensed out the area. The company replied by making a stressed moan in unison.

"How many?"

"Two, maybe three. But I can only sense one that appears to be at its fullest power," Apollos answered.

346

The company had dismounted and was huddled close together in a copse just off the overgrown yard of the dilapidated castle. It looked simple enough from the outside to get inside. There had to be an entrance way leading down into the caverns amongst all the rubble, hopefully it wasn't blocked off.

Kheane's gruff whisper broke the thoughtful silence, "In my opinion, the best bet is the element of surprise. I don't know much about dragons; but if it sees us coming, well, we'd probably not get anywhere near the element with all our limbs."

Alexa deliberated for another minute before deciding the basics of her tactic. "Warrior Eelyne said they were easily distracted. If we had a diversion on top of surprising them, we might have a chance to escape with the element. After all, we only want a little piece of the element. The dragons might give up chasing us to continue to protect the rest of their hoard."

"True. Estella and I would be good distractions," Apollos volunteered; and Estella bobbed her head, a glint of anticipation in her eyes.

"Are you sure you want to help by being bait, Apollos?" Alkin asked apprehensively. "To even think of unicorns as bait is beyond my comprehension."

The unicorn tossed his head nonchalantly. "I'm not worried for my safety. Estella and I can take care of ourselves. And, yes, I want to help. I *need* to help. You'd be foolish to pass up my help," he said with a twinkle in his chocolate eyes.

"I suppose you're right. Well, if you're willing…" Alkin resigned, feeling protective over his one-of-a-kind friend.

"Well, the details are vague. But if we can sneak down into the caverns without alerting them, and Apollos and Estella cause a distraction, I might be able to snatch the fire element and run. However a person snatches flames, I'm not sure…We did have to ask the dryad for the earth element. Though, I'm hoping this fountain of flame is something I can just approach and gather," Alexa contemplated aloud. Everyone nodded their heads in silent accordance.

Then the Master Sword spoke up a little icily, "Well, it sounds all good and well enough, straightforward as ever. Head-on is probably the best in this case; there's no other way it seems." Alexa felt an aggrieved shiver shock through her heart at his reminding words and tantalizing voice. But Bryan wasn't done speaking and he abruptly regarded her with a firm stare. "If what you say is true, then anyone can gather the element. I don't see where you're needed to go down into the caverns at all," he stated flatly to a stunned Alexa. Her features quickly turned into a dire glare, staring hard at the Master Sword, who continued to stare austerely back at her. She couldn't even form a thought in her mind she was so furious. What was his game?

The others contemplated this for a second. Then Alkin said in approval, "Yes, I don't see having her go either."

Alexa's temper got the better of her and she turned on the Prince like an angry cat, "You all can't stop me from going in there. I'm supposed to gather the elements," she hissed.

"No, you're the one to *use* the elements," Bryan stated. She opened her mouth to retort angrily back, but he cut her off stubbornly, "You're not going and that's final."

She snorted harshly. The others in the company watched her apprehensively. "And what? You're going down there?" she said insolently.

"I could," Bryan merely said.

"He does have a point, Alexa," Apollos' soft voice tried to console her. "You're too important in the matter of using the elements."

"I'm smart enough to do this. I know how to fight and can take care of myself." Her tone was imploring, but it had a dangerous edge to it. She utterly despised how the Master Sword was taking on such a calm demeanor while basically betraying her. This was her mission! This was her company!

"This is a dragon. It doesn't care what you can offer in a fight. It would roast you for its dinner. It can fly; and I don't see you sprouting any angel wings. Its tooth is probably bigger than you. Forget it, girl," Bryan said frostily, his eyes an icy blue.

Why was he doing this to her? She had to do this! He was doing it out of spite; she was positive. She clenched her jaw and scowled at him, crossing her arms. He glared back, unmoving. She then regarded a concerned Prince Alkin. His hazel eyes widened with apprehension. "Tell him he doesn't have to babysit me. I'm mature enough, I can handle this," she stated firmly. Alkin looked as if he didn't want to get in the middle of this argument. *Kind of cowardly for a prince.* Alexa stared sourly into his submissive eyes.

"Ha!" Bryan scoffed; she turned her blazing eyes back on the Sword. "Oh okay, Miss Temper Tantrum," he jeered.

Alexa's mouth gaped in utter indignation. The Master Sword merely stared at her smugly with a slight smile across his lips. She snapped her jaw shut. "I do *not* throw temper tantrums," she seethed through her teeth. Her sapphire eyes bored straight into Bryan's clear, blue obstinate ones. *Well, he isn't ignoring me by any means now!* What bitter irony.

"Like a two-year-old," he replied arrogantly.

"I do not!"

"Well…." Bryan snickered and held up his hands to show the obviousness of her display.

Any shards left of Alexa's composure shattered completely. "Well, you," she growled menacingly, "you're a chauvinistic, pigheaded, conceited, bossy, great big—"

"Whoa, now," he interrupted her with a casual laugh, but his eyes narrowed, the azure blue darkening dangerously.

His off-handedness maddened her all the more. She wanted nothing more than to punch him right in his smug face. She clenched her fist. But taking a quick glance around to the shocked faces of the company, she realized she was making a scene. She rapidly quelled her anger. Although, she glowered one more time at the Master Sword before she composed herself. "I guess we'll discuss it in the morning," she said tersely. Bryan shrugged, brushing her off self-importantly.

Alexa looked over to Zhan, who was pulling at some leaves on a nearby tree. She gave a low whistle, and the horse plodded compliantly over. Placing her hand on his sleek, white neck, her boiling insides calmed. She looked back to the company, who were now mounting up and mumbled, "I'm sorry…for my behavior." They all nodded in acceptance, except for the Master Sword, who just stared at her with penetrating eyes.

Prince Alkin, who was closest to her, smiled tactfully. "It's all right. I understand why you feel the way you do." She gave him an appreciative smile and swung up onto Zhan's back. She grumbled inwardly to herself the whole way back to the camp. She had a good feeling Bryan was punishing her for some reason that was entirely *not* her fault. It had nothing to do with protecting her. She didn't bother acknowledging the Master Sword as they split to go their ways to their private tents.

Chapter 33

Something felt uncomfortable and he was cold. Shivering a bit, Bryan tugged at his coarse blanket. His movement caused the rickety cot to creak. He had a stiff neck. He was vaguely aware that he was sleeping on his stomach, his neck cranked to one side, his right arm dangling to the ground. He groaned sleepily and shifted, opening his eyes just enough to see that it was dark out. He closed them and fell back to sleep.

The next instant there was a startling flapping noise coming from all around him, jarring him awake. Heart pounding, he jerked up. The cot rocked precariously nearly bucking him to the ground. His sword was in his hand before he was even fully conscious. The flapping noise hadn't ceased. He looked around, sleepily noting that his tent was waving violently as if it were in a wind storm. Then it abruptly stopped.

Lowering his sword and well aware of his surroundings now, he realized the situation. Someone had taken a hold of his tent and had shaken it. A small smile escaped his lips with a whispery, knowing chuckle. He rubbed the sleep from his eyes and sheathed his sword. He had an idea of who it was and he shook his head amusedly. He had better go out and face her. He stepped outside his tent into the dark, breezy night.

He could see her willowy silhouette. She was holding a tacked up Zhan and glaring blatantly at him. He felt a twinge of guilt upon seeing her. Though, he said in spite of his feelings, "What in the demon's name was that for?"

Alexa shifted her tense stance. "I'm leaving for the ruins. I'm giving you the option to come with me or not," she said frankly as she swiftly mounted Zhan. The white horse gave a snort and an excited toss of his head.

Bryan studied her for a second. She had all her gear mounted on her. Her quiver full of the black arrows and bow were strapped across her back. Her dagger was strapped around her thigh and the sword he had given her belted to her waist. She stared at him levelly, waiting for him to respond. Rubbing his face a tad exasperated, he sighed. "I thought I told you that you weren't going."

"You said we'd discuss it in the morning. It's morning and I'm discussing it. I've decided I'm going with or without your permission."

"You'd go alone?"

"Apollos and Estella." She pointed off into the distance to where the two unicorns stood watching their confrontation impassively.

"I never said we'd discuss it," he stated.

"You shrugged. That implies we would."

He stared at her, contemplating morosely. *I deserve her anger*. His command for her to stay behind *was* intended for her protection, but the guilty feeling he had derived from it also told him he had done it for other more bitter and selfish reasons. He had known she would want more than anything to gather the fire element herself. So he had taken that away, to anger her...purposely. And now he felt guilty. Yet, he still didn't want her in harm's way.

"Okay then. I'm leaving," she stated and reined Zhan around.

"All right, all right," he said, caving in for probably the first time ever. How was she doing this to him? He felt unnervingly vulnerable to her fury. He had slept out his own bitter anger that night.

She turned Zhan back around to face him, a triumphant smile spreading across her features. "Good. Let's go."

Bryan sighed and shook his head in denial of his weakness. "Give me a minute. Wake the others and have them prepare for the dragon just in case." He turned into his tent and readied himself.

By the time he was finished, he could hear the company rousing and the centaurs readying themselves. He stepped outside and went to Dragon, who was tethered on a nearby tree. The horse stretched his neck toward his master and puffed a small breath into Bryan's offered palm. The black stallion's dark eyes gleamed in the low dawn light. The Sword gave his mount an affectionate pat and began tacking him up.

Then, despite all his power to rein in his feelings, Bryan's thoughts washed over him like a tide pulling him down. He had been strongly endeavoring to resist all thoughts and feelings pertaining to Alexa in an affectionate manner. He realized he had been doing this for weeks, but now the situation between the two of them had reached a boiling point. He could no longer deny he had feelings for her, nor could he deny she showed feelings for him as well. Despite all his efforts in the beginning to not even like her, he had fallen completely for her, like she was some kind of seductive sorceress. He laughed ironically at his own thoughts. What if she had bewitched him? But deep down he knew she hadn't. He had been drawn to her the moment he had laid eyes on her; and he remembered blatantly resisting it.

Before he had met her, he had sworn off women. He had decided to willingly die an old, lonely warrior if he must. Because of his own bitter resentment toward women he had foolishly denied his natural partiality to Alexa. He had also resisted her because his sense of duty was so overpowering to him. Being her Sword-Guard was his first and foremost obligation with her. He couldn't think of her as a lover did. Such thoughts befuddled his mind, his judgment, weakening his ability to do his job. It would be dangerous for her as well as him and the company. But despite his best efforts, it slowly crept over him and ensnared him. His feelings for her had broken out and won over.

The night of the ceremony he had finally resigned to the fact that he indeed loved her. And allowing himself to delve deeper into his feelings that night he found he cared more for her than he had cared for anyone else ever. It was a strange almost liberating feeling to finally allow himself to be okay with this resolve. Then he had seen her and Alkin kiss on the terrace. By his former keen observations of Alkin and Alexa, which now he knew were because of his jealousy, he had known that the Prince felt some kind of attraction to her. But he never thought he would act upon it.

Upon seeing their kiss that night, Bryan had burned with anger and resentment…as well as betrayal. He had wanted nothing more than to march over and yank them apart and punch his friend and Prince square in the face. He was angry and bitter toward Alexa for allowing Alkin to kiss her. Although, Bryan knew deep down that was the last thing she had wanted. He knew by her ridged stature when Alkin had touched her and by the way she resisted looking himself in the face. He felt betrayed on some level by her. She had given him signs, or so he thought she had shown him that she reciprocated his feelings. He had resented her, but it was for only a short time; before he had realized that everything was all his own, foolish fault. He had allowed this to happen. He had denied his feelings so far that he had let her slip right through his ignorant hands.

Now she was out of reach. Sword Bryan would never, could never cross Prince Alkin. It went against his obligation as just a mere citizen of Shelkite. Even more so, he was the Head-Master Sword and was once Alkin's good friend. So, as always, Bryan's self-control and strong sense of duty toward his job won over. He had played his impassive part well. Apart from that one blissful minute when he had decided he didn't care about his duty, or about an irate prince; and he was going to take Alexa for himself despite all. He had been so close. If he had broken the flood gates and had taken her in his arms like he had wanted to and had kissed her and had—well, done many things—that would have been it. He wouldn't have been able to stop himself from loving her and he would've blatantly disregarded his duty to Alkin and Shelkite. But, he had had enough resolve to stop before her sweet, offered lips had touched his. Thus, making the distance he knew he had to put between them easier; or so he thought easier.

Yesterday, he had receded back into his old, bitter shell and he had wanted to punish her; despite his knowing that he was really at fault. But today, well, his own mood swings were annoying him; today he felt guilty and he would do anything to make her happy and not have her fiery sapphire eyes bore into him. He just wanted to make sure she came through this safely. He would be there for her as he had promised.

Bryan had long finished tacking up Dragon. He had mounted and gone to wait by the unicorns, inattentive to their open musings about Alexa and him. His mind was full of his own complex thoughts too much to care what the two conniving unicorns had to say. Alexa was over speaking with the others in last minute preparations. Bryan could tell Prince Alkin wasn't happy about her going. But he had relented, of course, the softy that he was.

Alexa glanced up and caught eyes with him. Bryan looked away coolly; she was punishing him and he didn't want to see her spiteful eyes. After another few minutes, when the risen sun was casting a dusty hew on their surroundings, Alexa rode over to join him and the unicorns. She looked stoic, ready for the business at hand. Bryan had to resolve himself to do the same. Wow, but he was falling to pieces under her power! He reflected bitterly. He couldn't let this jeopardize his job. He met eyes with her again; their blazing resentment was replaced with an anticipation that only had to do with the task at hand.

"Ready?" she addressed them all, her voice light.

"Yes. Let's go," he answered briskly.

They set off down the lightly wooded path, the two unicorns leading the way. The crude plan was the others would follow behind, but stay back, so as to not alert the dragons to their presence. Sword Bryan, Alexa and the unicorns were hoping to sneak up on the dragons. It would be easier and perhaps safer for all to have only a few creep down into the caverns. Even this plan would be farfetched, except that the unicorns had revealed they could cast an aura about their small party that would mask them from the dragons' senses, at least until the dragons spotted them. After that, well, it would play out. The unicorns would try to distract while Alexa and Bryan would gather the element and run.

The Master Sword tried not to think about how they were going to get out of the caverns alive. It seemed astronomical that they would make it without a scratch. But he tried to think positively; they had two clever unicorns helping them. That had to count for something. And, of course, he was a good warrior, and Alexa was definitely nothing to scoff at when she put her mind to it.

Alexa shifted her quiver of arrows on her back to a more comfortable position. Well, it was over before it had even begun; she determined as they made their way toward the ruins. She wasn't thinking about the dragons. It was her and the Master

Sword's potential love she was thinking on, much to her disgust. She couldn't even manage to extricate him from her thoughts even as they marched to face the dragons this very hour.

He rode just a half a stride behind her. Close enough to jump to action if something was to happen to her, but far enough away to make a point that he didn't want to have a conversation with her, let alone look at her. Well, she didn't care. She despised him. She sighed grudgingly at the lie to herself. She couldn't bring herself to hate him, even after he had hurt her so excruciatingly. How could a girl hate any man that had saved her from the certain fate she had almost obtained by the warm spring? And she wasn't just merely thinking of her death...

Enough, enough! Alexa squeezed her eyes shut to rid herself of all thought. *High Power, help me!* She pleaded desperately. When she opened them again she could see the ruins through the branches. Something stole over her and she allowed herself to be completely consumed by it. It was the lucid mid-set she needed to handle the task. She sighed in relief at the freedom from her imprisoning thoughts.

They halted in a thicket just beyond the overgrown yard of the old castle. Alexa and Sword Bryan dismounted silently and tied Dragon and Zhan near one another on a tree, hiding them from view of the ruins. The two crept to where the unicorns were peering at the ruins through the branches. They crouched down next to each other, forgetting all their complications and grievances with one another.

After a moment of fervent study, Estella said, "You two humans ready?"

Alexa and Bryan glanced tentatively at each other, their eyes briefly, unwillingly, scanning the other's face. They nodded stoically.

"Okay. We're going to cast a masking aura. Don't wander too far from us at first. We'll keep it snug around the four of us. The dragon will be less likely to notice the aura if it's small. It would get suspicious if there was a huge space in its lair where it couldn't sense anything," Apollos said in a whisper. Alexa and the Master Sword nodded their understanding, each feeling a twist of nerves in their stomach flare up.

"All right, let's find a way in," Bryan stated, risking a glance at Alexa. He was content to see she was already looking at him, impassively as it was.

The two elegant unicorns bobbed their heads and their horns lit up, glowing lavender. Alexa felt something close in on her. It was barely noticeable. She couldn't describe it any way other than it felt like a warm blanket being tucked in around her. She felt safe.

"Okay, let's go." Apollos' voice was muffled by the aura.

They moved together, crossing the grassy field and entering the wasted grounds. They searched as quietly and as quickly as they could. There was so much rubble, there wasn't much to see or find.

As the sun rose and warmed their backs, Alexa was starting to get discouraged. It was possible the entranceway to the caverns had been blocked by the castle's wreckage and it would be impenetrable. But after some more intense minutes of searching, they found a door. It was snuggled in a grassy knoll behind the ruins. It was in what would have been the old courtyard.

Alexa and the Master Sword quickly dug at the dirt covering the door and pulled at the long grasses to clear the front of it. The unicorns helped by pawing the dirt aside. Once they had the door uncovered, they pulled hard together on the handle. The humans thought vaguely to themselves that once this thing budged it was going to make an ungodly noise opening. But the unicorns stood close to the door and muffled the sound as it finally gave and popped opened. Crouched over the gaping entrance in the ground, they all peered curiously down in. The old stairway that led down in was crumbled into nothing but rubble.

"It looks like an old shelter of some sort," Bryan said, his own voice muted.

"Yeah, but it could lead to the caverns. It's hard for me to sense anything with the masking aura," Alexa replied.

"It's a good a start as any," Apollos said.

"No dragon could get down in here. It wouldn't fit," Alexa stated, thinking the dragon must leave the caverns once in a while.

She envisioned the dragon trying to squeeze its large girth through the small door and smiled childishly.

"There might be another exit in the woods," Apollos suggested.

"All right, let's check it out." Alexa swung her legs through the doorway and went to drop down into the hole, but the Master Sword put a firm restraining hand on her shoulder before she could. Her skin tingled pleasantly at his touch, much to her dislike. She gave him a small scowl. He was looking at her disapprovingly shaking his head.

"Let me or one of the unicorns go first," he merely stated.

"I'll go," Estella said from behind.

Alexa roughly shrugged Sword Bryan's hand off her shoulder and moved out of the way, not bothering to see his reaction as he too moved back to make room for the unicorn's leap.

Estella leaned back on her haunches and launched herself from a standstill through the doorway and down into the dark. They all rushed to the edge and quickly peered in. The unicorn was standing soundly on the ground maybe ten feet below, her body softly glowing, lighting the darkness. She looked up at them expectantly.

"I'll go now," Bryan stated without consulting Alexa.

He sat down in the grass, dangled his legs over the edge and pushed himself off. He bent his knees as he fell, preparing for the impact. He hit the rocky ground and stumbled a bit, his feet stinging from the impact. Estella moved aside to make room for him. He looked up at Alexa, who was now dangling her legs over the side. She pushed off, falling in one smooth motion to the floor. She landed with a light thud, crouched and one hand steadying herself on the ground. She stood up lithely and came to stand by Estella, not regarding Bryan at all as he eyed her a tad regretfully. The three moved aside to make room for Apollos.

Once he was down in, they took a look around. Alexa noted the area they were in was small and didn't have much to it. It was cold and damp and had shelves lining the walls. There was a door in the back and they moved to it. Alexa gave the door a firm jerk and it opened with a groan. The Master Sword stood with his sword drawn as they peered down the dark passageway. It was narrow and long and carved from the earth. The humans moved aside and let Estella take the lead into the corridor. Apollos took the rear.

They marched silently down the damp passage, the soft glow of the unicorns' bodies and horns providing the only light. It was a little claustrophobic; they walked in single file. The only sounds that could be heard were their light, muted footsteps and low, nervous breaths. They soon came to an opening. They were surrounded by stone shelves filled with dusty, rotting objects, along with scattered bones from some creature or two.

Without a second glance, they moved past the unsettling sight and into the passageway leading deeper down into the earth. They followed the twisted, narrow path for what felt like hours, but it wasn't. They started to sweat, conscious only then that it had gotten extremely hot. They stopped and glanced apprehensively at each other, realizing they must be getting close to the fountain of flame. Alexa swallowed over a lump in her throat, drawing her dagger as she followed behind the Master Sword.

After a few more bends they could see a flickering light ahead that wasn't emanating from the unicorns. Moving even farther, they heard a roaring, snapping and sizzling noise. Estella stopped abruptly, halting Bryan. Alexa bumped into his broad back; her body seemed to catch fire by the insignificant touch. He glanced over his shoulder at her, his blue eyes deep. She wanted to mutter an apology, but she stubbornly bit her lip.

"We're here," Estella barely whispered, craning her neck around to gaze at them piercingly. "I'm sure they're just around the next bend. I sense they're asleep."

Alexa's heart suddenly began thudding with such ferocity that it almost hurt. The blood it pumped came whipping into her brain so fast she began to feel light headed. She put a hand to her heart to calm it and leaned against the wall; the stone was almost too warm on her back. Bryan turned and regarded her pragmatically, his clear azure eyes wide with sincere concern for her. "You all right?" he whispered. His forehead was creased with worry, and sweat was gathering at his brow.

"I'm fine. You?" she choked as she struggled to gain
control of herself. She felt her own sweat start to trickle down her
hairline; the cavern was like the inside of an oven. They would be
baked alive if they stayed long.

"Yes, as much as I can be." He had the urge to reach out
and touch her face in reassurance. His hand rose up, but it fell to
the hilt of his sword instead.

Alexa eyed him for a second, gathering her bearings. She
thought vaguely that this could be the last time she looked into his
penetrating eyes, or saw his perfect square jaw clench in
apprehension. But why did it matter? He was not hers anyhow. She
felt herself come quickly back together at this distracting thought.
She straightened her stance. In a brisk movement she wiped her
hand across her face, attempting to clear the hot, slick sweat
gathering there. Her heart began to gradually slow its rapid pace
and her old confidence flooded into her.

Bryan waited patiently as she fought to gain her
confidence. It was slightly unnerving to see her so unsettled; it
wasn't her norm. He fought another urge to take her in his arms,
especially when he found it so surprisingly alluring to see that
when she had wiped her hand across her face she had left black,
muddy streaks from her dirt caked fingers. But he didn't have to
resist long, because a steely look came into her eyes and her stature
became rigid. She held her chin up haughtily, her sapphire eyes
holding a dangerous spark. *That's more like her.* He glanced
longingly at her soft, curving lips. Disregarding him, she placed
her palm firmly on his chest and shoved him out of her way; he
hadn't realized how close he had been. She pushed past him with a
dark look and walked to the bend in the passageway. He felt an
unexpected pang thrum in his chest; he ignored it. He followed her,
the unicorns at his heels.

They walked around the bend and found that the corridor
opened into a high domed cavern. On their left, the wall of the
corridor continued for several yards then stopped. But its height
was to the high vaulted ceiling and blocked them from the view of
the open cave. On their right, the rocky wall merged and became

the perimeter of the cavern.

The heat and light of the blazing flame of the fountain of fire filled the cavern with its intensity. It was brighter than daylight, leaving only scarce shadows flitting. They could see perfectly.

Alexa crouched down and slowly, very stealthily poked her head around the corner of the wall. The Master Sword was at her shoulder, the unicorns were standing abreast at his.

Chapter 34

At first Alexa was blinded by the shock of light hounding her pupils. Her impaired vision gave her a jolt of fear, but she quickly recovered and studied the cavern.

Her eyes thirstily drew in the scenery. In the center of the cave's stone floor was a wide, circular chasm with water-like flames spewing out of it. The fire was a brilliant conglomeration of colors: white, blue, yellow, orange, red and pink. It shot several hundred feet into the air, touching the domed ceiling of the chamber, scoring it black. It was smokeless.

Alexa noted with brave resolve three beasts on the far side of the fountain of flame. Two appeared to be asleep. One of the sleeping beasts was the largest of them. The smallest was pacing with its back toward her.

Fighting against the immense heat assaulting her face and sweating profusely, Alexa studied the animals, configuring her next move. So far they seemed unaware of their presence, thanks to the unicorns' masking aura. However, once the beasts spotted them, the sneaking around would be over. The unicorns could make themselves invisible, but they couldn't make the humans so.

Alexa could feel all too well Sword Bryan hovering over her shoulder, his breath hot on her neck, his sweat dripping on her. She forced herself to remain focused and appraise the dragons.

The one pacing was gangly. It reminded her of a yearling colt, not quite full-grown. It was roughly the size of two horses of normal proportions. The full-grown dragon, which she assumed was the mother of the two others, was larger, but not as large as she had imagined dragon to be. It reminded her of a beast she once saw a rich merchant riding, when he came to stay at their inn. The man had called it an elephant. It was an intriguing creature. She had liked it. But this dragon only compared in size and not looks what-so-ever.

The dragons' scales were metallic and iridescent, changing color when the light of the flame touched them. The tones changed from silvery green, to bronze, to a dark, dull blue and black. The reptiles had two ram-like horns curling out of their skulls. Their faces were lizard-like with small, swiveling ears, reminding Alexa of big mouse ears. Their necks were long and sinuous. Their front legs were slender, but muscular, ending in sharp four-fingered talons. Though their bat-like wings were folded, their span appeared immense. They had rotund girths and muscular haunches with even nastier looking talons on their hind feet. Their tails matched the length of their body and had sharp, boney spikes protruding all the way down to their tip.

The companions were abnormally quiet as they beheld the scene. Without a signal, they ducked back behind the wall to have a quick conference.

Alexa realized she was panting from the heat. Her mouth was parched, hot and sticky. She glanced at the unicorns; they seemed unaffected by the heat. They stood cool and collected as always. The Master Sword seemed to be having the same trouble breathing as she. He gulped and wiped away the pouring sweat from his brow and knelt down close to her, where she was crouched on the floor against the wall. His intense, azure eyes searched her face earnestly. Alexa quickly gathered her thoughts and whispered, "Hear any voices in your head?" she regarded the Sword.

Bryan stared perplexedly into her red face, studying her dark sapphire eyes, and then snickered in spite of the situation. "No," he replied.

Disappointed, Alexa huffed and agitatedly wiped away the sweat dripping in her eyes. "Humph. I was hoping you were a dragon whisperer, because I'm certainly not hearing any unfamiliar voices."

"No new ones aside from what you normally listen to, huh?" Bryan said with a wicked grin.

"This isn't time to joke," Alexa hissed. "You know what I mean."

Apollos cut in, "I'm not sure if that's how dragon whispering works anyhow."

"Okay, well, how are we doing this?" she retorted and pulled uncomfortably at her damp shirt.

Bryan's faced turned thoughtful as he sat back on his heels, realizing, upon seeing her annoyed eye, that he was once again invading her space.

They sat in contemplative silence.

Then Estella spoke, "There isn't any way other than to just go for it. Apollos and I will do our best to keep the dragons distracted while you run for the flame."

The two humans nodded apprehensively.

"I'm not leaving your side," Bryan said emphatically, gazing at Alexa with intense features.

Alexa was slightly surprised by his fervor; but she clenched her jaw and nodded resolutely, her eyes steel.

"All right then," Apollos said.

"Let's stop stalling and just do it." Bryan stood. Alexa followed suit.

For a moment the four of them stared anxiously at each other, the flickering light dancing around them in the chamber. The awareness that in just a few moments they could possibly die by being torn to pieces and eaten was powerful.

Apollos stretched his neck out and pressed his muzzle gently to Alexa's shoulder, his chocolate eyes encouraging and fretful all together. Alexa turned to the unicorn appreciatively. She took his equine head in her hands and gazed into his eyes feverishly. "Thank you," she said and was about to say more but the unicorn stopped her.

"None of that," he soothed, giving her another affectionate bump.

Alexa turned to Estella and nodded her appreciation. Apollos bobbed his head encouragingly toward the Master Sword, his eyes twinkling with fondness. Bryan nodded solemnly to him with a small, tense smile.

One more time Bryan glanced at Alexa to find her gazing at him intensely, a strange powerful look behind her deep, sapphire eyes. They held only warmth. His heart swelled; and he suddenly wanted to crush her to his chest and smother her with kisses full of regret and farewell. But he wouldn't resort to the fact that they might not see each other again. He returned her gaze with as much depth; and they silently fell into a resolve together. They were a team: she the warrior guide and he her warrior guardian.

Then, tearing their eyes from each other, they marched
defiantly around the corner into the chamber. Everything that
happened after went so quickly it was a surreal blur for the
humans.

The dragons didn't sense them, but the young one on guard
saw them straight away. At first he was stunned as still as a statue.
His lithe, gangly body poised tall, his head high, his eyes wild. He
looked like a young colt braced for flight, but he would not flee; he
would fight. He snorted a warning, arousing the others. Then he
hissed. His ears flattened and his eyes narrowed, glistening in
anger. His neck out stretched, he opened his mouth and sent out a
blast of hot air and flames. The friends scattered.

Bryan, his sword drawn, gripped Alexa's arm so hard it
would leave a bruise and pulled her toward the chasm. The
unicorns shot with amazing speed toward the dragons. All three
were now fully aware and prepared to fight. With arched bodies,
they advanced, hissing and spitting flames.

Alexa and Bryan ran as fast as they could, dodging the
spewing flames. Alexa fumbled with the vial, extracting it from her
pocket and readying it in her hands as they dashed to the fountain.
She vaguely wondered how she was even going to collect the
flame. She barely noticed the Master Sword's body harshly
bumping and pressing up against hers as they charged as one. He
ran with his torso turned from her, his back on her, his sword
drawn protectively.

Apollos and Estella were amazing. They dashed around
with such speed that it confused the dragons. The reptiles were
distracted all together by the strange, white blurs shooting black
bolts of pain at them.

Alexa and Bryan came to a skidding halt at the ledge of the
chasm, Bryan's grip tightened as Alexa's foot slipped over the
rocky precipice. Both were breathless from the thrill.

The flame lit their faces until their skin shone a brilliant
white. The heat was immense; save for the magic in the everlasting
flame, they would have ignited and turned to ash.

Alexa's eyes were alight as she gazed transfixed into the
fire. "Quickly!" Bryan urged as he watched the dragons hiss and

snap at the two lethal unicorns.

Alexa reached out, and Bryan held his grip on her with one hand while the other held his sword aloft. She leaned over the edge and opened the vial and without a second thought she stuck her hand straight into the colorful flames. They both watched in amazement as the flames swirled and rippled as if she had stuck her hand into a placid pond. The flames shone an even brighter shade of their ever changing colors and flowed swiftly into the vial as if they were smoke being sucked through a pipe. Alexa snapped the lid shut. And before she comprehended it, she felt the Master Sword tug her with such force away from the ledge it jerked her whole body into action.

"Apollos! We got it!" Bryan hollered at the top of his lungs as they ran. His interruption caught the dragons' attentions. They turned toward the humans with such fury it sent a jolt of fear straight through both of their visceras. The unicorns were on the creatures in a flash, blocking the vomited flames with powerful magic emitting from their horns.

"Run! Run!" Apollos yelled frantically. "We'll hold them!"

Looking on their friends with love and trepidation, the humans escaped to the corridor as quickly as their legs could carry them. One of the smaller dragons flew and landed with a loud thud behind them. It growled with a low accompanying hiss and spit another flame at the two frightened humans, but they were just out of its reach; it couldn't fit down the passageway. It gave a roar of fury.

The Master Sword and Alexa pushed themselves as hard as they could. Their hearts pumped with a passion that matched the dragons' wrath. Adrenalin raced through their limbs, sending them on farther and faster. They sprinted down the dark corridor blind, their breaths short and ragged. Their mouths were dry as if they were stuffed with wool; their lungs burned and their windpipes ached. Their minds were pregnant with worry for the two left behind.

Racing around another bend, the heat lessoned but their sweat didn't stop flowing. They were gripping hands now as they charged down the hall. Their eyes met on occasion, each brimming with small victory and immense fear.

They reached the door and crashed through it. The sunlight flooded the small storage chamber and the two welcomed its comfort. Releasing Alexa's hand, Bryan regarded her briefly. "I'll go first, then pull you up," he breathed fervently, his eyes wide and his face urgent. Alexa nodded mutely, gulping, attempting to moisten her throat.

Bryan clambered up the rubble without much difficulty. He scrambled onto the green, weedy ground, flinging his legs out and around so his torso was hanging over the edge. He stretched his arms out to Alexa's reaching fingers. She clambered over the dilapidated stairs only partially before she touched the blessed hands of her guardian. His strong grip closed around her hands, snaking down for a firmer grip around her wrists and heaved her up without much effort.

She scrambled onto the ground, momentarily sprawled awkwardly next to the Sword. They quickly got to their feet and upped their pace to a dead run, leaping over the rubble. Alexa tripped once, but Bryan caught her in reflex and they barely missed a stride.

They reached the horses breathless. The two animals were alert, having sensed the catastrophe underground somehow. They danced where they were tied and waited impatiently as their masters mounted them. The horses snorted enthusiastically and didn't have to be asked to charge into a full-fledged gallop from a dead stand. They sensed the urgency and thrived on it.

The two companions galloped abreast, speaking to their mounts encouragingly. Bryan knew they *must* get within the protection of the rest of the company awaiting them with weapons ready, or else they would have no chance of survival.

Then, with an anxious flutter of his heart, Bryan heard a great roar behind and above them. He glanced over his shoulder to see Apollos and Estella crashing, albeit rather quietly, through the forest to his left. The unicorns looked frantic and were glancing every so often up to the sky where the largest of the dragons was lazily circling lower and lower. They must have had exited from another entrance in the forest as Apollos had guessed.

Bryan urged Dragon for a faster pace. The warhorse dug in with pleasure and upped his speed, his nostrils catching wind of the predator chasing them. "Go! Go!" Bryan all but screamed at Alexa, motioning to the sky. She looked above and spotted the dragon; fear conquered her face. She glanced at Bryan with wide eyes and then leaned down over Zhan's withers and asked the horse for more speed. He responded with amazing swiftness. He dashed past Dragon as if the warhorse was standing still and sprinted down the treacherous forest lane with agility and purpose.

As Bryan fell behind, he watched Alexa's lean body move in perfect sync with Zhan. They were yards and yards ahead now. The dragon was closing in. It seemed to be taking its time, knowing it had the upper hand in flight. It circled lower and lower, heading for Alexa as if it somehow knew she carried its treasure.

The unicorns were now far ahead of the Master Sword and were leaping into the air as high as they could launch themselves and still hit the ground running. They sent black bolts of light out of their horns in the dragon's direction, each taking every other shot.

Soon, the unicorns were running abreast with Zhan. The great reptile in the sky was hundreds of feet in the air, screeching wrathfully when deadly bolts hit. Then, in an instant, the dragon shot down with the alarm and speed of an experienced predator. It charged right into the fleeing group.

Bryan let out a choked holler, "No!" But all he could do was watch in helpless horror as he galloped Dragon from way back. Ahead of him there was a tumbling mass of white and metallic. "Alexa!" he yelled with a piercing fear in his chest. He urged Dragon for more; the game stallion, his black body foaming white with sweat, laid his ears flat and pressed faster.

The tumbling mass grappled. White blurs zipped around, and the silver body flipped violently, giving off a vicious hiss. Then, suddenly, the dragon rose out of the heap, dragging with it a white lump in its talons. It roared in triumph as it rose into the sky.

Terrified, Bryan's eyes took a second to focus. For a moment he thought the creature had one of the unicorns, but he then realized it wasn't. It was Zhan. "Alexa," he whispered hoarsely under his breath as his eyes followed the dragon.

The unicorns were already up and pursuing, shooting never ending bolts of death. The Master Sword never felt a crushing so intense in his chest before now. He couldn't breathe. His eyes tore from the figure in the sky to latch on to a crumpled figure looming ahead of him on the ground. His heart jolted.

Alexa stirred on the ground ahead of him. She was dazed and struggling to stand, falling to her knees. But she was alive! The dragon hadn't carried her off with Zhan. The greatest relief flooded over Bryan like a tidal wave.

His mind and body only had seconds to react as her stunned figure came upon him. The Master Sword let go of the reins allowing Dragon to take control; the stallion galloped on obediently. Bryan calculated the distance and speed in his head at which they were moving. He leaned down over the left side of the saddle and reached out. The girl was on her knees, her head lolling slightly. As the stallion sped by, Bryan's desperate hands groped for her. He felt the touch of her and gripped onto whatever it was he had.

His left hand clasped tightly around her thick braid at the base of her neck and he yanked her up as hard as he could. She came up much easier than he had subconsciously thought. His right hand gripped her shoulder snuggly. With this grasp, he pulled her swiftly onto his saddle where she lay across her belly in front of him. She was scarcely aware and she struggled mildly against his hold. He gazed down at her with soft, intense eyes.

Bryan could now see the others ahead. They had gathered, and the centaurs were sending scores of arrows from their crossbows into the sky toward the livid dragon.

Once he reached the group, he dismounted with speed and agility, dragging a bewildered Alexa with him. Warrior Hazerk was suddenly at his side gesturing for him to carry her to the closest tent so he could tend to her.

Bryan barely noted the flames emitting from the sky, or the vile hissing and growling from the dragon. He gazed down into Alexa's befuddled, dirty, sweaty, bloodied face with such affection he could barely hide it any longer. He carried her into a tent and gently laid her down. He didn't notice a sudden cry from one of his own warriors in the background, nor the surprised exclamations from the rest of the company, nor the sudden strange silence from the dragon herself.

Chapter 35

"You're lucky Lil' Sis'. It's nothing too serious, just going to have to put up with a sore shoulder and neck, a few minor scratches and bruising."

"And a very bad head ache," Alexa groaned. She was perched on the end of a cot in Hazerk's tent, her head resting in her hand. She had a terrible throbbing behind her temples.

"And it looks as if you might get a black eye marring that cute face of yours—though the good news is it'll cover up some of those freckles," Hazerk said lightheartedly. She gave him a weak look of exasperation. He then added more solicitously, touching her shoulder, "Just take it easy for the rest of the night. It was a pretty bad spill."

Alexa looked up into the red-head's kind amber eyes. She noticed for the first time that he had laugh wrinkles at the corners of his eyes. She gave him a weak smile, still trying to not move her ailing head. "Thanks, Hazerk." Her voice was hoarse.

He smiled. "Didn't have to do much." He shrugged and glanced at Bryan who stood among the others crowded in the tent. "But if the Master Sword hadn't yanked you up by your hair, I figure your neck wouldn't be so sore," he joked with a wide grin.

Alexa looked up to her Sword-Guard. He was gazing at her with his face set impassively, but his azure eyes were tense with worry. Despite all, Alexa decided to give him a break from her ire; she attempted to muster up a grin at him. He merely returned her gesture with a weak, crooked smile. Then he fidgeted restively and glanced away from her gaze. Hazily, she wondered at this, but before she could think on it too much Prince Alkin stepped to her side demanding her attention.

"I think you should get some rest. You've done a good job today." His comment wasn't only meant for Alexa, it was directed at the rest of them hanging around to clear out; he eyeballed each one of them pointedly.

Alexa shrugged and was immediately remorseful for this action. A sharp pain shot through her shoulder and up her neck. She winced. "I'm fine, really," she said when Hazerk rushed to her side. "You all can go. I feel like I'm on display or something," she groused.

"All right," Hazerk snickered. "I'm off. If you need anything let me know. Take care, Lil' Sis'." With that he stepped over and planted a friendly kiss on her hairline above her temple. Alexa smiled gratefully at him. He departed.

Jadelin, who had been among the crowd, gave Alexa a concerned smile and came to place a quick kiss on her cheek. "Get well," she smiled, but Alexa noticed the empress' eyes were cheerless. Alexa watched her go, waving off Kheane as he nodded his get well, following the empress out.

"Okay, see you, kiddo." Warkan patted Alexa awkwardly on her good shoulder.

"Yeah," she said dryly, looking amusedly after him.

The Prince and the Master Sword were the last in the tent. Alexa's head ached so terrible she wasn't comprehending much, but after a few odd seconds of the men standing restively by she looked up from where she had been resting her head in her hands and realized that Eelyne hadn't been among the inquisitive party. She glanced from the Prince to the Sword, not even caring of her previous, sillier concerns of the two men. "Where's Eelyne?" she asked with concern. The two men glanced at each other anxiously. Finally, she caught on that something was awry. "What's going on? Is something wrong? Is he all right? The dragon's dead or gone, right?" she asked uneasily.

"He's fine, Alexa. We actually have something to tell you," the Prince said with forced enthusiasm. He sat down next to her, the cot creaking noisily at his weight. The Master Sword held his stance over by the tent flap, staring unnervingly at her with a quiet demeanor. Though, his brows were gathered in a tense way and his eyes bored into her with a guarded concern, his handsome lips turned down ever-so-slightly.

Alexa, now completely unnerved, flashed her eyes back and forth between the two of them. "Tell me what's going on," she demanded.

"Well, it's really good actually," the Prince forced another smile. She glared at him incredulously, but he pressed on. "After you passed out, the Master Sword brought you in here while the rest of us tried to bring down the dragon. It looked optimistic, but Eelyne suddenly started yelling at all of us to stop shooting at her. I guess he somehow connected with her, like a dragon whisperer would."

"Really?" Alexa was surprised and impressed and rather pleased. "That's good then. What're you all worried about? Did she stop attacking? Is she communicating back with Eelyne?"

"Yes, actually." The Prince finally looked sincerely happy. His eyes not clouded by that strange unnerving anxiety. "She stopped almost immediately. Eelyne explains it only as if he just plain understands her language and her his. He doesn't *hear* her speak human words, but when she hears him speak she understands him. He's explained everything to her and surprisingly and fortunately she's willing to comply with us."

"That's great!" Alexa's enthusiasm caused her to wince again; which caused her to note a pain throbbing near her eye. She lifted her hand to gently probe the tender area around her left eye. It was very tender and there was a cut.

"So, the dragon is assigning one of her two sons to be bound faithfully to Eelyne. He'll be Eelyne's counterpart for life. She can't leave herself because she's bound to guard the fountain of flame and pass on that duty to at least one of her sons. The other of her offspring will come to Eelyne's aid when needed. The dragonling will not travel with us. With Eelyne's whisperer connection with him, it will be able to hear his call." Alkin ended with a broad grin.

"This is good news." Alexa smiled, gently massaging her shoulder as she looked into the Prince's avid hazel eyes. He smiled and studied her features fondly for a second. He sat close. Suddenly, feeling the unsolicited attention as a threat, Alexa glanced discreetly away just as he reached up and pushed a lock of her tangled hair out of her eyes.

Alexa glanced up a bit victoriously into the Master Sword's now completely impassive face. She couldn't help but rub the Prince's sentiments toward her into the Sword's face, even if they were completely unwanted. *He'll be sorry for disregarding me.* She felt revengeful with all the hurt he had caused coming to mind.

She watched with a haughty glint in her eyes as Bryan's face turned from impassive to rigid and then into a scowl. She glanced away from him feeling triumphant and regarded the Prince once more with a coy smile. "I think I'll just rest here a bit. I think if I stand my head might roll off." She grimaced.

Alkin nodded with a small smile. He gave her a gentle hug, careful of her shoulder and pressed his warm, soft lips to her forehead. "Rest well." He stood and went to leave gesturing for the ill-tempered Master Sword to follow.

Alexa attempted to lay herself down into a more comfortable position on the cot and then suddenly remembered Zhan. How could she possibly forget to ask about him? She must have hit her head hard. "Hey," she said. The two men halted their exit and looked back at her expectantly. "You caught Zhan, right? Make sure he's comfortable and gets fed too, will you, please?" She laid her head back, assured that she needn't worry about the care of her horse.

The two men glanced nervously at each other and didn't speak. And this time Alexa truly understood all the odd, anxious looks in everyone's eyes. She jerked up, ignoring her swimming vision. Fear shot through her viscera. Her eyes bored into their troubled faces frantically. "You got Zhan, right? He's not lost in the forest is he?" She stood abruptly, ignoring her pain. She rushed to the door, but the men blocked her. She tried to push past almost in a panic. "What's going on? Where's Zhan?" she demanded.

"Alexa, sit down for a second." Alkin held her firmly by the shoulders, restraining her from leaving the tent, forgetting to be careful of her shoulder.

"What do you mean?" she growled, her blue eyes suddenly firing up into spitting flames. Alkin pushed her backwards toward the cot, Bryan followed with rueful eyes. Alexa glanced frantically between them. "Tell me what's going on," she commanded. She struggled against Alkin's hold and broke free only to be stopped abruptly by the Master Sword's iron grip on her good shoulder.

"We were going to wait to tell you…so you could get some rest," Alkin started hesitantly.

Alexa clenched her jaw. She felt her stomach give a violent

lurch filled with bile. Her throat began to constrict. "Tell me what?" she hissed through her teeth.

Both men looked at her with sad eyes, "Zhan…he didn't survive the dragon's attack. I'm sorry, Alexa," Alkin said sympathetically, his shoulders slumping, his hazel eyes fallen.

"What? No!" she cried pathetically. She felt an abrupt, sharp stab behind her eyes and unstoppable tears pooled and began spilling down her face. "No, that can't be. We just had a tumble! You can't mean…Oh, Zhan, no!" she wept.

She couldn't breathe. How could she breathe? Her throat had closed up completely. Her lungs burned for air. Her head swam. She felt as if she were going to vomit and faint. She couldn't see clearly, but she didn't care to see to the men's sympathetic faces. She pushed past them and raced through the tent flap before they could stop her again, but they didn't try.

Alexa sprinted out into the light and glanced around frantically, searching, searching adamantly for her friend. Where was he? He must be standing over by the other horses snacking on some juicy blades of grass. She raced to the tethered horses. He wasn't among them; she choked out another panicked cry. She raced to the other side of the camp, unaware of the company's sorrowful gazes on her. "Zhan! Zhan!" she screamed in panic.

Then she saw him. He was lying on the ground near where the company had gathered earlier to hold off the dragon. Her breath caught in the lump in her throat and she choked on a sob. He looked as if he were sun bathing. His body was spread lazily out for a nap in the warm, evening sun was all. She raced to him and fell to her knees at his neck where her eyes took in the dreaded realization.

Her hand flew to her mouth. Her eyes glistened with tears as they roved over his still body. His head was out stretched. His limbs lay limply down on the ground. His long, white, glossy tail sprawled out on the emerald grass. His mane was still slick with cold sweat as it stuck to his neck. Alexa gently laid her palm on her horse's shoulder. It was still warm, but cooling. It had only been a little while since the whole ordeal. She leaned down close to him and laid her head on his sweaty neck, diverting her gaze from his wide, lifeless, chocolate-colored eyes. "Oh my dear, dear Zhan. Where have you gone without me?" she whispered. Tears welled again and rolled down her cheeks to land warm and wet on his cool body. She held him for a long moment, not caring what the others thought of her. Her heart physically ached. She had never realized there could be so much agony imprisoned in a person before. She was broken and she couldn't find the lost piece. *It's all my fault...if only I'd listened and stayed back, you'd be here still. I'm so, so sorry. I'm sorry....*

After several long minutes, Alexa felt warm hands take her and pull her to her feet. She allowed this to happen only because Zhan's body was cooling faster by the minute and it didn't feel right. No, it didn't feel right at all.

She comprehended that the hands belonged to Prince Alkin. He guided her away from Zhan to her tent. The Prince was attempting to hold her and comfort her. But she didn't want to be comforted. She wanted to be left alone in her pain. In her sorrow she tried to pull away, but Prince Alkin wouldn't allow it. It was aggravating, but she didn't have the mentality to fight him. Dazed, she let him guide her to her own cot. Where he sat down and helped her curl up by his side, guiding her aching head to rest on his shoulder. Her fingers clenched around his arm in a harsh embrace. He soothed her, brushing back her damp hair. And that was where she cried until she had no tears left to release her surmounting pain.

Chapter 36

That night everyone felt Alexa's pain in some form or another. Most all had a connection with their mount they couldn't explain. None could imagine what it would be like to be abruptly and irrevocably parted forever. It would be like losing a close loved one.

As Prince Alkin held and comforted Alexa in her tent and as the sun slowly slid behind the forestry horizon, Bryan kept company with the horses. He was restless, aggrieved and annoyed. He was aggrieved for Alexa's pain; but he was also for himself, in that he wished he had been the one to take her in his arms and offer comfort. For that same reason he was annoyed. He was angry with his prince and friend. He knew full well he couldn't interfere now, especially now that Alkin's intentions were so apparent. In seeing Alexa's deep sorrow, Bryan couldn't even bring himself to be bitter about her revengeful actions against him. He supposed he deserved them. *How pathetic is that?*

Pacing along the line of tethered warhorses, he stared at the toes of his boots as he marched. Every once in a while a horse would crane out its neck and nuzzle his sleeve in curiosity. The Sword would then pat the soft nose and continue on with his restive pacing. Coming to the end of the line where Dragon was tied, Bryan paused his march and greeted the stallion. The horse tossed his head and stuck his nose in his master's face and whickered a breath. Bryan breathed in the sweet, grassy scented breath and smiled for the first time since that morning.

Giving his burly black horse a firm, loving pat, Bryan looked out over the hills of forest before him to the setting sun. It glowed a soft orange as the very tip of it finally sunk completely. He sighed, annoyed again. He clenched his jaw and thought momentarily of what Alkin's reaction might be if he marched into the tent and pulled Alexa out of his arms and into his own. Bryan snorted in derision at the thought. He could never do that; his duty wouldn't allow it. Though, he was discovering he absolutely hated he had to hide that he loved her and that he couldn't have her. Having her for himself was consuming his thoughts more and more every passing moment.

He sighed, trying to clear his thoughts and continued his ill-tempered march. After another minute of brooding, he gave Dragon one last pat. He would go to his tent and sleep. At least there his mind could have reprieve from the vision of Alkin and Alexa together; as well as the imaginary vision of himself and Alexa making love.

With that, he stalked off to his tent moodily. It took all his will power and self-discipline as he passed Alexa's tent to not charge in there and command Alkin to get out. He could hear them together in there still. He grit his teeth and ducked into his tent. Adjusting his sword so he wouldn't lay on it, he plopped down on his cot and cleared his mind of all thought so he could fall asleep in peace. Eventually his mind drifted, and he fell into a sea of happy nothingness.

Bryan's body twitched in his sleep. Then he snapped awake. He sleepily opened his eyes. It was dark out. It was late in the night. After midnight he guessed. He moved stiffly, rubbing his face. He sat up and reached for his water pouch and took a long drink. His ears caught a soft sound as he drank. He put the pouch aside and wiped his lips, listening; his innate warrior senses piqued. There should be nothing he should be concerned about; some of the centaurs were on guard as well as the unicorns and even a young dragon. He listened only for a moment more before he realized what it was. Alexa was moving around on her cot. It sounded as if she were tossing violently. She either wasn't sleeping well or she was awake and very uncomfortable, he supposed. But what could he do? He couldn't go to her. Or could he?

He stood abruptly, almost subconsciously, and was out the flap of his tent before he had time to even think about his actions. He took the few quick strides over to the entrance to her tent. He could hear her toss agitatedly and hear the creak of the cot clearly now. He was about to enter when he froze. He couldn't bring himself to go in. If he went in he would be working against the duty he held as her Sword-Guard. Could he contend with that? Could he interfere with his prince and friend?

The Master Sword sighed and turned around very annoyed with his sense of duty. But instead of returning to his tent he settled

378

to pace restively in front of Alexa's. He took in a deep breath of the cool night air and craned his neck back and gazed into the inky sky dotted with thousands and thousands of twinkling white lights. He relaxed a little at the heavenly sight. He furrowed his brow as he vaguely pondered why the stars reminded him strongly of the starry twinkle in Apollos' chocolate-brown eyes. This thought didn't last long as he was interrupted by another violent shifting sound emitting from Alexa's tent. He glanced at the tent tensely, his eyes troubled with a thousand tangled thoughts.

"Master Sword, there isn't any need for you to be on guard duty."

Bryan turned at the soft voice coming from behind him. He saw Apollos standing a few feet away, his snowy, velvety coat glowing dimly in the dark. The unicorn was looking at him with a curious pragmatic gaze. "Yes, I know. I couldn't sleep," Bryan answered.

Apollos lowered his head, his prismatic horn glinting in the low light still left from the hot coals in the fire pit. The unicorn eyed him thoughtfully and said, "It sounds as if Alexa is having a hard time sleeping, too. I'm afraid her sorrow and aches keep her awake. I wish I could go comfort her."

The Master Sword's brow turned puzzled. The unicorn's words were off compared to what his voice implied. "Then go to her. She'd be grateful," Bryan replied.

The unicorn flipped his mane, shaking his head, a twinkle in his chocolate eyes. "I don't fit in the tent," he said amusedly.

"Oh." Bryan looked away from the unicorn's confusing, penetrating gaze and began pacing again.

Apollos walked over to stand directly in front of the Sword's path. Bryan halted, gazing into the unicorn's equine features, trying to discern what the beautiful creature was attempting to communicate. Apollos stared at him levelly. Bryan stared silently back. What was the silly unicorn trying to say? "You, Master Sword, could fit in the tent," Apollos stated pointedly, giving him another pragmatic look.

Bryan glanced tentatively from Apollos to the tent, now realizing exactly what the unicorn wanted of him. He was

379

speechless for a second. He opened his mouth as if to make an excuse. But who could argue with Apollos? Instead, Bryan's wide, anxious eyes darted over to Prince Alkin's tent in a silent question.

Apollos bobbed his head, his horn glittering like the stars and said, "The affection he shows for Alexa is shallow in comparison to yours. Don't worry about your friend. He'll realize it all in time. You do what you know you must."

With that revelation, Apollos left the suddenly elated Master Sword to himself. All thoughts of duty had dissipated at the unicorn's words. He didn't care what his duty called for. He could handle it and he would handle it as it came. He didn't even care that he knew he may feel different about his decision in the morning.

Then Bryan, forgetting all self-discipline and reservation, walked straight over to Alexa's tent and went in. He was through the flap before he could have a second thought. He stopped at the entrance. He could see her lying on her cot, her body huddled uncomfortably and dejectedly. He was rendered still. His heart began to thrum at a quicker pace. He could feel his body warm at his anticipated rebellion.

Alexa thrashed and jerked around to lie in another position, not even noticing his presence. Her magical senses were obviously distraught, too. Her movement snapped Bryan in to action and he was at her side in one swift movement. He reached out to her and felt her warm skin brush against his rough hands. She groaned, startled at the touch, flinching from the unfamiliar hands; but Bryan hushed her quickly and gently scooped her up and into his arms where she hazily gazed into his face. She slurred something inarticulate. But he hushed her again. Her puzzled features softened as she comprehended his intentions. She let out a long, relieved sigh and snuggled closer, causing his heart to race with nervousness. He grinned despite himself and lowered himself with her in his arms gently down on the cot where he stretched out on his back. There was no room for the both of them on the cot side by side. So he positioned her so that she was lying on her side, partially on him.

Alexa snuggled up against him and Bryan felt like he

couldn't get her close enough. Her body was warm against his and it felt right. Like she was a piece of his body he had been missing, and now it was once again fully intact with her here, this close. He felt happy. It was strange to even think he actually felt that emotion.

Alexa slipped in and out of consciousness, her face nuzzled in his shoulder, her arms surrounding him, her leg draped over him. Every once in a while Bryan felt her twitch awake with a strangled sob and his arms would tighten around her small frame. She would bury her face in his chest, wetting his shirt with her tears for a short time before she drifted back off to sleep. She was sleeping more restful now with him here. That thought comforted him. He doubted he would be able to sleep at all. He was so wide awake with exhilaration. He knew she wasn't completely conscious of the situation, perhaps she wouldn't even remember in the morning. But he didn't care. He just merely cuddled her when she cried and soothed her hair back. It was silky. In her restlessness, her raven hair had come free from her plait and it lied over them like a silky shawl. He ran his fingers pleasurably through it.

He was content, more than content, to just lay there and hold her. Though, he knew he must rise and leave for his own tent before the others rose for the day. He still felt uneasy about the rest of the company knowing their feelings for each other. He especially didn't want Alkin to know. That would come in time. Bryan sighed with the thought, but it wasn't an aggrieved sigh. He couldn't feel such a feeling right now. He wrapped his arms closer around Alexa, giving her a tender squeeze. She responded readily, snuggling her face into the crook of his neck, sending chills spilling through his body.

His wishful vision of him and her together in a more personal manner roared up again. He remembered how lovely she had looked the night he had almost kissed her. And how he had hopelessly thought he would have liked very much to help her remove that elegant gown from her beautiful frame when she had stated so ruefully that she wanted it off. He smiled at his own memory. Then there was the morning he had found her bathing in the warm spring. Her eyes and skin had glowed; inviting in all his senses....Her figure was willowy, elegant and strong....

He had better be careful; he couldn't let his mind wander into such thoughts. It had been a long time since Bryan had held a woman in his arms. And he had never held one in his arms before he had felt this strongly about. But, he chided himself, he couldn't compromise her virtue. She held such a close relationship with Apollos, he couldn't upset that; not right now. Bryan loved her all the more for her being allowed to touch the unicorn without retribution. At the thought, he ran his hand tenderly down the length of her back. The feel of her beneath his palm was exhilarating. She mumbled incoherently in her sleep.

A smile twitched across Bryan's mouth. Alexa shifted again in her sleep and Bryan turned and pressed his lips gently to her head. He wanted to breathe her in for forever. He wanted her closer. He pulled her closer in frustration. He kissed her face fervently once, twice, three times. His lips touching her temple, he stopped, realizing sheepishly he was getting carried away.

Alexa shifted; her face was near his. But before she settled, he caught her eyes. She was awake. She held his gaze for a moment; he froze. Then a long, pleased sigh escaped her lips. "Bryrunan," she whispered into his neck, her breath sweet and soft on his skin. She fell into sleep once more.

Her tender touch sent stronger emotions coursing through him. He used to hate people using his birth name; but on her lips it sounded nice. The way it passed her mouth it sounded like music; and he found he didn't mind her use of it.

Bryan loved her. She had dispelled all his bitterness and brought him back down to earth where he belonged. He decided then and there that he wanted her to be his wife. Somehow he knew she would want the same. When this mission was over, they would stay together. Bryan smiled at the heartening vision of him and her. Not only them together forever, but their bare, warm skin pressed against each other as they lay entwined in each other's arms....

Then, suddenly, a shock of horrid realization ran through his body, chilling him. Bryan's face froze in dismay and he went ridged. He couldn't be with Alexa. He wasn't allowed to be with her. Despite all his qualms of going against his duty as her Sword-Guard and going against his duty as the company's leader and going against his friendship and his prince, he still couldn't be with her. And this was something that was irreversible, practically sealed with his blood. It was completely and undeniably permanent. He couldn't go against it or else it would mean his life, either by severe punishment or possibly death. It was his oath as a Master Sword. He had made an irreversible oath to serve Shelkite all his life and with all his blood. The strict oath of a Master Sword was to serve Shelkite in every possible way; that included he could only marry a woman born of Shelkiten blood, so she could bear Shelkiten children.

Bryan lamented the day he became a Master Sword. The thought of him falling in love ever again, let alone falling for a foreigner, had never crossed his mind when he had taken the oath. He had been so determined to be just a simple warrior for the rest of his days.

Bryan wrapped his arms around Alexa's slender body and felt how wonderful her frame was under his fingers as he ran his hands restlessly from her shoulders down along her back. He did *not* want to give her up. He clenched his jaw at the injustice. He couldn't give her up, especially now when he had allowed himself to succumb to her. There was no going back for his heart, or hers. But he honestly didn't have a choice.

The Master Sword squeezed his eyes shut with the immense sorrow for the loss he knew he had to bear. He didn't want to face it, but there wasn't an option. He wanted this night to last forever, for there would never be another for him and her. His oath restricted him from ever having her. He didn't want to admit its power of him. Curse it! He couldn't think of her in another's arms; but he must not hold her either! He would be forced to return to his passive indifference for both of their well beings; and continue to merely be her Sword-Guard as he was intended to be. It would be best to suppress his feelings and pretend this never happened....

Bryan pressed a desperate kiss to Alexa's forehead and

then another, his eyes alight with indignation, torment and sorrow. What had he done? Why had he allowed himself to come in here and discover how wonderful it felt to hold her in his arms, to find that this would be the first and last time?

Chapter 37

Unsettling visions swirled before Alexa's shut eyes. They danced and whirled, causing her sleep to be restless and pointless. All night she drifted in and out of agitated sleep and heartrending consciousness. One minute she would fall into the abyss of sleep only to awaken suddenly with such a crushing force of loss in her chest that it threatened to suffocate her and drown her in its depth.

Her woe over Zhan's death was so powerful it haunted her dreams and consumed her waking moments of the night. He was now only a memory, forever in the past, never again to awaken so he could make new. She yearned for a sweet oblivion to escape the sorrow and the hole he had left.

But sometime during the night, oblivion did come. It came to her in the form of Bryan. Or so she thought it was him. She couldn't be sure. Her mind was mangled with distress and her dreams were vivid and strong, seeming real for one infinitesimal moment and ethereal the next. But Bryan had brought with him an oblivion that numbed her pain unlike anything else could. True, she still had awakened with the same suffocating force, but it lessoned as he stayed deeper into the night and soothed her splintered heart with his comforting kisses and embrace. *Kisses?* Alexa was puzzled even in her half-asleep state.

His presence was as fleeting as peaceful sleep. His arms locked around her had chased away the abyss of her pain. Though as the rays of dawn seeped through the flap in her tent, reality and sorrow threatened to intertwine its bitter soul around her again. The Master Sword's warmth and comfort were absent. If it had even been there at all…perhaps her mind created the illusion of his presence to ease her pain. She pondered this in slumber.

But deep down, locked away in a casket, she knew, even in her sleep, that his presence *had* been real. She had wanted him to stay. But why did he leave, taking with him his solace? Would he now return with the dawn? Was he finally succumbing to his feelings for her? Would he now love her as she knew he wanted to?

Alexa tossed on her cot, tangled in her disturbing dreams and thoughts of the Master Sword. The bright morning sun threatened to peel its way behind her closed eyelids, but her mind was not done dreaming. It was exhausted from the restless night. And it yearned for time to recede and wallow in the dark, although its paths of dreams were anything but dulcet oblivion.

Alexa dreamed of Zhan. He was galloping joyfully in his pasture back home. The warm desert sun shone on his satiny back. He leapt merrily over the sandy terrain and raced up the side of a rocky cliff. The Alexa in her dream watched in admiration at his grace. But it turned to horror as she watched him leap splendidly over the cliff, falling to the ground. He flew through the air, down, down, and landed softly on the ground before her. She reached out to touch him, and he transformed into the white stag.

She stood in the dense forest of Carthorn. The stag with his grand antlers towered above her as if she were only a foot tall. His black eyes gazed fiercely at her. Then he spoke. His voice was like thunder racking the air around her, blowing her hair back in its gust. "Alexandra! The breath of the world dawns from the soil of your blood!"

She jerked awake. She found herself alone, the late morning light glaring through her tent. She rubbed the sleep from her eyes. Her eyes felt puffy from her tears of the night as well as her wounds. She looked hazily around, trying to absorb everything. She stared perplexed at the ground as she swung her stiff legs out and placed her feet down. Was Zhan really dead? Had the Master Sword really come to comfort her? Why did her dreams turn to the stag's mysterious words to her?

In thought, she ran her fingers through her tangled raven mane and reached for her battered brush in her sack. Brushing her hair and braiding it for the day, she pondered the words of the stag. *The breath of the world dawns from the soil of your blood.* She repeated the statement over and over in her head. Sitting and staring baffled at the wall of her tent for a moment, Alexa realized the stag had given her a riddle.

Her brows raised in comprehension. It wasn't a hard one. Slightly excited and pushing aside her inner pain, she worked on its meaning. The breath of the world: what would the breath of the world be? It meant the wind, of course. He was helping her find the wind element. *Okay.* She bit her lip, and then chewed a nail. *Dawns...ah...the beginning of the day, the origin...it comes from!* She felt a twinge of glee. She stood and began pacing. Though, she had to stop briefly to collect her bearings; her body was sore and stiff. She slowly and gently stretched her muscles as she thought. *The wind element comes from the soil of my blood?* She contemplated this confusing outlook cynically.

"Soil...Soil...land of course," she muttered aloud to herself. She licked her lips and took a swig from her water pouch, wiping the excess on her lips away with her sleeve. "Blood, my blood. It's inside me? No, it's my ancestry. The wizards have the element? No, that's not right." She growled in aggravation. The answer was there; it was just barely eluding her. "My father, my home...soil, home. My homeland! The wind element is in Kaltraz. Not just Kaltraz, but Eastern Kaltraz, my home. Dawn, where the sun rises in the east; it has a double meaning. It's in the far east of Kaltraz. That's it!" Alexa bounced on her heels in triumph, and promptly regretted it.

It had been so simple. How hadn't she seen the answer before? Well, it was most likely because she'd almost been murdered a bit later. And then she'd been consumed with thoughts only for the Master Sword.... Bryan. How would he act toward her today after last night?

Trying desperately to forget her sorrow and think only of her new found bond with her Sword-Guard and her knowledge of the wind element, she decided she would tell the others of her discovery.

She readied herself. But quickly found that even with her determination to forget her pain it still raised its ugly head. The gaping hollowness in her chest sucked all the good thoughts right into it like a vortex, leaving her feeling sour and low. She sighed in averseness to its power as she stepped outside. She would have to press on nonetheless and let the hollow vortex do its evil as she did her job. It wasn't something she could ignore or rid herself of. She would just have to tolerate it while it lasted; much like the aches still emanating from her body.

In the glaring morning sun, Alexa studied the camp.

Everyone was mingling around, preparing to depart. Obviously, the Master Sword hadn't rushed them to leave at the crack of dawn this morning like he usually did. It was probably on her account. She was grateful. Plus, as far as they were concerned they were unsure what their next step was anyway. She would fix that right now.

"Alexa! You're up. How are you feeling?" Prince Alkin broke from the throng of centaurs and warriors and came to her side.

She smiled at him, remembering his own attempt at comforting her. He had held her and allowed her to cry on his shoulder for a few hours; but really she would have rather been left alone, or had Bryan there instead. However, she would never say such a thing to the kind prince. "I'm fine, thank you." She forced a smile past the crater in her chest and endeavored not to look over to where Zhan's body had lain motionless the night before.

"I'm glad." His hazel eyes searched her solicitously.

Alexa looked at him, her blue eyes soft with appreciation. "Thank you for…for understanding."

The Prince smiled. "Of course."

"I have some good news," she continued, trying to sound upbeat.

Alkin seemed stunned; his eye brows rose. "Really? What?"

"I know where to look for the wind element. If you want I'll explain it to the company as a whole," she said struggling to place herself into a business-like mood.

"That's great news," Alkin exclaimed, and touched her arm lightly. "Come on." He took her hand and led her to where the rest of the company was gathered around the fire pit.

"Everyone! Alexa knows where to find the wind element," Alkin called, abruptly stopping all conversation and grabbing everyone's rapt attention.

Alexa searched the many faces looking expectantly at her and found the one she sought. The Master Sword was on the opposite side of the pit among the centaurs. His view of her had been blocked and he moved so he could see her better. They met eyes. Alexa took this brief moment to let loose her senses on him. To get a clear reading, it was always best if she looked directly in the other's eyes. She had to know instantly what he was feeling. She couldn't guess and didn't want to be surprised if he suddenly treated her indifferently.

The Master Sword gazed at her passively, his guarded eyes unwillingly meeting hers. She felt like a dagger was thrust into her chest at his avoidance. She almost became utterly overwhelmed with the crushing, entangled emotions of betrayal and sadness of her undeniable loss of him as well as Zhan. She couldn't take much more. Her soul would crumble to dust soon.

She narrowed her enchanting eyes at him ever-so-slightly, her jaw set hard with inner rage and hurt. The Sword tried to pull away from her dire glare, but she wasn't giving up so easily. She forced her senses on him, magically persuading the reluctant Sword to meet her eyes and hold her deciphering gaze. She felt him resist, but he bent under her power, swimming in the depths of her eyes. Strangely enough, she could feel strong, powerful, *good* emotions emitting from him concerning her. However, they were tangled and bound tightly with anger and sadness. Then slowly, as she had him ensnared, all his emotions became obscured with the old, bitter, dark sludge. This perplexed her and she let his fighting gaze go, feeling lost at the confrontations going on inside of him.

Once she released him, he let his passive azure eyes linger on her a moment longer. But she could read no emotion from him now; he had shut down. Quickly Alexa tried to decipher this knowledge with common sense, pushing her bewildered pain aside. Maybe she *had* dreamt of him during the night; and his visit was merely an imaginary vision of her wishes. She looked away from his broad stature feeling small and child-like. She was like a heart sick young girl filled with dreams of falling in love with a knight in shining armor. How ironic and sad. She had become what she used to detest in other girls her age, always dreaming of ridiculous romances.

But how could she have imagined that? It was unlike the vivid dream she had had while sleeping in Shelkite's hills. It had to be real. He was feeling emotions for her; she sensed it. Why wasn't he letting go? Why did he endeavor so hard to close himself off from her? She sighed; she wasn't only upset, but confused.

She glanced at the Prince, who was still looking fondly at her, his hazel eyes alight. She gazed into his handsome, kind face and pondered. Perhaps the Master Sword knew Alkin held affections for her, too. So the Sword's hands, and his heart, were figuratively bound. Why should it matter in the long run though? Unless he was only playing with her....

She nodded a solemn greeting at Bryan and left it at that. She was tiring of this game that involved the senseless interpretation of his emotions. They needed to clear things between them. But that was pointless considering it was obvious he had no intention of pursuing her. In a strange, heartrending way she understood. They both had a duty, and that was where their relationship ended. That was their unspoken understanding. Alexa left her musings there. She had a job to do and couldn't dwell on it.

Alexa's musings had run through her mind all in the moment she'd greeted Bryan. The others waiting expectantly for her news hadn't even noticed. She forced herself to switch to a business persona, determined to keep it there, lest she become distracted from her mission. She quickly immersed herself in the explanation of the discovery of the wind element. They listened with rapt attention as she explained about the white stag. The company expressed their approval at her decipherment of the riddle. They agreed avidly that it sounded as if the wind element were in Eastern Kaltraz. It was decided on the spot they would travel there next without delay.

Alexa didn't have to persuade them to continue on with their original plan to stop by her family's inn on the way. She wanted to speak with her father about the mission. Alkin and Bryan wished to hear the wizard's thoughts on Ret, and also wanted his opinion of the elemental usage and maybe a better explanation of it, too.

It was settled. They would pack up and head out of Carthorn toward Alexa's home. How comforting that sounded. She was pleased to be going home, even if was only for a little while. Being home with her family might ease her stress of losing Zhan, among other things.

Chapter 38

They had been instructed to stay away from the dragon. Alexa had been warned right after she had explained the riddle. Apparently the young male dragon was not safe, or tame in any sense. Eelyne was the only human that could approach him without being mauled or eaten. The horses were obviously not allowed close either. Although, the warhorses seemed to know on a prey level that they didn't want to be near the dragon anyhow; they kept their watchful distance.

Alexa stood with her arms crossed, glaring vilely at the dragon from a distance. She wanted nothing more than to shoot one of her obsidian arrows straight into his soft, beating heart. She was contemplating doing just this, even unknowingly drawing out an arrow and getting so far as to set it, when the Master Sword came up behind her and firmly pushed down her bow. She frowned up into his face, for he had been decisively ignoring her again. Her hard eyes locked on his features. His face was stern as he shook his head, but his eyes held a spark of sympathy and understanding. She sighed and lowered her bow, stiffly nodding her understanding, her jaw clenched and eyes aflame. Then the Sword stalked away to finish packing without another word or glance back.

As the company was preparing to move out, a heart rendering lover's goodbye took shape between the newlyweds. Kheane kept his composure well, however Jadelin fell to pieces. She struggled courageously to contain her racking sobs. Kheane did his best to soothe her even in his own gloom. Although, the empress knew he had a vow to keep in helping the company and he would soon return to live with her, she couldn't bear the idea of being separated from him again.

Eavesdropping, Alexa heard Jadelin say fretfully, "What if you die?"

In which Kheane replied, "Then I'll die happy. Something I used to think wouldn't happen." Alexa felt on Jadelin's behalf that this answer was perhaps not a fair one; but she kept her grumpy opinion to herself.

The company awkwardly endured the quarrel as they

gathered their things and tacked the horses and ate a quick meal. They never saw Kheane speak so many words since he had been with them, or look so distraught. He was frightening to look at even in his most comforting countenance. His raspy voice was lowered in a soothing tone that came across almost menacing, belying his words. His broad body was tense and his dark eyes held bleak encouragement; his scarred face twisted in agitation. But the empress seemed impervious to Kheane's unavoidable, frightful countenance, something that for sure had struck fear into many of Kheane's victims. She seemed to see through all his imperfections to his true intent.

Finally, their parting good bye ended. Jadelin held herself tall and dignified, although her eyes were still red around the rims. With the conclusion of their good bye Prince Alkin approached Jadelin to say his farewell and thank you. She expressed her pleasure at being able to help the company and was only sorry she couldn't help more. Her place was back in her small kingdom. Though, she did propose with great enthusiasm that two of her centaur guards accompany them on the mission. Alkin was pleased she and the centaurs were so willing to help. However, he was a bit hesitant in adding more to their company. It would make it more difficult for them to travel covertly. Still, the extra help would be welcomed. His indecision called for him to summon Alexa and Sword Bryan for their advice.

Alexa had been sitting morosely at the trunk of a great tree throwing her dagger at the earth repeatedly; reluctantly she stood and joined the Prince. The Master Sword stalked over from having been quietly taking his time tacking up Dragon. Apollos followed close behind in the Sword's steps.

In the end, between the four of them, they decided it would be beneficial for at least one centaur to join their company. Night Strider would travel with them. This pleased the empress and the centaurs. Though, they were still regretful they couldn't spare more help. They promised they would arrange to send what little help they could on ahead to the battlements in Galeon. Most of them would stay behind to protect the hidden kingdom. Many of the mystical creatures there were the last of their kind and unable to protect themselves.

Estella had been torn in whether or not she would join the company. The unicorn could of course, like Apollos, make herself unseen. She would not be a hindrance to the company's stealth, but, in fact, would add to it. However, she was bound greatly to Jadelin, as Apollos was to Alkin. The unicorn yearned be with Apollos, too, her own kind. After some debate, Jadelin finally insisted fervently that Estella go with the company. She released the unicorn from any vows to her. Estella was deeply grateful.

With the decisions made and without a single glance at Alexa during the whole conversation, Bryan went back to his grooming and tacking of Dragon. Alexa turned to return to her spot under the tree to await their departure; but before she did Prince Alkin clasped her hand and gave it an encouraging squeeze. She glanced impassively down at their joined hands, slowly raising her eyes to meet his sparkling hazel ones. She returned his squeeze, smiling cheerlessly, and left him to watch her walk away.

While the warriors packed to leave, Alexa merely sat at the base of the tree in a trance watching the camp turn back into a vacant valley. She allowed her eyes to wander every once in a while to the mound of dirt piled high over on the other side of the meadow beneath the low hanging boughs of a maple tree. Her eyes misted over with tears and she looked away, not being able to bear the thought of leaving Zhan behind forever. She was resistant in having to comprehend that his body now lay cold and still beneath the ground, where it would eventually become earth itself. Alexa had been grateful when she had discovered the company—either the Prince or Master Sword more likely—had had Zhan's body buried, so she would not have to bear the sight of it again. Surprisingly enough, they had done it with the dragon's help. Eelyne had instructed the dragon to dig a hole and to move Zhan in it without any problems. The dragon was willing under only Eelyne's command.

It was only a few moments before they were ready to leave that everyone realized Alexa didn't have a mount. Alexa had noted this problem, obviously, from very early on. But she hadn't bothered, or cared to discuss it. By this time the empress and centaurs had left to return to the kingdom and the camp had been completely packed up and most of the company was mounted.

Alexa rose from her position under the tree and came to stand amongst them. All mounted and circled her, looking contemplative. Alexa off-handedly suggested she just walk. She didn't mind walking. But the Master Sword was quick to shoot down that idea. She would slow them down and be more vulnerable to danger. Then someone suggested the pack mule. But the poor animal was already burdened with all their supplies. There wasn't any way he could carry Alexa, too. And no human was daring enough to ask Night Strider to carry her. The centaur was carrying his own supplies. And the company could tell by his defiant countenance he was very averse to carrying a human, half-blood or not.

Night Strider announced regretfully that there were no horses back in the hidden kingdom either. The mystical creatures didn't have any need of them. Then Prince Alkin suggested Alexa ride double with one of them. He proposed she could either ride with the Master Sword, since he was her guardian; Dragon could bear them both without a problem. Or she was welcome to ride with him.

Alexa baulked at his idea. She didn't want to ride with either of them for more than one reason. First off, riding double was entirely uncomfortable, especially for the distance they had to travel. Secondly, and most of all, she didn't want to have to be in the constant close proximity to either of them, for different reasons for each.

She glanced impulsively at the Master Sword on the Prince's suggestion for her to ride with him. Bryan finally looked at her. His features, as always, were set austerely. But oddly, after avoiding her eyes all morning, he allowed her to hold his gaze. He stared at her a bit unnervingly, his azure eyes full with an unspoken opinion on the matter. She couldn't tell by the clenching of his jaw and his hard set, boring eyes whether he wanted her to come join him on Dragon, or that he would rather her not come near him period. She looked away coolly, not even bothering to use her senses on him to understand. She then spoke up and opposed the idea vehemently.

After another minute of contemplating, Apollos came forward. To everyone's great surprise, he offered generously to carry Alexa. No one had even dreamed of asking him or Estella to carry her. It was unheard of to ride a unicorn. They were fiercely independent and divine-like creatures. They were beyond such things. It surprised no one more than Alexa herself. She felt she should not ride the unicorn; she wasn't worthy of such an honor. But Apollos assured her it didn't bother him to carry her. He would carry her willingly and happily.

Hesitantly, she finally yielded to his insistence that she was welcome to ride him. However, it was under the condition that she didn't use her tack. She agreed readily to this. Although, Apollos did consent to her placing a blanket underneath her seat in order to help ease the discomfort of riding bareback. She would leave her tack behind, set up like an adornment with flowers by Zhan's grave. It would be too much trouble to take along with her.

With all their mundane problems settled, the company continued steadfastly on with their journey.

Those tense events were days behind them now. The company was far from the meadow and was traveling northeast toward Kaltraz. It would take several days to get out of the territory of Carthorn. As far as they had traveled at this point, they were now only passing the heart of the forest. Ever since they had entered the boundaries of Carthorn it felt as if they had been there years; so much had transpired in their travels and in their hearts while there. Everyone was anxious to leave.

Riding Apollos was the strangest thing for Alexa, strange but heavenly and wonderful all together. It was like they were gliding over the forest floor. Alexa could barely feel his smooth gait as he placed his hooves down; they never made a sound. He never stumbled. He never knocked her head on a branch. He slinked smoothly around tight places, much like a cat. His bare back was also peculiarly comfortable compared to a horse's. Her backside wasn't even numb. He was a very comfortable ride. Beneath her thighs she could feel his sleek barrel move and sway; it was much like what she thought riding air would be like.

Her senses were heightened to him. She felt every smooth, tone muscle of his ripple under her. She sat astride him tall and confident, her legs gently wrapped around his barrel as he took her fluidly over the ground. She could feel his power, too. The consistent touch of his body beneath her seemed to absorb the magical vibes emitting from him. She could feel the intense, potent magic he contained, as well as his physical power. It energized her. She could easily tell that at any given moment he could spring into a gallop that would leave any living horse far behind, and it would be nothing to him.

The strangest thing of all, though, was that while she rode him she always felt calm and relaxed. She constantly ran her hands down his satiny neck and through the silky, iridescent threads of his mane. She couldn't help herself. He had a draw to him that no one could resist. It was like he was a piece of heaven here on earth. It was normal for anyone who had ever laid eyes on a unicorn to have an inexplicable desire to be as close as they were allowed to the creature, always wanting to touch and feel a piece of paradise. However, few were ever permitted; but Alexa was, and she reveled in it. She didn't understand the draw of unicorns no more than she understood the draw of merpeople on humans, nor any more than she understood magic itself or the High Power. No one did.

The more she touched him, patted him, the calmer she felt. It was magic. She knew this because she had tried to think of her task and worry about the coming days, and even tried to think of her lost love on the Master Sword, but she could never dwell on anything negative for long. It just didn't last with him beneath her. The despairing thoughts were always evanescent and quickly replaced with a sense of peace. The hollow vortex in her chest felt muted; it was still there, but its power was infinitesimal. Did he do this for her sake? Or was this something everyone felt when they touched a unicorn? It didn't matter really.

At twilight, they stopped for the day and made camp. Alexa dismounted Apollos and he went his own way while she went hers. She instantly felt all her cares settle back down on her where they thought they belonged. Maybe she could snuggle up next to Apollos during the night. Would he mind so much? She doubted he would deny her that.

As she helped collect dry wood for the fire she thought about the last days and how Bryan had acted toward her. At first, he had completely ignored her. They all rode, made camp, slept, rose and rode again. That was how it went. He had paid her no mind beyond his Sword-Guard duties. Then, slowly, he began acting as if nothing had ever transpired between them. He spoke to her like he'd always had and treated her much the same. This infuriated her. But what could she do? She hated this foolish game he was playing with her. She was tiring of it. She didn't understand it. As much as she had tried to explain his actions away because of his hard core sense of duty, she found she just did not care anymore about giving him excuses. Wasn't there ever a time when one took their duty too far? Her heartsickness was allowing her temper to get the better of her, obliterating her earlier resolves of tolerance and understanding toward him to ashes.

She remembered vividly that he had once very much wanted to kiss her. She *knew* he had come to her during the night she mourned Zhan, bringing solace to her because he cared. She knew he had feelings for her, because he had allowed her to see it in his eyes and actions every so often when he was unguarded. There was no way he could talk himself out of the real reason why he had held her in his arms that night and had placed soft, consoling kisses on her brow. Unless, she was somehow greatly mistaken on the normal relationship of a Sword-Guard and his charge, this kind of behavior was not the norm. Because she was very certain the Head-Master Sword Bryan didn't ever relate to Prince Alkin in this manner when he had been *his* Sword-Guard. She smirked inwardly at the assurance this thought brought her. He couldn't fool her, and she wouldn't allow him to fool himself any longer. She would put an end to this madness, starting right now if she must. Despite her love for him she was beginning to loath him for all he had done, or hadn't done.

By the time she had made this staunch revelation to herself, she had collected the fire wood and had helped make a snapping fire. She plopped down next to the flame and gazed into it, deep in thought. She felt a large, warm body come to the ground next to her. She glanced over to see Apollos lying with his legs tucked beneath him and Estella alongside him. He was watching her closely, his chocolate eyes discerning. She gave him a half smile and leaned up against his warm, sleek side. He bobbed his head and said nothing. Here she stayed and let his calming effect spill over her, right down to her toes.

Night Strider had gone out to catch fresh dinner. The rest of the company, after feeding their mounts for the night, joined Alexa and the unicorns around the fire. A few of the men groaned as they lowered themselves to the ground. Everyone was stiff and tired from the long day of riding. At least they had had no trouble with the uncanny forest lately. This was the advantage of having the added company of an extra unicorn and a formidable centaur; not to mention a dragon on call.

Bryan finished brushing Dragon and came to squat by the fire. He looked at Eelyne and Alexa, who refused to regard him even though she knew he was gazing at her. "All right, I think I've given you both a long enough break. We need to get back to practicing your swordsmanship," he stated.

Eelyne shifted and grimaced at the thought of not relaxing, but he stood obediently and stretched, preparing for the bout. Alexa didn't move. She continued to lean against Apollos and stare passively into the fire. At her inaction, Bryan merely gave her an amused look. He then stood and went to a designated spot for the bout with Eelyne.

"Okay. Where'd we leave off?" he thought out loud, still regarding both Eelyne and Alexa. "Right. We left off at three on one. But I think I'd rather work on team practices tonight," he said. He called over to Alexa, "Come on, Sand Queen, let's get moving. We don't have all night to wait on you," he said evenly, but his eyes and features were firm in his command as if he were expecting some kind of defiance.

"I'm not going to sword fight tonight, thank you," she stated offhandedly. She leaned forward to gaze into the fire, pointedly not looking him in the eye.

Bryan stared at her exasperatedly. Her curt comment had caught the attentions of the rest of the company. They stopped their conversations to listen. "There's no doubt that you're getting better in your fighting, but I still think you need to practice. You've a lot to learn. Now, come on," the Master Sword said more sternly. The company was watching them anxiously, noting the scowl across Alexa's face.

"I don't have to. I don't feel like I need to. If I'll be using the counter magic I don't think perfecting my swordsmanship is necessary," she stated arrogantly, her sapphire eyes firing up.

"What do you mean you don't have to? I told you to; so get over here," Bryan growled.

"No, Master Sword," Alexa said brusquely. She glared at him defiantly from where she could see his braced, broad stature across the fire pit.

He took a tense step toward her. His jaw was clenched angrily at her disobedience. His hand grasped the hilt of his drawn sword so tightly his knuckles showed white. His azure eyes narrowed dangerously. "You'll do what I say," he said forebodingly through his teeth.

She had never before heard him use this tone. Alexa felt a flutter of anxiety in her chest, but she held fast to her defiance. The whole company seemed to stop breathing as they watched the confrontation with wide eyes. "Are you going to make me, Sword Bryan?" Alexa said condescendingly. Looking up to hold his dire glare with her own. "I thought it had just been an off-hand idea to train me. Warrior Eelyne is the one who originally asked for your help. Being my Sword-Guard you're not required to train me, only to protect me."

Bryan stalked over to the edge of the fire to stare down over it. Alexa mustered as much courage as she had and stared resolutely back into his formidable face. He looked intimidating and dangerous. Despite her actions she couldn't help but at that moment feel so very attracted to him in this state. He looked as if he wanted to wallop her head off with his sword; though inexplicably and foolishly she felt ever-so more drawn to him for it. But she couldn't let her guard down. She had to not only push aside her feelings for him, but she had to find a way to make them completely disappear. It was impossible.

"I gave you that sword so you could learn to protect yourself with it," he said lividly. "Now—"

"Sword Bryan," Alkin suddenly cut in, "If Alexa doesn't feel like fighting tonight, I think it's all right if she passes this time."

Bryan snorted a response. His features looked rebuffed and furious. He was not used to someone blatantly refusing his commands. He clenched his jaw, shot Alexa one last glare that would have knocked her unconscious if it had been something physical, and turned stomping back over to where Eelyne was standing frozen by his shock. "Come on. Fight me," Bryan commanded.

"Ah, okay," Eelyne stuttered, his eyes wide. He probably feared for his life as he took in the menacing stance of the Master Sword and how he held his sword aloft with a death grip on its hilt and a vile spark in his darkened eyes.

Eelyne fidgeted anxiously for a second; then with the Master Sword's apparent impatience he decided he had better obey immediately. So, he threw himself bravely into a match he had no chance of winning.

They fought viciously. Well, the Master Sword fought viciously, apparently taking his frustration out on poor Eelyne. The young warrior had no chance up against the Head-Master Sword. He definitely was learning to defend himself tonight, quickly and efficiently; for the Sword wasn't playing around. Bryan's blows were hard, quick and precise. His foot work perfect.

Alexa watched the heated match feeling satisfied. He would have no power over her. He knew how he was playing with her, and she wasn't going to allow him to get away with what he had done to her heart without any punishment. This was his punishment. She wasn't going to be compliant to his whims any longer. He had to have known what she was doing, or else he would not have gotten as angry as he had. Or would he have? Alexa sighed. She didn't understand him at all.

She realized she had leaned away from Apollos' side. This must have been why she was able to think and act in the insolent manner she had intended. She glanced over her shoulder and found the profile of Apollos' equine head inches from her. His big, round, chocolate-colored eye was staring right at her, very much reproachfully. As he eyeballed her, she suddenly felt ashamed for what she had done. The unicorn huffed out a soft, sweet smelling breath and shook his head, his penetrating eye still on her. She glanced shamefully away toward the brooding Master Sword. He was pounding Eelyne in the fight. Alexa could tell the young warrior was tiring. His defenses were weakening. He was sweating notably and was grimacing whenever Bryan landed a blow. She should go over and give him reprieve.

By that time, the rabbits Night Strider had caught were skinned and roasting over the open flames. The scent of them filled their small camp. The rest of the company had now long forgotten the argument and were partaking in other conversations.

Overhead, clouds rolled in and the thick smell of rain was on a warm, mounting breeze. Off in the distance they could hear thunder. The company groaned simultaneously. There wasn't room in this small clearing to set up their tents to escape the storm. They would have to huddle under the boughs of the trees and hope they wouldn't get too wet.

The forest was thick in this area and the trees were broad and tall, with beautiful vines hanging from the branches. This would provide some cover for them and they were grateful. The ground was mossy and spongy, which would be good to bed on if they could find a space unbroken by the plethora of roots breaking the surface.

By the time they had finished eating and had readied their bed rolls and climbed in for the night, the rain had come. The thunder was soft and the lightning was dim. It wouldn't be a harsh storm. The rain was merely drizzling. The pattering drops on the forest floor and the quiet rumbling of the distant thunder acted like a lullaby and lulled the exhausted company into a deep contented sleep, except for Alexa.

She laid awake, feeling troubled. Apollos was on guard duty. He was up and moving silently and vigilantly around the camp. So she couldn't snuggle up against his warm, sleek body and find comfort there. She didn't dare ask Estella.

She layed on her side, staring at her Sword-Guard's back, feeling every so often the pleasant plop of a warm rain drop on her exposed face. Of course, despite his anger with her, he had stubbornly unrolled his bed roll near hers; so he would be protectively close by.

Alexa allowed herself to sigh heavily. She felt sorry for her treatment of her Sword-Guard now. How could one love someone so much one second and then hate them so vehemently the next and then find that their hate was suddenly replaced with love again? She took a deep breath, inhaling the heavy moist air, pleased by the wet soil smell filling her lungs. She felt restless. She needed to think. She needed to walk. She had to get away so she could sort through her feelings.

She sat up and quietly extricated herself from her bed roll. She peered around, stood and crept to the edge of the camp, heading for the dark woods. She wouldn't go far. She would go just far enough to where she could feel some solitude and sit and think, gather her senses and recollect her magical senses. She felt that they had somehow been scattered by her emotions.

She glanced over her shoulder to find Apollos perked up, watching her fixedly from across the camp. His head was high, his tail arched and his horn glittered in the low light. She stopped and mouthed silently, "I won't go far. Need to think. Keep your senses on me."

The unicorn was still as a statue for a second as he considered. Then he lowered his head in acceptance, but his eyes held a sharp warning for her to be careful. She nodded her understanding and crept into the forest where it wrapped itself like a dark shroud around her.

Apollos watched her disappear. But he wasn't the only one watching her disappear into the forest. Bryan had been awake. He hadn't been able to sleep. He had only been pretending to because he knew Alexa was awake still. He glared at her back as he watched her retreat alone into the woods. After he could no longer see her dark silhouette, the Master Sword quickly untangled himself from his bed roll and stood. He would follow her silently and keep an eye on her and then maybe tell her off, too. She was such a fool-headed girl. Why would she do such a thing? Being her Sword-Guard was becoming more of a difficult task than he had ever imagined; considering how he had come to feel for her as well as her reckless behavior. He threw a glance over his shoulder as he crept into the woods. He found Apollos gazing impassively at him. He paused; and shook his head disapprovingly at the lenient unicorn for letting her go. The unicorn gazed at him with wide, innocent eyes. Bryan softened; and Apollos bobbed his head, thrusting his muzzle outward in a gesture to tell him to get going. Bryan turned to the woods and let the dark swallow him.

Chapter 39

Alexa took Apollos' warning seriously and allowed her senses to run rampant as she crept through the forest. Her boot falls were silent on the mossy ground. She brushed the harsh bark of the trees with her fingertips as she passed by, breathing in the damp air with relish. She lifted her face to the sky and allowed the light rain drops to wet it. The forest was quiet and soothing. It didn't seem bothered with the company's trespassing right now.

The thunder roiled in the distance and every now and then a strong warm breeze would whip through the branches bringing with it a kind of ethereal presence. Alexa found a sheltered spot under a great oak tree and sat down. She leaned against the rough trunk and let her head roll back against it. She closed her eyes. And felt out her magical senses, collecting them and reveling in them. Someday she would learn how to control and use them better. She would be powerful...someday. She sighed. Then slowly among the healing power of nature, she relaxed. All her troubles dissolved in the rain.

With her eyes closed and her ears and mind focused on the soft, delicate noises in the forest around her, her unchecked witch senses latched on to something approaching. Her eyes popped opened. She rose up stealthily, her back hugging the tree. She drew out her dagger, knowing she could throw and use it better than her sword. She peered into the dark woods. Her keen eyesight caught a movement in the distance approaching from the direction of the camp. Soon she could clearly see the silhouette of a tall person. She held her breath and clenched the dagger tighter. Her body braced for action.

As the figure moved cautiously closer, her senses recognized him before her eyes did. *How ironic.* She knew him well enough to recognize him through her senses, yet she could never really figure him out.

The Master Sword paused several feet away. He didn't speak, but Alexa sensed his irritation. She closed her senses off. She didn't want to feel his bitterness. She didn't feel like deciphering all his complex emotions right now. It was him and thoughts of him she had been trying to escape; and now here he

405

was tormenting her. This was a cruel game. Whether he was playing it on purpose or not didn't matter anymore.

Lightning flashed and lit his broad stature for her to see. He saw her, too. His hand rested lightly on the hilt of his sword. His face was impassive. *Why does he still play the austere part of the Head-Master Sword in only my presence? It's wasted on me.* She sighed and returned her dagger back to its sheath at her thigh. "Come to give me a thrashing, my precious Sword-Guard?" she asked sourly.

"Maybe. You definitely deserve it. You shouldn't run off like this, especially after dark. How many times have I told you that?" he huffed.

"Not enough." Alexa raised her chin haughtily and kept her stature tall and confident.

"You're so infuriating," he growled and stalked toward her. He lessoned the distance between them to barely a step. It was dark, and his angry eyes hungrily sought out her face.

"And you're not?" she retorted in his face. He took a half a step back.

"What are you doing out here?" he demanded.

"Thinking. I just needed to get away and clear my mind," she stated.

"Get away? Get away from what? You could be eaten out here," he said flatly.

Alexa pursed her lips and stared him down defiantly. "From you," she snapped.

"Me?" he scoffed. "What for?"

Alexa clenched her fists and growled agitatedly. He stared bewildered at her. He was still standing rather close to her and this annoyed her even more. She didn't want him near her. She released her pent up frustration and gave him a brusque shove on his chest. He glared at her, abruptly pushing her hands off himself.

"I don't understand you," she blurted. Her eyes were aflame now, and she felt her witch temper taking hold of her. All her hurt and confusion were bubbling to the surface. She feared she wouldn't be able to control her anger.

"What isn't there to understand? I wanted you to practice

tonight like we've done almost every night," he said indignantly. "It doesn't warrant you running off and putting yourself in danger."

"No, no." Alexa began to pace, her eyes troubled. She ran her fingers agitatedly into the crown of her hair, pulling locks loose from her tight braid, giving her a slightly crazed look.

The Sword stood back and watched her closely as she paced and snarled, apparently holding more anger back. Her fists were clenched. Her jaw was tense and her body nearly trembled from head to boot.

"Just—just please leave me alone before I lose my temper!" she groaned after a minute, turning to regard him severely.

"*Before* you lose your temper?" he snorted in derision. He allowed himself to give her a wry, crooked smile.

She stopped her pacing to glare exasperatedly at him. He could see her clearly now that his eyes had adjusted. Her eyes looked dangerous and bewitching; he suddenly felt a light, unnatural chill spill through his body. He held up his hands in surrender and gave her a boyish grin; his own anger rapidly dissipating upon observing her in this stressed state. He didn't budge at her request though. He merely stood there watching her. He was willing to wait out whatever was bothering her so they could return to camp. Perhaps she was mourning Zhan, or stressed over the mission; he lied to himself.

Alexa was so busy mumbling to herself, pacing and trying desperately to hold in her horrible temper that she hadn't notice the Master Sword had calmed. He was now gazing at her astutely. After another minute, she glanced up at him as if surprised to see him still there. She narrowed her eyes. "I'm not going back with you. I can take care of myself," she stated pointedly.

"Yes you will. I'm not leaving without you," he said quietly.

"I want to collect myself first."

"What's going on?" he finally asked, but deep down, in a place he kept locked, he knew exactly what was going on. It had taken him to calm before he could clearly see what was distressing her. He just didn't want to address the impending, painful subject. Everything would be best if she thought him indifferent. Then they could all together avoid proclaiming their feelings, thus avoiding the desolation of their unpermitted love.

She begrudgingly eyed him like a harassed cat. *I've fallen in love with you, and for some reason you won't love me....* But she couldn't bring herself to say it. Instead, she said, "I'm just sick of...the game."

"Game? What game?" he asked stubbornly, though his voice held no malice.

"Nothing. Never mind. I'm just a silly girl." She waved him away and bit a finger nail.

"Sometimes, but—" he started in attempt to lighten the mood, but he stopped abruptly on seeing her resentful sapphire eyes turn on him.

Alexa paced again, faster and faster. She wanted to run; to run far away from him until her lungs burned and her mind was utterly cleared of him. He was playing the game again. As if he had no idea there was something between them. How wicked of him to think he could fool her! It was all so mystifying and heartrending to believe he cared one moment only to find out the next he didn't. Then again, perhaps she had *really*, honestly fooled herself into thinking he loved her....

"Alexa," Bryan began hesitantly; his voice held the tone of an adult soothing a child. It irritated her. "We've forgotten our pact. We need to be on good terms...in order to accomplish this mission."

Alexa snapped her head up to regard him flatly. She hated to admit to herself that she had been half hoping he was going to finally declare his love for her. How stupid to think that! Her jaw tensed, her eyes glossing over with suppressed tears. She fought them, not trusting herself to speak. She merely stared dourly at him.

Bryan took her silence as an okay for him to continue. "There are good reasons to explain...my behavior," he faltered, but he pressed on courageously as Alexa's unreadable eyes bored into him, "I haven't been the best Sword-Guard to you." Alexa's countenance changed to a quizzical hurt. Her mouth curved ever-so-slightly, but she didn't speak. Her troubled eyes were fathomless and dark. "I have sworn a duty to you and to Shelkite, and on many levels I have failed."

"You have not," she whispered, lowering her eyes, her anger dissipating.

"I can't allow anything to compromise my responsibility. Anything that would jeopardize my obligation to you puts your success at severe risk. I would like to renew my promise to you." He paused and came to stand closer.

He regarded her tenderly, his aloof words strongly belying his eyes. She didn't move away. He was so close to her she could almost feel the heat from his skin. He smelled enduringly of campfire smoke and woods.

"There's no need to renew any promise. You've never failed me. You've given your best from the start," she whispered, looking up into his face, her eyes landing on his intent ones. He parted his lips as if he had decided to speak some sudden truth, but he paused, studying her face, her lips. Alexa ached for his touch, but his countenance was conflicted. His whole being acted as if he wanted to be nearer to her than he was allowing. His eyes held a forgone yearning as he leaned closer to her, his eyes on her mouth. Alexa's breath stopped as she waited for his touch; she could just barely feel his soft exhale on her skin. But to her once again dismay, his brow furrowed desolately and he pulled away.

"Our connection," he continued huskily as Alexa looked away sorry, "Can't be personal." He fought to set his features stoically. Alexa felt something in her chest slip to the depths of defeat. "I am solely your Sword-Guard; that's where our connection begins and ends." His inflection grew firm, "When this is finished we will part as only Master Sword and charge."

Alexa stared at him with lost eyes. He swallowed anxiously and looked away. So this was how it was to be. She finally understood. Their feelings were banned. Their love was never to be. It would only be a hindrance to him, to her…to the mission. He was plucking it from its very new and tender roots. If he would not love her, she couldn't make him. And he was right; they both had a responsibility to concentrate on. Alexa nodded numbly in resignation.

"Alexa," Bryan suddenly looked sorry, an untypical expression of him; it didn't suit him. His clear, azure eyes were sad, and he shook his head regretfully. Alexa pursed her lips and jerked her head curtly to silence him. He had said all she wanted to hear. She needed no more from him. He clenched his jaw and nodded in silent accord. He also had to bear with his statement now that it was voiced.

"Fine then, dear Sword-Guard," her voice was brittle, "I'll be from here on out a more dutiful charge of yours." She gave a slight, mocking bow at the waist. Straightening, she added cynically, "Though, I shall still admire your gallantry from afar in agonizing solitude." Bryan gave her a wry look; an amused glimmer came into his eye at her dramatization. She continued, "Perhaps someday when you're a crusty old Sword, sick of attending all the dreary councils and the repugnant parties with dull ladies, you will think back on me with some nostalgia…and regret," she ended bitterly.

"Alexa…." Bryan sighed stubbornly. He felt as if somehow he was going against the grain of fate by lying to her. But he must; he must for her own good!

"Master Sword," she silenced him with a sour smile, "I've heard all that I need to. You made it clear; we are guardian and charge only. Pact?" She held out her hand brusquely. He glanced down at it, unsure at her sincerity. Then resolutely, he gripped her hand and gave it a firm shake. They both quickly released their hold, neither able to bear the touch of the other.

Alexa knew all her hopes of their love had been slaughtered with that hand shake. Even though Bryan's eyes said differently, he had never said out right that he cared for her in any way other than as his charge. To Alexa, this decision of forbidding their feelings was all the more worse because it was an absolute conscious rejection.

They stood in silence for a moment, listening to the sound of the soft thunder and the gentle tap, tap of the drops of rain on the leaves. The damp wind rustled the tree tops, bringing with it a consoling atmosphere.

Bryan moved awkwardly to speak, "You must understand that I do ca—"

Alexa silenced him abruptly with her hand, staring avidly into the dark of the forest to the left. "Something is near. And it's not friendly," she whispered anxiously, her eyes wide and alert.

The Master Sword's broad stature tensed into defense mode. He drew his sword, coming to stand even closer. Alexa already had her dagger in her hand. She cursed herself for leaving her bow behind. What had she been thinking?

The creature approached. The two still couldn't discern it. Alexa could sense it clearly. It was a creature of stealth, a predatory animal, but it also had a mystical nature. Her slender fingers wrapped more snugly around the hilt of her dagger.

"I think I see som—" Bryan began to say, but his words were gulped up by a ferocious snarl. The creature was on them before they could discern it. It came out from behind a nearby tree and hammered straight into Alexa, knocking her forcefully into the Master Sword. Then, just as quickly, it bounded off back into the dark. Befuddled for a second, they quickly collected themselves. "What is it?" Bryan asked, grasping Alexa's arm a bit hard, dragging her right up next to him. He held his sword drawn in the direction the creature had disappeared in.

Alexa had her dagger drawn in the arm opposite of the one he held; she squirmed against his bruising hold. "I'm not sure. But you need to allow me to fight! It's large whatever it is, and you can't fight it on your own." He released her. And they stood back to back, peering into the dark, scanning the forest floor fervently.

This time the creature gave them a warning. Straight to the right of them, it growled; it had circled. They snapped around to face it, and found themselves feet away from an enormous hellhound staring them down. They both inhaled a shocked breath and uttered a curse.

The hellhound was a distant cousin of the howler; although hellhounds were much larger and meaner. Unlike the howlers' disgusting hairless bodies, hellhounds had shaggy, smoke-gray coats. This hellhound may have actually been cute if it weren't for its red eyes and deadly glare; hellhounds were much more dog-like than howlers.

The hound crouched down and slowly inched toward the two companions, its shoulder blades protruding pointedly. Locked in its alert eye, Bryan and Alexa braced themselves for action. The Sword whispered through his lips, "What is it?" He had never seen a creature like this.

"Hellhound. They're smart. Be careful," she whispered warningly. "To our benefit they fight solo. I think…" she added as it crept toward them, showing its pristine white fangs. It eyed them each one at a time, apparently trying to decide which one of them to take out first. It decided on Bryan.

In an instant, the hound set back on its haunches and launched itself into the air straight at Bryan. The Master Sword was quick, but not quick enough for this animal's predatory instinct. Its massive bulk crashed into Bryan knocking him to the ground faster than Alexa could react; yet, the Master Sword was miraculously able to keep a hold of his weapon.

In a brief scramble, for she had been knocked aside, Alexa jumped forward and plunged her dagger into the hip of the hellhound. It howled and turned, plowing right over her, knocking her to the ground, denying her a chance to free her dagger. By that time Bryan was to his feet and charging the creature. Vaguely aware her face had been trampled into the dirt, Alexa leapt up to help. She had only her hands now, but she wasn't about to surrender.

Bryan was making wide swipes at the darting hound. It dashed closer each time, attempting to take a chomp out of the Master Sword. Alexa raced toward them and skidded to a stop realizing she still had a knife in the hidden flap in her boot. She quickly pulled it out. Bryan landed a few blows with his sword, but the hound was only becoming angrier as it got bloodier. Alexa approached them, holding out her knife.

"Stay back!" Bryan hollered at her. The hound snarled and bit down onto his sword, its teeth making an appalling sound on the weapon. Bryan jerked his sword as hard as he could and the creature came away with a mouth gushing scarlet.

Trying to make herself useful, Alexa took aim and threw her knife with all the strength she had in her arm. It flew straight and hard, but the hellhound suddenly darted and the knife buried itself into a harmless spot in its flesh. Now Alexa was completely unarmed.

The hellhound, seeming to decide Alexa was more of a threat than it had originally anticipated, dashed around Bryan to take a bite at the his ankles to incapacitate him. Luckily Bryan's boots protected him, but the creature jerked its massive head and the Sword crashed abruptly to the ground. Then in a decision showing it had uncanny intelligence, it left Bryan in his momentarily weak state and went after Alexa.

It leapt on top of her. She felt the boulder-like heaviness of its shaggy body plow into her. She hit the damp ground hard on her back, knocking the wind out of her lungs. As she choked for air, she was unable to react as the hellhound bit down on her left arm. Once she had breath, she cried out in pain. It began to rapidly drag her away. Bryan was back on his feet, chasing them down frantically.

Alexa squirmed and thrashed, but the more she jerked the deeper the hound's teeth went. It felt as if her arm might tear right off. The hellhound was dragging her at a pace much faster than she thought possible. She could see the Master Sword charging after them, fear apparent across his features. As Bryan neared them, the creature stopped right at a creek's edge and thrashed his head violently side to side, tossing Alexa like a rag doll. She became disoriented. Then the shaking abruptly stopped, and she felt the hound disengage its teeth from her arm.

Bryan was close, but he had paused, his sword at the ready. Alexa could smell and feel the hound's putrid breath on her face. It was standing possessively over her, snarling menacingly at the Master Sword, daring him to approach.

"Alexa, are you okay?" Bryan asked fretfully, his azure eyes peering anxiously into her dirtied face.

"Yes," she croaked, "he just twisted my arm a bit. No real damage."

"He's playing games with us. He could have killed me back

there, but chose not to. Now he *wants* me to attempt to rescue you again."

Alexa tentatively rolled her eyes up to look into hellhound's face. It looked as if it was actually enjoying itself; its tail was even wagging. It hovered over her like a dog with a toy, gazing tantalizingly at Bryan.

"Be ready," Bryan said, and then charged. The hellhound pounced on Alexa, grabbing her shoulder and began to drag her again. But this time the Master Sword was quicker and more precise. His sword came down hard on the creature's neck, severing it and barely missing Alexa as she rolled swiftly out of the way.

Bryan fell to her side instantly, dropping his sword. He braced her as she hazily sat up. "Are you sure you're not hurt?" he asked earnestly. He pryingly checked her over with his hands. Without thought his anxious fingers brushed her hair from her face.

Mutely, she nodded her head, rubbing her injured shoulder. She prodded her arm. Though it had felt like the teeth had pierced her skin, she found they hadn't. The hound had been only playing with them. That wouldn't have lasted long. He would have soon killed them both.

"Are you bleeding?" Bryan persisted.

"I don't think so." She looked herself over. No blood. The blood from the hellhound's mouth was on her, but unlike howlers' blood it wasn't poisonous. Overall, she was just a bit rumpled and dirty from being trampled and drug.

"You have some claw scratches on your arm, but they aren't bad," Bryan said inspecting her arm.

"Are you hurt?" She looked him over.

"No," he replied simply, and then went to the creek and wetted down the sleeve of his overcoat.

Alexa rose and walked, rather more easily than she thought she might, over to a nearby weeping willow tree. Its long, slender leaves were draped over the creek. It formed a kind of curtain around her as she sat down, her back against its stocky trunk. Bryan came to her, having cleansed his sword, and took a seat beside her, handing her his overcoat with the wet sleeve.

"For your face," he said. She nodded gratefully and took the coat and wiped her face.

He shook his head disapprovingly at her, "When will you learn not to run off?" She merely shrugged, not meeting him in the eye. "What would you have done if I hadn't been here?"

"I would've managed."

He gave her a skeptical look.

"And if not, you would've been rid of a lot of trouble," she stated.

He sighed reluctantly after a moment of quiet, "No. My troubles would've just begun...at losing my charge."

She paused her cleansing and looked up to meet his eyes, wondering if his statement was more personal than what he implied. He stubbornly stared impassively at her.

They sat for a few long minutes in companionable silence, listening to the nighttime forest sounds around them. The woods had calmed in an instant. Deep in her thoughts, with a clear and relaxed mind, Alexa heard the Master Sword heave a sigh beside her; one she would have called aggrieved sounding. She moved her sapphire eyes to gaze at him wonderingly. She was quite stunned to see him studying her face with a strange, conflicted expression across his features. She realized he was unnecessarily close to her. With a thoughtful, furrowed brow he gazed at her. Then his azure eyes turned unguarded and peaceful, as if he had suddenly made some sort of resolve inside.

Alexa's breath caught in her throat as he gently reached up and brushed away leftover smudges of dirt from her face with his fingertips and said softly, "That hellhound made me panic." She merely stared at him entranced. He let his thumb trace over her lips, which were parted slightly in surprise. His eyes lingered on her mouth for a moment, mesmerized it seemed.

Alexa studied his face bewilderedly, feeling shivers run through her body at this unexpected touch. His eyes flicked up to meet hers; they were unmistakably full of longing. Then, as if without thought, he leaned in and placed his lips softly on hers. Alexa returned his tentative kiss. He pulled back and glanced at her as if he questioned his actions. When she didn't protest, he kissed her again, more fervently this time. She responded the same, falling back to lie in the plush moss. He hovered over her, his insistent, warm mouth still on hers.

Alexa hesitantly reached up to gently touch his face and damp locks of hair. He kissed her deeper, slipping his tongue over hers. She grasped his hair tighter, entangling it in her fingers. His hand was at her jaw and she felt him run it down the sensitive skin of her neck to clutch her shoulder. His palm was rough, but his touch wasn't. *Oh man, he kisses even better than he handles a sword.* She was beside herself. Then to her confusion, he suddenly stopped and pulled away. *He's the most aggravating person I've ever met.* She tried to control her frustration. She was baffled. He had just gotten done telling her they could be nothing more to each other than business, and then he had kissed her, and now this again....

His countenance was conflicted. He traced his fingers down her chin, giving her a sad smile, letting his hand fall into his lap despondently. He leaned back and looked up at the clearing night sky. The rain clouds were slowing drifting away. The sky was midnight blue and unspoiled.

Alexa sat up and faced him. "What is it, Bryrunan?" she whispered. At the sound of his real name, his eyes snapped back to hers, an unmistakable yearning glowing inside them again. He leaned into her and she came in to meet him. He rested his forehead against hers. His demeanor was troubled. She could feel his breath on her. And she waited anxiously for his lips to touch hers again, but they didn't. She leaned away from his strange embrace in puzzlement to study his features better.

His normal impassive façade had completely melted down and he looked rather dejected. His normally bright azure eyes darkened and were wreathed with gloom. His handsome lips were turned down in a frown. He gazed sadly at her. She was rendered still at the sight of him. She knew now without a doubt that he absolutely cared for her. She was speechless.

"Alexa, the truth is..." he said huskily. She waited, holding her breath. His words seemed to trip over his tongue as if part of

416

him didn't want them said, "I want you to marry me…but it isn't possible."

Chapter 40

Alexa was taken aback. She leaned back and stared astounded at him. That wasn't exactly what she'd been expecting. It surpassed all she had wanted, demanded, from him. Her mood brightened a great deal and hope poured into her wrinkled soul. Her wry humor came back tenfold. She snorted an uncontrollable chuckle; the Sword's eyes narrowed defensively. She gave him a half-smile and said dryly, "You could at least ask me and not tell me. You may be in command of me in some ways, Master Sword, but definitely not in who I decide to marry."

Bryan ran an agitated hand through his tousled hair. He seemed lost for words. His broad body was slumped and he seemed vulnerable. Alexa found this nearly irresistible; she had never seen him in such a dismal state. She regarded him warmly, her sapphire eyes bright and hopeful. She moved closer to him and he didn't move away. She came close enough to him where her senses were engulfed completely by him. He merely watched her with soft, unguarded eyes. Peering beseechingly into his face, she whispered, "So, all this torturous time you've been disregarding me and confusing me was only you not allowing your dedication to your job yield to your feelings?"

"Yes and no," he answered solemnly. "There is something else…"

But she silenced him with her eyes and said quickly, "I love you, Bryrunan." He looked at her with a bittersweet expression. "I have for a while now, ever since we made that ridiculous pact. I want you more than anything I've ever wanted. I *would* marry you," she said confidently, her eyes searching his face earnestly.

Bryan felt his heart swell with elation a thousand times its size, despite his distress. "I've tried to resist you for many reasons ever since I first saw you, but I can't. I can't deny I love you any longer."

Alexa smiled sweetly. She yearned to reach out and take his coarse, unshaven face in her hands and taste his mouth again. However, the dismayed look in his eyes brought her reaching hands to a puzzled halt.

"You don't understand. I said it's impossible for us to

marry. I'm bound by my oath as a Master Sword. I would be disgraced and exiled if I were to break it. I can only marry a Shelkiten woman. It was impulsive of me to accept the offer to become a Sword. I didn't even want it. I never realized I'd fall in love with anyone again, let alone a Kaltrazian enchantress." He smiled humorously, though it was bound with sorrow.

Finally, Alexa fully comprehended his logic for everything he had done. He was such a loyal, steadfast and rational person. It all made sense now. He was isolating himself from her for good reason, to protect both of them. Buried in the back of her mind, she remembered hearing of the strict Master Sword's oath Melea had explained to her in her chamber at the Shelkite castle. She lowered her eyes feeling lost, sad and trodden. She couldn't have him still. This was utterly unfair. Her body felt torn asunder. Her soul fell, rumpled.

"I know," he said at seeing her fallen countenance. "That's why I've distanced myself. It's for both our sakes."

Then with an unexpected fire blaze up in her eyes, she gazed at him with fierce hope, "We could be lovers."

"In secret?" He was skeptical; he looked at her askance.

"Yes." Her sapphire eyes were as light as the morning sky.

"That's not really fair to either of us," he said slowly, his blue eyes dark and full of distress.

"What do you mean? We'd be together," she replied.

"Alexa, you have to be rational. Over time we'd tire of it," he explained.

"Rational? You're too rational. When is love rational? We wouldn't tire of it. Not if we really loved each other," she countered.

"You don't see." He shook his head hopelessly.

"We could travel to each other. I'd come to Shelkite to be with you—"

"To stay for how long?" he cut her off bitterly. "People would suspect. We'd be found out and your honor would be ruined."

"I could visit occasionally for short periods. I'd tell whoever asked that I was just passing through to visit relatives in the west. I'd tell my family that I'm visiting a friend. I don't care about my honor." She was nearly pleading with him now. She was losing him slowly, and it was more painful this time, because now she truthfully knew how much he did care.

"You always traveling?" he said skeptically, resisting the urge to brush a lock of hair from her face. He mustn't touch her again, lest he couldn't stop. "I could never come to Kaltraz. You know that, right? My duty ties me to Shelkite. I travel the countryside sometimes for months at a time. And when I'm at the castle I always have some kind of business to attend to," he said solemnly. He dropped his blue eyes away from her face as if he couldn't bear to look at her because of the pain he was inflicting on her.

"So?" she merely replied. Her persistent resolve pulled his eyes back to her face. He looked bewildered, amused and pleased all at once. She continued, "I'd come to you when I could. Who cares if anyone discovered us?" She was adamant. She *would* be with him. She would let nothing keep them apart.

The Master Sword gave her a cheerless half smile. "And you don't see how this would be wearing on us? We'd become an obligation to each other. You always traveling, alone and in danger, always at *my* beckoning."

"It wouldn't be like that," she retorted, her eyes sparking up flames with his unrelenting resistance.

"It wouldn't be at first. Then eventually it would come to that. Trust me…" He sighed, feeling frustrated himself. "I refuse to use you. If we can't be together lawfully, then we shouldn't allow ourselves to be together at all. It'll save much pain later." He lifted his hand as if to gently brush her cheek in reassurance, but he made it fall short.

They sat silently facing one another, close, but neither reaching out to the other. Alexa because she realized he was unwilling, and Bryan because he feared if he did he wouldn't be able to resist anymore and hold to what he knew was the right thing for them both.

After a moment Bryan spoke, still trying desperately to convince her and make her understand his side, "Don't you want a home and a husband that can be with you always? Would we do this until the day we died? And what about children? Don't you want children?"

Alexa's pondering eyes shot up to his down cast face. "Yes, of course. But I'd give up all that to be with you," she said earnestly, almost frantically.

He sighed a bit exasperated, trying to stay resolved in his decision. "You say that now. You'd change your mind."

"Stop making excuses! No, I wouldn't. I'm a very determined girl," she said firmly.

Bryan ground his teeth in frustration and breathed out. "All right. So what if we did become lovers, despite the difficulties, and then you became with child? You would be ostracized. I wouldn't do that to you," he said forcefully, his own eyes were now ablaze at her foolish stubbornness.

"There are herbs to prevent me from conceiving," she countered quickly.

Bryan sighed and smiled forlornly at her. "You have a solution for everything."

Alexa gave him a weak smile and then said, "It sounds as if you'd feel I was the obligation."

"You'd never be an obligation," he said with frustration. "It's just that we can't be with each other in a way that will be easy. It'll be hard on us and perhaps detrimental to us in the future," he explained, beseeching her to understand and be logical. He searched her face, struggling against his desire to reach out to her.

"Prince Alkin is kind. Don't you think he'll allow this for you? He wouldn't force his power over me," Alexa stated.

Bryan pursed his lips. "It's part of the oath. The other Swords would become angry and malcontent. And don't think that I haven't notice how Alkin feels for you. He won't be so thrilled to grant me permission to marry a woman he cares for. He may be kind, but he's still a man. And he can do as he wishes. I know him enough to believe he's capable of begrudging someone."

Alexa pondered the oath and tried to think of another way around the Master Sword's stubborn way of thought. Then she suddenly remembered Melea and how in love Melea was with the Master Sword. She felt a twinge of guilt. "I'd forgotten."

"What?"

"Melea. She loves you."

Bryan sighed and rolled his eyes. "I suspected it. It doesn't matter. She'll find someone new. You shouldn't care; it's not her I care for."

Alexa raised her eyes perplexed. "Why shouldn't I? You've been spending all this time convincing me we shouldn't be together."

He gave her a boyish grin. His smile faded, and he cocked his head, raising his eyebrows at her. "Now, *you* tell me that you were only playing games by acting coquettish with the Prince and Kheane," he demanded gently, his eyes intent.

She merely grinned sheepishly at him, "I only ever wanted you."

All his qualms melted away.

Deep in their troubles and falling into thoughtful silence, the two loves hadn't noticed when the stars had come out to sparkle in their entire grandeur. Or when the moon's silvery rays started spilling down through the branches to cast eerie, white shadows all around them. They looked around themselves and saw a quiet, woodland paradise. They were shielded by the curtain of the willow; and the forest felt content. It seemed to request that the two new loves be left undisturbed.

"Well, I could just bewitch you and have you anyway," Alexa finally broke the silence. Bryan turned his gaze back on her from where he had been observing the woods.

"I was afraid you'd already done that." He smiled, nervously eyeing her enthralling eyes.

She grinned crookedly at him and shook her head. There was another moment of silence and Alexa studied him as he once again studied the intriguing forest around them, lost deep in his thoughts. She loved his steadfastness, his loyalty and even his infuriating rationality and stubbornness. And, oh, how she loved that face with his strong square jaw, high cheek bones and bright azure eyes. She loved his tousled dark hair and his broad, well-muscled body, and how she loved, *loved* to watch him sword fight. He was irresistible on all accounts. She wanted him for always. She bit her bottom lip. She couldn't resist any longer. She leaned toward him, reaching out to him and touching the edge of his jaw with her fingertips, wishing she could dispel the conflict in his heart.

He turned to look at her, surprise across his face. She smiled coyly at him, her eyes twinkling in the white light of the moon. He gave her a sad, crooked smile. Alexa's heart started beating like she'd run a mile. Her breath came short and quickly as he held her gaze intensely with his shining blue eyes. She could see in his eyes he had lost the battle he was fighting with himself. He hesitated, lightly touching her fingers resting on his face. Then he gathered her face in his own hands and placed his mouth on hers, kissing her determinedly.

There was several seconds of blissful, fervent kisses on both their parts, along with feelings of regret for all the time they had lost in resisting one another. But they couldn't think of that now, or their uncertain future…

Bryan pulled away from her soft lips and mumbled quietly in her mouth with a regretful groan, "Alexandra, your lips are as foolishly reckless as you are. How much I've kept myself from…" He landed a few quick, ardent kisses on her face, his eyes troubled, feeling extremely tormented by his oath. Breaking away, he studied her for a moment, still fighting the battle inside against his rationality. He loved every part of this girl, no matter how infuriating she was a times. He loved her courage, her spirit, even her recklessness. He gazed into her face for only a second longer before he could no longer contain his desire. He had her back in his arms in one quick motion, wrapping his arms around her waist and pulling her up close to him. She didn't protest and he didn't care anymore about resisting. She had ended up convincing *him* and it was done.

Her willowy body pressed against his as she tilted her chin offering her lips to his. He placed his yearning mouth on hers like he had imagined so many times; and she responded to his touch like straw to flames. Her touch liberated him from all his responsibilities and he allowed himself to become utterly unconstrained, reveling in the rare sensation.

Alexa's lips were warm and luscious. Her touch was invigorating. She clung intensely to him as if she couldn't make up for the time she'd lost in not having the privilege to touch him. Everywhere she touched he was aware of her heightened magical power racing into him. His skin simmered with the alien feeling. Her body shuddered and melted beneath his hands, and he melded with her. He thrived from the realization that she was finally in his arms.

He wanted to touch her to know it was real. And touch her he did. He drew her warm, firm body close to his, pressing his lips beseechingly on hers, tasting her sweet tongue on his. Intertwining his fingers into her hair, he drew her deeper into his kiss and heart. His body ached for more. His hands desperately wanted to discover more of her. She was so lithe, warm, soft and lovely. He wanted her under him, where he could feel her smooth, bare skin touch his. So they could wrap themselves around each other and become one permanently. Though he knew it couldn't be that way now, he craved for that day. He just wanted her ever closer. He yearned for the day her soul would become a piece of his for always.

Alexa felt as if Bryan was high above her, like a god; and here he was loving *her*. His kisses were so sweet and ardent; she felt intoxicated. His lips were full and precise in their ever changing charm as they whisked over her throat and features. She felt thrill after blissful thrill fall from her head to her toes every time she realized it was really him finally pulling her closer to embrace her and kiss her. She ran her hands over his shoulders as her lips reveled in the taste of him. The muscles in his arms were taut as he drew her close. Through his shirt she could feel the firm outline of his torso. When his fingers brushed her skin, and his light breaths tickled her neck, she felt as if she might fall straight into heaven…or hell.

He gently lowered to her to lie back on the ground. She laced her fingers around his strong neck and clung to him, still drinking in and returning his fierce, insistent kisses. His light hands brushed dangerously along her thighs, seemingly shooting enough flames through her to ignite the fabric between them. He was beautiful, exquisite, inside and out. She wanted more of him, all of him…

Taking his unshaven chin in her hands, she kissed him with deep, solid affection. Her heart was beating as if a thousand horses were galloping through her veins. She could sense his rapid heartbeats and she drowned rapturously in the certainty of his love.

Holding his exquisite body dangerously close to hers, he hovered over her, his lips making a sweet trail from her neckline to her ear. She breathlessly peppered his pleased features with gentle kisses. He had finally surrendered himself to her; and she felt victorious. She had desired him above all else in the world and now she would never give him up from this moment.

She traced her fingers perilously along his trouser waistline, feeling the warmth of his skin on her fingertips. They both felt the tense, caged desire within the other. Bryan pulled slightly away, though he still kissed her tenderly. She froze in apprehension. "We should stop," he groaned reluctantly into her mouth. She relaxed. "You need Apollos too much right now to hinder your relationship," he said hoarsely, his mouth going from her lips to land a soft kiss on her forehead. He paused, his azure eyes searching out hers. She gazed into his handsome face a bit starry eyed.

"I understand," she replied quietly. He grinned at her, flashing his nice teeth. There was a moment of silence between them. They studied each other as if they couldn't believe what they had just done. They had fallen down into a mysterious new world. "So I take it you've chosen to be lovers?" she asked.

"More like surrendering. Since there's no other way to be with you," he answered honestly.

"In secret then?"

"Yes."

"Forever?"

"For as long as you wish." He brushed aside a loose lock of her raven hair that had fallen in her eyes. He found her so enchantingly pretty.

"Then," she said contemplatively, "That will be until my death."

He gave her a small, cheerless smile. He looked unsure and forlorn. He watched her features for a second and they turned from determined to distressed. "What is it?" he asked solicitously, his brow puzzled.

She bit her lip, her bright sapphire eyes were round with a dreaded realization. She glanced away from his intent gaze. He waited. "I just realized something," she began slowly, looking out to the moonlit forest around them, unable to look him in the eyes. "I will outlive you by almost two hundred years."

Bryan felt his heart plummet to his feet. His breath caught in his throat. He swallowed, trying to get his bearings as he let this reality sink in. He stared at her, unclenching and clenching his jaw in thought. She turned her eyes back on him. All her earlier fervor had dissipated. Her eyes looked frightened and he couldn't help but want to take her again in his arms and kiss all the trouble away. Wordlessly, he bent down and pressed a gentle and reassuring kiss to her forehead.

"I won't live to the age that my father will, only being half-blood, but I'll live a long time," she said morosely, glancing away again from his sympathetic eyes. This was possibly the first time ever she wished that she weren't a witch....

"Well," he started quietly, hesitantly, "Then maybe you could find someone...after I'm gone, that you could marry. Unless, of course, you change your mind and we just...go our separate ways." He nearly had to choke out the words, but he had to say them. She wasn't something he could capture and bridle and hoard away for only his pleasure.

A determined look came into her blue eyes and she sat up taller, looking him in the eye again. "No. I will have you. I'll endure...somehow, when that time comes. I won't give you up while I can have you."

Bryan smiled cheerlessly at her. "Fate isn't too charitable to us is it?"

Alexa snorted in derision, her fiery spirit resurfacing. "Fate? I don't believe in fate or destiny. I think something, like the

High Power, prods us and guides us. But ultimately we decide what we're going to do with the circumstances and we decide our own future."

"How do you explain us? I kept resisting and I know you tried to forget about your feelings, too. But we couldn't ignore *us* no matter how we tried. And what about the naiad giving your name, isn't that destiny?"

"I could've have fought the Shelkiten warriors when they came for me. Could've said no and ran away. I could have still chosen to turn around and go back home after I met with the Prince...but I didn't. Kaltraz is in danger. It's my home. What kind of person would turn their back on their country and allow people to suffer? It was *my* choice to do this. Sometimes we just have to listen to the quiet, persistent prodding we feel inside of us and then everything will fall into place from the choices we make from there. You'll see. It's more like providence, guidance. Nothing is forcing us to do anything; though we have to be willing to accept the consequences from our choices," she replied confidently.

He chuckled and reached out to her, pulling her into an affectionate hug. She snuggled into his chest, breathing in his scent. He rested his chin on her head and breathed her in, too. He heaved a sigh. "You're smarter than you act at times," he teased, and then added sincerely, "and brave." He gave her a soft kiss, which she returned graciously. "At least I won't have to endure losing you because of old age," he said.

She pulled away to look thoughtfully up at him. "You talk as if I might leave you. Do you think I'm a silly, scatterbrained girl? That I'll someday bore of you, and I'll take off, forgetting all about you like a broken toy?" she said heatedly, her eyes narrowing in defense.

He sighed again. "I just don't think you realize what a difficult situation we're getting ourselves into." His eyes searched her face unhappily.

"Don't worry you're handsome head about that." She smiled good-naturedly at him. "Just concern yourself with being my Sword-Guard and leading the company right now." He glanced away from her avid face in thought, his brow creased in concern.

His blue eyes troubled and unguarded. Alexa allowed herself to sense out his emotions. "You're thinking about what will happen when we finally meet up with Ret, aren't you?" she asked.

He looked at her, troubled. "Yes."

"Don't be anxious, my beloved Sword-Guard, my uncle won't turn me into a breathing corpse that bears abominations. I won't allow that to happen. I promise. We'll all make it through this okay. This is where I choose my own fate," she said confidently.

He gave her a small smile and shook his head in amused disbelief at her. "You're not lacking in confidence or courage that's for sure." He hugged her and kissed her one last time, savoring it; he knew they had to be heading back to camp.

She grinned up at him as he stood. "Never been a problem."

He shook his head, giving her an amused, crooked smile, "Come on, girl, we need to get sleep." He wrapped his arm around her shoulders as she stood.

He began walking with her back toward the camp. There was a moment of silence between them where they both reveled in the midnight paradise the forest had created for them. They looked wistfully back to the weeping willow tree they had sheltered under. It alone appeared like a haven, as its long, slender leaves swayed gently in the night breeze.

Carthorn was truly an enchanting place, angry and aspiring to destroy one moment, and then a blissful haven for lovers the next. Maybe Carthorn and its strange magic and hidden presences condoned their love from its ire. And had allowed them this time to finally come together the way they should have months ago. Perhaps the willow's dryad had tenderly protected them from the forest's dangers. In memory of two lost, forbidden loves. Maybe fate was charitable to them after all.

"Oh," he broke the silence, "Could you just try a little harder to be indifferent toward Alk—Prince Alkin," he corrected himself. He looked at her warily, raising an eyebrow.

She smiled knowingly without looking at him. "Yes, I'll try." She glanced slyly at him and he gave her a warning look.

Then she added more seriously, "How are we to act now?"

He shrugged and smiled crookedly. "Well, let's just refrain from making love in front of the company, shall we?

She laughed merrily and marveled in the warmth of his arm around her. Her witch and human senses were dazzled and consumed by him. The sensation of him was everywhere, dancing on the wind. She was determined to keep it that way.

About Alicia

I grew up in a pastorate and military family, the younger of two daughters.

As a child I enjoyed writing. I had an adventure series about a Queen Alicia and her nameless husband, the King. Today, I enjoy reading, archery, spending time with my family and hanging out with horses.

I live in Michigan with my husband Don and three highly entertaining cats. I'm currently writing the sequel to Remnants of Magic as well as percolating other novel ideas. Visit Remnants of Magic VOL I's Facebook page for updates!